Advanced Praise for *The Big Red Herring*

In his truly wild first novel, Andrew Farkas smashes history straight through the looking glass to offer a world of Orwellian chill and Strangelovian élan. Indeed, the whole beautifully complex, carnivalesque bundle dances with uncommonly light and dexterous step. Even when it gets dark. And man does it ever. **The Big Red Herring** *is a revisioned century's worth of truth and hoax, pain and fun.*

- Laird Hunt, author of
In the House in the Dark of the Woods,
The Evening Road, and *Neverhome*

It is thought the Earth (beginning with the invention of radio) pulses when regarded from the vastness of outer space. Our broadcasts broadly broadcast, an electromagnetic soup to nuts, every transmitted signal still expanding outward through the ether. **The Big Red Herring**, *Andrew Farkas's vibrant pulsar of a book, generates accommodating light, both particle and wave, piggybacked and packed with rich dense packages of info and intel. Not a mere novel but a kind of juiced and jumpy step-up transformer, its radiation bands, like our universe, inexplicable accelerating, irresistible, multidimensional (quantum and string). Farkas is the new Newton of narration, standing on the shoulders of giants, yes, but double clutching this shift of the novel's paradigm. There's no stopping this novel Novel, this new New.*

- Michael Martone, author of *Brooding*
and *The Moon Over Wapakoneta*

The Big Red Herring
Andrew Farkas

KERNPUNKT • PRESS

Cover Art: Scott Schulman
Book Design: Jesi Buell

1st Printing: 2019

ISBN-13 978-1-7323251-3-5

KERNPUNKT Press
Hamilton, New York 13346

www.kernpunktpress.com

Andy: Lewis, this story you're telling me, I know it's not true. You made it up.
Lewis: Well, sure. I know you know that...
Andy: But you're gonna tell it anyway?
Lewis: That's right, Andy.

Your theory is crazy,
but it's not crazy enough to be true.

- Niels Bohr

Zero

The Point Before the Point of No Return

"*This*... is London," says a voice. Though who can tell, since all is black...

In this stagnant darkness, for now, ladies and gentlemen, there is time. Today's program, *Vayss Uf Makink You Tock*, will begin shortly, but for now... there is time. If Captain Ahab had written *Moby-Dick*, it would've been half as long, a novella, a short story, a short short, two words: *The Whale!* But for now...

"London," says the voice again, and maybe it's telling the truth. Very well:

Down stately crescent-shaped Regent Street, along Shaftesbury of theatre fame, into Charing Cross Road, London's Tin Pan Alley, and so to Trafalgar Square. Roving there, airfoil lights shining, is Edward R. Murrow; yes, the chief narrator at CNS, that's the Columbia Narratorial Services, in his black, rocket-like 1942 Chrysler De Soto. The 1942 Chrysler De Soto, tomorrow's style today... though admittedly that today has already passed into yesterday (tomorrow's style yesterday?), and that tomorrow never came to be—a history of yesterdays' tomorrows today...

But still, there is time. Edward R. Murrow can just do a little night driving, can tell us this is London (whether it is or not), can even turn on the De Soto's radio.

The radio says: *This is KDRG. K-Drag: Always headed to commercial just*

1

as you tune in. We'll be back right after these words…

According to our prophetic correspondent, in the future, when *Vayss Uf Makink You Tock* begins, when our man Ed Murrow starts narrating, there will be characters: a femme fatale bent on destroying her husband, a master of disguise who seeks to reveal an awful conspiracy, a patsy attempting to avoid a horrible fate, a CIA agent with his own private agenda, a matron willing to do anything to save her family, a company man betrayed by his employer, a former KGB agent who's playing both sides against the middle, an assassinated senator who was never an actual senator, a paranoid CEO who has gone missing, a mysterious informant who may only be trying to help (though his motives are unclear), and, without doubt, Nazis. There will be Nazis. So we can rest easy knowing precisely who the bad guys are…

The radio says: *Diplomatic Immunity Liquors–just say 'Diplomatic Immunity,' and they'll let you off every time.*

"The noise you hear at the moment is silence," says Edward R. Murrow over the commercials on the radio. "There are no air raid sirens, and there won't be any later. Of course that doesn't mean there aren't machines flying over London at this very moment, machines carrying darkness, the final darkness that'll blot out all we've ever known. But since the alarms are silent, we feel safe… I'm driving past St. Martin-in-the-Fields and the National Portrait Gallery, two neoclassical buildings. In front of me now I can just see Lord Nelson in his Napoleonic stance on top of that big column. And all is quiet…"

The radio says: *Milk of Amnesia–the cure for whatever the problem was.*

"…When that inky blackness does fall, there will be no warning. The search lights will not burst into action. They'll remain inert, unilluminated, unswooping, projecting beams of oblivion into the ether. The airborne machines will remain cloaked in night. The people… Later, there will be no shelters for the children or the adults…"

But in the present we needn't worry about the characters or even the events. We, gentle people of Radioland, have the luxury of aimlessness. And it is a luxury. For, according to our various in-house critics and scholars, *Vayss Uf Makink You Tock* has sex, drugs, violence, conspiracies (terrestrial and extra), artistic forgeries, Antarctic exploration, lunar exploration, sport, alcohol, interrogations (violent, chemical, psychological), espionage, the inner workings of secret societies, the inner workings of rogue television stations, an alien abduction, murder, and not only Nazis, ladies and gentlemen, but Nazis! In! Space! With such a full program, later, we might just find ourselves blissfully recalling this moment in time when nothing seemed to have happened yet, when nothing seemed to be happening, though everything, unbeknownst to us, is already underway.

The radio says: *Just when you thought there was no narrative at all, Narratol.*

"As the shade descends, it'll be obvious this isn't just twilight. The taller buildings will fall under the shadow and disappear with no hope of return. Then the ink will splash down over the people, the neighborhoods, the roads, yes, the ink will fall, it will fall until all of London has been engulfed. London? Before I even have a chance to see the town, the jaws of darkness do devour it up."

And so, farewell Trafalgar Square, I guess...

Apprehensive listeners of Radioland, having just been unLondoned, it is only natural that we feel cast adrift, asea in the formless void. Our clairvoyant correspondent has informed me that Edward R. Murrow feels the same way, lost on an anonymous road in the pitch black, wishing right this very moment that he was in London at the beginning of World War Two because at least that'd mean he was somewhere where something real was happening, uncertain now of where he is, where he's going, what's occurring (if anything), uncertain of his surroundings because his surroundings appear to be uncertain of themselves, appearing to have not yet decided whether they wish to come into being or whether they wish to remain abstract or whether they were already and are no longer, ladies and gentlemen, whereas I cannot help our man Murrow, I do have it in my power to help you, though I hold back. Please, dear listeners, do not think I am being coy. The reason I refrain is because once I tell you the setting for today's program, we will have passed the point of no return, we will go sliding down the slippery slope and our luxury, our aimlessness, will become a thing of the past, we will fall lockstep into whatever is to come.

Good people of Radioland, who knows what grim revelations await us there?

3

And so there is darkness. And the road. And the radio.

The radio says: *A. Parachroni—We don't make the reality you believe in. We make the reality you believe in better.*

But it can't last forever. By now, ladies and gentlemen, much like Murrow, you perhaps want form, structure, events that span time, that indulge in cause and effect. And so, soon to be sated people of Radioland, I tell you that *Vayss Uf Makink You Tock*, although utilizing various locations, takes as its primary setting the general vicinity of Lincoln County, Nevada. Let the inertial slide begin...

The darkness up ahead lightens some for Edward R. Murrow, listeners, and for you too. Now, in the distance, barely visible, weakly lit from behind, is a hill. It isn't much, but it finally is something, luxury be damned. Our body language correspondent has just pointed out that Mr. Murrow appears excited. And yet, how does the primary narrator from CNS know that this hill is meant for him? Couldn't it be any old hill? A hill in a series of unremarkable hills? But no, according to our resident clairvoyant, Murrow knows this is his hill, and he knows because (in his mind) the radio tells him so:

"There will be a sign. You will know... when you are in the right place... the place where the story begins, though you are only the narrator, because there will be... a sign... at the top of a hill. The sign will ignite, will be a beacon for you, and when you read it... you will understand."

The radio actually says: *Pilgrim & Pagan Donuts—Make a Holy Quest for this Decadent Delight.*

Indeed, awestruck listeners of Radioland, at the top of the hill, there is a sign. It says: Pilgrim & Pagan Donuts. Could that be it? Our future narrator appears to think so, since he roars into the entryway, jams on the brakes, slides, and comes to a squealing stop, the De Soto, somehow, aligned perfectly in its parking space outside of this 1940s-inspired eatery. Then Murrow lights a cigarette and gazes intently through the windshield at a different sign that, when lit, should say Hot Now (indicating when a new batch of donuts is done), but this one looks different, like it says something else. A disembodied hand comes into view, hovering near the pull chain that will ignite the neon. It pauses for an agonizingly long time.

The radio actually says: *Coming up next on K-Drag–music. Hours and hours and hours of music. Hope you can stay with us...* as Ed switches it off.

But what the man from CNS heard, again, according to our resident clairvoyant, is:

"This, Edward R. Murrow, is an important sign, yes, a sacred sign. It will inform you what time it is, what it's time for, it will be the sign you have forever been seeking. Though your... life before may have been cast into the... chaos of the void, your existence from thereon out will... cohere... once again. Now there will be structure, form, order, real momentum that you can ride... to the holy land. And you will know you have reached your true destination when you see the neon that reads:

"PLOT NOW."

One

The Ancient Achaean Order of the Nobles of the Puppet Regime

That knocking at the door is the Gestapo.

Already partially awake from the continual, morning-long telephone klaxon, Dogfaces in green camouflage rocking back and forth to the metronomic knocking, an infinite room, say Tick-Tock, say Tick-Tock, the earlier ringing unanswered, the knock ongoing, the Dogfaces' camo doing nothing in this white expanse, if anything makes them stick out more, and while the room may be illimitable, at the front (front?) you can see the leaders of this mob, but something tells you they have hands up their backs, a puppet regime. Wall doesn't ignore his visitors, sitting up in his flickering room lit only by the Philco Predicta television set, letting them pound on till the door comes down, till the guy's hand is black and blue, maybe sprained badly, maybe nerve damage, meathook unusable, a claw to forever remind…, but no, though it would be, yeah, poetic justice, Jesus, where'd that come from? Really, Wall? Ugh, time to get some shuteye, few more hours, maybe few more days, but…, well, sure, this enormous room with the Dogfaces, turns out to be a restaurant *called* The Puppet Regime, waitstaff dressed like the Vichy police force weaving between the rocking POWs, and, hate to break it to ya, buddy, but everyone's looking at you, your turn to order, what do you want? Come on already! Never an easy decision, and none of your fellow diners have been very helpful since it just went duck, duck, duck. You look down at the menu and order the first thing there–Red Herring, please, yeah, the Red Herring–at which point everyone at the table goes mad because who knows what twists and turns the waiter'll have to go through to get *that* dish, are you fucking kidding me? The *Red Herring*, seriously? *Seriously, that, that's what you're getting?* The waiter seems delighted, as he vanishes into the enormous room, and you think, as your "friends" go insane, that maybe you should run after him (you don't), maybe you should be a good boy and tell him, "I'm sorry, I meant the goose" (your order remains unchanged), maybe years later you'll look back on this moment and say, "I aborted my bad decision and that made all the difference" (instead of what you'll likely say: "If I knew then what I know now…"), but, maybe what you should actually do is something about that goddamned knocking.

The Predicta shows the Nazi ship *MS Ablenkungsmanöver* on the ocean, and sez, *When Nazi Grand Admiral Karl Dönitz said, "The German submarine fleet is proud of having built an invisible fortification for the Führer anywhere in the world, even in the midst of the eternal ice," few knew exactly what he meant.* Then the words New Swabia appear on the screen, as the camera pulls back and shows that beyond the freighter the Antarctic coast is lined with Nazi flags. *The Neu-Schwabenland Empire, a two part series, next on ICU.*

Looking around, Wall gets the distinct feeling he's never been here before, immediately trumped by the distinct feeling that he's never been anywhere before. Hangovers.

No choice in the matter, so Wall gets up (is that the remains of a white tux you're wearing?), stretches suspenders over shoulders, rubs scalp, makes for the door, tripping over the couch in the process, revealing, uh, oboy… You don't see it, pal, as you regain your balance and shuffle on, but now that the couch has moved, yeah, turns out there's a dead body underneath… Maybe he's not dead. Maybe he's your drinking buddy from last night. And he's sleeping it off. Without breathing.

And those aren't bullet holes in his head. No. Not at all. In a few minutes, he'll sit up, run his hands over his face and through his hair and, sure, he'll still look a little rough, but he'll be alive, saying, "The reports of my death have been… mildly exaggerated." Yeah… Not very likely. But we're pulling for you, Wall. We really are…

At the spyhole there's nothing to see, been broken since the beginning of the lease, since God only knows when, meaning nobody knows. Shrugging, suddenly feeling like maybe this is a momentous occasion, not sure why, Wall throws the door open…

The Predicta sez: *Remember, it's the year of World War Two. Everything, no matter what it may be, must be based on, or make reference to, or be in some way connected to World War Two. And then, after this year, World War Two goes into the Vault…*

… and standing…

… this is the International Channel of Uchronie…

… on the other side of the door…

… formerly the Allohistory Channel, formerly the Alternate History Channel…

… (as if They belong there)…

… ICU, the history of this world…

… are the Gestapo.

… and others.

The Gestapo.

Another door down the hall banging open and slamming back? Seems so, as a man with a bag over his head is led away by two leather trench coated goons, phone still ringing, uh, what the hell is going on? Confronted by the Gestapo, probably best to ignore everything else. Easier. And there's no choice, right? That's just how it goes.

With the Gestapo.

There are two of them. One obviously the Leader, the other the Muscle. The brute rubs his knuckles, stares a kind of Neanderthal menace in your direction. The Leader raises a hand to his black fedora, lifts the hat, replaces it, smiles an unnerving smile, smoothes his leather trench coat.

You have nothing to say. The Gestapo are content to crack knuckles and grin, respectively. For now. For now. Wonder if maybe this is nothing, just some silly hangover dream. Hope is a beautiful thing.

"What's it all about?" sez Wall.

The Leader grins, sez, "Ein Geheimnis."

"I guess you don't know either," sez Wall.

"Persönlichkeit!" from the Leader.

"Excuse me?"

"Name!"

"Wall."

"Full Name!"

"Wallace Heath Orcuson," frowning as it comes out of your mouth.

"WHO?! Vell, guten Tag, Herr ... Orcuson. May ve come in? Hmm? If not, perhaps ve can take care uf zis at der Hauptsitz. Headquarters. Hmm? Vhat vill it be, Herr Orcuson? *Vhat*... vill it be?!" The Leader's voice rises to a spiking pitch, accentuated by his wan sunken cheeks, red lips, piercing blue knowledgeable eyes peering from behind round, steel spectacles, black gloves, silver watch, your eyes are safe nowhere, Wall, nowhere, and what with the corpse right behind you (that you still haven't seen, sure), probably... well, we hope you pick *Their* place, not...

"Uh, yeah, come on in."

Damn.

And so the Gestapo come in, you in the lead, never one for ceremony, and, well, here you go sprawling again, hangovers turn this guy into Jerry Lewis, but as luck would have it your clumsiness, Wall, sends you into the back of the couch which slides forward and, once more, hides the dead body from sight. After what you see as a hard day's work, and finding no other reason why you'd be on the ground, blithely ignorant of the shitstorm avoided, you, Wall, figure it's time to go back to sleep...

The Predicta sez: *In 1938, Captain Alfred Ritscher of the Kriegsmarine led a secret expedition to the area of Antarctica now known as Queen Maud Land, but which was then called Neu-Schwabenland, or New Swabia after the Swabia region of Southern Germany.*

The Gestapo march in, goose-stepping, of course, until the Leader and the Thug position themselves overtop of Wall, who's still not completely awake, wondering who left the Predicta on and why, for fuck's sake, is it showing that cracked out ICU channel? *The stated goal of the expedition was to found a whaling station that would produce fat for margarine and soap, Germany being the second largest importer of Norwegian whale oil.* The Gestapo tower above you, but at least the phone has stopped ringing. Small favors. A professor on the Predicta sez, *"But why would they have to go all the way to Antarctica for whale oil? Wouldn't it be just as expensive to ship the 200,000 metric tonnes from Antarctica as it would be to buy it from Norway? Not to mention how treacherous and unpredictable the Antarctic can be. Even though they knew they were about to enter another war, there has to be a better answer. Why were the Germans really going to New Swabia?"*

"Voult you like to get up, Herr... Orcuson?" sez the Leader.

"Not really," you say and maybe it's better that when you let your head lull to the side your eyes close, Wall. Seeing the dead body would only make this worse.

The Gestapo, not actually interested in what you want, pick you up and haul your ass over to a chair, the Leader and the Thug planting themselves on the couch that hides the dead body.

"What's...?"

"Order!" shouts the Leader.

"What's it...?"

"Zilence! Order! Zilence!"

"For what?"

"Ze Erzählung! Narration!"

"Narration?"

"Ze proper Beschreibung! Description!"

The Leader marches over to the Philco Radio-Phonograph Model 42-1016P (uh, has this behemoth always been here?), twists the volume knob, and...

DESCRIPTION OF THE APARTMENT: *A rectangular loft composed of one room plus a bathroom. The left-hand side of the rectangle has the door, the top of the rectangle has a bathroom and a kitchen nook (which separates the cooking area from the rest of the flat). The right-hand side of the rectangle has four large windows and the bed (unmade). The right bottom of the rectangle has a vintage Philco Radio-Phonograph that bears a picture of the historical Edward R. Murrow atop. The left bottom of the rectangle has a vintage Philco Predicta television set (currently showing the Nazis getting closer to Antarctica) in front of which are two mismatched couches and a torn up leather chair situated in a V, with the chair at the vertex. The wall behind the Predicta is a mirror which... [static]...*

§

But, ladies and gentlemen of Radioland, there's no static at the Pilgrim & Pagan.

Sitting at a booth, unalone thanks to the doubling created by the donut shop's lights and the blackness beyond the window, is our man Edward R. Murrow deep in contemplation–of his twin, of the darkness, of nothing, nothing in particular. Before him on the table is an RCA Model 74 microphone with CNS stenciled white on the shaft plugged into an Ampex 601 reel-to-reel, a red pen, a Sharpie, an unlabeled bottle of what appears to be aspirin, a brown Old Fashioned sinker, an empty coffee cup bearing doggerel:

The Optimist's Creed
As you ramble on through Life, Brother,
Whatever be your Goal,
Keep your Eye upon the Donut,
And not upon the Hole.

and a well-thumbed, red-and-black marked manuscript. According to our radio critic, Loman Drab, the manuscript is called *Vayss Uf Makink You Tock*. Judging by the eye-rolling and heavy sighing, Mr. Drab doesn't approve of this title.

12

Murrow, for the umpteenth time… Umpteen, says Professor Brahma Gupta, our mathematics correspondent, is a number equal to at least one more than you wish it were… Murrow, for the umpteenth time, reads the doggerel on the cup, but only now looks down at the center of his donut… It's difficult to tell what…

KHRYPTYMNYZHY: I believe I can help.

Ladies and gentlemen, joining us is our resident psychic, Madame Khryptymnyzhy. Madame, perhaps you can tell us what our primary narrator, Edward R. Murrow, is going through right now.

KHRYPTYMNYZHY: Mr. Murrow… Mr. Murrow is trying to reconstruct… reconstruct the night. This is what I believe… yes… reconstruct… the night… because he sees himself as if… as if in a… movie. Third person. A camera. In his mind, he is looking at himself.

Madame Khryptymnyzhy, can you tell us what he sees?

KHRYPTYMNYZHY: Yes. Dressed in his conservative, gray suit. Smoking a cigarette… Yes. He is in a room… at the Hyperborean Arms… a room very similar to the one we just… we just heard him describe. It is… yes… it is… almost… almost identical. He sits in a chair similar… similar to the one Mr. Orcuson occupies… occupies now. He sits in a chair and… and he stares. He stares. But there… there is something wrong with… with the light … the light in the room. It must… it must be the light. Your Mr. Murrow… the light… his skin looks waxen… yellow… your Mr. Murrow… full of… of fear… The room… the room looks… There is… there is something in the room with Mr. Murrow. Something… something…

Madame Khryptymnyzhy?

KHRYPTYMNYZHY: I'm afraid I have lost my connection with Edward Murrow… for now.

Thank you, Madame, for that very… dramatic report. Dr. A.O.K. DeMent, our resident psychiatrist, has just joined us. Could you shed some light… I mean, could you explain *what* is troubling our narrator?

DEMENT: Indeed. Your primary voice-over man, Edward R. Murrow, has a fully developed sense of narrative identity, meaning he has integrated his life experiences into an internalized, evolving story (starring Edward R. Murrow, of course) that provides him with a sense of unity and purpose. This is nothing new. Lots of people do it. Murrow's problem, however, is that he's especially susceptible to catatonia. When he becomes catatonic, later, in order to explain to himself what was happening while his brain was switched off, he must invent transitions that, for all intents and purposes, are not truthful, are not made of the truth, are not even based on the truth, and yet he is thoroughly devoted to the Truth.

Of course. But when he loses his narrative grasp on reality, when he allows his life to become amorphous…?

KHRYPTYMNYZHY: The darkness… the darkness… out the window… an indescribable wall of black… The ink… the ink's not falling… not falling from the sky… like rain… but draining from it… oozing… Are you there, Mr. Murrow? Mr. Murrow? Come in! Come in! Where are you, Edward R. Murrow…? I have lost him again…

So, compassionate listeners of Radioland, when Edward R. Murrow returns from a reality hiatus, he wants to comprehend the entirety of what has happened, the whole, unwilling to accept that part of the donut is the hole. Without the hole, the donut is not whole… Ladies and gentlemen, may you never think so much about an inscription on a coffee mug.

DEMENT: In order to reestablish a link with his structured reality, being a narrator after all, Murrow will often record narration about his immediate surroundings…

Murrow flips the switch on the Ampex reel-to-reel, and so come in, Ed Murrow:

MURROW: *This*… is Pilgrim & Pagan Donuts. Under me there's a black & white tiled floor. Small hexagons. To my left there's a chrome-fronted counter topped with black & white formica shards. The donuts, of numerous varieties, are in a display case hidden from where I sit, though I know they're there. On the counter is a steel behemoth made by the National Cash Register Co. The register appears aged, but it's fully digital and computerized, able to process any plastic you may have. Behind this mammoth is a big galoot named Arty Magam with his long, unkempt, shaggy brown hair bulging out from underneath a vintage Washington

Senators baseball cap turned backwards. Occasionally, it seems like he's warming up to pitch a ballgame. A dry spitter, maybe. A knuckleball. If you come into the Pilgrim & Pagan tonight, he'll be there, behind the counter, ready to take your order, and refill your coffee…

"You, like, need some, uh, more java, man?" says Arty Magam.

"No thanks," says Murrow, popping a couple aspirin.

"By the way, man, what's your, like, name?"

"Murrow."

"Good to meet ya, man."

Yes, this is where Edward R. Murrow is right now, ladies and gentlemen. To hear him describe it, well… Reality is fixed, objective, verifiable. Norton Thales, our resident physicist, says that Murrow's narrated world is composed of and governed by laws, instead of loosely described by first principles and questionable theories. Sir Isaac Newton, admiring the clock ticking on the wall, would be right at home in this Pilgrim & Pagan franchise, says Professor Thales. And, should we let Murrow continue on with his narration, it would all make perfect sense. Following the chain of events, before this donut shop, where was Ed Murrow? He was in his car, a 1942 Chrysler De Soto. And before his car, no comment is necessary. Madame Khryptymnyzhy has already told us that he was in an apartment like Wall's. Listeners of Radioland, the illusion of cause and effect appears to be fully operational for our man Murrow… for now. But what about for Wallace Heath Orcuson out at the Hyperborean?

Munn E. Pitts, our real estate analyst, and Sirius Simoleons, our financial analyst, have more on Wall's residence and the corporation that owns it. Gentlemen…

PITTS: The Hyperborean Arms is, to be frank, a mystifying property. It's located in an undisclosed and unincorporated part of the American Southwest. The one time I saw the place, on the way there, I honestly thought I was being taken to a drug deal or an execution. When we arrived and they removed my blindfold, here was this building looking rather like the Mendelssohn Palace in Berlin, as if it'd been picked up by a whirlwind and dropped into the desert. Above the door, in a Gothic font, was carved THE HYPERBOREAN ARMS. *Hyperborean.* Because it was so out of place, the name made sense... at the time, anyway. Afterwards, it was a very long drive home. Longer than the trip there. At some point during the return, we stopped at a donut shop. I have no idea why...

What *is* the property, exactly, Mr. Pitts? It's an apartment building, correct?

PITTS: That *is* what the deed says. But why would anyone want to put an apartment building in the middle of the desert? And at that such a lavish apartment building, since the Hyperborean Arms is almost identical to the Mendelssohn Palace, which is itself an English country house–or in that style, I should say. Your literary scholar, Dr. Anne T. Epifanik, could speak more to this, but the Hyperborean kind of reminds me of a murder mystery setting–impossibly remote. So isolated you wonder how any of the construction workers got to the job site, how any of the materials were transported, how anyone in his right mind could've ever said, "Of course *this* is where we will break ground," without being met immediately by mocking laughter. No, the Hyperborean Arms couldn't possibly've been built in any normal way. If you saw it on the horizon, you'd think it was a mirage, but somehow this mirage forgets to disappear on closer inspection. It's solid. A completely material hallucination. Sounds crazy, sure. But I find that argument to be more convincing than the idea that a bunch of carpenters, masons, plumbers, electricians, roofers, foremen, engineers, and architects all trucked out here to go about the workaday task of building the Hyperborean. Now if that were the case, well, whoever planned this colossal folly was either the greatest con man or the biggest fool...

SIMOLEONS: I can speak to that, Mr. Pitts. The business that owns and runs the Hyperborean is every bit as mysterious. It's called A. Parachroni, a conglomerate that's filed its preliminary paperwork with the SEC to become a corporation, but right now only has a red herring prospectus...

A red herring prospectus? Could you please tell our less financially savvy listeners at home what that is, Mr. Simoleons?

SIMOLEONS: Of course. A red herring prospectus is a document produced by an issuer that intends to offer stocks. It's a preliminary record, however, and does not yet include all of the necessary information a company needs in order to have an IPO. The reason it's called a 'red herring prospectus' is because the document is designed to drum up interest in a company that, technically, no one knows much about. Not yet, anyway. This *red herring* draws investors away from more stable ventures (well-known securities) by generating interest (normally via arguments to novelty) much in the way mystery stories generate interest by planting the seed of suspicion at the beginning.

Do we know who owns A. Parachroni?

SIMOLEONS: That's part of the mystery. The company was allegedly founded by one Renato Fregoli, who has been missing for just over seven years now and is therefore presumed dead, meaning his business transfers to his children who have the unlikely names Iam and Ima Fregoli. A brother and sister. Little to nothing is known about this family, making A. Parachroni's red herring prospectus very much a red herring.

PITTS: If no one lived in this building, it'd probably be easier to understand. But there is a resident: Wallace Heath Orcuson. Sounds like a fake name.

SIMOLEONS: Probably is. All of this, the Hyperborean, A. Parachroni, the Fregoli family, Orcuson, it could be an elaborate front. But the question is—a front for who or for what?

PITTS: That makes sense. We all know what it's like to walk into a front organization. There's always just some guy sitting there, chewing on a toothpick or smoking a cigarette...

SIMOLEONS: He eyes you with contempt. He goes out of his way to be unhelpful. He gets paid to stifle progress. He knows nothing about anything. You marvel at his lack of knowledge...

PITTS: ...and ambition. Other people, even stupid people, even lazy people, they know a few things, they want something, no matter how small, no matter how trivial. But him...

SIMOLEONS: ...he only wants you to leave, so he can go back to collecting his paltry paycheck that keeps him in smokes, that allows him to continue on knowing nothing, wanting nothing. It's only when someone comes in that, with a heavy sigh...

PITTS: ...yes, his sighs are ample, denoting physical weariness, connoting the weight of the entire universe be upon his shoulders...

SIMOLEONS: ...that he swings into inaction, making it seem like nothing can be known, nothing can be done, unless, of course, you leave him and his front alone.

PITTS: That sounds like our Mr. Orcuson...

That was Munn E. Pitts and Sirius Simoleons, ladies and gentlemen. The story so far seems much more ambiguous than previously thought, as if it took place in a null zone. Yes, there is an apartment building, but why does it exist?

According to our investigative reporter, Eve Z'droppe, the fog may be clearing. Ms. Z'droppe...

Z'DROPPE: This is Eve Z'droppe reporting. Although the account at this time is uncorroborated, we have an anonymous source that claims Wallace Heath Orcuson was frequently seen days and even weeks before the murder with Greta Zelle, wife of one "Senator" Kipper Maris, gentleman of leisure. We now think that Zelle had something to do with bringing Orcuson to the Hyperborean, possibly for a tryst. Since there's no road that leads to the apartment building, we have no idea how they arrived, or if Zelle was ever there at all. For now, that is all we have. I will bring you more as the story develops...

Thank you, Eve Z'droppe... Ladies and gentlemen, I am sorry to skip from one report to the next, but our resident clairvoyant, Madame Khryptymnyzhy, has connected once more with Edward R. Murrow. And so...

KHRYPTYMNYZHY: I believe... yes... I have connected again... yes... with Edward Murrow. He sees himself still. Now, as if projected on the darkness beyond the donut shop, he sees himself... he sees himself in the apartment... sitting... staring at the floor... as a red stain spreads... spreads across the carpet... toward him. But then there is only his reflection from the Pilgrim & Pagan again...

Brave listeners out there in Radioland, why is our primary narrator, Edward R. Murrow, so tormented by this project? A brief description of his job history should help explain. Ed Murrow is, of course, a narrator for CNS. And according to the *Columbia Narratorial Services Handbook,* we know that whatever a narrator says comes into being. For instance, if a narrator speaks the words "a murder has been committed," then indeed a murder has been committed. But we also know that a narrator can either be a diegetic or a non-diegetic entity. Foax, that just means he can exist within the story or outside of it. Thus far in his career, CNS has allowed Murrow to be embroiled in the action, rather like a character in a radio play, commenting as he acts, commenting upon things he's just witnessed. Everything, thus far in his career, has either been real or at least appeared real. In the case of *Vayss Uf Makink You Tock,* Murrow himself is not involved in the action and none of it appears real. Our psychiatrist, Dr. A.O.K. DeMent, has more.

DeMent: Edward Murrow is suffering from a sense of detachment. Even the donut shop, where he currently sits, seems unreal to him, never mind the Hyperborean apartment from earlier. *That place* belongs to the realm of mythology. His ordered universe is gone, if he ever actually believed in it. With no sense of the past or the present, Ed feels lost, like a disembodied voice. That's what he always is to us, the listeners, certainly. But never to himself. Until now. A narrator is like a genie: great power, but he must obey his master–the script. His job is to read the words, to convey the ideas and sentiments he's been given no matter what they may be. And so if this program, *Vayss Uf Makink You Tock,* doesn't sound like Edward R. Murrow, it's because it's not Edward R. Murrow, even though the vocal cords you hear vibrating are his. The narrator's place in the world, the narrator's beliefs and opinions, the narrator's personality: moot. Some have no problem dealing with this. Others, like Murrow, have a great deal of trouble. Perhaps the only saving grace for Ed Murrow is that, speaking with the voice of authority, what he says becomes truth…

"It's a nice day out," says Edward R. Murrow, back in the Pilgrim & Pagan.

"If you, like, say so, Murrow. Murrow, Murrow, Murrow. You mean, like, uh, Edward R.?" says Arty Magam, pouring more coffee for the man from CNS.

"Well, for now, any…"

"But I mean, right, you're dead."

Looking at his reflection, Edward R. Murrow appears to be floating in space. There are no stars. There is no moon. The darkness outside a black hole consuming everything. But perhaps Arty is right and this is an afterlife with oblivion to come. In the Pilgrim & Pagan the clock keeps ticking, but the numbers run backwards, the minute and hour hands remain stationary, while the second hand clicks back and forth between the 12 and one second away from the 12 in both directions. Outside everything is devoured by the black hole, the hole, the hole that is part of the whole at the center of it all…

And now this:

MURROW: The wall behind the Predicta is a large mirror which, unbeknownst to Mr. Orcuson, is a two-way. Behind the mirror sits the narrator reading the script into a microphone as the events unfold before him. The narrator senses something is wrong with Mr. Orcuson, something beyond the Gestapo…

§

[static ends]

… The floor is covered with wall to wall carpeting the like of which is normally only seen in casinos: bursts and swirls, strange attractors everywhere. On the walls, tastefully framed and hung, are propaganda posters from World War Two. They say: "A CARELESS WORD… A NEEDLESS SINKING" and "A CARELESS WORD… ANOTHER CROSS" and "…BECAUSE SOMEBODY TALKED" and "SOMEONE TALKED!" and above the bed a weathered original "LOOSE LIPS SINK SHIPS." Again, at the bottom of the rectangle, Mr. Orcuson sits in the chair at the vertex of the V, the Leader sits on the corpse couch, while the Thug has moved behind the facing couch. Mr. Orcuson wears darkish suit pants and a lightish shirt. He is of medium height and build and youngish. There seems to be nothing specific about him. He is neither flesh, nor fowl, nor a good red herring. The Leader and the Thug both match their previous descriptions, having aged very little in the interim, though both wear an armband with the usual Nazi insignia:

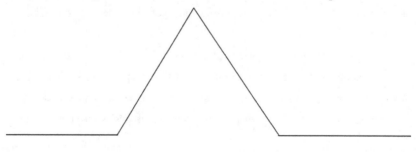

The Leader and the Thug snap to attention, give the Roman Salute, then the Thug resumes his position, while the Leader turns the radio down.

The Predicta sez: *We've always thought the Nazis' intent was to conquer Europe because that's what we were supposed to think. Actually, the Nazis, from the very beginning, wanted to conquer far more than that. But they knew, in order to be successful, they'd have to be patient, their scheme unfolding over the course of decades, not months or years. And so, the Nazis came to realize that in order to cover up their secret plan, they were going to need a red herring big enough to mislead everyone, even most of their own people. Once this grand diversion was in place, the Nazis would begin the search for what they really wanted. The camera enters a vast, Antarctic cavern. An entrance to the Hollow Earth.*

"Was the radio describing my...?"

"Nefer mind, Herr... Orcuson! Ve must begin with ze...!"

"Do you just scream all the time?"

The Leader slumps down a bit, smooths his pants with his hands.

"You are right. It ist schwierig. Difficult. Ja. To be ze Gestapo zometimes. Ve haff to be menacink, cruel. Ve haff to sprechen vith zese outrageous Akzente. Accents. Who voult belief us if ve speichen. Spoke. Like an Amerikanische? No vun. Unt zen vhere voult ve be? Lost! Vanderink in ze colt for no reason, vhile..."

"I'd like to make your jobs easier, agents of the Gestapo. Really, I would. But think about it like this: if I understand the situation correctly, you're here to interrogate me. So you can hardly be surprised if I complain about your methods."

The Leader and the Thug exchange a look. And, Wall, well, they almost seem, uh, proud of you?

The Predicta sez: *To most people, the New Swabia Expedition seemed like a waste of time and money. Frivolous. Of course, this was the genius of the plan. Even amongst the Nazis there were few who knew the actual objective.*

"Ve like you already, Herr... Orcuson. Ve shall go easy," sez the Leader, removing a cigarette and a holder from his pocket. "But ve must begin vith die Fragen. Ze qvestions. First, vhere ist your Pistole? Gun?"

"Why would you think I have a gun?"

"Zis ist Amerika, Herr… Orcuson, eferyvun has eine Waffe. A gun. But no matter. Second qvestion: do you haff ein Licht? A light?"

"I certainly would if I smoked," sez Wall.

"Do you zmoke?"

"Don't you know?"

"Don't you?! " The Leader is not amused.

"I don't feel like a smoker, so I don't think I do. But can you really trust a smoker? (Present members of the SS excluded.) Here's a person committing ritualistic suicide right out for everyone to see. Doesn't seem like the most trustworthy kinda guy, you know? Say, if you walked up to someone who was slowly sawing into his own wrist and asked where the post office was, whattaya think? Could you trust the directions? What does he care if you find the post office? The jerk! I'd kill that guy if I got the chance and if this wasn't a civilized society and if he wasn't dead from bleeding all over the place already, telling me, me!, the post office is just around the corner, when it obviously… So, anyway, I'm not sure you could rely on a single thing a smoker says. Except, of course, if you ask him what he'll be doing later, and he says, without pause, smoking."

There's a green ashtray on a chrome stand next to Wall.

"You don't *sink* you zmoke?" sez the Leader, grinning at the ashtray overflowing with cigarette butts.

"No, but maybe I have friends who smoke and I have no problem with it."

"Ja, Freunde…"

"That is, if I can believe they are my friends, being smokers and all."

The Leader inhales deeply on his unlit cigarette, scrutinizing you, almost… amused?

The Predicta sez: *From the outset, the New Swabia Expedition faced difficulties, though now it can be told, the difficulties were manufactured. Hitler, himself, publicly declared the mission of minimum importance, and on paper it appears that Captain Ritscher and his crew were receiving orders from a dizzying array of naval and government officials. As a part of the front, confusion and stagnation reigned.*

"Very vell, Herr… Orcuson, you haff had your fun vith ze Gestapo.

But… Herr… Orcuson, please, more fun, ha ha, zis Name, it zounds fake. Vallace Heat Orcuson. A fake name. Ja. Wie sagen Sie? Wie sagen Sie?"

"I don't speak German," sez Wall.

"Made up. Yes. No vun has zis Name. You aren't pullink ze leg, ze leg uf ze Gestapo, are you? Zis voult be a… bad idea. Come now, you can tock to us. Vhat ist your name?"

"What would you like me to go by?"

"Ve cannot begin vithout your Name."

"The name I was given?"

"Your birth Name."

"My Christian name?"

"Are you a Christian, Herr?"

"I wish to God I knew."

"Your true Name."

"You wouldn't want me to make one up?"

The Leader smiles, taps his glasses, and the Thug leans in, intimidating the empty couch.

"Zat voult be a bad idea, Herr… Orcuson, for it appears you haff done zo already!"

"Okay. My true name."

"Ja."

Wall stands up, smiles, extends a hand toward the Leader, sez, "Hello, my name's Wallace Heath Orcuson, but my friends, inveterate smokers to the last, public ritualized suicides to a man, like to call me Wally, I'm sure. But I hate the name Wally, and I don't actually recall having any friends, so I go by Wall."

A pause.

"Ve belief you, Herr… Orcuson," sez the Leader with a sigh. "But you must admit, your Name, ha ha, zounds fake. Ja. Vhen our report is read, no vun vill belief it. Vallace Heat Orcuson. Nein. He ist not real. An alias, maybe… But, as you might zay, try zis on for size—vhat do you sink your Name voult be if it veren't… Orcuson?"

"I guess, since you're the Gestapo, it'd be something like Stein…"

The Predicta sez: *Finally, on December 17, 1938, the New Swabia Expedition left Hamburg in the freighter MS* Ablenkungsmanöver, *a ship capable of carrying and catapulting aircraft. Unless whales began flying in 1938, why did the sailors need an air presence?*

The Leader stands, joyously takes your hand he'd left hanging, Wall, and sez: "Herr Schtein! Ja! Uf course. Eine Jude! A good choice. Ve learn more about you by die Sekunde. Ze second. Now, voult you please zit down here on ze divan?" The Leader's eyes look kind, inviting, his head nodding toward the Thug's couch as if you had come over to his place.

"You mean the one your boy is behind?"

"Einleitungen!" The Leader points to the Thug and, "Zis ist Oberschütze Lorenz Schmetterlink, my partner in ze SS."

Schmetterling clicks his heels together, salutes.

"I am Major Gustav Freytag."

He takes a bow.

"Now! Vill you please…?" he sez, gesturing toward the couch.

"No, I like this chair," Wall sez, sitting back down. "It has fewer thugs behind it. Now normally, sure, I'd sit on that couch, no problem. It is mine. But when the Gestapo want me to sit there, it makes me see that couch in a new light. Maybe there's something wrong with it. Something's off. Maybe it's a morally inferior couch. Maybe it's the kind of couch, who knows?, that'd turn you in just to save its own upholstery. What the fuck?! I'm disgusted by that couch! I'll never sit on it again! How did it even end up in this apartment?!"

"Ja, der Stuhl. Ze chair. Zis ist ze better Entscheidung. Decision. But you understand vhy I had to…"

"No explanation necessary, Gestapo agents. I would like to know why you're here, though," you say, yawning. Maybe, Wall, your rope-a-dope jackassery will get rid of the Gestapo before they find out there's a corpse under your couch, huh?

"Ve are establishink Ihr Hintergrund. Your background. For instance, how lonk haff you liffed here?"

"I can't remember having ever lived anywhere else…"

"Ist zat zo? Das Gebäude. Ze buildink ist new."

"…and yet this feels like my first day here. Luckily, I managed to bring all of my World War Two propaganda posters along."

The Predicta sez: *From December 17, 1938 to January 19, 1939, the MS Ablenkungsmanöver made its voyage to the Princess Martha Coast. Although their trek was short, crew members believed they were lost the entire time. Many of them began to believe they'd entered some other dimension…*

"Zen vhen vere you born?"

"It was a year rife with both tragedy and comedy, a year remembered for its august events, its heroic leaps, its grand scope, a year so often listed as being part of a Golden Age that not only is the wish to have lived during that time considered a cliché, but pointing out that cliché has become its own cliché. Yes, to this very minute you can hear politicians demand that things were done a certain way then (and everyone knows when then was) and we should overturn none of the decisions from then now; we would do so only at our own folly, at our own peril even! And to this very second friends who lived through that year together greet each other with We Will Never Forget Where We Were When…"

"Ze year, mein Herr. Ze year!"

"I don't recall. I hadn't learned my numbers or my months yet. You see, I was just a little baby. And anyway, why do we number our years the way we do? Didn't this system begin when most of what people thought and believed in was hooey? Isn't the earth something like 4,540,000,000 years old? I tell ya, next year should be 4,540,000,001, and so on. We'd even have thirteen months that are each twenty-eight days long to match the actual lunar revolution. The new month would be Freytaguary or Gustavember. It'd be the Orcusonian Calendar. And from now on we'll remember the years because they'll make sense, instead of being completely arbitrary. Come on, we don't believe in nearly so much hooey anymore. Only a little bit. Let's get things right this time. My plan has novelty going for it, that's for sure. What else do you need? Who's with me?"

"Very droll, Herr Schtein. Oh ze Gestapo does luff to laugh!"

"Really?"

"No, you svine! (Vell, I do, but ze Gestapo does not…) Vhere are you from?"

"The place was new to me, I'd just arrived, there were no signs, no recognizable language, no way of knowing. One second there was nothing, and then here I am without even a marker saying you are here. Not that I could've read it if there were…"

The Predicta shows the *Ablenkungsmanöver* approaching a permafrost coast. *In his journal, Captain Ritscher admits, when the frozen continent was finally spotted, he wasn't convinced it was Antarctica. It was cold, full of ice and snow, but it seemed otherworldly to the sailors. When Ritscher and the crew planted flags along the shore, it wasn't because they expected the Norwegians to come and reclaim their land; it was to convince themselves that they were still standing on planet earth.*

The phone starts ringing again, Wall, and I mean, come on, who could it be? All morning rattling off the hook.

"Aren't you goink to answer das Telefon, Herr Schtein?"

"Would you like me to?"

"Aren't you curious who it might be? Who keeps callink unt callink you?"

"Should I be?"

"Nosink has happent up to now, Herr Schtein. But perhaps zis vill zignal a beginnink for you. It may be important. Zis call may lead to zomezink, zomezink unexpected, zomezink even ze Gestapo doesn't see comink!"

"It couldn't be anyone important. I don't know anyone important. I wish I did. I really, truly do. But somehow, as soon as I get acquainted with somebody, even if they were important before, they immediately stop being important. I'm like an importance vacuum. Whatever became of? Whatever happened to? Where are they now? All questions that could be asked about my crew, except that they've become so unimportant no one would bother asking them…"

"No vun important, you zay. Vhat ist ze first sink you remember?"

"The telephone ringing," you say, as the telephone stops ringing. "I suppose this morning…"

"Unt now ze Gestapo are here."

"…or whatever time it was. I have no memories before that."

"No past. How do you know you are who you zay you are?"

"Because I say it."

"Not even a present, Herr Schtein. Zere ist only ze future. Your life is abzurd."

"What's it all about anyway?"

The Predicta shows the men of the New Swabia Expedition wandering across the tundra: *Over the coming weeks, there was great hardship. Some of the sailors starved to death, many ended up with frostbitten fingers or limbs that needed amputation, while others succumbed to hypothermia. And still the entrance to the Hollow Earth was nowhere in sight. The expedition appeared to be a failure.*

"You zee, Schmetterlink. I told you he knew nosink. He's perfekte." The major pats his arm holding the Nazi insignia, and only now does it look odd to Wall. "Such a promizink beginnink, ve are in zight uf ze Pyramide." At mention of the pyramid, Freytag jumps to his feet, clicks his heels, and both he and Schmetterling give the Roman Salute.

"Herr Schtein, I am sorry, but do you happen to haff a light?" spinning the holder with cigarette around on his hand.

"Sure."

An insidious smile and: "Vhen did you ztart zmokink, Herr Schtein?"

"Since the last time you asked me. I'm a pack a day man, now, Major."

Schmetterling glowers at you through his bushy eyebrows. Major Freytag frowns, removes his hat and gloves, drops them on the threadbare couch, runs a shaking hand through his blonde, slicked hair. No more smiles, Wall. He taps his spectacles with the cigarette holder. Schmetterling leans in over the vacant couch, intimidating, towering, hulking, a puissant marionette. You're rather disappointed for the superfluous goon… But after this routine, they, uh, relax? Relax. The Gestapo agents, and you should tell us if this is preferable, or if it's unnerving, Wall–the Gestapo agents smile at you. Why? Maybe it's a little scratch my back and I'll scratch yours. After all, the way these SS operatives've been looking at you, pal, they're fascinated. Like they were observing some rare animal they'd only read about, Latin name in the caption, but had never seen in the wild. Beforehand, they adjusted their expectations, only to stumble upon, well, you, buddy. Doing absolutely everything they ever wanted, ever dreamed you could do. And so, returning the favor, they put on this performance in your honor. I guess you're welcome?

The Predicta sez: *It was only when his ravaged crew was on the brink of mutiny that Captain Ritscher finally informed them of the* Ablenkungsmanöver*'s secret mission. He told them about the Hollow Earth.*

Beginning anew, Major Freytag sez: "You are probably vonderink vhy ve are here."

"I *am* wondering why you are here."

"Ve…"

"Which is why I asked."

Annoyance, utter annoyance, and then that smile again.

"*You are probably vonderink vhy ve are here.* Vell, Herr Schtein, ve are here because zomezink zuspicious has happent…"

"But then isn't it always suspicious when the Gestapo stop by? What with World War Two over for more than half a century and all?"

"…or ist about to happen," sez Major Freytag. He's obviously loving every second of this, Wall. Schmetterling, meanwhile, has begun pacing the room, looking rather like a boxer psyching himself up. "You zee, when ve begin vork on a case, ve haff, yes, different amounts uf… information. By ze Ende, make no miztake, Herr Schtein, ve vill know all. But at ze beginnink… zometimes ve know a great deal, unt zometimes ve know very little. Zometimes ve know all about ze principal, all about ze zituation, zo ve are merely zere *to vatch ze insect sqvirm!* Unt uzzer times ve find ourselves in alien zurroundinks among Unbekannte. Unknowns. However, no matter vhere ve end up, zomezink zuspicious has just happent, or ist just about to," sez Freytag, getting up, moving behind the couch. "For instance, how vell do you know your Nachbar. Neighbor?"

Schmetterling runs into the Philco Radio-Phonograph, the volume spiking, a voice sez, *He has a neighbor? I thought he was the only resident,* before the Thug shuts the thing off, Freytag directing his inferior back behind the couch with his eyes.

"You mean the guy I saw your boys take away?" sez Wall.

"Ist zat vhat you saw, Herr Schtein? Are you sure?"

"I saw them with my own eyes… So, uh, you're not here about… me?"

The Predicta sez: *But why would the Germans go in search of a myth? Isn't this just more evidence of Nazi madness? The answer is: no. Thanks to a clique in the Thule Society, the Germans knew the Hollow Earth existed. They knew all along. And they also knew whatever group went in search of the entrance would have a tough time finding it. But they would find it just the same.*

"Oh, ve're here about you, too, Herr Stein," sez Major Freytag, pulling the couch back, revealing the corpse. "But ve are also here about your Nachbar. Neighbor."

Now they have you, Wall. And what red herring can you use to throw them off your trail?

§

Our eminent drama critic, Blaise Algonquin, describes the scene at the Pilgrim & Pagan this way:

ALGONQUIN: Tableau–Magam and Murrow reflected in the window. For now, they are the epitome of two *guys* in a donut shop. Ha-HA! Not necessarily men of import, nor men of action. Just a couple a *guys*. If we didn't already know better, we'd take them for extras: Waiter #1 and Coffee Drinker. Soon the named characters will grace the stage, the principals will demand our attention, and these two will become so much scenery. But no! Not here. Arthur and Edward may, briefly, appear superfluous, but that's only because they stand and sit, respectively, agape, contemplating the nothingness beyond…

"S-so dark out there," says Arty Magam. "Man, you know? Wow. I mean, right, just look out there. What's, uh, you know? What's the setting? If you were givin' this as a, right, movie pitch and the bigwigs asked you, when the cameras fade in, Jackson…"

"Ed."

"Huh? Oh, yeah. When the cameras fade in, Jack, just where the hell are we? What's the dateline? Could you lay it on 'em? Could ya lay it down? I mean this ain't even sci-fi. It's… I dunno what it is, man. Hell, you'd have to tell them bigwigs,"

Magam straightens up, sets the coffee pot on the table, makes a movie screen with his pointer fingers and thumbs. "The camera doesn't fade in, gentlemen; it cuts in. A hatchet right to the frontal lobe. And when that silvery picture suddenly flickers onto the screen, we're nowhere. Not the middle of nowhere, sirs. Not some cornfield or desert or frozen wasteland or redneck town. Not lost at sea or floating in outer space. The setting, gentlemen, is nowhere… That's what you'd have to say, man. An' what about us? Where are we, Jack? Like, are we in this donut shop, or are we out there? In that nothing? Maybe we're out in that darkness thinkin', 'Fuck, man, if we were at least in a Pilgrim & Pagan, that'd be something,' you know? Exactly. Ex–actly. And that right there… that… right… there… that's… that's what you call… I dunno what you call it."

Ed Murrow slowly turns and looks in marvel at his companion, as Algonquin reports that our big galoot will be performing his one-man show, *Arty Magam: The Fuck?*, all next month.

"It scares me that I know what you're talking about, Arty," says Edward R. Murrow, taking a couple more aspirin. "There was a time when I wouldn't have. There was a time when I thought I knew where I was. Now I'm not so sure. It's as if there were an era when the world and everything that was going on in the world… when it was all so real. But at some point we were blown off course. And so we wait and hope for someone to come along and tell us the truth, to put us back on the right path once again. In the meantime, we reach back to…"

Murrow trails off as he finally notices Arty has started putting on a dumbshow: a pitcher warming up before a ballgame. Our primary narrator, watching this spectacle, appears to be without words.

Ladies and gentlemen of Radioland, according to our theorist, Theo Reticle, there's a problem out at the Pilgrim & Pagan for our man Ed Murrow. That problem is this: the present and the past. Professor Reticle has more in his report.

RETICLE: The major difference between the present and the past, at least for Edward R. Murrow, is permanence. In the past, you were somewhere. It can be proven. There's evidence. But where are you right now? Right now. Suddenly, we're on shaky ground. It's difficult to talk about the moment in the moment. Later,

later all places and experiences get situated, all thoughts made part of the report. The rest is forgotten, edited out by the boys back at the station, and anything left on the cutting room floor never even happened. But that log is the expurgated version. The present, the *actual* present, like a fog, hovers over the past, obfuscates the future, always threatening to dissipate, never quite evaporating, leaving you lost in its opacity…

Professor Reticle, could you give our listeners a more solid example?

RETICLE: Take your Arty Magam. If asked what he was doing right now, right this very minute, he probably wouldn't say he was preparing for an imaginary baseball game between the Minnesota Twins and the Texas Rangers; I don't figure he'd say that he was warming his arm up and tightening his grip on his signature pitch: the knuckleball; and I can't imagine that Magam would tell anyone at all that this particular imaginary game was to be a throwback, both teams wearing uniforms from 1942, meaning both squads are dressed as the Washington Senators (since each team began in the District of Columbia as a Senators franchise before moving to their respective cities). And yet, based on his actions and based on a report from Madame Khryptymnyzhy, that's exactly what's going on. Certainly, if Arty's boss asked him what he was doing, the donut clerk'd say he's waiting on customers, sweeping up, preparing another batch of sinkers, brewing more coffee. But if you or I, Mr. Station Manager, or anyone else asked him, Arty would probably say, "Nothing. I was doing nothing."

Well, other than his job, Mr. Magam isn't doing anything important right now.

RETICLE: And that's just the point. The reason we so often claim we're doing nothing is because we believe what we've done is of little historical import. Certainly this moment won't be included in the log of the past. The pristine, beautiful, knowable past. Instead, it'll be blotted out. The present is our reality; the past is our mythology. By saying "nothing" when asked what we're doing, we continue to worship the concreteness, the importance of the past and shrink from the difficulty of the present. And yet, how often are we really, truly doing nothing? Rarely, I daresay, if ever.

Thank you, Professor Reticle. Joining us once again, people of Radioland,

31

is our own Madame Khryptymnyzhy who has reconnected with our primary narrator. Take it away, Madame…

Khryptymnyzhy: Your Edward R. Murrow… yes… he is still trying to process the scene at the… Hyperborean… the Hyperborean. The point of view switches back and forth… yes… back and forth between the camera view… the third person view… and his own perspective. In the Pilgrim & Pagan, he stares out the window at the darkness. At the Hyperborean, he sees himself staring out the window at the darkness. But …but sometimes… sometimes there is… there's only darkness. Darkness. And then… there's a large man in the room… in the Hyperborean room… with him… with Edward. Murrow… Murrow is… not unhappy to see him… Maybe relieved… yes… relieved. Here, says the big man… and hands a bottle to Murrow. Drink, drink, says the big man… His name… the big man's name… is Kuzma…

"Kuzma," says Murrow back in the Pilgrim & Pagan. "Kuzma Grigorovich Bezopasnosky." Ladies and gentlemen, I do apologize, Ed isn't usually this… odd. We will have a report on his mental state as soon as we can get one together. In the meantime, he has removed *Vayss Uf Makink You Tock* from his reel to reel and has replaced it with another spool. Inquisitive listeners of Radioland, he has pressed play, so let's listen in…

I remember drinking with the big Russian, Kuzma. We were in some basement bar. It wasn't a nice basement with a fireplace and brick walls and wooden columns supporting the ceiling. It looked like an unfinished wine cellar. A cracked stone floor, smell of mildew and mold, almost no lights, every part of the room a shadowy corner. Other than me and Kuzma, the only inhabitant: a curmudgeonly bartender who'd get you anything you wanted as long as it was cheap vodka. Once he served you, he'd forget you were there, forget you ever existed. Probably preferable to the few customers he had. He was part ghost, a poltergeist who moved glasses and liquor, and who spoke only in a dialect of disdain. You were invited to disappear into your own alcoholic oblivion as soon as possible, so he could get back to cursing the world.

Kuzma and I ordered a bottle, washed our glasses out with our own spit, and drank toasts in spite of the place.

"Na zdrovye!" I said.

"Thees ees not vhat you say," said Kuzma.

"No?"

"Nyet. Za vas!" he said, and raised his glass. We drank.

"Za fstryetchoo!" he said, and raised his glass. We drank.

"Za nashoo droozhboo!" he said, and raised his glass. We drank.

"Za zhenshsheen!" he said. We looked around. There were no women. Even the bartender was missing, though we could hear echoes of the old poltergeist's curses. We were alone in a dank basement drinking, the shadows seeming deeper than before.

"Payekhalee!" Kuzma said, and raised his glass. We drank.

We left the bar, taking the bottle with us, but not the glasses. We stumbled through the city lit only by the quarter moon, the color washed out of everything. It was a beautiful and lonesome city that appeared abandoned. Except for us. Maybe everyone else had been evacuated.

We were next to another bluish building, could've been a ruined cathedral. It had a giant mound of dirt next to it and a lone church pew, looking as if the night had excavated this temple from the earth. I sat down on the pew. The Russian stayed standing, holding the bottle of vodka with his long, thin fingers.

"I doan like plan," said Kuzma.

"You don't think you can do it?" I said.

"I can do. But I doan like plan. Eet eesn't... Eet doesn't..."

"There isn't much choice. Think of the consequences if we don't."

"Ve should be engineers of souls, not..."

"Look..."

"Ve need to elevate, to transform. Look at vorkers. How ees deefferent? Proletariat struggles, farmers and fact'ry vorkers, and ve must..."

"Your 'boy meets tractor' style would be fine, but this isn't..."

"You know vhat you ask me to unleash?!"

"What? You hardly have room to talk. I mean, you worked for..."

"I know! You seenk I forget? You seenk I ever forget? I know."

"Look, it's better this way. We'll be in charge..."

"Een charge? Een charge! You seenk... Whole country ees veesible from

Kremlin." *The Russian smiled an unnerving smile.*

"Don't worry. I have it under control."

There was a long pause. Kuzma took another swig from the bottle, backed by the unearthed unearthly cathedral, lit by the bluish light of the quarter moon. We could've been at the beginning or the end of the world.

"Once Comrade Khrushchev say, 'Communeesm ees on horizon.' 'Communeesm ees on horizon,' he say to whole Soviet Union. Beeg speech. Aftervards everyvhere you go people say, 'Communeesm ees on horizon, Communeesm ees on horizon.' You hear everyvhere. I say too. Ve are proud. Ve are excited. Ve seenk ve are close. Communeesm ees on horizon. Communeesm ees on horizon. I dunno vhy. One day I look up horizon in book. In deectionary. You know vhat say?"

I shook my head.

"Horizon ees eemaginary line… zat retreat vhen you approach. And Communeesm ees on horizon."

"I…"

"You seenk you are een charge? Of zem?!"

"Right now, it's my ass on the line. I came to you for help. You said you could help."

"Ve, ve are not een charge of zem!"

"There's no choice. Think of who's driving us to this. Think of what he's done already. We have to take control. You may not like my methods now, but if he's successful, you'll wish you'd…"

"Hokay," he said, and handed me the bottle. "Hokay. No more argument. Hokay."

We stared at the sky and were quiet.

"Za vas!" *I said, drank, and handed the bottle back to him.*

"Davajte vypem za uspekh nashego dela!" *said Kuzma, and drank.*

"What does that mean?"

"I dreenk to success of project."

"Don't you worry. We'll succeed."

"Da. I know. Success ees on horizon," *he said, again with that smile.*

For the rest of the night we wandered the city, passing the bottle back and forth. We drank toasts to the decay of the old because we figured the new, the better, was within sight. I knew Kuzma wasn't thrilled with the way we had to work. I wasn't either. But bad stories can lead to good as long as they are modified. All material has value.

At some point we split up, Kuzma and I. The clouds covered the quarter moon, the bluish light got dimmer, the darkness had snuck up, and when the clouds finally dispersed, he was gone. I was standing in a square, or what was once a square. The remnants of buildings in the Stalin Baroque style surrounded me. I had no idea where I was. The moon no longer in sight, the crumbling architecture seemed to glow. But Kuzma left me the bottle of vodka. That's the kind of man he is. Life doesn't seem real to him unless he can give you something. I felt bad for having to force his hand, but there was no other way. I downed the rest of the vodka and, just before it all went black, had no doubt that our poltergeist bartender, if I wanted more, would move another bottle in my direction, cursing the entire time.

Edward R. Murrow switches the reel to reel off and stares back out the window, immediately thinking, according to Madame Khryptymnyzhy, of himself and Kuzma in freeze frame at the Hyperborean… Ladies and gentlemen, if you've been wondering why an apartment building in the middle of the desert is called the Hyperborean Arms, you're not alone. Dusty Buchs, our resident mythologist, and Water Wordsworth, station philologist, have asked the same question.

BUCHS: Hyperborea comes to us from Greek mythology. It was supposed to be an idyllic place where the sun shined constantly, where people lived in happiness to the age of 1000. To a modern listener, the constant sunlight makes it sound like Hyperborea should be located in the Arctic Circle. But that's not entirely accurate. The Greek god of the North Wind was Boreas; Boreas supposedly lived in Thrace. *Hyperborea* therefore means any place beyond Thrace. Consequently, at different times, it was thought to be in Northeast Asia, Dacia, Britain, Gaul, near the Danube, beyond the Alps, north of Scythia, in the Ural Mountains, between Iceland and Greenland, among other places. The most honest account of its location comes from Pindar, who tells us that you cannot reach Hyperborea by ship or by foot…

WORDSWORTH: Pindar's description certainly fits the Hyperborean Arms, but otherwise the name's a linguistic red herring. It could be that Renato Fregoli, former owner of A. Parachroni, thought it'd be ironic to build an apartment house with the name "Hyperborean" far to the west of Athens. That is, if we can even believe anyone named Renato Fregoli ever existed.

Dr. Wordsworth, why do you question his existence? His name is on the prospectus for A. Parachroni.

WORDSWORTH: Because of the Fregoli delusion. After Pitts and Simoleons mentioned him, I did some research and learned that it's a condition wherein the sufferer comes to believe that different people are all the same person, one single person, in disguise or with a changed appearance. Dr. DeMent, of course, would know more about this ailment than I do, but from what I've read, Renato Fregoli could literally be anyone or everyone.

BUCHS: Or no one… I also looked up Mr. Fregoli, and it turns out that he may be a myth from the intelligence community. He was supposedly a USSR prisoner after World War Two. Later, he was accused of sabotage and implicated in a conspiracy to overthrow the Soviet government. Before he could be brought to trial, however, he miraculously escaped to Singapore. The KGB claimed he was a CIA mole; the CIA disavowed him. The KGB believed that anyone disavowed by the CIA was an agent; the CIA figured that anyone who bothered the KGB this much *should* be an agent. And so both sides began hunting for him. And yet, even at that time, as the major intelligence firms started planning their respective manhunts, there was a general belief amongst Soviet and American operatives that Fregoli didn't exist, that he was invented by one side or by both sides for a purpose long forgotten, if it was ever even known.

WORDSWORTH: This reminds me of a rarely told story about the linguistic history of the term "red herring" and how it came to mean "diversion." Up to this point, there have been two camps: those who think the definition's connected to escaping prisoners (who used the fish oil to cover their tracks), and those who claim red herring was used to train fox-hunting scent hounds (the dogs first learning to follow the sardine trail, then the fainter fox odor, and finally the red herring would be re-introduced as a test). Turns out, both might be right. In the seventeenth century, or so goes the folktale, an escaped convict happened to wander through the center of the Bilsdale fox hunt. Since he was using red herring to divert his pursuers, not only were the guard dogs fooled, the scent hounds lost the fox. Now, any sport that's been around long enough is going to attract gambling. Realizing this and realizing what he'd done, the jailbird went to each huntsman, privately of course, and offered his services… for a nominal amount of coin. "Count on me, and your dog will catch the quarry." But at the next hunt, the fox went to ground again. Afterwards, the gentlemen discussed how this could've happened. When they all admitted they'd tried to tilt the contest in their favor, that they'd hired a certain man who had certain skills, they laughingly accepted that they'd been bamboozled. Hence, the Bilsdale huntsmen decided to call that particular outing, "The Hunt for the Red Herring." Afterwards, it became common practice to train scent dogs with fish. As for the con man, no one ever saw him again.

Thank you, Dusty Buchs and Water Wordsworth, for your report. However, we still haven't adequately answered why Wallace Heath Orcuson happens to live in the Hyperborean Arms. Our investigative reporter, Eve Z'droppe, believes she knows.

Z'DROPPE: This is Eve Z'droppe reporting from Jamais Vu, a French restaurant that, strangely, serves an equal amount of German cuisine. According to our own food critic, Colon Bownde, a meeting took place here at Jamais Vu between Greta Zelle, Agent Kuzma Grigorovich Bezopasnosky, an unidentified man in black, and one MR. SPEAKER. Yes, that's a small audio speaker like an intercom with MR. SPEAKER written across the top in what appeared to be Sharpie. Mr. Bownde says that during the meal, the group was having a heated discussion, emphatically pointing to something on the table, until MR. SPEAKER said, *He's the man for the job*, although the intercom did not specify what job. Immediately after MR. SPEAKER spoke, the man in black stared at Greta Zelle, who finally said, I know what to do… I'll have him eating out of my hand. At this time, Mr. Bownde managed to close in on the table and see what the group had been pointing at: a picture of Wallace Heath Orcuson. Although my earlier report was speculative, I'm now certain that Zelle, on the orders of these three mysterious individuals, enticed

Orcuson to the Hyperborean Arms. *How* he got there, we're still not sure…

Thank you, Ms. Z'droppe. Meanwhile, over at the Pilgrim & Pagan, our man Ed Murrow has rewound the reel to reel and, yes, it appears that he's recording a new ending to his report about Kuzma. Ladies and gentlemen, let's listen in…

MURROW: We spoke of the past, when things were better. We spoke of the present, where things are uncertain. We spoke of the future, when things would be different. We talked about bringing everyone together into a community that wasn't falling to pieces like this one, this one, where everyone was separated and many were even afraid to go into the streets. Kuzma and I weren't afraid. We knew something greater was to come, something real. Then the people would return. They would… Kuzma finished the vodka, all but a swig. He threw me the rest. With a salute to each other, we parted ways. He admitted he was skeptical. It might lead to catastrophe. But we agreed that catastrophe was better than the nothing we had, the indeterminacy of right now. And anyway, it's better to go with the devil you know. Even if you have to pull him out of cold storage.

Murrow snaps off the reel to reel, looks over at Arty Magam who's now running through a dumbshow of interacting with the other pitchers and catchers in the bullpen.

"Arty, what… what're you? What's happening?"

Pause.

"Aww, nothin', Jackson. Nothin'."

And now this:

§

The Predicta sez: *The Thule Society, originally called the Study Group for Germanic Antiquity, was an occultist and folkloric group in Munich, named for the capital of Hyperborea.*

"So, I figure you want an alibi. You want me to stop holding back. If only I'd tell you where I was last night, then you could either eliminate me as a suspect, as a character in your drama, or you could discover that I'm lying, which would make me even more interesting because I'd be a suspect, or I'd at least be connected to the suspect. But I got a problem. An alibi's only worthwhile if it *sounds* believable. Doesn't matter if it's true. For instance, let's say some poor bastard is getting killed right now, and this particular poor bastard happens to be the husband of a woman I'm sleeping with. Sooner or later, the cops are gonna come around to me and ask where I was. And let's say I immediately chime in with, 'Well now, officers, I couldn't possibly have murdered that man, I was being interrogated by the Gestapo at the time you say he was killed.' That's what's happening right this very minute, but no one would ever believe me on account of the world thinking you guys went defunct, oh, back in 1945. On the other hand, what if, instead of being interrogated by the Gestapo, I was sitting here all by myself watching a ballgame. Once upon a time, maybe that would've played. Not anymore. Why? Because so many guys have used it. To a cop, it's more likely that you were out on a murderous rampage, rather than watching a game by yourself. It's so innocuous, it's unbelievable. Like when you knock on somebody's door and it takes them forever to answer, and when they finally *do* answer immediately they say, 'Oh, I was cleaning the place.' No one believes that. Everyone thinks…"

"Herr Schtein, you are stallink."

The Predicta sez: *The Thule Society is primarily known for its sponsorship of the Deutsche Arbeiterpartei (DAP), which Adolf Hitler later reorganized into the Nazi Party.*

"There's a reason for that. The story I'm gonna tell you, my alibi, it's like something out of a dream, even though it's not a dream, and I know because I never have dreams. Or, I never remember them, anyway. I wouldn't know what dreams are like, except I've heard people describe theirs to me before. I find them to be completely… unbelievable. I listen while they say, 'I had the strangest dream last night,' and as they relate it to me, I think, 'Are you making this up?' But they're not making it up. In a manner of speaking, it's something that actually happened to them, even though it only happened to them in their minds. And while I listen, I'm forced to accept this story as completely real, even though it doesn't sound real at all. The experience, of listening to someone describe their dreams, it's like a, well, it's like a dream…"

"Herr Schtein!"

"Okay, okay…"

"Get on vith it!"

The Predicta sez: *According to the minutes of Thule Society meetings, Hitler never attended. And later, in various speeches, he denounced occultism. But Rudolf Hess, Hermann Göring, Heinrich Himmler, and other Nazis were members. And they subtly and later not-so-subtly incorporated Thule Society ideas into the Party. Especially once Himmler created the Ahnenerbe. The Ahnenerbe, it's important because it sponsored the New Swabia Expedition.*

THE ALIBI

"I cannot remember everything. I must have been unconscious most of the time," said an almost robotic voice from what I assume was the limo's radio. I think it was an electronica remix of Schoenberg's *A Survivor from Warsaw* and Beethoven's *Victory Symphony*. But slowed way down. Only one note at a time. Discordant. Full of echoes. Chilly. Out the window, the world was frozen. The intense light of the micromoon blaring from a cloudless sky, reflecting off the ice and snow, made it seem even colder. All of the color had been drained from the world except blue. I would've asked the driver where we were going, but I couldn't see him through the partition. It didn't matter. What could he say? He wasn't important. The script writer hadn't even given him a name. If there were a script writer. And the casting director, enigmatic, told me nothing at all. At least, I assume he's the one who sent this '42 Cadillac Limousine. I can imagine him saying, "You'd be perfect for this role," even though I've never met the guy.

The Predicta sez: *We can see the Nazi origins in the Thule Society's racist blood declaration of faith: 'The signer hereby swears to the best of his knowledge and belief that no Jewish or colored blood flows in either his or in his wife's veins, and that among their ancestors are no members of the colored races.'*

As we drove, I noticed the same scraggly, ruined tree kept passing by the window every two minutes, just like in cheap movies where short loops are used again and again to simulate movement, in the hopes that the audience would just acknowledge that the car was motoring along without further scrutiny. I supposed it was possible that we weren't *moving* at all. Whatever feature I was in, it was low budget, a B film, maybe a C-. Likely to be full of poorly written characters with unbelievable names, likely to star actors who chew the scenery or use outrageous accents, likely to focus on an inexplicable plot. Maybe that's where I belong anyway. I don't feel at home amongst things that are realistic. They don't feel real to me. My homeland is outlandish. If you visited where I'm from, you'd say none of this could ever happen as you watched it happening. You'd turn to leave and find there's no way out. Your nostalgia for the real would manifest itself in a monument; you'd refuse to believe anything else existed.

The Predicta sez: *But the Thule Society was even more exclusive than its racism indicates. In fact, the group was a front for another secret organization that went by various names: the Society for Truth and the Vril Society being the most often used. This inner circle sought to find 'vril,' a mystical essence introduced to the world by Edward Bulwer-Lytton in his 1871 novel,* The Coming Race.

We finally arrived at our destination: The Puppet Regime. It was a mansion/restaurant. Later I'd hear this swanky eatery was originally called Jamais Vu. To my knowledge, I was never there when it went by that name, though everything looked both familiar and not.

The driver (I think) opened my door, and I was immediately hit by a blast of hot, dry air. I stepped out into this foreign climate, not sure where the cameras were shooting from, giving my best red carpet wave to no one, which was when a song I can't remember ever hearing before started playing in my head.

> The herring is the king of the sea
> The herring is the fish for me
> The herring is the king of the sea
> Sing foller o' diddle o' day

This replaced my usual intrusive thought, which is that I never get intrusive thoughts, a fact that always bothered me.

The Predicta sez: *This quest for vril led the Society for Truth to the locations of the Hollow Earth and Hyperborea.*

The Puppet Regime was situated next to a lake, and I'd say that the moon was reflected by the water, but there was no water, nor was there snow or ice—there was only salt. I scanned the horizon, trying to find the hills we'd driven over, or a line of scraggly trees stretching on into infinity, but they, like my limo, like my driver, were gone. I might've stared at this alkaline flatness forever, but I felt the director getting nervous, even if I couldn't see him, and then I heard a phone ringing from a booth just outside the entrance. My cue.

"Other than those who normally listen in, who is this?" I said.

"It's me," said the distorted voice. So maybe it was the eavesdroppers finally dropping the pretense.

"Oh. *You.* Hello, you."

"No, I'm *me.* *You're* you."

"I'm you?"

"More than you know. Now listen…"

"No no no. Right now, I feel like me. You have to give me a lot more to start acting like you."

"But you already are."

"How do I know?"

"Faith."

"Faith? I have no faith."

"In humanity? In the deity?"

"In you."

"Ah, I see. Then it's all a…"

"Who are you?"

"…mystery."

"Mr. E.? I don't get it."

"Never mind. You have a job?" I wasn't sure if he was asking a question or letting me know I'd been hired somewhere.

"Oh. Mr. E. You're the casting…"

"You know, a job. A place where they force you to arrive at inconvenient times, where they require you to dress in clothes you can't stand" (I was in this same white tux) "where they coerce you to do things you don't want to do, where they treat you in ways you normally wouldn't allow, and for this you're granted a pittance you use to purchase alcohol to block out a world you'd rather not live in."

"A job. A job. Oh, yeah, being you. That's becoming a full-time job. Look at these clothes. Look at this phone booth. Look at this restaurant in the middle of nowhere. What's going on? Are you even here?"

"I am here. I was early. Too early. And don't worry. You're perfect for this job. I'll call again later."

"Look, I don't want to be…" But I couldn't finish because the phone was making that racket, the one that tells you to hang it up already, so I did, then I barged out of the booth, slamming into a man who, as he crashed to the ground, didn't seem to be bothered by the collision at all. Hitting the deck, he almost instantly got back up, dusted himself off, helped me up, dusted me off, and then asked me to join him. It happened so fast, if I didn't know any better I'd think it was planned. But then, I guess I don't know any better because I'm certain it *was* planned. What a lousy movie.

Inside, everything was marble, plush carpet, brass, mahogany, Art Deco. In this world, even the curves made you think they were straight lines. Triangles and perfect circles repeated everywhere. Where I come from, the entire town's failed geometry; at The Puppet Regime, Euclid and Pythagoras could maybe get jobs as fill-in dishwashers. If they were lucky.

The Predicta sez: *While the actual secret organization was trying to locate the Hollow Earth and Hyperborea, the Thule Society was engaged in what amounted to political diversions. During the German Revolution of 1918-1919, the Thulists were accused of attempting to overthrow the government. Seven members were later apprehended and executed, including Prince Gustav of Thurn and Taxis. No one from the Vril Society was even questioned.*

It smelled like seafood was on the menu tonight. But for such a high end joint, the aroma was wrong. Cheap. What was this, Smell-O-Vision? Gimmicks. The low budget again. Same excuse for why the ballroom sounded packed, even though there wasn't a single automobile parked outside. I quickly tried to find Mr. E. to complain, but he wasn't around, or I still didn't know what he looked like, possibly both.

The only person who was around: the maître d'. I've always wondered, how do ritzy restaurants hire a maître d'? I'm thinking it's not the want ads. Maître d's have to be summoned. That look, that maître d' look, what? It's something the guy picks up during training? No. Not a chance. One day, out of the blue, he just arrives, takes his position behind the standup reservation desk, wearing the perfect suit, menus in hand, towel over an arm, a face ready to welcome the important, banish the insignificant, and there's no question–he is the maître d'. Really, he's always been the maître d'. His name's even on the schedule. He works from four to close.

"Good evening, sir. Do you have your invitation?"

My new companion said that unless he stepped on some in the john, he didn't have a scrap of paper on him. A look spread across the maître d's face, untaught, natural as a wildfire, says your number's been drawn and it's 86, but the blaze was extinguished as quickly as it flared up.

"You must be Mr. Stein," said the maître d'. "You, of course, do not need an invitation. *You* are expected."

His line must've been a cue because we were immediately mobbed by men in tuxes, women in cocktail dresses, who all swept us into the ballroom, as

The herring is the king of the sea
The herring is the fish for me
The herring is the king of the sea
Sing foller o' diddle o' day

continued playing on the payola-accepting station in my head, finally jammed by the torch singer who went into "Somebody Else Is Taking My Place." I still couldn't find the cameras, but the shots had to be tight in on our group, tight in on the torch singer, tight in on the bartender, because there was no one else around, though from the sounds of things you'd think we were in a packed stadium, Game 7 of the World Series.

Stein was a big deal at The Puppet Regime, so everyone wanted to buy him a drink, and if they weren't talking to him, they were talking about him, saying how important he was to the plan, that he was a major player, that he was the type of person who just seemed to know what to do in any situation, a kind of savant really, that without even realizing it he did so much work, that they couldn't go on without him, that he made their lives infinitely easier, that there was a name for their luck and it was Stein.

Watching everyone drink nonchalantly, too nonchalantly, and engage in this forced banter, I could see where everything was headed. From this point on, it would be chaos. Very cinéma vérité. There'd finally be cameras. Handhelds, of course. Only the shakiest, most disconcerting shots. And I'd still wonder why I was here, why I had to witness this performance, why it continued no matter where I was. Tired of my fake fellow partiers already, not above begging the director, the assistant director, the producer, the goddamned best boy, Mr. E. to get me out of here, if only I could find them, I studied the walls looking for an escape. With a little luck, I got the feeling, I could probably walk right off the set and out of this movie.

But the designer was better at his job than that.

I soon found myself in a room dominated by fishing paraphernalia: nets, lures, hooks, poles, tackle boxes, hats, it was everywhere. There were also composite pictures, as if this were a fraternity, though the composites on one wall had photographs of people, while the facing wall just had silhouettes.

The Predicta sez: *When we scrutinize the setup of the Nazi Party, look at the nests we find! It was based on the German Workers' Party which began as the Thule Society which was a front for the Vril Society. The SS, run by the occultist Heinrich Himmler, may have been based on the Jesuit order, but that's because it was a front for Himmler's actual interest, the Ahnenerbe, a Vrilist institute.*

"It's a secret society with many orders," said someone from behind me. His voice sounded familiar, but I was more interested in the fact that this Chapter Room somehow had a Vermeer: *View of Delft*. "An antediluvian and ancient secret society. Tonight is an initiation."

"Right, Stein," I said, fascinated with the boats in the painting. I have no idea why, but it felt like there was something sinister about them.

"Do you see the composite pictures? The ones with actual photographs. Those are only half of the members. The, we'll say, public order of the society. They

45

are nominated without their knowledge based on certain criteria."

"Who nominates them?" I said.

"The private members," he said.

"What criteria do they use?"

"The criteria are secret, but mostly pertain to how well they'll perform as members."

"If the criteria are secret, how can anyone hope to meet them?"

"Public members are born, not bred."

"What do the public members have to do?"

"Just be who they're supposed to be. Likely, who they already are. Whether they like it or not."

"What if a potential public member doesn't care about this secret society?"

"Then he's much more likely to be selected. Think of it this way: although a great honor, almost no one would consciously choose to be a public member, though it does lead to a level of fame. The biggest perk: public members never die unknown."

The Predicta sez: *Since the Nazis started the war, it should come as no surprise that World War Two itself was a front.*

I turned around and found I couldn't see the man who was talking to me. He seemed blurry. I could only take in an outline.

"Woh, friend. Maybe you've had enough to drink," he said.

"I haven't been drinking at all," I said, gesturing at him with a glass that slipped out of my hand and shattered on the tile floor just as I got sick, though luckily there was a toilet beneath me. In the stall next door, I could hear Stein, between wretches, saying that he may not be well now, but soon he would be invincible, and maybe he had become invincible, since he was up, washing his hands, while I was still on the ground next to the john.

"What are you doing here?" someone said to Stein.

Stein said that he was the man of the hour.

"Then you must've been invited."

Stein pointed out that he was expected, even the maître d' said so.

"Can I see your invitation?"

From my vantage point on the floor, I could only hear Stein feeling around in his coat pockets.

"Mr. Stein, you need to come with me."

As quickly as I could, which, granted, still wasn't very fast, I got up off the tile, wrestled with the stall lock, kicked open the door, stumbled out of the men's room in time to see Stein surrounded by men in fish masks singing

The herring is the king of the sea
The herring is the fish for me
The herring is the king of the sea
Sing foller o' diddle o' day

the full film crew on hand with cameras and lights and microphones and director's chairs, the song continuing, listing the things you could make of the herring, each verse ending with, "And all sorts of things," and either this was too much for me, so I returned to the safety of the bathroom floor, or I had to get sick again, or I never left, I just don't know, because the next thing I recall, after the mermen serenading Stein, is hearing a knock at the door and the phone ringing and the Gestapo here to interrogate me.

END OF "THE ALIBI"

Major Freytag sighs deeply; Oberschütze Schmetterling sits with his head in his hands.

The Predicta sez: *Fascists always seek to convince an entire country to hate a scapegoat. Our country is the greatest, our people are the best, but this* red herring *is trying to destroy our supremacy. The goal is to make your populace hate the fall guy so much, no one can think about him. For the Nazis, that patsy was, of course, the Jews. But as we've seen, it wasn't in this government's nature to operate so simply. In fact, those who focused mostly on the war were like Thulists. Meanwhile, the real leaders, the Vrilists, found the Hollow Earth, found Hyperborea, executed plans to colonize both, and covered it all up by unleashing their own red herring on the world: Adolf Hitler.*

47

"Herr…"

"It's Orcuson, but, agents, you can call me Wall."

Another sigh.

"Mein Herr, do you happen to haff ein Licht? Light?"

"No."

"Because you are out uf Streichölzer? Matches? Because you lost your cigarette lighter?"

"Nope. I quit. Cold turkey."

Schmetterling begins sobbing.

The Predicta sez: *Lost in the Antarctic, with shipmates dying, daily amputations, if you're Captain Ritscher or one of his crewmembers, you probably start thinking, at some point, about the Thulists, about the Vrilists, about the Hollow Earth, about vril, about Hyperborea, and wonder, 'How did I fall for this… fiction? How did I end up at the South Pole looking for something that couldn't possibly exist?'*

"Very vell. I vill now tell you vhat I sink uf you, Herr… You are a vorthless zlacker. You like playink zilly games. You have problems vith Behörde. Authority. Honestly, I can't zee you as der Mörder. Ze killer. Because zat voult take plannink, initiative. Perhaps you are ze vacky Nachbar, ze kooky Freund, but definitely ze *minor* player in zis Prozess… It started off zo promisink. Ve vere goink somevhere. But now, Schmetterlink, now ve are flat on den Boden. Ze ground. Gettink novhere! Unt ve can't even zee die Pyramide…"

Freytag and Schmetterling rise, give the Roman Salute, but they look dejected, two soldiers hailing their country at the end of a lost war.

The Predicta sez: *In current day Nazi ideology, it's believed that Captain Ritscher and his crew were being tested, their faith was being tested. Only true Teutons could enter the promised land below. But before they could reach it, as with any grail quest, they had to conquer their own despair.*

"Oberschütze! Wir gehen! Ve haff vasted der Tag. Ze day. On zis," a disgusted gesture at you, Wall. "I toldt to you, Herr, zat vhen ze Gestapo appear, zomesink has just happent, or zomesink is about to happen. Ve shall investigate your ludicrous story, but maybe, maybe on zis occasion… nosink has happent. A first Zeit. Time. For everysink, I zuppose. Even for nosink."

The Gestapo file out of your apartment, Wall, just in time to let a legion of trenchcoated goons in, who shove aside the couch, pick up the corpse (doesn't really look like they plan on, ya know, processing the evidence), revealing…

"Eine Kreidefee!" sez one of the goons. "A chalk fairy." And there it is, like in the old TV cop shows. The chalk outline. They cover it back up on their way out, Major Freytag adding as they go, "You are not to leaf ze flat for any reason until you haff our permission."

The apartment is yours once again, Wall. Feeling smug after your defeat of the dreaded Gestapo, are ya?

Victoriously, Wall slumps down into the chair, accidentally sitting on the remote, channels changing, a chaos of flipping, one station briefly showing Dogfaces rocking back and forth and back and forth, while a man looking at a menu… before you can finally stand up and grab the clicker from off the cushion.

Sitting back down on your throne, do you even think about the fact that you have no idea when the Gestapo might give their permission? And what about in the meantime? Do you dare defy Them? You can't. You have to stay right where you are. Imprisoned in your own castle. Or they'll find out. They're the Gestapo.

And that's just the way it is.

With the Gestapo.

Still feeling victorious, pal?

§

"Arty, I think it'd be better if I just let 'em have the land. They've been moving the boundary stakes around that show where their property ends, and it's not my lot anyway, so I think I should ignore it and move on with my life."

"Oh, is that what you're gonna do, huh? You're gonna appease your neighbors because it's not your land. You know who else had an appeasement plan, don't you?"

"No. Who?"

"Neville Chamberlain."

Mechanical laughter.

"I hardly think that applies here, Arty. I mean that was countries during a…"

"Go on, Neville. I'm listening. I'm starting to feel appeased already."

More mechanical laughter.

Arty Magam sits in the manager's office of the Pilgrim & Pagan running an imaginary call-in program, while Edward R. Murrow paces and smokes.

"This is *The Arty Magam Show*. As always, we're brought to you by A. Parachroni. And remember, at A. Parachroni, we don't make the reality you believe in. We make the reality you believe in better."

"How, how could this've happened?" says Murrow, picking up the bottle of aspirin, then putting it back down.

"What?" says Arty.

"Nothing," says Murrow.

Madame Khryptymnyzhy, can you give us some insight into what Ed's thinking about right now.

KHRYPTYMNYZHY: Yes. There's… there's a swirl of images moving through Edward R. Murrow's mind… a ghost-like hand reaching out from beneath the couch at the Hyperborean… a hallway… a familiar hallway extending out to infinity… a man in a very loud outfit, a very loud Hawaiian tourist outfit… it's "Senator" Kipper Maris sitting behind the director's desk at Columbia Narratorial Services, his feet up on the table, drinking some kind of cocktail… there's a man all in black… perhaps the same man Colon Bownde and Eve Z'droppe told us about from Jamais Vu… and then Murrow sees himself sitting alone at the Hyperborean once more… yes… alone and calm… yes… calm… until… Do something, Ed! A hand comes out from underneath the couch! It's pulling him down into an intense light! But the hand… it looks like… like… like an outline?

Thank you, Madame Khryptymnyzhy, for that unsettling report. We are now joined by our station rhetorician, Gorgias Georg Sofiztri. Thank you for being on the program today.

SOFIZTRI: My pleasure, sir.

Tell me, you were listening to *Vayss Uf Makink You Tock* and the beginning of *The Arty Magam Show* and you said both Wall and Arty make extensive use of red herring arguments. Can you tell us what those are?

SOFIZTRI: A red herring argument, also known as the red herring fallacy, is when you answer an argument with another argument that's not directed at the original issue. We see these all the time in political campaign commercials and debates. Appeals to emotion, appeals to force, appeals to the majority, appeals to abstract consequences, appeals to tradition, ridicule, straw man attacks, argumentum ad hominem… On this last one, there are the famous World War Two examples that I believe your Arthur Magam is cycling through right now.

"…reminds me of someone. Oh yeah! It's the Chief of State of Vichy France, Marshal Philippe Pétain, ladies and gentlemen. Right on the air with us. So, how'd you like that treason trial, Marshal?"

But you were also telling me about the Great Arguments.

SOFIZTRI: Oh, yes, we do like to have our fun. The Three Great Arguments are Argument/Schmargument, Argumentum ad Moronum (where you call your opponent a moron), and the last one, speaking of World War Two, the last one is where you compare your opponent to…

KHRYPTYMNYZHY: The man in black. The man in black. Edward R. Murrow sits in the Hyperborean… Yes… But he thinks of the man in black.

Excuse me, Professor Sofiztri, but it appears that Ed Murrow has re-spooled the reel-to-reel and is playing one of his old reports. Let's listen in.

Our first meeting took place in a parking garage that was demolished the next day. There were no cars. There was barely any light. I never saw his face. Even when he held a match to his cigarette, somehow no details emerged.

"You know, cigarettes, they'll kill you," I said. "What's your name, by the way?"

To be honest, I have no idea what I was doing in that abandoned garage. Kuzma had told me he couldn't work alone, that he needed the help of a former collaborator, that this collaborator would want to interview me before he took the job. But we had no appointment, and I had no reason at all to be in that crumbling carpark.

"Don't worry, I'm… protected." He paused inhaling a great deal of smoke. "Asbestos," he said. As it turned out, C. Irving Asbestos.

We met irregularly over the span of a few weeks in buildings that would be dust and rubble the next day: an ancient shack used by fishermen, a decrepit and mammoth tavern, the former Hall of Records, the clubhouse of a condemned baseball stadium, even a decaying diner. At one point I said to him, "If we keep this up soon everything will be leveled." He seemed unconcerned.

"Kuzma... tells me you have a job for us," Asbestos said.

No matter where we were, I always tried to find out a little bit more about him, tried to determine who he was, what he was up to, tried (at the very least) to catch a glimpse of his face. I was never actually sure if he was sent by Kuzma, or if he was a spy.

"But if I'm going to work for you, I need you... to work for me."

Of course none of the usual institutions had ever heard of him. The one piece of information I finally tracked down was that his father was a man named Owen G. Asbestos. But everywhere I went, I was told he worked at some other government agency.

"Murrow... what I'm going to ask ... you to do, you'll be tempted ... to play detective. At first... there will be no... problem. But then... you'll see clues. The clues will... compound. A vast conspiracy. And when you're not able to put it... all together, you'll decide the clues weren't real... clues, but red herrings. Everything will smell fishy. You'll be... positive that you must've... missed something, that you must've missed... someone. And you will drive... yourself insane trying to figure it all... out. Don't play detective.

"You... need me. You've laid out exactly what you... want Kuzma and I... to do, and we'll do it. And I've laid out... exactly what I... want you to do. So do it."

Although it was early in the going, I felt like I'd already lost control. Or maybe I'd never had it. I started to think this plan had been orchestrated long before I arrived on the scene, that ancient, chthonic forces had set the original stages of this plan into motion. I wanted to ask, if that were the case, who was I and why was I necessary, but I knew the questions were irrelevant. I was in it, so I was necessary. That was all. Or, that's what I thought then, anyway.

"Even our... prime operative won't know what's... been done when... it's been done. Safer that way."

"But how can he or she not know?"

"Well... detective... I'm not... sure."

"Never mind."

"That's the... spirit."

Kind listeners of Radioland, Edward R. Murrow has switched off his reel-to-reel for now, perhaps contemplating the report. While we wait for him to continue, we'll send you out to A. Phil LeBustre, esq., our legal correspondent, and I.M. de Mann, station anthropologist, who have more on the Fregoli family.

LeBustre: Each known member of the Fregoli family has a birth certificate and passport from the tiny Pacific island nation of Wainiwidiwiki. For such a small island, covering all of eight square miles, Wainiwidiwiki is as corrupt as any major power, with the legal history to prove it.

de Mann: It certainly does. But our story starts off innocently enough with the British finding phosphate on the island in 1900. Before that discovery, Wainiwidiwiki was tribal, practicing aquaculture, growing coconuts and pandanus fruit. After the discovery... Well, it turned out there wasn't just a little phosphate; the entire surface of the island was made of it thanks to thousands of years of birds stopping there for a bathroom break. And so, from 1900–1966, at different times, Germany, Great Britain, New Zealand, Australia, and Japan operated mines on the island. Once free of foreign rule, the residents continued the practice themselves under the aegis of the Wainiwidiwiki Phosphate Corporation.

LeBustre: An entire economy based on the age-old droppings of sea birds. Understanding that their lone resource wouldn't last forever, the islanders invested their money in the Wainiwidiwiki Phosphate Royalties Trust, presumably so they could move elsewhere when their homeland was gone. Unfortunately, the trust was mismanaged, including investments into collectibles like coins, stamps, baseball cards, stuffed animals, and a Broadway musical about the Puritans called *No Singing, No Dancing*.

de Mann: If nothing else, the title was entirely accurate. Well, almost. It should've been called *No Singing, No Dancing, No Paying Customers*. But isn't it fascinating how quickly the Wainiwidiwikians adapted? In the late nineteenth century, they were still tribal. By the 1980s, they were completely caught up to the Western world. If it weren't for the fact that this actually happened, Wainiwidiwiki could be seen as a microcosm for capitalism itself. But it did happen.

LeBustre: And during this oh-so-real time period, Wainiwidiwiki showed just how advanced it was. With depleted phosphate reserves, empty coffers, and a post-apocalyptic-looking homeland, Wainiwidiwiki became a tax haven and one of the biggest money laundering centers in the world.

De Mann: And since, if you had the money, absolutely anything could be bought, this is likely when the Fregolis had their Wainiwidiwikian birth certificates and passports made.

LeBustre: And scattered across the island is evidence that "proves" the Fregolis "always" lived there–pictures, plaques, newspaper stories, birth certificates, passports, other government documents.

De Mann: I even talked to the only tour guide on Wainiwidiwiki, who proudly informed me that he and Renato Fregoli had worked for the Resistance during the Japanese occupation. That was World War Two! The tour guide couldn't've been older than 25, and he was telling me about something that happened seventy years ago! After his story, I said, "It must be exhausting recalling things you couldn't possibly have witnessed."

LeBustre: It's the same with the supposed "evidence" that "proves" the Fregolis come from Wainiwidiwiki. All of it is faked. In pictures, the Fregolis never look the same twice and they're often very obviously pasted into pre-existing photos, their names written by hand or typed in a different font in the descriptors at the bottom.

De Mann: Being so blatant, it's as if those who planted this bogus "evidence" wanted you to know, immediately, that it was counterfeit. Here's the problem, though–if the island were full of clever forgeries, then we could debunk them and move on. Since the island's full of obvious forgeries, we have to ask why? Why would anyone go to all that trouble to plant so much "evidence" that is glaringly phony?

LeBustre: And we have a possible answer... a theory. Walking across the island, talking to people, looking at pictures, plaques, government documents, everything connected to the Fregolis is so ridiculous, it's like going to a Ripley's Believe-It-or-Not Museum. No one's fooled. But in this case you are fooled. You're fooled, and again, this is only a theory, because what these counterfeits cover up is the fact that the Fregolis actually lived on Wainiwidiwiki for a time.

DE MANN: Furthermore, this cover-up might also be covering up something else. But what that might be we have no idea.

That was A. Phil LeBustre and I.M. de Mann, ladies and gentlemen. And now, it appears that Ed Murrow is ready to hit play on the reel-to-reel. And so, we return you, live, to Pilgrim & Pagan Donuts…

"So, do we have a deal?"

He held out his hand; we shook and I came up with a set of car keys.

At the time the deal seemed innocuous, a means to an end. But now I wonder if it would've been better to've done anything else, no matter how unsavory.

"You have… ten minutes… to get out of here before the building… comes down."

"What about…?"

"It will be… waiting for you at… the place where plots begin. You have your… instructions."

As I motored off, the building imploded. And I drove. Away from it all. Away from mysterious backgrounds. Away from uncertain motives. Away from dark pacts. Away from meetings in locations that would soon be no longer. Away from Asbestos. Away from "Senator" Kipper Maris. My then-client. All of this, calling on Kuzma, agreeing to meet Asbestos, setting the plan in motion, it was all an attempt to get away from Maris, away from his manuscript. I knew every last bit of this stunt was against CNS's rules. But then, I had a hunch that ever since Maris appeared, the rules had changed.

Patient listeners of Radioland, Ed Murrow has switched off the reel-to-reel once again. But joining us now, to better explain what our primary narrator is going through, is a former employee of CNS who goes by the codename Heidi Larynx. To protect his or her anonymity, Larynx is using a voice modulator.

LARYNX: Narrators, from what we can tell, are assigned manuscripts at random. Consequently, each CNS employee handles a wide array of styles. Because of this arbitrary distribution, there are times when a particular narrator will end up with several work orders that are all of the same type. Murrow, for instance, has always been assigned projects that are more "realistic" (or in that vein), until

Vayss Uf Makink You Tock. Now, it shouldn't surprise anyone that narrators are susceptible to conspiracy theories just like anyone else. Most are ironic, but some really take them seriously. Think of a roulette player who laughingly tells you he has a system, and then think of a nut who keeps saying, "Oh, you have no idea," and you'll get the difference. Murrow, he believed CNS was perfect before Maris came along and corrupted Central Opps. Never mind that no one knows how Central Opps operates, for Murrow, CNS was flawless. The Senator destroyed all that. Now, in an attempt to bring back the past, your primary narrator is breaking the first law in the CNS *Handbook*–he's reworking a manuscript without the author's permission. This isn't just a fireable offense. It's something that's forced narrators into hiding in the past.

Thank you, Heidi Larynx.

When I arrived at the Hyperborean Arms, I felt like I'd achieved escape velocity, that I'd finally managed to liberate myself. But inside, I knew... I knew... that I was wrong.

KHRYPTYMNYZHY: Blood! Edward R. Murrow is being pulled underneath the couch by the outlined hand, the ghostly hand, and there is blood, he is being pulled into blood and light, blood and light, and... and... and as he's being... yes... as he's being... pulled under... he... he thinks... he thinks he'll never be able to clean up all this blood.

Inside, I knew I hadn't escaped anyone. Not Asbestos. Not Maris. Not the new corrupted form of my once beloved CNS.

Z'DROPPE: Mr. Station Manager, I hope you don't mind me cutting in, but from a number of anonymous sources, we are now being told that Murrow cleaned up the apartment after the murder was committed. And we can now confirm that the dead body is "Senator" Kipper Maris, husband to Greta Zelle, CNS client assigned to Edward R. Murrow on the *Vayss Uf Makink You Tock* project.

...Looking down on the body, completely unrecognizable, and on all that blood, I realized I wouldn't put it past Maris to get himself killed as long as it meant making my life more difficult. And I thought, "The place where plots begin? All I care about is where this one will end."

Ladies and gentlemen, I know that was a flurry of information, but I believe we have reached the calm. In the Pilgrim & Pagan, Arty Magam wanders out to check on his customer, right as Murrow switches off the still-spinning reel-to-reel and downs a couple more aspirin.

"What's this thing you're like working on, man?" Arty says.

"A manuscript," says Murrow.

"Oh, you're like a writer, sure."

"No, a narrator."

"A narrator? Looks like you're editing or somethin'."

"Reorganizing."

"'s not yours, right man?"

"I have a better plan. A much better plan."

"Oh! You have like a plan. Sure, man. You're, I guess, reorganizing. You're like working on this book here. This book, sure, probably shows how, you know?, things should be, like, run. Am I right? Probably, ya know, out lookin' for recruits. Maybe you even, sure, have your own salute. Seems like you're taking power, man. And what's this, I mean is that an ugly little Chaplin mustache I see you like growing there, bro?"

"I haven't had time to shave. I've been working on this manuscript, on this narration."

"I get it, I get it. Sure. It's all like a part of the plan. But you know, man, who you remind me of?"

"Who?"

"Oh, I think you like know. Sure. Ya know perfectly well. I mean, like who else could you remind me of, man? Doesn't even need to be said. And that's *The Arty Magam Show*, foax! Thanks for tuning in. Next week we'll have…"

And now this:

§

That presence lurking in the dark, waiting patiently, is the Gestapo.

The telephone rings. It's the new moon, meaning there is no moon.

Stumbling, moving through the apartment, now a Cimmerian domain (oboy, where'd that come from? been reading Poe and Lovecraft to pass the time, buddy?), you, who do not fear the dark, fear this dark, this spectral atmosphere that can only be felt and never seen, mental images running amok thanks to no visual input, flickering, flickering, say Tick–Tock, Tick–Tock, the ringing continuing, and somehow, what's this? The phone.

"A good day to the various secret agencies tapping this line. Oh, and who's this?" sez Wall. From the smell of things, must be standing in the kitchen.

"It's me," sez the distorted voice.

"Me, me, me, me…"

"Are you prepping for your solo?"

"…me, me. Hmm. Nope. Doesn't ring any bells. Maybe you have the wrong number. Who were you trying to reach?"

"You."

"You. Ya know, I think I finally get it. Years ago, you lost touch with yourself. How do these things happen? Where does the time go? No way of knowing. Could it really be that long? Fuck… That's right, it'd been ages since you had a chance to sit down and shoot the shit, and you wondered how you were doing. You needed to know how you were doing. But there was a problem. Whenever you called yourself, the goddamned line was busy. 'Who's that bastard always talking to?' you said to yourself. 'How can I get ahold of him if he's on the phone every frickin' time I call?' That wasn't the worst of it, though. Naw. The worst came next, when you wondered to yourself, 'What if he's trying to call *me* everytime I'm trying to call *him*?' After that brain-melting thought, the old rotary was off limits. Wasn't any other way to catch up with yourself, and you really wanted to catch up. And so you circled the damn thing day and night, constantly wishing you could just pick up the handset, dial, and… No. Can't do it. *He* might be having the same dilemma on the other end; he might be weaker than me, so I gotta wait. Probably that glorious ringing will start any second now…" The Predicta makes a fizzing, imploding sound and warms to its bluish life, showing an icy landscape, the camera approaching the entrance to a cave. "Only it never came. Sure, you couldn't stay in your place forever, you finally had to go out, buy something to eat already, do the goddamned laundry, and when you returned, you could tell, you could just tell the phone'd been ringing not a nanosecond before, it had that look, implacable, smug, and right when you're ready to show the old black rotary who's boss, you came up with a solution: 'What if he only calls me when I call him?' Understanding neither of you'd ever get through, well, that was a depressing realization until you landed on another solution: you'd hire someone to play the part of you. And that's me. Now, at long last, you can talk to yourself, you can see what's up, what's new, what you've been up to for all these years; the waiting's over, my friend, soon you will know exactly how it's going."

"It's not going well."

"And there you have it. Hope it was worth the wait."

"It's *really* not going well."

"Aw, shucks, you think you got problems, me, you'll never guess, I got the goddamned Gestapo on my…"

"The interview. It's not going…"

"Hold on, hold on. I thought I had the job."

"You don't have a job."

"I've been fired? Really, that's a load off. It ain't easy being you. Frankly, I have no idea how you do it."

"The second part of the interview is approaching. I'm not sure you can…"

"I thought you said I was fired."

"Do you know how to succeed at interviews?"

"Well now, Mr. E., I'm not sure I'm that kind of guy. But then maybe I am. Only you would know. But since I'm you, that means only I would know. And I dunno."

"What are your strengths?"

"That I have no weaknesses."

"What are your weaknesses?"

"That I can't name my strengths."

On the Predicta, the camera enters a subterranean cavern, a team of United States servicemen appear, moving through the rugged, underground landscape that becomes more easily traversable with each step, until the grotto transforms into a futuristic temple, at the center of which is a platform holding a tiny block no larger than a die.

"I don't think this interview is going to go well for you," sez Mr. E. There's an audible click and then a creaking sound, as if a door were swinging open only a couple feet away. But what door? No telling in this blackness, the TV not quite helping (who turned it on again?), somehow making it seem even *darker*, a tenebrism neither Caravaggio nor Gentileschi ever imagined. "You need to get out of there."

On the Predicta, the four servicemen approach the platform that holds the small cube, the camera zooming in on it, freezing the mysterious fetish on the screen until it explodes into blinding light, inhuman figures printed on retinas, too tall, too broad, too angular, silhouettes of horrifying gods which vanish when the illumination calms, revealing the servicemen's ash shadows and an unforgettable insignia on the altar.

At the same time, Wall, you're assaulted by a radiance in the neighborhood of, oh, we'll go with a million watts.

"See you found yourself a light," you say, turning away from the source, but, oops, wrong way, as you crash through the new opening in the floor, the trapdoor slamming shut behind you, the phone back in your apartment making that awful racket, *Would someone hang it up, for fuck's sake!*, and somehow you can still hear the Predicta as if it were underground too:

In 1947, when Rear Admiral Richard E. Byrd, Jr., returning from Antarctica aboard the USS Mount Olympus, *warned that the United States, based on his own experience, could be attacked from the polar regions, no one was quite sure which enemy would utilize such tactics. Little did the Americans know that the adversary was all too familiar.*

But that's not the only friend who's followed. Stepping forward, as if introduced by the Predicta...

The Hollow Earth, part two of the Neu-Schwabenland Empire...

...in titanic silhouette...

...ICU, the history of this world...

...is the...

...and others.

...the Gestapo. Oberschütze Schmetterling shrugs a titanic shrug; Major Freytag brandishes a swagger stick.

"Vell hello, Herr Schtein, you veren't expectink ze Gestapo zis evenink, vere you? Hmm? No, you most certainly vere not!"

An echoing sound like tearing paper, a flaring, the smell of sulfur and then burning tobacco–probably Lande Mokri Superb.

"Unt, ja, ve found ein Licht. A light."

The Predicta sez: *One question we must ask ourselves: why were the Nazis constantly shipping supplies to New Swabia when those supplies were desperately needed in the European theater?*

Orienting yourself, Wall, you find you're in an underground passage, dimly lit by electric lights that look like torches, leaving plenty of shadowy corners. And whoever decorated this place maybe spent a little too much time in grease pits like Long John Silver's and Captain D's, or maybe they just grew up in a nautical theme park, because the salty seadog kitsch level has gone all the way to eleven down here. Luckily, the shadowy version of your Gestapo friends seems to've been a symptom of your mild concussion; they're nowhere to be found. Better make sure, though.

"Isn't this when we shut the lights off? Isn't it past the Gestapo's bedtime?"

Out of the corner of your eye, Major Freytag's shadow inhales on its cigarette holder. Does the ash, even in the peripheral silhouette, flare? Wall...

"Do ze Gestapo sleep? Are zey sleepink now? Or, Herr Schtein, perhaps you schläfst. Sleep. As ve speak. Perhaps ze Gestapo are in your Verstand. Your mind. Tinkerink vith your brain. Perhaps ve are now die Schattenleute. Ze Shadowpeople. Pursuink you through das Labyrinth. Ha! He sinks ve vere sleepink, Oberschütze! Zat ve vere slumberink avay, content at home all snug in our Gestapo beds. Zat our scrutiny had come to an Ende because uf our comfort. Oh, Herr Schtein. Ze Gestapo nefer sleep! Nefer! Vhile you sleep, ze Gestapo are vide avake, gazerink information. Ve accumulate more unt more information all–ze–Zeit. Time. Ve are insatiable. Ve vill do anysink. Anysink. Zat ist how ve know zo much. Isn't zat right, Schmetterlink?"

The enormous umbrage grunts its approval, though it's difficult to pin the two of them down, never appearing right before your eyes, always off to one side or the other and then... gone. One thing, though: you have no problem hearing the Predicta or Freytag. The acoustics in here are amazing!

And, yeah, creepy.

The Predicta sez: *We now have evidence that proves beyond a shadow of a doubt that the supplies were used to sustain massive underground complexes like those constructed in the Harz Mountains and Thuringia, but most importantly like the one found by archeologists at Chavín de Huántar.*

Yes, perhaps they were comical before, Wall, but look at the Gestapo now! Just look at them! Well, right, if only you could see, really see them, instead of being left with the Schattenleute towering in your periphery, surrounded by smoke, and ever more smoke.

"Oh Herr Schtein, it voult haff been better for you if you hat listened to us. Ve gafe to you simple Anweisungen. Instructions. Do not leaf die Wohnung. Ze apartment. Until ve giff permission! Unt vhat has happent?!"

"To be honest, nothing has happened."

"Lies! Vhen you gafe to us your Alibi, it vas disappointink because it vas not beliefable. It vas not beliefable as eine Geschichte. A story. Zat explains ze events of Gestern. Yesterday. Nor vas it beliefable as a clefer cover-up to fool us..."

The Predicta sez: *Why is Chavín de Huántar so important? Because the underground portion, the so-called Gallery of the Labyrinths, is based, or so we believe, on the Antarctic entry to the Hollow Earth. Both of them have fascinating acoustics...*

From room to room, each more full of nautical and undersea kitsch than the last, you notice this place does a good job of amplifying and distorting sound. Sometimes it's like Freytag and Schmetterling are far off and you're only hearing echoes.

"...but your Alibi, as it turns out, Herr Schtein, vas not zo bad after all. Unt now, you zee..."

...other times you get the feeling they're right behind you, Wall...

"...our interest has been piqued! Unt it continues to be piqued because..."

…and then there are the times when you get to thinking that, probably through division or budding, the Gestapo have replicated themselves, legions of Freytags ready to fuck with your mind, while brigades of Schmetterlings prepare to pulverize you.

"…as ve speak you are tryink to escape! Zere ist no escape, Herr Schtein! No escape from ze Gestapo!"

Granted, that "minor" concussion ain't helping matters any, but you should try to think the way old football coaches did–at least you didn't hurt a knee. Just got your bell rung. Shake it off, buddy. Keep moving.

"Seriously, nothing's happened, agents. Ever. Yesterday, to my knowledge, nothing happened. And the day before, still nothing. Last week? Nothing. Last month? Nothing, for thirty or so days. How about last year? I'm not sure about you, but I don't remember last year. Not a bit of it. I'm not even sure what numbers we used to indicate what year it was, or if we bothered with the numbers. I suppose three hundred and sixty-five or so days went by, but how could anyone tell them apart?"

You know, Wall, incoherent babbling is a symptom of concussions. As is confusion. And tell me, buddy, have you been keeping track of where you've been in this maze? Do you even have a clew? Seems more likely you're wondering when they're gonna bring out the fried fish already. Come on! I need me a grease fix pronto! And how come no one's put a cardboard pirate hat on you? Long John Silver's, indeed!

The Predicta sez: *Obviously, we don't know much about the entrance to the Hollow Earth yet. But why did the Chavín build their acoustical marvel? What purpose did it serve? And how did the Nazis connect the Gallery of the Labyinths to Antarctica? These are questions we can answer.*

"Now, Herr Schtein, tell to us vhat happent today vhile ve vere gone. If you do, maybe ve go easy on you. Maybe!"

"Today? What? You think it was any different? Lemme tell you, today seems quite a bit like yesterday, which seemed like everyday last week, and that week brought to mind the entirety of last month, a month that reminded me again and again of last year, a year I don't recall at all. So why should something happen

63

when, to my knowledge, it never has before?"

"Vere ze Gestapo here yesterday, Herr Schtein?!" echoes from all around you, as if there were a Freytag at the entrance to each one of these rooms, rooms that seem to be getting more sinister in their nautical kitchiness, Wall, though you're not quite sure how, everything being rather hazy down here, thanks to the bad lighting and your pulsing head.

"For all I know, you were."

"Vouldn't you remember?"

"No."

"Why?"

"Because I wasn't here."

"Zo, today ist different after all." You can't see it, Wall, since he's still a peripheral silhouette, but you can feel Major Freytag smiling.

The Predicta sez: *The Vril Society learned about Chavín de Huántar early in archaeologist Julio Tello's excavation. The intelligence gained from this find would be vital to the New Swabia Expedition.*

"Is this still about my hypothetical neighbor?"

"Nachbar?!"

"Yeah, you remember, the dead guy?"

"Ve shall get to him, Herr Schtein. But for now, zis ist about you!" sez Major Freytag, the impossibly tall shadow pointing in your direction.

"What a surprising twist," yawns Wall.

"Ze motto uf ze Gestapo, Herr Schtein: Ve Aim To Please."

The silhouette bows. By the way, how, exactly, are the Gestapo projecting themselves into this underground maze? The slam of that trapdoor sounded pretty final, as if it would never be opening again, even with someone like Schmetterling pulling on it.

"Ve are not alvays about zurprize. Zometimes ve do exactly vhat you voult expect in ze precise vay you voult expect it."

"I'd never expect you to do exactly what I expect."

"Zat is vhy ve do it!"

"So sez the Gestapo, a brilliant source of information on their own operations. Really, who *doesn't* trust the SS?"

"Ja, it is difficult. No vun ever beliefs ze Gestapo. But zis ist die Belastung. Ze burden. Ve must bear because uf our Macht. Power."

"…Anyway, I was being sarcastic. I would expect you to do anything."

"Can't keep your story straight, hmm? Unsurprisink. You zee, zis ist vhat ve learnt from your Alibi. You are a Lügner. Liar. But you are unbewussten. Wie sagen Sie? Wie sagen Sie?"

The Predicta sez: *The Chavín, through their visual art, claim that visitors from the sky taught them how to build the labyrinth. Julio Tello assumed this was part of their mythology and therefore fictional. The Vril Society and later the Ahnenerbe disagreed.*

"Agents, think about my dilemma. You're the Gestapo, right?"

"At your zervice, Herr Schtein." Major Freytag's shadow bows.

"And I'm the person being interrogated, right?"

"Ja."

"Since we agree on our definitions, I think we can also agree that it's your job to ask questions, while it's my job to avoid answering your questions. I can't be surprised that you continue to threaten me with abstract menace, any more than you can be surprised if I give you nothing of use. It's the way we are, Major. If only we were different! Then, then I could tell you what you want to know, you would have your information, and we could all get on with our lives, maybe even stopping off at the pub for a schnapps. But that's just not the way of the world."

Maybe it's the concussion, but your skin is starting to feel… well, odd. Slippery. Scaly. The air in here, oppressive. Difficult to breathe. And, Wall, yeah, you can't help but think you'd give both your arms if you could go for a swim. To cool off? Uh, sure, keep telling yourself that…

"Oh, Herr Schtein, you are wrong. You haff given to us much that ist uf use, zough you do not know it. Unt ve shall help you giff to us more."

"You're gonna help me? I've loved what you've done so far. Really, I can't think of a time when things were better for me than when the Gestapo entered my life. I'm sure you hear this pretty often, but if only the Gestapo would've found me earlier, to have them alongside every step of the way…" Which, buddy, they kind of are, but… "Ahh, alas, to be able to go back and have the SS cross my path when I was younger, more impressionable, before I became the man you see before you, or to the side of you anyway, then, then, I could say…"

"Zilence your zarcasm, Herr Schtein. Zo far ve haff been lenient vith you. No longer! You haff lied to ze Gestapo! Ve vill learn vhat ve neet to know. Ve vill do vhatever ve neet to do. Sprechen ze truth, Schmetterlink?"

Schmetterling, so predictable. And then you hear an enormous, echoing clank of metal, Wall, along with a sibilant hiss of electricity, blue lightning filling your periphery, it's time to move faster, but this foreign atmosphere is slowing you down.

"So, tell us vhere you vent today."

The Predicta sez: …*the visitors taught the Chavín to initiate new cult members by using the Gallery of the Labyrinths…*

"I suppose I should feel honored. It's not everyday the Gestapo stop by."

Throughout, you've noticed that none of the humans depicted in the kitschy paintings and diecast models and, well, sculptures remain human, instead becoming a kind of fish/human hybrid, and something is just plain revolting about a fried fish shack advertised by mermaids and mermen, Wall, don'tcha think? What exactly am I eating here?!

The Predicta sez: *And we know that Chavín de Huántar's labyrinth was used for initiations because the sculptures that were found there depicted humans transforming into animal deities…*

"Vhere vere you today, Herr Schtein?" The Schattenleute are closing in, they're tall enough now that their shadows should be bending up onto the ceiling, but the room's gotten bigger. You can even feel the hair on the back of your neck standing up from the electricity, Wall, though that might be the feeling of your hair falling out. Whatever's going on, you have to keep moving, and so you do, your own voice sounding foreign to you now, speaking fluently in a language spoken by no one, not even, technically, you.

"Not since the 1940s, right? You know, we've missed you guys, from the day the Nazis disappeared, we've tried replacing you with Hispanic drug dealers, Banana Republic despots, Middle Eastern terrorists, Irish Republican

Army bombers, Eastern European dictators, Victor Charlie, various criminal organizations, and the group that maybe came the closest: Russian Communists, but all the Soviets could do is approach your éclat, and, hell, they showed their anxiety of influence by using East Germany as the setting for some of their vilest works, they wanted to be better than you, they really wanted to, but they just didn't know how to go about it. Maybe the Soviet problem was their craziest leader was eclipsed by the Grand Master of All Villains, the Archfiend himself."

In a sing-song: "Herr Schtei-ee-ein?" Schmetterling's shadow hands clamp down on your shoulders, Wall, the electricity so close you can feel it burning, you can *smell* it burning your, well not your hair. Scales? Where did that come from? Answers don't appear to be forthcoming. In the meantime, keep on with the jackassery. Certainly that'll save ya.

"No, the Soviets couldn't pull it off, even their demise–the Berlin Wall *fell*, it wasn't blown to pieces after an epic war involving the entire world, and then, quietly, the Soviet Union became Russia again, Leningrad turned back into St. Petersburg, Stalingrad had been renamed Volgograd years before, all of those small Eastern Bloc countries got their freedom, as did Eastern Europe, and the Iron Curtain, well it wasn't so much lifted or ripped down, it rusted away, disintegrated, and when we could finally see through it, we turned our backs like you would for an old woman whose dressing screen has rotted and fallen apart."

The Predicta sez: *We also know that the Chavín used psychoactive drugs similar to mescaline to enhance the initiation experience.*

"Tell ze Gestapo vhere you vere today, Herr." The Schattenleute are colossal (though somehow still in your periphery), and it's impossible for you to imagine them as mere Gestapo agents any longer, they've transcended that level. You get the feeling that if you turned to the left or to the right, you'd be confronted by their new, gargantuan forms, encircled by the blue flicker of electricity, by the haze of smoke, but the funny thing is that's not what you're actually afraid of, naw, you're actually afraid of seeing your own shadow, for what aberrant form has it assumed now? And if your eyes took in that figure, and if your brain processed it, would you go stark raving, or, or even worse… maybe you'd see it as your true self, pal, the self that was always there, encased in the flaccid meatsack that was

Wallace Heath Orcuson, now irrupted into this dimension, torn from its chrysalis by the Schattenleute, an unearthly creature unleashed prepared to do… uh, what, exactly? Lemme tell ya, buddy–you'd rather not know.

"Now we've focused on you, our books and movies and television shows about… well it makes it seem like we want the Nazis to return eternally, because we have absolutely no problem killing you, hating you, we want to resurrect you over and over, so we can immediately destroy you and feel good about ourselves again, and we haven't just written stories about your actual or potential exploits during World War Two, no! We've shipped you to the past, we've brought you to the present, we've sent you to the future, and we've even launched you into space…"

The Predicta sez: *We speculate that the Nazis who found the entrance to the Hollow Earth went through a similar ritual using the substance they found under Antarctica: Explodium.*

"I vill ask vun more time: vhere vere you today?!" The voice of the Gestapo is everywhere.

"I get it now! That was Hitler's triumph! He really did install fascism! But not for the Jews or the *inferior races* or whatever, but for the Nazis–the one group we can all agree on! forever and ever we will all as an entire race, the human race that is, we will all hate the Nazis! Oh, guys, really, I can't wait, I just can't wait, you're gonna spring something on me that I didn't see coming, and then I'm gonna have to figure out a way to escape from you, this should be good. *This* should be amazing!"

But what's that up above through the shimmering haze? An exit? Surrounded by fish-gods, you know what to do, Wall. As the shadow Oberschütze's about to bring the electricity down on you, you slump forward just enough to throw Schmetterling off balance, and you're free, Wall, free, the Schattenleute lumbering after you, but for the first time you're showing some verve, swimming through this atmosphere, your atmosphere, slick as greased lightning, you make it to the ladder, to the trapdoor, slamming it down, locking it before the slow-motion Nazis can overtake you.

The Predicta sez: *The Ahnenerbe learned about the Antarctic labyrinth by way of Chavín art. They were initiated by exploring what everyone else thought was a fictional maze – Hyperborea, Thule, Hollow Earth, Vril – that led them to another maze in Peru, that led them to another in New Swabia. When initiated, the Chavín were secretly transformed. The Nazis took it a step further.*

"Herr Schtein, can you hear me? Today, against our orders, you left your Wohnung. Apartment. Unt met Greta Zelle, die Frau. Ze vife. Uf your Nachbar. Your Nachbar who vas murdered! Zat ist not all ve learnt, however. Ve also learnt zomesink about your Alibi. Zomesink important. But I von't tell you vhat, Herr Schtein. Not yet. Zat voult spoil der Spaß. Ze fun. Unt anyvay, you vill find out soon enough…"

And you get the feeling, Wall, that if Major Freytag were to crack that sinister smile from a town away, a state away, from Antarctica, from the moon, you'd be able to feel it, no problem, the sensation shooting through your sensory receptors, binging into your central nervous system, lighting up your relay neurons, until it exploded in that dome of gray matter between your ears; it's the sense that says there's something wrong in the world, the sense that says you've fucked up, the sense that says even after you've escaped the SS by slipping into and out of a secret passage, the Gestapo still have you exactly where they want you, Wall. Exactly where *They* want you.

§

According to George Euchre, the radio voice of the Washington Senators, Arty Magam has a ritual before each game he pitches.

EUCHRE: I caught up with Arty Magam recently, and he… he has that weird way of talking, and he told me, "Man, before I go out there, right?, I like to read the, ya know, the most intense parts of mystery novels, the parts that really get you going, see? I read 'em again and again, and again and again." And I said, Arty, buddy, that doesn't sound like somethin' that'll calm ya down before a ballgame. But he said, "George, that's, like, just the thing. The characters in those mystery novels, you know, right?, they're about to die. Gonna get killed any second. An' when I'm, like, out there gettin' all intense man, wondering what's gonna come next, you know, I calm myself down when I think, probably, whatever happens,

69

home run, error, wild pitch, right?, I'm not gonna die. Ain't like a whodunnit at all, you know?"

For now, Ed Murrow shuffles through papers, occasionally eyeing his bottle of aspirin, while Arty Magam leans against the cash register reading an Agatha Christie novel translated from the original racist into *And Then There Were None* (1940).

EPIFANIK: That book Mr. Magam is reading, it's known for an extensive use of red herrings.

Ladies and gentlemen, joining us now in the studio is our station literary critic, Anne T. Epifanik. But I'm afraid we'll have to put Dr. Epifanik's report on pause because we have just received an update from Madame Khryptymnyzhy, the strangest she's filed thus far. And so, Madame, take it away…

KHRYPTYMNYZHY: Up to this point, I've been giving you live reads of Edward R. Murrow to see what he was doing at the Hyperborean Arms. However, this time I stumbled onto something big, and so I decided to organize it into a complete report. What I have found is a narration by Ed Murrow that he has no conscious memory of performing. That's right–he has no conscious memory of performing this narration. Why he doesn't remember the project, I do not know. It's like a repressed memory, only he hasn't repressed it. Someone else has… You'll see why I believe this. And so, in a matter of speaking, I turn it over to Edward R. Murrow. Ed…

Agents C. Irving Asbestos and Kuzma Grigorovich Bezopasnosky sit facing each other in a small, metal room lit by a bare, yellow light bulb sticking out of the wall. Quality of the light: cancerous. They might be in a ship below decks, they might be in a submarine. The fact that the cell pitches back and forth indicates a ship, but the sub might not've gone under yet.

There is a large, two-way mirror to the respective right and left of each agent.

"How much longer?" says Bezopasnosky.

"An eon," says Asbestos.

"Vhere are ve going?"

"Antarctica."

"Da. I know zees much, but…"

70

"If… you tell me what you know, and… I tell you what I know, then we'll both know… where we're going."

Beat.

"You first."

Asbestos removes a cigarette from a pack and lights it.

"I veesh I breeng vodka," says Bezopasnosky.

"Just what I… need. You drinking… singing… and then getting…"

"Do you know vhat ve are doing?! Do you?!"

Asbestos glares at Bezopasnosky, his fingers poised to pull his cigarette from his lips. He finally removes it, taps the ash on the floor.

"Have you ever… seen them?"

"Vhy are ve doing zees?!"

"To ward off the… inevitable."

"Eef eenevitable, can't be varded off."

"No, but it can be held… at bay. And you haven't answered my… question. Have you… ever seen… them?"

"Nyet. I've never seen."

"I haven't… seen them either. How… do we know anyone will be… waiting… for us at the end of this… voyage?"

"Entire heestory of…" Bezopasnosky is interrupted by a knocking. "Vhat ees…?"

"Opportunity."

"Da? Vill anyvun be vaiting for us?"

"Even if… there's not, we can… make it seem like… there…"

"Vhere are ve?!"

"We … have arrived," says Asbestos.

"Has eon passed already?"

"No… an era has. But with any luck, we can make it… come back."

The two agents file out of the ship, of the submarine, of the room, as the light flickers, flickers and then plunges everything into darkness.

Thank you, Madame Khryptymnyzhy, for that in-depth report. We now, at last, take you to Anne T. Epifanik, who is here to tell us about the literary use of the red herring.

EPIFANIK: In the narrative sense, a red herring is when a clue or some piece of information is intended to be misleading. Granted, some mysteries plunge the reader (and normally the detective character) into the dark, so we never quite know what's happening until the plot is explained at the end. However, other mysteries operate by making us think that a particular character committed a murder, when indeed that character had nothing to do with it. Diverting our attention away from the true killer and toward someone who's actually innocent, that's a red herring–but that's not the only type. There is also the false protagonist. A false protagonist is a character we follow from the beginning who is suddenly killed, or...

We interrupt Dr. Epifanik to take you to our prophetic correspondent, C.U. Tomorrow, who has *this* pressing report...

TOMORROW: Lookin' into the future, my wild and wooly amigos, is like duckin' into a stoners' party, the smoke so thick you couldn't possibly hope to see, and as you glide on through the room, bumpin' into foax (hey, sorry, Brosephus), runnin' into futons (Godfrey Daniel!), you think maybe those orbs in your noggin'll never be worth a damn again. Only sometimes, that's right, the mist clears just enough, just enough, my fine feathered friends, and you get a vision, a vision like this one... Right there, it's that Wallace Heath Orcuson I do believe, lookin' lost and scared, stumblin' around like as if he were blind, and in the distance, it's unmistakable I'm afraid, I am afraid, it's the cocking of guns, Wall maybe pleading, maybe taunting his executioners, not for me to know as the bouncers of the hereafter won't let me all the way in, and the riflemen fire! Just before a wall of white descends, makin' it seem like February there on the prognostication channels, since they're all full of snow. And so, that's it for me: C.U. Tomorrow.

EPIFANIK: It sounds like there's a chance that Wallace Heath Orcuson is a false protagonist.

Or the killer and Mr. Tomorrow just described his execution. We thank you, Dr. Epifanik and C.U. Tomorrow, for your reports... Knowledgeable listeners of Radioland, with a dearth of information about the Fregolis, we now turn to their company, A. Parachroni. Because its purpose is vague and its existence is somewhat inexplicable, we've assigned our ambiguity expert, Polly Semmy, to the case. As per usual, we are not entirely certain who contributed to the following; we are not even certain if Polly Semmy, herself, had this to say…

SEMMY [?]: A. Parachroni's first venture was a chain of for-profit museums dedicated to World War Two, the Cold War, and art (not all in one building, mind you–separate museums for each). The interesting thing about their collections, though, was that they were all bogus. In the World War Two and Cold War museums, the various machines, uniforms, pieces of pack gear, spy devices, what have you, they could all fool a layman, yes. But only a layman. Anyone even remotely versed in these time periods would be able to spot the inaccuracies. And yet, each museum was so full of this junk, there was just so much of it, you started to feel like it was real. No, not real here, where we live, but *somewhere,* maybe somewhere you could never go. As if World War Two or the Cold War took place on a different planet, or maybe elsewhere. Wherever that may be. In the art museums, the art was all forged, but none of the pieces were copies. Walking through, the styles looked familiar, but when you got closer, when you looked at the placards next to the works, the names were completely foreign. Who were these people? Did they influence the masters we know? Were *they* the masters? These museums, no matter how oddly mindbending, were always located in the worst parts of town, and they never lasted long, appearing and disappearing like mirages in the desert, until they all vanished together, leaving a strange impression on a small percentage of the population. A strange, powerful impression that doomed those who felt it to a lifetime of questioning how truthful any historical account was. Next, A. Parachroni ran a chain of tiki bars known for being jammed full of more island kitsch than any other Carribean or Polynesian themed joint in the world, but none of them operated under the same name, so no one knew they were connected. Not to mention that these lounges were always so crammed to bursting that people actually got lost inside, search parties needed, some foax never heard from again. But those might be rumors. Now, A. Parachroni owns what appears to be an apartment building, the Hyperborean Arms. A lavish place located in the Nevada desert. It doesn't even have a road leading up to it. None of this sounds like it could possibly be real. *Everything* about A. Parachroni screams dummy corporation or front organization. But a front for who? Whoever it is, they must have a hell of a sense of humor. After all, A. Parachroni *does* have an advertising slogan: "We don't make the reality you believe in. We make the reality you believe in better."

Thank you, Polly Semmy, for that obfuscating report. Back at the Pilgrim & Pagan, Magam looks up from his book.

"This, uh, manuscript you're working on, is it, like, a mystery?"

"I suppose you could call it that."

"Ahh, but, right?, I probably already know who did it, man."

"Really?"

"Yep. Sure. I know. Know all too well," nods knowingly at Murrow.

Pause.

"Are you going to tell me?"

"Wouldn't want to ruin… ahh, you asked. It's the same every time, man. The butler did it."

"The butler? There isn't any butler."

Magam picks up the coffee pot and walks over to Murrow's table, pours; Ed downs another aspirin.

"I'm tellin' ya, man. You're gonna be like furious," shaking his head.

"I am?"

"Sure. When you find out the butler did it anyway."

And now this:

§

After escaping from an apartment that seems less and less like your own apartment, like the place you, once upon a time, wandered up to, having read the ad, appointment scheduled with the building manager the day before, who made you believe you were worthy of a viewing (you weren't), who incomprehensibly had something to say about everything in the place as if this were the tourist sector of a major city where events of historical import had actually occurred, your experience being identical in that you only remembered the most inane details (it has a kitchen and a bathroom!)... No, it doesn't feel like any of that ever happened, because certainly if it had you would've been thrown out during the credit check, some very unprofessional words hollered after you, "in this town again" becoming a suffix for each potentiality that could be imagined. No matter, you, Wall, now find yourself in a men's clothing store.

How's that working for ya?

Innocuous, unidentifiable music playing. Suits. Ties. Shirts protected by impenetrable plastic. Collars of these shirts protected by yet another layer of impenetrable plastic. Socks that are either navy blue or black, indiscernible by the purchasers, obvious to absolutely everyone else. Shoes that make you think going barefoot would be more comfortable even when walking on gravel. Underwear that costs more than your entire wardrobe. Undershirts that look better than any T-shirt you own. Cufflinks. Tie clips. Vests. Button extenders. Pocket squares. Racks of sport coats or sports jackets or blazers. Who knows the difference? Not you, buddy.

But that guy does.

Coming at ya, Wall: a silver fox who would have to provide an egregious amount of documentary evidence, supported by an army of witnesses to prove he hadn't emerged from between his mother's legs offering to assist in updating the medical professionals' wardrobes, him already wearing polished black dress shoes, slacks (the man cringes at the word pants), a crisp shirt with top button buttoned, a tie in a perfect Full Windsor, a blazer, and equipped with his sole incongruity– the fact that he's forever chewing a small piece of gum. Perhaps it relaxes his more skittish customers. That's you, pal.

Feel relaxed?

Let's take a look, Wall. Sure, at one time, anthropologists, archaeologists even might theorize that that was a white tuxedo, but after your underground, maybe even undersea (is that water damage? erosion?) adventure, it's descended a number of layers in the social strata. And whatever you were swimming in, was it a school of sardines? Filthy, filthy sardines.

Gross.

The silver fox, unflappable in his manufactured nonchalance, ushers you to the back of the store, strips you of your supposed white tux, directs you to a shower, shaves you with a straight razor afterwards, leads you to the usual multi-mirror display, measurements, measurements, measurements, this Ur-clerk never needing to ask you a single question, time to hit the fitting rooms, try everything on, showtime, alterations marked, the outfit put on a hanger conveyor belt that goes through one wall and almost immediately returns through the other, back to the fitting room, and here he is, ladies and gentlemen, Wallace Heath Orcuson!

Shoes: black and white.

Pants: brown plaid.

Belt: silver.

Shirt: copper.

Tie: silver.

Blazer: red, crested (the crest bearing a picture of a fish).

Pocket square: gold and in the shape of a crown.

He stops to look at you. Not really you, Wall, but the you he has created. It's obvious, no matter the resources provided, you could never have made this you yourself. Actually, you'll probably never be this you again. But right now, you're perfect. Well, almost. He brushes something off your shoulder. Runs the comb through your hair again. Eyes sparkling. The silver fox turns you around and shows you to yourself. His masterpiece. For a second, Wall, you think it's someone else, that you've been transformed into someone else. But it's you. All you. And, really, can you complain? Like a sculptor, he's carved away all the dreck (the dirt, grease, and slime in your case, buddy), and presented the world with the best version of...

The silver fox knocks on the central mirror in the display.

"Who goes there?" comes the reply from the other side of the glass.

"I have a candidate without," sez the silver fox.

"Is he appropriately attired?"

"He is. His suit of white has been replaced with one befitting a man of his station."

"Is he prepared?"

"He is not, nor will he ever be."

76

"Then permit him to enter," sez the voice as the mirror swings inward, the silver fox nodding at you approvingly, Wall, letting you know (without saying a word) that you have his confidence, letting you know (like a grandfather might) that you've turned out well, letting you know, in short, that he's proud (who knows why?), before he sends you sprawling into the black corridor (guy's stronger than he looks), you barely catching your balance, almost crashing to the ground, almost ruining all that hard work, the door slamming closed behind you. In the hallway, you're grasped by hands that lead you through the darkness into what feels like a room (no telling, really, but that slight sense of claustrophobia's left). You're then set in place, and the hands leave.

Somewhere the Predicta sez: *Underneath Antarctica, the crew of the MS* Ablenkungsmanöver *found the remains of an alien empire. Amongst the ruins they found designs for superior new vehicles and a map showing where the richest deposits of Explodium were to be found.*

And Wall, here you are in the dark, maybe feeling like a lone actor in a theatre, maybe Bugs Bunny's crickets chirping, afraid to speak for fear of an echo, not entirely certain if you're waiting for something to happen, or if this is it, you've been stuffed in a room-sized closet and forgotten. You should be so lucky.

Somewhere the Predicta sez: *While the red herring, Adolf Hitler, was directing World War Two for the Nazis, the Ahnenerbe was conducting experiments around the world, shipping supplies to New Swabia, and generally preparing for the future. By 1945, all of the major players were in Antarctica. The patsies stayed behind and either committed suicide or went through the Nuremberg trials.*

When the lights finally come up, you imagine a script somewhere saying FADE IN, as if you were briefly inhabiting the black space in a movie, though that doesn't actually save your orbs any, the rods and cones going through their usual difficult shift change, before you come to realize, Wall, once your eyes begrudgingly start doing their job again, that you're looking at two boats in a painting. The boats are black. No sails. No mast even. For the time period, what could possibly propel them through the water? That emaciated poleman, barely visible in this cityscape? Not a chance. And yet, he's all they've got. If the artist had chosen to zoom in on this thin man, the effect would be completely different—comical, campy, possibly sad. A naturalist work of art like *The Stone Breakers*. But because the scope is so much larger, there's an unsettling, even supernatural quality that makes you think the upright buildings standing before you are the reflections in the water, that the reflections in the water are the actual buildings, that the world of this painting is not at all the world we know, but some other, and the only being who isn't lost in this oil on canvas is that slim boatman.

Somewhere the Predicta sez: *After Hitler committed suicide, in a shocker, he was replaced by a relative unknown. Everyone just assumed it'd be Göring, but it wasn't.*

"Those are the herring boats," sez a voice from behind you, Wall, a voice that sounds familiar, though you have no idea who it is. "They're symbolic for this secret society. They represent one of the three orders. The oldest, the most well known, but not the most prestigious. The most prestigious is the Ancient Achaean Order of the Nobles of the Puppet Regime." To your right, you see a composite picture full of silhouettes. "They took on the name Achaean because the Achaeans in Homer are an ethnos with no actual living people in the world. Later, however, a group came along and called themselves the Achaeans. The members enjoy this subterfuge—a people that does not exist represented by another people who had nothing to do with them. The Puppet Regime, they're the second order. The Knights of the Antediluvian Order, that's the group you're about to be initiated into, is the first order. The third order is unknown, possibly myth…"

"Who are you?" sez Wall.

"No, I'm me. You're you," sez the voice just as the lights go out again.

Somewhere the Predicta sez: *After an early version of this story was leaked, an interesting conspiracy theory arose: that the Nazis never existed. We've heard of racist Holocaust deniers, but Nazi deniers?!*

…and the hands return, guiding you back into a hallway, to what you think is a door (impossible to tell), and whereas last time FADE IN was the appropriate sobriquet, this time there's darkness and then light reflecting off of miles and miles of salt—why not? This world's so protean you're almost afraid to turn around, Wall, thinking it's likely miles and miles of salt in all directions, and then miles and miles of lava or space or gumdrops, but when you slide backwards, ah, there it is, the old Hyperborean Arms… assumedly.

In the distance a phone's ringing.

And, Wall, you have a decision to make:

1. see how long you can walk in a straight line out into the salt, or
2. return to the mansion.

Both options have their charms. The latter gets you back inside, Wall—the safety of shelter and modern conveniences. The former, however, has a Biblical quality, pick your favorite testament, what with the wandering in the desert, maybe becoming a prophet, maybe running into the devil, maybe a land of milk and honey on the other side (you're not diabetic or lactose intolerant, are ya, pal?). Religious delusions aside, though, the first choice likely leads to certain death, while the second choice certainly leads to continuing uncertainty.

With options like these, huh, Wall?

In the distance a phone's ringing and then stops like someone answered it.

Luckily for you, the decision's made, as you see a mammoth whirlwind of salt (a salty whirlwind? "Be ye thar when I was makin' the heavens and the earth, yarrrgh?") form out in the desert, and even Wall can't help but listen to nature's neverending message: "Given any chance at all, I will fuck you up." Hauling ass, Wall cuts around the building, sprints across the front, hits the red carpet, careens into the ground, popping back up almost as fast as he went down, not seeing the sign that sez Jamais Vu (why? what else would it say?), vaults up the steps two at a time, barges through the door, and…

Somewhere the Predicta sez: *But the Nazi deniers' view of history is far too simplistic. Everything that happened from 1939-1945 was real, but this reality has its basis in fiction. A fiction so omnipresent, the reality would've been impossible without it.*

…and is it Art Deco in here or is it just me? Everywhere you see brass circles and triangles, straight lines. Wall, are ya getting this feeling like you've never been here before? Then how come in those pictures on the wall, well, you're featured in some of them? Is that you? In the white tux? Maybe it just looks like you. The resemblance *is* uncanny. Straight up doppelgänger…

"Good evening, sir. Do you have your invitation?"

…and there he is–the maître d. What else could be said about him other than his job title?

"Unless I stepped on some in the john, I don't have a scrap of paper on me," sez… sez… did you really just say that, pal?

A look spreads across the maître d's face, though not the one you immediately expect.

"You must be Mr. Stein," sez the maître d'. "You do not neet an invitation. You are expected. In fact, ve haff been vaitink for you for a lonk time, Herr… *Schtein!*"

Somewhere the Predicta sez: *In the meantime, Nazi scientists had mastered the use of Explodium. Normally an inert solid, when exposed to climactic situations, its explosive force is several orders of magnitude greater than any other fuel on earth.*

"Guy could be a Tibetan monk, head shaved, wearing a kasaya, and if he didn't have the right papers, you'd think he was Jewish," Wall sez, but nobody hears him, as the room is flooded with men in tuxes, women in cocktail dresses, the mob engulfing you and Freytag then redirecting you back toward the ballroom. "What the hell is going on, Major?!"

The ballroom's packed, only one empty table, and your gang takes it, immediately surrounded by Dogfaces rocking back and forth, and back and forth, saying Tick–Tock, Tick–Tock.

"You vant to know vhat is goink on, Herr Schtein? Ze motto uf ze Gestapo: Ve Aim to Please. In your Alibi, you lied…"

"I told you I didn't remember anything. That wasn't good enough for you, so I made something up."

"Do not interrupt again, Herr Schtein!"

Somewhere the Predicta sez: *When exposed to climactic situations. That's why we use those overly dramatic countdowns.*

"I vill continue. In your Alibi, you lied, but not ze vay you belief. You lied

80

to yourself, makink yourself sink zat you vere lyink, zat you vere tellink lies to ze Gestapo, vhen actually your Geschichte. Story. Vas true! Except for vun part–you haff alvays been Herr Schtein."

Whereas the rest of the Dogfaces keep saying Tick–Tock while they rock back and forth, first left leg then right leg, now left leg now right leg, the one closest to you, Wall, just sez Tick.

"Fine! I don't care. I'm innocent! I demand that you let me go. Holding me any longer, it's unjust."

"Unjust, Herr Schtein? Unjust?" sez Major Freytag with that sinister grin, Schmetterling appearing out of nowhere. "Ve are not ze police, Herr Schtein. Ve are die Geheimpolizei. Ze zecret police! Ve do not care about Justiz. Ve care about Schauspiel. Spectacle."

Somewhere the Predicta sez: *One of the Ahnenerbe's missions was to find Hyperborea. And even this secret arm of the government was originally subject to the expected racism. But once reports came back from the New Swabia mission, they realized there weren't going to be any ancient Aryans, and that whereas Hyperborea was certainly beyond the Borean realms, it wasn't to the north…*

"You couldn't possibly think I'm the killer!"

"No, Herr Schtein, ve do not belief zat you are der Mörder. Ze killer. But you are still wichtig. Important."

Waiters arrive, weaving in between the rocking Dogfaces, placing covered dishes in front of each diner. Everyone else at the table is so sloshed from the cocktails, they think you and Freytag are quite hilarious, Wall.

"How? I couldn't be less important."

"Herr Schtein, zis ist not true. You are very important. You may not be der Mörder. Ze killer. But ve sink you are die Heulboje. Ze patsy. Or die Ablenkungsmanöver…" Freytag lifts the cover off Wall's meal, " …ze *red herrink.*" And there it is, that fish, that fish, and you think about the mermaids and the mermen in the underground labyrinth, about the nautical and undersea kitsch, about the black boats in the Vermeer, about the angling paraphernalia, about all those brass circles and triangles swimming beneath the Art Deco waves spread throughout this mansion, and you realize that amongst all the oddities in the

Hyperborean Arms or The Puppet Regime or Jamais Vu, what smells fishiest is you, Wall. *You.*

Somewhere the Predicta sez: *At the end of World War Two, on earth's surface, for all intents and purposes, the Third Reich had fallen. But underground, it was thriving. And soon, with the help of Explodium, it would expand even more, going where no man had gone before...*

This is ICU, the history of this world... and others.

"That's it, Freytag. I'm not helping you anymore. From here on out, I won't even talk."

"Tick... Tick... Tick... Tick... Tick..." sez the Dogface.

"Oh, but Herr Schtein, zat *voult* help ze Gestapo. For you zee..." collective gasp from the partiers, "...*ve haff vayss uf makink you TOCK!*" The ballroom erupts, an orgasm of applause and cheering, every attendee roaring with joy, the moment absolutely everyone (present company excluded, Wall) has been waiting for, and they all surround you, buddy, every invited guest wearing a fishhead mask obscuring their faces (who are these bastards?), the MC announcing, "The newest member of the Antediluvian Order of the Knights of the Red Herring, ladies and gentlemen..." but before the master of ceremonies has even finished, this lushed-up mob begins to sing:

> The herring is the king of the sea
> The herring is the fish for me
> The herring is the king of the sea
> Sing foller o' diddle o' day.

§

Meanwhile, back at the Pilgrim & Pagan, Arty paces all around, goes into his pitcher's motion, but ends up with a phantom fishing pole cast instead, frowns, then smiles.

"Hey, narrator, do you like to fish?"

"I could go fishing," says Murrow.

"Right on, right on. We gotta, you know?, put like a fishing trip together.

Get outta this place, sure, for a while. I dunno, pack up some poles and… you gotta pole?"

"No."

"No problem, man. No prob. We'll like get you a fishing pole. You know? Sure. And some like tackle, maybe even, I dunno, some nightcrawlers. Man, you totally need one of those hats."

"All right," says Murrow, "whatever you say."

"Most important part, man: beer. Big old cooler of beer. Right on? You drink beer?"

"No, not really. In the past it's only been gin or vodka."

"Vodka? Vodka! What're you, like, a communist, man?" says Magam, leaning in to where Murrow's sitting, mock gravity evident on his face. Ed takes a couple more aspirin.

"A communist? Earlier you just about called me Hitler, now you call me a communist. Get your politics straight. Anyway, like that old movie says, communism's just a red herring."

Arty chuckles, says, "Slike, uh, what I'd expect a Nazi communist to say, man. And by the way, right?, sometimes a red herring's like just a red herring, bro." Snapping his fingers, "I got it! That's what we'll like go fishing for, man! Red herring!"

Our food critic, Colon Bownde, has this to say about the food red herring.

BOWNDE: The red herring is a curious little dish because it is a particularly strong kipper that has been heavily smoked and/or cured in brine–although it's normally a herring, it doesn't have to be, it can be any number of smallish fish. The process of smoking and curing the fish turns its flesh red, but there isn't any actual species known as the red herring. Contrary to what your Arthur Magam says, then, a red herring might not be a red herring. It's all just a red herring.

And now this:

TWO

The Original Singapore Sling

"Tastes just like the original," says a voice from far off. But ladies and gentlemen, who could see anything in this jungle?

Moving through the dense flora, beset by palm trees of silk, cardboard, aluminum, polyethylene; by plastic bamboo and large leafy "plants" of unknown pedigree; past walls covered in synthetic tapa and grasscloth designed to keep the outside out, rather than bring its simulation in; kept to his slight path by lava rock that erupted from factories and then delivery trucks, a consumerist Ring of Fire always on the ready to eruct for its customers; the way lit by flickering electric torches, almost but not quite reminiscent of actual flame; surrounded by the rushing of waterfalls flowing into lagoons with gurgling fountains, all creating an effervescent sonic resonance that nearly disguises the sound of the automated pumps which control the waterfalls and fountains; beneath canoes and woven fish traps soaring above, as if they belong there, as if some race of antigravity Islanders for whom air is like water were angling for food below a canopy of molded greenery; welcomed by Hula dancers who appear so authentic, ladies and gentlemen of

Radioland, it's a given that they will come to life, will beckon to those beleaguered souls who have found their way here, will dance slowly to the twangy guitar music the tropical forest plays itself, no, broadcasted from speakers hidden throughout, possibly behind or even inside the inscrutable tiki gods who simultaneously appear to approve and disapprove… Listeners, traversing through and now exiting this faux-jungle, approaching a bar with a thatched roof, encircled by rattan furniture, flanked by stoic, enigmatic mo'ai, yes, ladies and gentlemen, here is our narrator, our man…

"Edward R. Murrow," says the voice from earlier, its owner standing behind the bar, scribbling on a pad, then turning his attention to the moon.

On today's program, Edward R. Murrow meets his employer, "Senator" Kipper Maris …

"So, you want *a Singapore Sling?" Barely a question.*

"Is that what you're drinking… Kip?"

"It's what I'm always drinking, Murrow."

…the Gestapo send their prisoner on quite a trip…

"You zee, Herr Schtein, since you vill not tock, ve must coerce you," said Major Freytag, filling a syringe, brandishing it before Wall. "Zis ist Narratol, eine Droge. Drug. Zat ve haff been vorkink on for zome Zeit. Time. No more zlacker routine, Herr Schtein. No more! Now you vill giff to us ze information. Ze Pyramide ist in zight!"

…Greta Zelle makes her entrance…

"And now you have your decision to make, Wall. I need a hero. Are you my hero? If you are, you'll follow your orders and kill my husband. Sure, maybe you'll get caught. Maybe you'll get the death penalty. But you'll die a hero… Or you can try to flee. He already suspects me of cheating on him. And sooner or later he'll get it out of me, he'll find out who I was with. And when he does, you'll wish he was only sending you through a minefield. You know this about me. You know this about him. So which one are you? Are you brave, or are you a coward?"

…Ben Blotto, professor of mixology, the doctor of doctoring, will give us the strange history of the Singapore Sling…

BLOTTO: *You know the movie,* The Man Who Shot Liberty Valance, *right?*

Course ya do. That's the one where Jimmy Stewart says, "When the legend becomes fact, print the legend." He's talkin' about the West, but I bet you can see how that line goes double for the history of li-bations. Comes as no surprise, particularly to those of us who've tilted a glass or two, that when we look into the inebriate past... inebriate past, gotta remember that one... when we look into the inebriate past with a sober mind, no doubt, we learn: myth is reality.

...And we'll have reports from Mortimer Pestel, Dr. A.O.K. DeMent, Polly Semmy, and Blaise Algonquin on the drug Narratol. All of this is coming up today, along with, of course, Nazis in space.

But returning to Edward R. Murrow and Kipper Maris, the Senator stands with his hands behind his back, staring out the glass dome ceiling, dressed in an outfit best described by our fashion correspondent Kelvin Klone's reaction to it...

KLONE: If an ensemble could kill, I wouldn't just be dead. There'd be nothing left of me. Vanished. Atomized. Not even an ash shadow remaining. Some people commit fashion suicide. But Maris' neutron bomb wardrobe should get him an invitation to The Hague because it's made him a fashion war criminal.

...Yes, Maris wears a Hawaiian shirt composed of every potential color, a neon green Panama hat, a pair of plaid chinos, black and white wingtips, and dark aviator sunglasses with side shields (the quarter moon reflected in the right lens). In front of him, on the bar, are bottles of gin, cherry brandy, Benedictine, Cointreau, Grenadine, Angostura bitters, lime juice (in a plastic lime), lemon juice (in a plastic lemon), pineapple juice (in a plastic pineapple), and a jar of maraschino cherries. Tacked up on the wall over the Senator's shoulder is a signed poster of Charlie Hough ("For Kip, a man who'll never knuckle under. Charlie"), and to either side respectively a picture of Ernest Gantt and Victor Bergeron. At the end of the bar, on a desk, is a pristine manuscript titled *Vayss Uf Makink You Tock.*

Murrow looks at Maris. Maris looks out the glass dome at the moon.

There is a long pause.

Dead air filled by your station manager.

Our resident psychic, Madame Khryptymnyzhy, senses that Ed Murrow wants to talk, but isn't sure what to say. He is filled with a knotting and re-knotting tension, anxious that he's supposed to say something, ladies and gentlemen, but positive any false start would spell absolute ruin. And, yes, everyone out there in Radioland, at this very moment rises the grim suspicion that with each second he, our now neurotic narrator, is sinking in Senator Maris' estimation. Murrow should've walked up to the bar, introduced himself, and began with the business-at-hand immediately.

KHRYPTYMNYZHY: How… how can I act… can I act confidently when I barely know where I am… why… why I was hired for this project? And now I'm being asked to go by… to go by Edward R. Murrow. Edward R. Murrow. That's not… that's not exactly my name… My name is…

"I have a good idea," says the Senator, still staring out the glass dome. He shakes his head slowly. "You ever notice how *I have a good idea* never leads to ideas that are any good? Good ideas just don't start with *I have a good idea*. You think Abner Doubleday said, 'I have a good idea: baseball,' and then people started playing baseball? Not a chance in hell. Probably no one would've played a single goddamned inning of baseball if Doubleday had said, 'I have a good idea: baseball.' Of course reasonable people claim that Abner Doubleday didn't invent the game of baseball, but I find reasonable people and reasonable ideas to be suspect. In any situation, the *reasonable* is really a tiny percentage of what could happen, or what could've happened, and you know that I'm right! So the way I see it, reasonable things don't happen very often. It's unreasonable to think they do. In fact, *I have a good idea,* that's a line any reasonable person would say. Let me ask you, what kind of jerk would lead off with, *I have a bad idea,* now tell me, what kind? A fool. We'd run him out of town on a goddamned rail, see if we don't! And yet, *I have a good idea* is no better. Maybe when we hear someone use that goddamned sentence we shouldn't get all attentive, prepared to have this asshole learn us an education, hell no. Instead, we should immediately realize the bastard has entered a wholly uncritical frame of mind, a fantasy world where everything is cotton candy and lollipops (which sounds like a nightmare world to me, goddamned sticky), a place where their moronic scheme is worthwhile, praise the lord Jesus Christ as he passes by on his pogo stick! Let's get something straight, from now on, when someone says *I have a good idea* what we're going to hear is *I have gone completely fucking insane!* Any reasonable person would agree with me." Senator Maris pauses, looks down, grabs a drink from behind the bar. "But who are the reasonable? And where are they?" he mumbles, sipping from his hurricane glass. "But you don't have to worry. You don't have to worry about me. I don't have any ideas. Not a one. None. None at all. Zilch. Well, except for one. And at least it's a good idea. That's right. I wouldn't waste your time with a bad one. No, I would not. I have a good idea for a restaurant. A restaurant, and no one's come up with this one before, prove to me they have! At this restaurant we will have the best food anywhere. Our beef will drive the greatest Chicago steakhouses into bankruptcy, will convince Texans that all they've ever eaten is low grade hamburger; our barbeque will expose all the best shacks in the South as frauds; our crab will make Marylanders wonder if they've actually been eating armadillo in the desert their entire pathetic lives; and all the chefs in the entire galaxy will fall under two categories: those who work for me and fast food grease monkeys! Yes, our cuisine will be the best there ever was, the best there ever will be. But there will be no theme. No theme. My restaurant will have no décor. None. Just a glass dome... I'm gonna put this restaurant on the moon. And our slogan will be, *Great Food, No Atmosphere*."

The Senator, still staring at the moon, drains the rest of his drink, sets the glass down, and finally looks at the narrator. Ladies and gentlemen, he is sphinx-like behind his sunglasses. Madame Khryptymnyzhy says that Murrow has no idea how to respond. Listeners out there, if you thought Ed was nervous before the Senator spoke, well, he's downright mortified now.

KHRYPTYMNYZHY: The... the CNS... CNS building... he sees Maris... Maris outside the CNS building with a... a can of... gasoline... a box of matches... and Maris lights a match on his thumbnail... and he... Maris...

Maris erupts into laughter. Aggressive laughter. Threatening laughter. His body convulses as he makes this inhuman sound. For a moment he himself appears animatronic. And just as abruptly as it began, the Senator's laughter stops and he stares at the narrator.

There is another long pause.

"You want a Singapore Sling?" says Maris.

Dr. Blotto, can you tell us more about this drink?

BLOTTO: The Singapore Sling belongs to that worldwide heavyweight champeen class of myth makin' drinks: the tiki. An' just mentioning the sacred tiki, you can already feel that breeze, a salty breeze, makes the palm leaves swish back and forth, cocoanuts swaying, feet in the sand, sun shining down, the blue, look right out there at that crystal, ever seen blue like that before? Pure Polynesian, I mean it don't get more Caribbean than that, no sir, and here's a drink brought to you by a beautiful Islander, a cocktail and you sip on that concoction invented likely by Ernest Raymond Beaumont-Gantt or his friendly rival, yeah, you've heard of him, Victor Bergeron, Trader Vic, you got it, well they invented those drinks, most of 'em anyway, back in California in the '30s, exported 'em to the islands because, says I, the myth has become reality, a mythical reality, then you near the bottom of the mug, an' a wave sidles in, an' you think you just might never leave this place, wherever it is, however you got there.

Sorry to interrupt your intoxicating account, Dr. Blotto, but we must now send our listeners to the Hyperborean Arms, where, we are told, the Gestapo are about to return. So, take it away, Ed Murrow.

An ominous look on his face, a scowl that means business, the old man points and demands, in no uncertain terms, I WANT YOU. This spectral progenitor is, of course, Uncle Sam, attributed to J.M. Flagg, though it's more likely the other way around, more like Sam appeared to J.M. and demanded his quintessence be illustrated for the world. And what could Flagg do but comply? These avuncular avatars surround that sleeping galoot (WHO?!) on floor-to-ceiling posters neatly covering every inch of wall space, a phalanx of red, white, and blue, a legion of game show hosts no one ever wants to stand in front of because this ain't a show where you win cash or prizes, oh no, it's one where you avoid... *unfortunate outcomes,* and Wall, hate to tell ya buddy, but they're waiting for your answer. The clock's ticking. Tick tick tick.

The Predicta makes that hissing, imploding sound and warms to its bluish life. On the screen are astronauts planting a flag into the moon.

Wall awakens, tries to get up, notices his hands must've been tied to the bedposts, wild night, pal? But the restraints aren't so tight now, so it's easy to slip out.

On the Predicta, as the camera pulls back, something seems wrong. There are the astronauts, a flag, some indistinct vehicles in the distance. But something's... off.

Wall walks over to the door, stumbling, maybe not quite cognizant of the world around him, and tries to open it. Locked.

The Predicta sez: *Reaching the moon is one of mankind's greatest accomplishments.*

Wall, since he can't budge the knob, knocks on the door. No answer. There's no one home in the world...

The Predicta sez: *What was greater still was the coverup. Created by a well known filmmaker,* The Lunar Landing *was released worldwide on July 20, 1969. This short picture depicts the Americans winning the Space Race, having journeyed to the moon with the help of a modified V-2 rocket and a capsule. Just like the rest of this director's cinematic endeavors, however,* The Lunar Landing *is fiction...*

...but he doesn't get to think about his newfound isolation for long because the phone starts up, maybe you're not the last man after all, buddy, an idea you question when you reach for the handset and all there is is silence. Was the ringing in your ears? Now over to the chair, only just as he's about to sit down, the phone brays again, and again stops when you reach it, pal. Time to take a load off, about to sit down, and, well, now it's, and I mean come on, Wall, are you gonna let that damn thing ring off the fucking, oh, huh, little red-faced rage seemed to take care of the problem. Quiet. Quiet. Until someone starts beating on the door, the phone's klaxon blaring, are they communicating with each other? Are They in on this whole thing together? Why exactly did you get out of bed, again?

Wall moves back to his comfortable vertex, ignoring the knock, ignoring the ring until they both stop of their own accord, replaced by a high-pitched creak, one of the Uncle Sam posters swinging like the door to a restaurant kitchen, and now the apartment, well there are tables and chairs and patrons and a counter and food under and behind glass, it's not quite a *restaurant,* more like a coffee shop, except it's also the apartment, seems as if some madman of a contractor said, "They won't tell me where they want their fucking coffee shop? Fine! Slap the motherfucker onto this loft, and let's call it a goddamn day, boys!" so even though behind Wall is the Predicta (maybe wondering who turned it on, maybe wondering just who that actually is on the moon), and there's the antique radio with the picture of Edward R. Murrow on it, and there's the Uncle Sam posters, and the bed, and the couches, and the chair, in short his flat… his flat that's also, yeah, an open-air café, maybe it'll all go away if you keep shaking your head, maybe we'll get that return to normalcy (whatever that is), while back on the Predicta the moon is surrounded by a fleet of flying saucers *For the real date of the lunar landing was February 14, 1942. And the victors were none other than…*, and the flying saucers, well sure, bear familiar insignia, the men on the cratered surface turning towards the camera, their tanks in the distance, their flag unfurling like it's in slow motion revealing that pyramid, and here's the Roman Salute, as two waiters head in your direction, Wall, and really, maybe you should complain, because what kind of place is this where the waiters are very obviously…

The Predicta sez: *Das Mondreich, the Lunarian Empire, next on ICU.*

…yes, unmistakable, who else?…

The Predicta sez: *ICU. The history of this world…*

The Gestapo. Looking like a seasoned server and a trainee, white shirt, black pants, no points for guessing who's who.

"Vell hello, Herr Schtein, voult you like to hear ze specials for heute. Today?" sez Major Freytag.

"No."

"Ze specials for today are as follows: ze information. But you vill find at zis Kaffeestube. Coffee shop. Ve do not vait on you. Ve do not brink to you ze food unt drink. Oh no, Herr Schtein. You zerve us! Unt ve haff made sure zat you vill follow orders zis Zeit. Time. Yesss, yess ve haff."

Maybe you remember now, Wall. You remember that the Gestapo tied you to your bed, and, well:

"You zee, Herr Schtein, since you vill not tock, ve must coerce you," said Major Freytag, filling a syringe, brandishing it before Wall. "Zis ist Narratol, eine Droge. Drug. Zat ve haff been vorkink on for zome Zeit. Time. No more zlacker routine, Herr Schtein. No more! Now you vill giff to us ze information. Ze

Pyramide ist in zight!"

"What's Narratol?" sez Wall.

Major Freytag quickly points to the antique radio and Schmetterling, on double time, reaches to turn the dial:

Do you feel like the comic relief at parties? Are people constantly laughing at you instead of with you? Do your hijinks really only exist to briefly distract others from the drama of their lives? If so, maybe Narratol is right for you. With its patented blend, Narratol builds a proper arc out of the apparently random events you experience every day. No longer will you be the butt of jokes. No longer will you serve as a hilarious warning to others. No longer will cream pies be launched in your direction. With Narratol, you will throw the cream pies. With Narratol, people will laugh with you. With Narratol you will no longer be the comic relief, but a comic hero.

Just when you thought there was no narrative at all, Narratol.

Brought to you by the fine people at the Gestapo.

When the commercial ends, Schmetterling turns the radio off, rejoins Freytag.

"Look, I don't know anything…"

"You know nosink. Zat ist vhy ve are zo glücklich. Happy. Vith you. You haff no employment. You haff no history. You are ze perfekte Heulboje. Patsy. Ve shall haff no qvalms with torturink you, vatchink you stumble through scene after scene toward your Schicksal. Fate! Unt as you do, ve vill get our information vhether you like it or nicht. Isn't zat right, Schmetterlink?"

With another guy, you might think this grunting signaled inattention, that the grunter's focus was elsewhere. Not with Schmetterling.

"Look, you're the Gestapo. You lie all the time. So let's cut the shit. I know why you're actually here."

"Oh? Vhat a surprisink tvist," sez Major Freytag yawning, mocking you, Wall. "Ze red herrink ist tryink to divert our Aufmerksamkeit. Attention."

"But my name isn't Stein."

"Is it Vallace Heat Orcuson?"

"No. That sounds like a character in a bad old radio play. My name's Frank Dolas."

"Frank Dolas?" Freytag is confused.

The Predicta sez: *During World War II, there were frequent reports of floating balls of red, orange, gold, or silver that looked like Xmas ornaments. These unexplained orbs of light were called "foo-fighters."*

"Yes. Frank Dolas. And you're not here about any murder. You're here about something much, much bigger… You're here about my grandpa."

A ghostly figure straight out of the 1930s, bespectacled, balding, carrying a leather medical case, enters the "coffee shop" attached to your room, Wall, and sits down.

"Großvater? Grandfazer?" Freytag looks very confused now; Schmetterling has always looked confused.

"Yeah, and don't bother with your bullshit Gestapo tactics. You know who he was. You know what he did." The 1930s ghost opens his case, smiles pleasantly.

Freytag collects himself, and: "Humor us vith ze details."

"Still trying to catch me in one of your traps, huh? Fine. My grandpa started World War Two. It's all his fault." The ghost folds his hands, still smiling pleasantly, but if you zoom in on the face, you'll see salvos, the barrages of battle yet-to-come reflected in the glasses of the man who (supposedly) started it all…

We interrupt Edward R. Murrow's narration of *Vayss Uf Makink You Tock* to speak with our pharmacological expert, Mortimer Pestel. Mr. Pestel, whatever is currently going on, it seems to have something to do with Narratol. Can you tell us more about this drug?

PESTEL: At the correct dosage, Narratol helps the patient construct a coherent narrative out of his or her life. The medication does this by 1) stimulating the left temporal cortex (the part of the brain that processes narrative), which, in turn 2) encourages the patient to structure their past experiences into a ground situation and seek out events that will propel this narrative onward and upward.

But do people really need to have a specific narrative?

PESTEL: In order to be fulfilled, in order to develop fully as a person, we must act as authors writing autobiographical novels starring ourselves as the main characters experiencing the plot that is our lives. Take, for instance, an accountant who lives alone, spending most of the day at work, while passing the evening unsure of what to do until it's time to go to bed, until work begins again tomorrow. This person, after a while, might begin to think that any one day is the same as any other. And if our accountant lives in a mild climate, he might not even be able to tell that time's passing. Maybe the Second Law of Thermodynamics has, itself, gotten bored and bellied up to a bar, meaning the clock can move either forward or backward or just remain still. If anything does happen, and that's unlikely, our accountant is apt to find the occurrence accidental, or random, an arbitrary blip that goes further to explain just how meaningless everything is. In such a funk, the potential patient loses all sense of narrative, coming to the conclusion that if I were not here, anyone else could fill in for me, if, indeed, a replacement is even necessary. However, if this hypothetical person (and he will see himself as a poor hypothesis, one that needn't be taken on to the theory stage), if this hypothetical person were to take Narratol, he might, for example, see himself as absolutely integral to his company (a careerist narrative), or the drug might lead him to pursue a love life (an erotic and/or romantic narrative), or he may be spurred on to seek excitement both in his hometown and in remote corners of the globe (an adventurer's narrative).

Narratol sounds like a wonder drug, until you look at the effects it's having on Mr. Orcuson.

PESTEL: First, most people who take Narratol want to find a story in their lives. Your Mr. Orcuson is being forced to find one, and he's rebelling. By spinning this yarn about his grandfather starting World War Two, Wall is trying to derail the Gestapo's intended narrative. I assume whatever tale he tells next won't just be a pack of lies, it'll be the whole carton. Also, remember that I said "at the correct dosage." The SS agents, what a shocker!, aren't exactly concerned with giving Mr. Orcuson the correct dosage.

Does Narratol have any side effects?

PESTEL: It can become habit-forming, leading to delusions, even hallucinations. Of course, all of us operate under a certain level of delusion. With Narratol, our accountant might begin to see himself as important to his company, meaning that every single day at work is a justified struggle against the forces of chaos, represented by cooked books, sloppy balance sheets, embezzled funds, unpaid taxes, etc. He might even start to see himself as a detective, finding errors, chicanery, malicious intent. But the drug in some patients creates an excessive yearning for narrative. Yes, it's nice having more respect at work, making more money, dating someone who is attractive and interesting, even going on the occasional excursion, but what if I took more Narratol? Before a mild-mannered accountant, now a power-hungry entrepreneur willing to resort to murder if anyone gets in his way. And that's when the patient begins ascending the Napoleon Scale.

There's a scale?

PESTEL: Indeed. At the low end the patient occasionally talks about troubles in France. At the high end he or she attacks Russia in the dead of winter.

"You… you claim your Großvater is ze reazon for der Krieg. Ze var?" sez Major Freytag.

"As if you didn't already know. Maybe you don't. Maybe your superiors didn't tell you. In Poland, my grandpa was Franek Dolas, a traveling salesman. (If I've changed my name now, you can hardly blame me, thanks to my family.) In the Fall of 1937, Grandpa Dolas was selling a headache medicine in Germany called Diverticil. Being a good salesman, Grandpa managed to unload more units than any of his fellow representatives, making Diverticil the most popular pain reliever in Eastern Germany, and he was able to do this without ever taking the medicine himself. By the Winter of 1938, Grandpa had moved on to Austria, where sales of Diverticil continued to soar. On March 11, 1938, Grandpa left Austria and entered Czechoslovakia. After selling Diverticil to the Czechs, Germans, and Slovaks who lived there at the time, Grandpa Dolas returned to Poland only to learn that the Germans had annexed Austria and the Sudetenland. Fearing the Nazis would come back to reclaim the territory they lost to Poland after the Great War, for the first time, Grandpa Dolas bought himself a bottle of Diverticil and took a couple of 'em, almost immediately learning how this headache medicine worked. As it turns out, the idea behind Diverticil is that you can't worry about a minor headache if various other parts of your body are in *excruciating pain*. He'd later tell me that as he sat in his front room there in 1938 feeling the effects of Diverticil, his arm branded with red hot steel, his foot stabbed with pins again and again, the nerves in his face flaring up the way they do when you need a root canal, that he realized what'd happened. Eastern Germany, twitching from the terrible malady that was this medicine, wanted to find the person who'd made the sales; Austria was more than happy to relinquish their entire country to have that man caught; the people of the Sudetenland were willing to be allied with anyone who'd bring this charlatan to justice. Unsurprisingly, a campaign was launched. It took less than a year for the Wehrmacht to learn where Grandpa's company was located, though the Germans still didn't know who the huckster was. When the Nazis invaded Poland on September 1, 1939, Grandpa Dolas joined the army. He fought against the Axis. And he was a decorated soldier. And just like everyone else, we, the Dolases, blame Hitler and the Nazis for the war. But then we look at Grandpa, and we know. We all know. The whole family. To this day, maybe we curse the Nazis all the louder because we understand that without Franek Dolas, the war never would've happened. And now, more than fifty years later, you know too."

The Predicta sez: *When I first saw the balls of light, I had the terrifying thought that a Nazi on the ground was ready to press a button and then that would be the end. But there was no explosion. No attack. They just continued to float like Will-o'-the-wisps.*

Major Freytag holds the bridge of his nose, shaking his head. He signals to Schmetterling, who retreats back to the kitchen through the swinging door.

"Vhat ist zis act, Herr Schtein? Do you sink zis vill safe you from ze Gestapo? You are fightink die Droge. Ze drug. Aren't you?!"

"Drug? No. I only took it once. Everyone in the Dolas family has to take Diverticil when they turn eighteen, that way, well, we can comprehend the pain we visited upon the world. One of my uncles, when he took his dose, experienced such awful seizures that he spilled his guts to a Polish filmmaker named Tadeusz Chmielewski, hoping his confession would be cathartic, would bring an end to the Diverticil horror. But instead, Chmielewski's movie *How I Unleashed World War II* (1969) was such a farce, it did more to discredit my grandpa's story than any amount of interference we could've run. Other folks, people who aren't Dolases, probably can't understand. Why don't we let the whole ordeal blow over? Why don't we just let history forget us? But the fact is, we assumed we'd get caught someday. And what we didn't want, we didn't want anyone to feel like they were being unjustly accused, a victim of mistaken identity. So each generation braced the next, steeled them against the day when the Gestapo would appear with their usual bag of tricks, pointing the finger in our direction, proclaiming the guilt we've felt *all these years*, directing us to our trial and inevitable punishment. Yes, we knew you'd come someday. Each and every one of us. We've been preparing for your arrival our entire lives. And now... here you are."

"Nein, nein, nein, nein! Herr..."

"I am Frank Dolas! And my grandfather caused World War Two!" he sez, standing up, knocking his chair over. "You can't imagine how happy I am to see you. The feeling can only be described as... I don't think this is overstating the point... the feeling can only be described as that relief, oh that blessed relief, once the Diverticil wears off, when the punch to the kidneys mellows briefly into a backache, when that boiling stomach ache becomes the alcohol burn of cheap whisky, when that sensation of being drawn and quartered transmogrifies, *finally*, into the strain after a good workout..."

Speaking of outrageous stories, Dr. Blotto, you were telling us about Ernest Gantt and Victor Bergeron.

BLOTTO: My friends, Gantt and Bergeron, they were men, let me tell you, who didn't need any a that, was it Narratol? Yeah, Narratol. They were Narratol incarnate. Good ol' Trader Vic, when the time was right, he'd gather everyone around, right there in his bar, his audience knowing good an' well that they were in for a real humdinger, and he'd tell 'em about how he was born on a tiny, South Pacific island, Vic! Born out there in paradise! And he often wondered what it woulda been like if he coulda stayed his whole life, not that he'd wanna be anywhere but right here, in this bar, right now, surrounded by all you friendly people, but at certain times, even Mr. Bergeron's mind could wander off and get lost out there in the What Ifs, only, an' he normally skimmed over this a bit not wanting things to get too, you know, dour, the decision was made for him by fate, on account of a plague, never coming out with which plague, but a plague, leadin' on that it was a disease never been diagnosed before or since, yes, a plague wiped out the entire island, an' he alone... no, it ain't time for that just yet, because his story went on. On the high seas he spent had to be... well, who rightly knows, being without a watch or a calendar, never quite sure if he'd see land again, not even certain what other lands were out there, if there were any, maybe he was the last man on earth, an' wouldn't that be boring, I mean who'd I go to the bar with if I was the last man on earth, couldn't even complain about the lousy service, I mean just what does a man have to do to get a, and so there he was, out on his little raft, living off versions of his later famous dishes, cooking them up on the float using the sun and a magnifying glass that'd washed ashore. While he was adrift, certainly a would-be tragic moment for others, but Vic always played it for laughs, ya see, the hero of this harrowing tale was attacked by a shark, only in his performance Bergeron insisted the giant fish, get this!, was on the brink of starvation, 'bout to roll over and get flushed down that big toilet bowl that empties out into the sky, when our friend Vic up and convinced the beast, can'tcha just see him puttin' his arm around the shark, coaxing that cartilaginous bag of teeth... woh! *cartilaginous*! where the hell did that come from?... that a human leg would be a delicious and, stay with me, Sharkey, a delicious and life-sustaining meal, I mean, it's like it's happenin' right before your very eyes. An' after, guess you might say it was a symposium between the great white and the venerable Victor Bergeron of Paradise, a symposium, I don't mind tellin' you, that I believe belongs in the annals of philosophy, the animal feasted, although begrudgingly, upon Vic's wicket, later replaced by a wooden version on the deck of the United States ship that picked him up, and to prove his tale Bergeron would have his customers stab his oaken prosthesis with an ice pick right at this point in his tale, as he'd say, "And I alone escaped to tell you about it," a show he'd put on from time to time at his joint there in San Francisco, his hometown and birthplace. The city where he spent his entire life, really.

Phenomenal. But it seems unlikely that any of that story is true.

BLOTTO: Nothing gets by you, huh? Well I heard that story with my very own ears, jabbed the ice pick into his peg right when he told me to.

That hardly proves...

BLOTTO: Ernest Gantt, his story's a little more difficult to put together.

Birth certificate says New Orleans. But I have it on good authority that *that* is where he was first *seen*. Maybe he landed there after leaving the Caribbean. Even his name is questionable. Like I said, there's a birth certificate, but who knows if it's his, or if it's a little misdirection? Anyway, once the Great Depression hit, Gantt left the Big Easy. Made his way across the country taking odd jobs here and there, bouncing from place to place. That is, until he found himself in Hollywood. Got a gig washing dishes at a restaurant in Chinatown. One night, as he emerged from his immersion into the cinema... *emerged from his immersion*... hmm ... as that flickering haze was wearing off, an' anyone who's ever been to a movie knows what I mean... Gantt met a man by the name of Donn Beach who was down on his luck. Many were in those days. An' Beach, he offered to provide spoken entertainment, a story, if Gantt bought him a drink. The panhandler's yarn was about an adventurer named Don Beachcomber, a man who, even while the country was suffering, as it was told to me, "the trials and tribulations of economic stagnation," was able to explore the Caribbean, have run-ins with pirates, rendezvous with native girls, break Voodoo curses, befriend chieftains and headhunters, amass treasure, yes sir, beyond your wildest dreams, and generally live a life most people only saw in swashbuckling pictures of the era, the like of which Gantt had just taken in. Later, Gantt hired Donn Beach to bartend at his restaurant which he called Don the Beachcomber in honor of that famous captain and rake of the high seas, an' anytime you stopped in to that there tiki bar, you might find Ernest Gantt, or Donn Beach, or, if you were really lucky, Don the Beachcomber himself, but you'd probably find that any one of them would answer to the name Don. After World War Two, Gantt settled in Hawaii. An' plenty of folks believe that's where he spent the rest of his life. Me, I think it's like his being "born" in New Orleans. Hawaii's the last place anyone ever laid eyes on him, that's all. Sure, my pal Trader Vic, he's the hero of the tiki, but Gantt or Beach or Don, he's the mystery. One day he appeared, he brought the tiki culture to us, and then he was gone. Just like that. Makes you wonder, don't it?, if he was ever actually here, if he was ever actually anywhere, and it makes ya hope, I know I do, foax, that someday there in the future, when he's needed, he'll return. Ladies and gent'mens, I like to think he will...

Thank you, Dr. Blotto. We now return you to the Hyperborean Arms, where the Gestapo seem to have retaken control. And so, to Ed Murrow...

"You are right, Herr *Schtein*! Ze Gestapo are here. Zere ist no ezcape. Zere ist no time for zilly ztories, eizer. Diverticil! Narratol is ze only Droge you shoult vorry about. Unt ve vill giff to you more if ve neet to! Now, in ze last Verhör. Interrogation. Ve learnt zat you haff been meetink vith ze victim's vife. Unt zis ist ze Kaffee. Café. Vhere you haff met her... Greta Zelle... zo many times. Now ve vill zee vhat has happent in zis place. Schmetterlink!"

The Oberschütze returns carrying a tray with two cups of coffee on it, sets them both in front of, is it Frank? Not for long...

"Finally, ve are gettink somevhere, Herr Schtein!"

The Predicta sez: *Renato Fregoli, a member of the Axis engineering corps, later revealed that the foo-fighters were actually Germany's first attempt at developing a flying saucer. Called Projekt Feuerball, the craft was pilotless, remote-controlled, and designed to knock out radio equipment on Allied airplanes.*

The Gestapo agents disappear behind the Uncle Sam door as Greta Zelle enters, and Wall, buddy, you look shaken, confused. When's this happening? When did it happen? The past? The present? Certainly not the future. It was... *was?*... the past.

Wall, letting history wash over him, or maybe letting it wash him away, hugged Greta, then the two looked at each other, Wall the actor who's forgotten his lines at rehearsal, Greta the tolerant actress waiting for him to remember, the Gestapo, watching from the kitchen, threatening to come out, when the couple finally sat down.

The Predicta sez: *Fregoli claims that Projekt Feuerball was built at the aeronautical center in Wiener Neustadt with the assistance of Fluggfunk Forschungsanstalt of Oberpfaddenhoffen (F.F.O.). Hermann Göring himself inspected the project's progress a number of times.*

"Can I ask you a question?" said Greta.

"Can you ask me a statement, an interjection, a conditional?" said Wall. "Those would be tougher to prove."

"I mean I know I *can* ask you a question..."

"You've just answered your own question. Was it directed at yourself?"

"But I mean can I ask you a question…?"

"I'm not sure who you're talking to."

"…that you will… that you will answer in the future?"

"Not if you beat me to it."

"Is this right?"

"Is this the question?"

"Are you nervous?"

"Is this the future?"

Long pause.

"This isn't right," said Greta.

"Again?" said Wall.

Greta stood up and left, the Gestapo confused, ready to rip their captive a new one, when Greta came back, Wall rising once more. The two embraced, sat down.

"Why are you drinking two cups of the same coffee?" said Greta.

"I am not drinking two cups of the same coffee: one is caffeinated, and one is decaffeinated," said Wall.

"Then why are you drinking one cup of coffee, and one cup of decaf?"

"My doctor told me I need to cut down on the caffeine. So I drink the caffeinated coffee and my blood pressure skyrockets, the whole world moving faster and faster. But then I drink the decaf and everything slows down."

"I don't think it works like that."

"This is the problem with the world. Nothing works the way we want it to. Oh, everything looks like it works. Everything appears to work. But secretly, it's all broken."

The two stared at each other, until Greta stood and left…

The Predicta sez: *In the evening, the Feuerball looked like a foo-fighter. During the day it was a disc rotating on its axis. According to Fregoli, when the Feuerball was pierced by a bullet it was rigged to hit maximum speed. If unable to reach maximum speed, the Feuerball would self-destruct.*

…and returned.

"Again," said Greta. "We should sit down."

"Yes," said Wall. "We *should* sit down."

"So the waiter will come."

They sat down.

"Yes, so the waiter will come. But…"

"Hmm?"

"The waiter will never come."

"Why?"

"Because we are sitting down."

"Why does that matter?"

"The waiter here never arrives if you are seated. I'm not sure if he's malicious, or if it's even purposeful. But the fact remains: at this café, when you are sitting, the waiter never arrives."

"I'm sure he'll be here any second."

"Hope."

"Faith."

"Delusion."

The Predicta sez: *But Projekt Feuerball was only a preliminary stage for what Germany actually wanted: Projekt Flugkreisel–the disc the Nazis believed would take them to the moon.*

"Again," they said together, Greta standing, leaving, returning, sitting.

"I know exactly what I'm going to order," said Greta.

"And what will you order?" said Wall.

"Coffee without cream."

"Coffee without cream? I see. I'm getting steak and eggs without steak or eggs, but *with* a bagel."

"Are you making fun of me?"

"Do your orders always come with negatives? What else would you like to be absent from your order? Sugar? Spare ribs? The Gestapo?"

Greta laughed; the Gestapo don't.

"It hardly matters anyway," said Wall.

"Why?" said Greta.

"Because they don't have cream. They only have milk."

"I'm not sure I want coffee without milk."

"That hardly matters either."

"Why?"

"Because we're seated. So you can't have coffee without milk."

"But why?"

"Because the waiter will never arrive."

The Predicta sez: The Brisant, *a newspaper whose name translated means "Explodium," reports that the first Flugkreisel flight was launched from Prague, the vessel reaching 2,000 km/hr, and topping out at 12,400 meters above the earth's surface. After this test run, the team planned and executed its most ambitious project. And on February 14, 1942, the Nazi flying saucer lifted off for the moon.*

Greta left and returned, saying, "Can I have one of your coffees? You know, for while I wait."

"Well, what kind would you like," said Wall. "We have caffeinated and decaf."

"Either is fine with me," said Greta.

Wall didn't move.

"Are you going to give me one of your coffees?" said Greta.

"Not while you're seated," said Wall.

"You mean…?"

They laughed and laughed, but then there was a pause, a long, long pause.

"I liked that one," said Wall.

"Me too," said Greta.

"It's good to talk to someone. I admit, I'm out of practice."

"You're getting better. But next time…"

"Again?" said Wall.

"Again," said Greta. "Only not yet."

"What are you waiting for?"

"The waiter."

Wall nodded. The two of them sat there, in the café, in Wall's apartment, the Gestapo watching. They sat on and on. But the waiter never arrived.

The Predicta sez: *Renato Fregoli says that the engineers were ecstatic, that they wanted to tell the world. But, of course, they could tell only their superiors.*

The apartment in its original configuration, the café gone, Greta gone, Wall pulls out a flask, sips, falls out of his chair, while Freytag and Schmetterling look down on him twitching on the ground.

"You know," sez Wall, "there are those of us, in my family I mean, who don't just take Diverticil once. No. We go on and on. Again and again. We're addicts. And even though that drug's supposed to be a reminder of the horrible thing we did, we can't get enough. We think it's hilarious! Absolutely fucking hilarious!"

The major pulls out a cigarette, puts it into a holder, flicks his lighter.

Wall is wracked with spasms as Major Freytag squats down, breathing smoke in the prone man's face. "But ze Gestapo are not laughink, Herr Schtein."

"I've got no clue why you want me here. I don't know anything about this… whatever it is. And I sure don't remember any of it happening to me," sez Wall. "But I do remember Diverticil. I remember the whole thing like I was there. Why…?"

"Because ve prefer you in der Dunkelheit. Ze dark. Herr Schtein." And the lights, Wall, really do go out, even the Predicta dying, though more slowly.

Back in the tiki bar, Senator Maris rips a piece of paper off a pad, hands it to our trustworthy narrator.

"Read that," says Maris.

"What is it?" says Murrow.

"It's the recipe for our meeting. That way, if you like it, you can mix one up yourself sometime. It's from the Vicomte de Mauduit," as he pours the various liquors and juices into a cocktail shaker.

Edward R. Murrow clears his throat, and in his best narrating voice says:

"Speaking of intoxication, it is curious to note that it embraces five stages: jocose, bellicose, lachrymose, comatose, and morotose. The first two are not only respectable, but very, very nice; the third not quite so respectable and not quite so nice; the fourth not respectable at all, and not a bit nice. As for the fifth,

105

well, it finishes one."

"There you are. The recipe for our meeting."

"It doesn't sound very auspicious."

Maris turns his gaze back to the moon, agitating the stainless steel container, a cacophony of rattling ice, then he pours two red drinks into hurricane glasses, shakes his head, ladies and gentlemen in Radioland, looks back at the narrator, and says, "No, no it doesn't."

And now this:

§

The full moon shines in lighting a stage adorned with three enormous Uncle Sam posters. It sounds as if a great audience is hidden in the dark, everyone murmuring, incomprehensible voices that never quite speak a coherent word, let alone a sentence. Finally, there's a clear, "Ten hut!" and the room goes silent. Onto the platform ascends a man in a yellow plastic construction helmet turned backwards decked out with four star stickers, an ill-fitting Boy Scouts uniform covered in every conceivable badge, purple Doc Marten boots, khaki dress pants five sizes too big tucked into the boots and bloused at the top. He's equipped with two orange-capped cowboy guns and a whiffleball bat swagger stick. On every finger he wears rings that came from plastic gumball machine bubbles. The theme to *Patton* (1970) plays, but the man on the stage does not salute, he sneers.

"Be seated.

"Now, I want you to remember, that no bastard ever got anywhere by following someone else's plot. Make another poor dumb bastard follow your plot. Or even better, ignore sonuvabitchin' plots altogether.

"And let me tell you, this stuff some sources sling around about character, about how you're just another lost, existential nightmare, about how you're unwilling to commit to some goddamned realistic mold that fits with how *life is actually lived*, about how you're unwilling to fight for who you are, is a crock of bullshit. Traditionally the Hun, they are the ones who won't fight. *They* fear the sting of the real battle.

106

"When you were kids, you watched the Hun fall in line. The ball players, the cheerleaders, the brawlers, the glee club singers, the computer geeks, the council members, the stoners. If you can't say who you are, you're a worthless cocksucker. Everybody loves a somebody and will not tolerate a nobody! And just so you don't forget, they'll remind you who they are all the time. *I'm a Christian, a Jew, a Muslim, a Buddhist, all hail L. Ron Hubbard. I'm a Democrat, a Republican, a Communist, a Libertarian, only Lyndon LaRouche can save us. I'm from Boston, Brooklyn, Joisey, the South Side of Chicago, South Central L.A., South Philly, the South, God Bless Texas! I'm fucking Irish! German! Italian! French! American! African-American! I'm a Yankee fan, a Red Sox fan, a Laker fan, a Celtics fan, the Cowboys are America's team, goddamnit! I'm a mother, a father, a grandmother, a grandfather, I'm your monkey's uncle. I'm a lawyer, a doctor, an actor, a writer, a software developer, a stock broker, a farmer, a goddamned artiste. I mean, don't you know who I am? Cuz I never heard of you before!* Well, we never heard of you either. Now, I wouldn't give a hoot in hell for someone who sticks a bullshit label on themselves without questioning it. That's why you're so odd to the Hun. Because the very thought of lacking a simple identity is hateful to them.

"It's true, an army may be a team, but you're not an army. You're on your own. And any bilious bastard who tells you that we're all a part of the same big family probably wants to bend you over and show you how families are really made. You might not be an island, but too much of this grand togetherness horseshit usually comes from someone who plans on fucking you. Maybe several times.

"You know, I actually pity those poor bastards you're up against. I really do. They think sooner or later you'll join the rest of the sons of bitches who have fallen in line all over the world. That's the Hun's mentality. And that's why I don't ever want to hear that you're holding your position. Let the Hun do that. That's what they do the best–hold positions they know nothing about. You're not holding a goddamned thing. You're always moving. Always bouncing. Always advancing. In your mind, wade through them. Don't let 'em slow ya down. Leave *them* behind! Now, I know you're wondering if you'll chicken out under scrutiny. Don't worry about it. When they almost break your spirit, when you smell the stink of capitulation, when your iron resolve almost turns to goo… you'll know what needs to be done. You're not going to knuckle under, you're gonna kick the hell out of them all the time! The Nazis are the enemy. You're gonna break their structure, you're gonna go through them like shit through a goose!

"Now, there's one thing you can say at the end, and you'll only have yourself to thank for it. When someone asks you, 'What did you do in the great World War Two?' you'll be able to say, 'I wasn't there, wasn't even born yet, though I lived in a culture obsessed with it. But instead of World War Two, I fought my own war, a war no one else believed in, a war no one else could see, a war I was told to avoid, while the rest shoveled shit and told me it was Shinola.'

"All right, you sons of bitches, you know how I feel.

"That's all."

Thunderous applause? Well no, not quite. Only as thunderous as two people can be, clapping slowly, sarcastically, yes, mockingly, and when you look out there, is it George now?, who do you see? Your audience, of course. Your biggest fans. Sitting front and center. You think *They* would miss your show?

"Very impressive, Herr Schtein. Very impressive… should I say… Generaloberst Patton? You show us zat you are adept at actink. Vhat's der Name? George C. Scott. So ve vere right to not trust you. Oh, ve vere zo right, don't you sink, Oberschütze?"

Schmetterling, loyal to a fault.

The Predicta sez: *Pictured here are four of the five men who designed the Flugkreisel: Klaus Otto Habermohl, Richard Walter Miethe, Georg Klein, and Flugkaptain Rudolf Schriever. Renato Fregoli, for reasons unknown, was never photographed. At the end of the war, Breslau, where the flying discs were being made, was captured by the Soviets. The Russians took the rest of the discs and two of the engineers: Habermohl and Fregoli. Later, Fregoli would escape. Habermohl remained.*

Only now, Wall, there's no stage, no murmuring, no parodic Patton costume. There's just Schmetterling carrying you to… is that a, is that like a rollercoaster? Well, sure. This is Climax Park (the Gestapo must really love you, young man, taking you here), and you, Wall, are just about to ride a classic attraction: The Perilous Pyramid! Things sure are getting exciting, maybe Narratol's to blame.

Oh, but look, attached to the coaster scene is the rest of the apartment. And if it isn't Major Freytag standing right next to the antique radio.

"And then one day. And then one day. And then one day. And then one day. And then one day. And then one day WHAT?! What happens next?!"

Does your life lack action? Do you keep waiting for something to happen, but nothing ever does? Do you think your story should finally make a turn, even though the road ahead looks flat and straight? Would an empty channel broadcasting TV-snow technically be more interesting than a show about you because at least there'd be a lot of movement on the screen?

If so, Narratol is right for you. With its patented blend, Narratol will eliminate the waiting and plunge you into the thick of things. With Narratol, you will grab the wheel of your life, spin it in any direction you wish, and take off at blinding speed—even into the unknown. With Narratol, your very existence will be an explosive, death-defying adventure worthy of a primetime slot. With Narratol, you can tune out the boredom of your Public Television reality, and tune in to a Nielsen hit.

"And then one day. And then one day. And then one day … I took Narratol."

Just when you thought there was no narrative at all, Narratol.

Brought to you by the fine people at the Gestapo.

Shutting off the radio, Major Freytag jumps in next to Wall, Schmetterling riding right behind.

"Yeah, I don't think I want to be on this…"

With a crack, Freytag smacks you, and—"Younk man, you are goink to haff fun. Or else!"

Only right now, ladies and gentlemen of Radioland, no one's having fun in the tiki bar. The full moon illuminates "Senator" Maris who stands like General MacArthur, arms behind his back, one foot up on a rattan chair, corncob pipe clenched in his jaw. He pulls out a match, lights it on his thumbnail, and sets fire to the tobacco. Sitting before Maris on the other side of the table is our humble narrator, manuscript open, drink still full.

"'Senator' Maris…"

"Call me Kip."

"Kip, sir?"

"Kip, Murrow. I'm not a senator. Just a nickname," says the Senator, reaching across the table, taking Murrow's glass as if it were his. And it is.

"Very well, Kip. But my name isn't... Just call me..."

"*Edward R. Murrow!* " moving in, threatening, intimidating, the smoke from the pipe circling his head, mirrors for eyes thanks to the sunglasses. Listeners, our fisticuffs correspondent, Professor Punchman, himself, Baron Monopoly, says this is a classic Maris tactic, and you can catch all of the action live from the Dustup in Dusquesne on pay-per-view. But for now, Maris pulls away and knocks the cocktail back. Ladies and gentlemen, the Senator does not appear to guzzle, no, instead, as if through some sort of magic, he just makes the liquid disappear. No human can drink that quickly.

"You won't answer to any other name."

"Is that part of the job?"

Maris reaches back, grabs the apparently bottomless cocktail shaker, and says, "Singapore Sling?" as he pours one for himself.

"Well... Kip... if I'm on the..."

"You work for me now, right?"

"I..."

"I hired you, didn't I? That's why you're here?"

"I..."

"You're not some vagrant off the goddamned street, are you? Wandered in, thought you'd score some free grub, maybe brain me and take my change purse for good measure? If you are you'll find yourself back in the great outdoors before you can say Jack Robinson, see if you don't."

"I..."

"There are twenty-five other letters in the alphabet, why don't you give them a try?"

"Uh..."

"So, you work for me. Do I have that right, Murrow? Try to phrase your answer in the form of a sentence."

Pause. "Yes, Kip, you have that right."

"Did I tell you you couldn't drink on the job?"

"N…"

"Back to single letters and monosyllables, huh? We better get a goddamned manuscript in front of you soon, or you'll be grunting like a caveman. Try this on for size: rule number one in your training manual, which you'll start on right now. You got a pencil handy, Murrow?"

Murrow, submissive, holds a #2 aloft.

"Good. Rule number one: you drink on the goddamned job. Got it? Simple enough? No room for interpretation? No need to get the lawyers involved, am I right? So… you want a Singapore Sling?" Barely a question.

"Is that what you're having, Kip?"

Kip's laugh sounds like he's been punched in the solar plexus, like all the air's being squeezed out of him, ladies and gentlemen. But as Professor Punchman tells me, it's Maris landing the body blows.

"That's what I'm always drinking, Murrow," setting a glass in front of our harried narrator, clattering the shaker's ice right in poor Ed's ear, and then pouring.

Dr. Blotto, you've told us about Gantt and Bergeron, but what do the two tiki inventors have to do with anything at all?

BLOTTO: Every morning the day begins here in the ol' U.S. of A. when the sun rises on Point Udall, St. Croix down there in the Virgin Islands and ends when the sun sets on Point Udall, Guam out there in Micronesia. So no matter where you are in this country, the sun is shining on Point Udall.

Fascinating, Dr. Blotto, but what does that have to do with…

BLOTTO: Think about it like this–the feeling of being in the islands any time of day, 'swhat Gantt and Bergeron brought to the world, an escape from their lives in the 1930s, Great Depression pulling everyone down like gravity'd been doubled and redoubled, folks who were more 'an likely looking at ledges, gun barrels, and lengths of rope with longing could forget, could wash up on an idyllic landscape… somewhere far from here, far from their troubles, far from their fears, far away from it all.

Certainly the alcohol helped.

BLOTTO: Well, sure. But Prohibition was over. You could get booze anywhere. Tiki bars sold you strong drink and a smooth story, a fairy tale that began as soon as, soon as you walked through the cane doors of the thatched hut: palm trees, waterfalls, girls in grass skirts, exotic carvings. When you enter a tiki bar you walk right out of the world. It's paradise, 'swhat it is. It ain't the way things are, it's the way they should be. 'At's why they serve your drink in a mug you can take home. So later, when your sittin' all by your lonesome, back in the way things are, you can make a cocktail in that mug, reminds you, reminds you of the bar, no, not a bar, couldn't just be a bar, more a vacation to some far off place, not on any map, if only I were there right now, if only I could go back... But you can go back. The tiki isn't as far off as all that.

To everyone out there in Radioland, if listening to Ben Blotto hasn't made you drunk yet... well, you ought to be...

And I guess this is as good a time as any to remind you that our Singapore Sling segments are brought to you by Diplomatic Immunity Liquors. Just say Diplomatic Immunity, and you'll be let off every time.

Meanwhile, back in the tiki bar...

"Tastes just like the original," says Maris.

"I heard you say that before," says Murrow.

"Your point?"

"Are they different drinks?"

"What did I tell you I'm always drinking?"

"Fair enough, Kip," and he shrugs. "Onto business. I got your brief, and it took me a while, but I think I understand..."

"Understand? *Understand!* I hired you because I need a narrator. I didn't hire you to *understand* a goddamned thing. You got that? I could give a fuck what you understand. And if I think this *understanding* is getting in the way..."

Murrow begins packing up his things.

Ladies and gentlemen, as Heidi Larynx has informed me, this tactic by Murrow is a feint. When a narrator has been assigned, he can only leave if he is fired or if he is taken off the project. He can't quit. Again, narrators are like djinni, they may have great power, but very limited means. It is true, in the past, Murrow was always given assignments he agreed with, assignments that might just as well have been written by him. But there are people higher on the totem pole than our man Ed Murrow.

"Hell you think you're doing?"

"You're drunk, and I'm leaving. I won't work in these conditions. And if you're actually serious about this project, you'll have to contact CNS for another narrator."

Kip throws his corncob pipe on the ground, grabs Murrow's drink, glowers overtop of his sunglasses. But then he advances in another direction, falls back into a chair, motions for the narrator to stop packing. When he doesn't, Maris punches the table.

A crashing sound. A thunderstorm on its way to the Hyperborean Arms. Is ordnance being fired? Are tanks advancing toward an objective, trucks roaring forward, soldiers on the march? The sound is rhythmic.

The Predicta sez: *But according to Fregoli, the Soviets didn't get the real Klaus Habermohl. Instead, they ended up with a spy who was so effective, the only name he was ever given was Pseudo-Habermohl.*

But wasn't there a rollercoaster? How are you back in the apartment, Wall? Amongst the explosions, in the background you can hear the clonking of a chain, but where is it? Maybe the band leader can help. Hey, wait a minute, this looks like a strip club. Smells of vanilla, coconut, and… just stick with vanilla and coconut. No reason to let your inner hound dog take over in this place. And that band leader. And the bassist. Right…

"After your successful Rede. Speech. To ze troops, ve belief you neet zome R unt R, Herr Generaloberst. Zo first, disarm."

"Disarm?"

"Vhere ist your Pistole?"

"I still don't have a gun."

"Zis ist Amerika! Eferyvun has guns. Nefer mind. Allow me to introduce to you, all ze vay from Paree, Frankreich, Mätresse Mata Hari!"

With her spotlight the moon, and her key light the Predicta, Greta stood hands on hips, head turned to one side, now the other, as if she were giving seductive orders, alluring commands, and who would disobey? She wore a tricorn

113

hat, an Amazonian tailored suit, a low cut blouse, white gloves, and high heeled boots. Her phantom army ready, she held back for effect.

The Predicta sez: *We now know the real Klaus Habermohl escaped Germany with Josef Mengele, made his way to Neu Schwabenland in a submarine, and finally reached Neu Berlin on the moon in a Flugkreisel. We also know that even though Rudolf Schriever was called Flugkaptain, Habermohl, had he taken his rank, would have been called Flugadmiral.*

Finally, releasing some of the tension, she pointed to Pharaoh Phreytag and his Great Pyramids, who struck up a version of "The Dog from Andalusia Tango," her first advance a linear move, but soon her slide steps and crosses took her to the left and right, less like an over-expenditure of energy, more a flanking of her opponent, coming at him from all sides, now crouching down on one leg, the other spinning her around, and when she sprang forward, Greta held her coat in her right hand, her hat in her left, flinging the Amazonian at Wall, who watched it bounce off his body, completely lost, can't we just play Axis & Allies or something?

The Predicta sez: *Pseudo-Habermohl, some believe he was one of Dr. Mengele's experiments. Others believe he was Klaus Otto's twin who'd been hidden from the time of his birth. Whoever or whatever he was, Pseudo-Habermohl kept the Nazis abreast of Soviet plans and operations, informing Neu Berlin on the Cold War hoax. He might've even conned Renato Fregoli into sabotaging the American-Soviet moon invasion.*

The music wasn't sensual and as Greta slid her hat back on in one fluid movement, there were a legion of Gretas, tracer Gretas still moving across the battlefield, and with fury, the goddess of war or lust looked down upon her sworn enemy, the object of her desire, shrapnel everywhere, the music now faster, the explosions closer as her blouse came off, rent, destroyed, buttons like sparks ticking to the ground, her skirt a trampled flag, the clothes behind shredded not in defeat, not in submission, but a victorious army burning what it didn't need, leaving the detritus in its wake with Marshal Zelle at the fore, looking like some teenage boy's wet dream, only this dream doesn't wait for you to have it, oh no, it has you. Wall looked terrified as she got closer, as if he had no idea what to expect, as if he were hoping for a miracle to stop the oncoming tide, though at the same time welcoming the attack, desperately and passionately awaiting his demise, summoning his climactic defeat.

Free of her hat, jacket, skirt, blouse, she was left only in her lingerie and boots as she approached Wall, suddenly innocent, kind, what was this? Right, a ruse, that Wall couldn't decipher, as she spun and kicked into his shoulder, sending the obviously Peter Principled "general" sprawling backwards.

The Predicta sez: *After years of spying, Pseudo-Habermohl was finally outed by a most unlikely source: Renato Fregoli. Why Fregoli outed Pseudo-Habermohl was never made entirely clear because, soon after, Fregoli disappeared. It is, of course, assumed the KGB executed Pseudo-Habermohl when they learned what he was.*

But Greta caught him, led him into the dance, Wall holding on for dear life, each step, each cross, each spin dictated by his instructor, his superior.

"During World War Two, the Nazis were successful at first because of their encryption machine: the Enigma. No one could crack their codes, so they could communicate more efficiently. But like anything else, the code becomes a kind of routine. Those who use codes most effectively are those who can constantly change their ciphers," Greta switches up the step, Wall barely keeping pace. "Part of the problem, usually, is hubris. We came up with an uncrackable code. No one will ever decipher it. This was the Germans' mistake, since the Poles and the Brits built the Bombe. But believe it or not, hubris is less dangerous than the other problem: nostalgia," she sat on the edge of the bed, her legs tightly together, an innocent look on her face. "Our pride can be hurt, absolutely. However, once upon a time we invented an exceptional code, so a better one can be found. Nostalgia, on the other hand... when we're nostalgic, we're not intellectually injured, we're emotional," Greta pushed back against Wall until he fell into a chair, then she sat on his knee. "Why can't things be the way they used to be? Everything was so perfect. Everything was so easy." Greta leaned in and kissed Wall deeply, but then pulled back, slid off him, and spun away. "Think even of our coded methods of control. It's inevitable that the ways we invent to control others end up controlling us," she bent over Wall, his eyes immediately darting to her cleavage. "Before we had the corset," she inhaled, held her breath, her hands pushing in at her hips, "which controlled women by giving men what they wanted: a slimmer, bustier girl, never mind if you could breathe. Then we got the bra. It worked similarly on the breasts, but you weren't always on the verge of suffocation," exhaling and overdramatically wiping off her brow, then she spun around and reached back for the clasp. "The first brassieres were purely functional, but they got fancier and fancier over time," hers was bejeweled, more a burlesque costume than a bra. She unhooked it, sliding her arms out, looking over her shoulder, her eyes, sultry, then she held up the bra and dropped it, twisting around, her hands now acting as a top. "Next we entered the cyborg age, and we got the breast implant," flexing her pectorals, keeping her hands in place, "For men, this meant they could build their own wet dreams. What they didn't know: they were building their own Maginot Line." She stopped dancing, and advanced on Wall. "Oh, there was a time when corsets, bras, breast implants were all a system of control created by men to manipulate women. Those days are over. Now, we turn your Maginot Line," Greta said, moving her hands, finally!, revealing, yes, her tits to Wall, "against you." Wall reached up, ready to spring the attack from his own feint. Greta looked down on him, shocked, until she became a Valkyrie. Her hand cracked across Wall's face, stunning him, his hands back at his sides having never reached their goal, Greta's eyes full of rage, her overdone makeup no longer part of a slutty costume, no no, that's the empyreal look of an avenging angel, Greta bigger than she possibly could be, possessed of an unworldly strength, the chair slammed backwards, Wall rolling to the floor, Greta pouncing on her prone victim, straddling him, kissing him, and, gently, she took his chin, Wall unable to move, how could she look so sympathetic? "Why can't things be the way they used to be? Everything was so perfect. Everything was so easy."

Her opponent dominated, pinned to the ground, as Greta rode on high, the ordnance getting closer, the rhythmic crashing had arrived, the explosions shook the furniture, the tanks roared, the trucks, the soldiers, unstoppable, the guns fired, and at their lead, on top, commanding the scene completely, at the climax, Greta, goddess of all, victorious.

The Predicta sez: *The fallout from the execution of Pseudo-Habermohl has never quite been sorted out. Some say the Nazis predicted it'd lead to the inevitable war and began sending Flugkreisel scouts. Some say the Soviets and the Americans began upping their production of flying discs for similar reasons. All of this could explain years of UFO sightings.*

"You know," sez Wall, a phantom Greta still on his lap, "it isn't just that my family started World War Two. With Diverticil, we created it. We created all of it, everything connected to it. All of the radio, literature, film, all of the paintings, sculptures, TV shows, we should get a credit. We should be thanked. If you think about it, Major Freytag, we even invented *you.*"

The major smiles, and really, come on, how is it possible for a smile to be that evil?

"It zeems zis vas a bad idea after all, ja, Herr Schtein?" sez Freytag, as the phantom Greta disappears.

"Well, was that as good for you as it was for me?" you say, still climbing the first hill of the rollercoaster. The Gestapo don't answer. They let the clank, clank, clanking of the chain speak for them.

DeMent: That clank, clank, clank, that's just the problem…

Ladies and gentlemen, Dr. A.O.K. DeMent has joined us in the studio to discuss Narratol. Dr. DeMent, you believe the drug is harmful, is that correct?

DeMent: Indeed.

How so? Because Mortimer Pestel has already given a very convincing…

DeMent: Mortimer Pestel is a corporate shill. Of course he thinks Narratol is beneficial.

Are you saying people are not naturally narrative in their thinking?

DeMent: Quite the opposite, I'm saying people are narrative. Think of an actress who plays the same role over and over again. Taking on a part for the first time, she gets to explore all of the facets of the character. Who is this character? Why does she do what she does? What goes on in her mind? How does she move through the world? But that's the first time. With each subsequent portrayal, the actress loses more control. No longer does she seek to define the role, now she must ask: what does the audience expect me to do?

A psychiatrist who's against people being coherent, ladies and gentlemen.

DeMent: Ah, but how often are we *so* coherent? Do we follow the same plotline our entire lives? And if so, what is it? Who gets to decide? Do our characters remain stable? And if they do, for whom? Your Mr. Orcuson is a fine example. He appears to be as skeptical about this narrative business as I am, and so he's trying to show the Gestapo the absurdity of narrative. One way to do that is to introduce a preponderance of competing narratives. First he used *How I Unleashed World War II* and then *Patton*. Who knows what he'll use next? I assume he's trying to prove that we are different people at different times, instead of coherent characters. But the Gestapo, much like all of those Narratol addicts, refuse to see this incoherence and continue to think of Wall as following a particular storyline that they control, even though they simultaneously wonder what they should do to please the audience. They themselves have already said so.

"Hell is other people," then, Dr. DeMent?

DeMent: Why is anyone else necessary? As long as we generally think our lives should follow a narrative, the only audience we require is ourselves. What is it that I think I should do? We even move toward the general: what would a person like me do in this situation? I ask: how can we ever get to know ourselves if we're constantly performing for an audience that is either real or imagined?

How does this have anything to do with Narratol?

DeMent: One of their commercials says, "Narratol will put you in the role of your life." That most definitely is the case. Narratol will take you out of your life, with all of its absurdities and its meaninglessness, and put you in the role of your life, where everything follows a smooth, obvious pattern, where everything happens for a reason, where everything is deterministically controlled by the drug. You will no longer be a human being; you will be a character.

"I'm not sure where in this operation I'm supposed to come in," says Edward R. Murrow. "Senator" Maris drinks straight from the cocktail shaker now, sitting slumped down in a rattan chair, facing away from our narrator, though occasionally shooting him the evil-eye. Our body language expert, Aiya Noh, informs us that whereas the narrator sounds confused, he appears excited, less sitting on his chair than squatting, ready to pounce on an idea. "Why am I here? Which access agent told you I'd be good for this project? Here are my problems: 1) the Gestapo, 2) the target, 3) the whole assignment. I'm tempted to say the entire affair is rolled up before we even get started. I mean, *the Gestapo*? We are in the twenty-first century…"

"Is it that late already?" says Maris, looking at his nonexistent watch.

"…so I have no choice but to ask what safehouse they've been in that we can contact them now."

"They're just a part of the operation, Murrow. That's all."

"So it would… Wh-why?… How?… Are we to assume someone dropped a note in a dead letter box that said, 'Dear Gestapo, it's been ages, absolutely ages, since we've seen you. How are things? Yes, we've been meaning to talk about that unpleasantness in the middle of the twentieth century. It couldn't be helped. Sure you understand. But we should've been in touch before now. Anyway, if you're free, we do have a project for you. Get back to us as soon as possible. Yours sincerely, etc. etc.' Is that what we're to assume?!"

"Getting a bit insub…"

"I mean you couldn't exactly swing by their headquarters. I believe, Kip, they've been out of business since, oh, 1945."

"They should work cheap then," says Maris. "Unemployment musta run out ages…"

"Look, I have an idea."

"I can hardly wait to hear it."

"Really?"

"No."

"Too bad. I have a friend…"

"There you go bragging about having friends again."

"I have a friend, and he has plenty of other friends…"

"For fuck's sake, is this a Quaker meeting? Your friend, where's he from?"

"Moscow."

"Defected?"

"He was going to, but then the Cold War ended, and there wasn't much point."

"Seems perfectly reasonable."

"I kn…"

"Which makes it goddamned suspect! Guy's probably set to lead you right into the meat grinder sometime, what with you swallowing all his reasonable horseshit, see if he doesn't. Hell, bastard probably knows a CIA agent who was going to be his handler, help him defect, if only there'd been time, Cold War being a brief affair and all. And, what?, you're probably gonna have them play the Gestapo agents, is that all?"

"No. That will only make it easier for me to swallow the SS's presence. Now another idea: explaining why the Gestapo are there."

"Gosh darn, we sure do need a lot of these here explanations."

"Yes, sir, we do!"

"Kip."

"Kip... But Kip, you have to understand, we do need explanations, otherwise we have no meaning, and then what's the point?"

"Keep going."

"So here's the product: our target, Wall, is obsessed with World War Two, but not just any World War Two story, he is obsessed with alternate histories. So Mr. Orcuson constantly watches the International Channel of Uchronie."

Our television critic, Davenport Starch, has more on ICU. Take it away, Mr. Starch...

STARCH: ICU is the strangest station in our media multiverse. In reporting on things that never happened, ICU works harder to appear legitimate than most history professors, citing reams of sources, interviewing an ever-expanding list of experts, referencing vast amounts of physical evidence. ICU's is a world where everything is known or knowable, making even their wildly disparate narratives more plausible than reality. To watch ICU for an hour is comical. To watch for a day is confusing. To watch for a week is hypnotic because even if the worlds described don't exist, you wish to hell they did.

"I see no reason at all why I haven't punched you yet. Name one reason this very instant, and don't tarry, cuz all I have to do is slap some mayo on this knuckle sandwich and..." Our body language correspondent, Aiya Noh, believes Kip is too drunk to stand.

"Never mind... Fuck is the International...?"

"International Channel of Uchronie. It's like an Alternate History Channel, reporting on alternate histories as if they actually occurred."

"If I get what you're saying, Orcuson, who's obsessed with the Alternate History Channel..."

"Inter ..."

"Whatever. Anyway, Orcuson, who's obsessed with ICU, gets a visit from the Gestapo, who are being played by a KGB agent and a CIA agent..."

"Maybe a CIA agent, I'm not sure yet. I only know the KGB agent."

"Right. Knowing you, you have a reasonable explanation for why all this is going on."

"I do."

"And I don't give a fuck what it is."

"What...?"

"I don't want to hear anymore of this outta you. Look, there's going to be the target, Orcuson, this honey trap, Greta, a dead body, and the Gestapo. If we make everyone take on second and third identities, who knows how all the dots will be connected? Who knows what direction any of this will go in? Your rationale is like most constellations: people say it's a goat, but fuck if it looks like any goddamned goat I ever saw before."

"But I don't understand..."

"Good!"

"...why any of this is happening. None of it makes any sense! A world with few reliable definitions, fewer reasons, and no meaning... that's just absurd!"

"Ain't it, though?"

Back in our studio with Ben Blotto, the question is, and we've been having trouble getting a straight answer out of the good doctor today, were the drinks invented on the islands, or not?

BLOTTO: I want you to...

Because it seems like what you're telling our audience at home is that Gantt and Bergeron merely used some clichés about island life to sell mixed drinks they cooked up themselves.

BLOTTO: Well I'm telling you...

Sounds like the tiki is just a manipulative marketing campaign, Dr. Blotto.

BLOTTO: If you want, you can go drink in your basement by yourself, ya jerk! It's a story. A fantasy. Who's dumb enough to think the islands are actually full of headhunters and medicine men and beautiful native girls? Congratulations, sir! You figured it all out. Don'tcha feel proud? Aren't you the Great and Powerful? The Mai Tai, the Zombie, the Swizzle, Planter's Punch, no, your highness, they were not invented *on* the islands, they were invented *because of* them islands, an' if they fit in so well there now, it's on account a the light of inspiration, a light that shines on and on, that infuses everything, even the lunar surface, and if you're at Point Udall, that light can never quite be eclipsed (no matter the moon-faced bastard who might stand inna way).

And now this:

§

It is… it is with great sadness that I address you today, ladies and gentlemen, as we have received… we have… here in the studio what we believe to be the final report from Polly Semmy. Yes, Polly Semmy, our ambiguity expert. We cannot at this time verify, as is to be expected, that Ms. Semmy is actually no longer… has actually pas… is actually dead, nor can we verify that the dispatch we have received is hers, but the preliminary accounts are trending heavily… well… as heavily as one might expect when dealing with our ambiguity expert. Of course we have many questions, as we often do… did… with Polly Semmy. What convinced her, listeners, that this message, of all the messages she's ever sent, was so important she needed to risk her life? And why did she need to risk her life in the first place? After an untold number of opinions delivered, what about this one put her in death's purview? Especially since, at this time, we believe the communiqué to be about, yes, Narratol. Again, we cannot at this time verify it is hers because, ladies and gentlemen, her report, as is normal, arrived thanks to various sources, some notable, some unknown, some with great reputations, some disreputable, some deserving of our respect, others the vilest members of the criminal underworld, some everyday salt-of-the-earth type people, others the most outlandish freaks one could imagine. Unsurprisingly, Polly Semmy never uses… never used the same network twice, but amongst her past confederates are… were hitman Vinny DeFenestrato, counter-espionage agent Citronella Fogge, madam to the stars Libida LaVish, garbageman Ray Fuse, professional gambler Wolf Shepherd, temperance league president Constance Snoar, American brewmeister Nucky N. Canoe, counterfeiters Benjamin Pranklin and Alexander Shamilton, orchard keepers Uncle and Auntie Occidents, conspiracy theorist and anomalistician Charlotte "Char" Le Tannes, and many, many more, too numerous to list.

At this time, ladies and gentlemen of Radioland, we have not yet completely decoded Ms. Semmy's communiqué, her… final report. When we do, we will bring it directly to you. Until then, unless a miracle… and wouldn't that be just like old Polly Semmy to… but, barring the completely improbable, our ambiguity expert, Polly Semmy, dead at the age of… heh… characteristically, none of us know how old she was… or, for that matter, if she was a *she* at all. So, from all the information we have been able to amass, on this day, our ambiguity expert, Polly Semmy, is dead.

To honor the deceased, we ask you for a moment of silence…

Silence. The silence continues as he lies in bed, a man who has been coerced to relive things from the past, things he perhaps did not want to relive, things too painful to remember, having now returned to the present, not completely free of the past, still flanked by Gestapo agents. When would it ever stop? The SS, it could be that, at first blush, there appear to be more of them, an entire audience, shadowy characters whispering in the background, repeating their sibilant organization's name, what are they actually saying?

The Predicta sez: *It has long been believed that the American moon landing was a hoax. But if it was, who was the hoax directed by and who was it directed at?*

As the past washes away, you feel the chaos of the present return, don't you, Wall? Have you grown comfortable in your old life? Don't you worry. They'll be sending you back soon. The rollercoaster ride isn't over yet. Clank, clank, clank. And struggling, buddy, sorry to tell you, it just won't help. However much They need… There will only be more Narratol. More Narratol.

Schmetterling this time on cue at the radio:

[The sound of crying runs throughout.]

Do you wish you could weep over something? Do you long for the release bawling brings? Do you yearn to wail, to lament your situation? But do you think it's impossible because you've already resigned yourself to the dizzying incoherence that is your life? Do you accept the fact that if you burst into tears right now it would only confuse you even more until you were finally forced to wonder why your face is so wet? Then Narratol is right for you. With its patented blend, Narratol will lead you into situations worth genuine sadness. No longer will your constant state of mind be classified as flabbergasted befuddlement. With Narratol, you will feel real emotion.

Just when you thought there was no narrative at all [crying crescendos], Narratol.

Brought to you by the fine people at the Gestapo.

The needle enters the man's arm, and all of the Uncle Sam posters spin around revealing paintings. And who are those men trying to look the part of inconspicuous guards? Sigh. Sure.

The room is now a museum, museum, was in a museum, an art museum. You remember there was an art museum. The Van Meegeren Gallery, which boasted a fine collection of works "by Frans Hals, Pieter de Hooch, Gerard ter Borch, and the finest example of a Vermeer in the world," according to the pamphlet. The window showed an early morning where the last quarter moon was still visible, the light doing more to drain the color from the scene than to illuminate it. Everything looked obliterated, bombed out, crumbling, decimated, destroyed, all of reality a montage of World War Two photos, the war itself an eternity away, a fantasy realm of good and evil, of glorious black & white. He (for there were no names here) shambled along through the grayscale. But were the population of the Second World War to see the man, the city, what would they say? That this post-apocalyptic dystopian science fiction film about the far-off future was obviously an assemblage of World War Two photographs, a future constructed of the past? Probably.

The Predicta sez: *First, we must accept the fact that the Nazis journeyed to the moon in Flugkreisels and landed on the surface February 14, 1942. But then we also must accept the fact that there was a joint American-Soviet mission to our only satellite in the 1950s.*

The entire afternoon continued on in this vein, a progression of stills, even when the man met the woman there was no linear logic to it. The man was alone, and then the man and the woman were looking at *Christ and the Adulteress,* the aforementioned "finest example of a Vermeer in the world." Everyone in the museum wore headsets. No one spoke, there was only narration.

In the museum, as they stood in front of *Christ and the Adulteress,* the man and the woman likely realized their predicament was not so much a cliché, but a trope that had appeared in visual art, poetry, theater, fiction, radio drama, and cinema throughout the ages. It was a trope that showed no signs of vanishing into a cloud of its own irrelevance, remaining brazenly germane even in life, luxuriating in its incomprehensible endurance. They were, of course, in love. The woman was, of course, married. And the husband was, of course, volatile. He had not been violent before, but the woman felt, if he saw fit, her husband would, either on his own or more likely through an associate, and, of course… The man and the woman, trapped in this immortal scenario, felt themselves separated not by space, for they were side by side, nor by time, for the events of their lives followed one after the other, but by space-time, for they felt they inhabited closely situated parallel dimensions.

The Predicta sez: *The American-Soviet 'sneak' attack on the moon was made possible by Renato Fregoli who'd been fooled by Pseudo-Habermohl into divulging that the Nazis had used Flugkreisels to fly into space. Before, the Americans and Soviets just thought of the discs as more attempted secret weapons. Believing they could easily defeat the Nazis, the two former Allied powers headed for the lunar surface. It was, as we now know, a trap.*

The headset informed them that *Christ and the Adulteress* had originally been owned by Han van Meegeren, who then gave it to his agent, probate attorney Grant A. Boon, for sale. Boon found a buyer in Nazi banker Alois Miedl in 1942. Later that same year, Miedl sold the painting to Reischsmarschall Hermann Göring for $625,000.

To distract them from their dilemma, the woman, on previous occasions, had expounded upon her job at ICU. At ICU, she'd explained, no one was allowed to use the words "as if" or "perhaps" or "seemingly" or "possibly" or any of their synonyms. The employees could not say, "Perhaps Stalin orchestrated the Roswell UFO Incident." Instead, everyone had to speak directly. "Stalin orchestrated the Roswell UFO Incident," someone would claim, and from there the various writers at the station formerly known as the Alternate History Channel would prove the assertion correct. They'd discover evidence that showed Stalin recruited Josef Mengele–slightly blurry photographs of a meeting in Leningrad, poor recordings of a conversation between two men who could be Uncle Joe and the doctor (complete with transcripts and reenactments that made everything crystal clear), cryptic quotes which if interpreted in such a way obviously corroborated the theory that Dr. Mengele had genetically engineered humans who looked alien, that Pseudo-Habermohl and Fregoli had built another Flugkreisel, and that Stalin had directed the flying disc and its crew toward the United States. Next, ICU would hire experts who were convinced that Stalin, with Josef Mengele's help, had orchestrated Roswell, experts who had written papers and books on the subject, and the ICU agents would interview these Soviet Flying Saucer Theorists at length. Finally, the station's writers would find gaps in the logic that Stalin did not orchestrate Roswell, and use these gaps to establish, once and for all, that Soviet Flying Saucer Theorists had been right from the beginning, and therefore Stalin, without a shadow of a doubt, had orchestrated Roswell.

The Predicta sez: *To stem the tide of the coming war, the Americans and Soviets put on one of the greatest performances in history: The Space Race. Decided by coin flip before the operation even began, the Americans won, meaning they would reach the moon first... At least in this cinematic display.*

The headset told them that Göring proudly displayed *Christ and the Adulteress* at his estate, Carinhall, lamenting it was his "only Vermeer." Later, in 1943, the Reichsmarschall hid his collection of looted art, along with his only Vermeer, in an Austrian salt mine. Göring would never see his painting again.

The woman had said that it took a while for the new hires to get used to the rules, not saying "as if" or any synonym, believing they'd been hired into the business of "as if." This was not true. "As if," she explained, is the historical fiction mindset that doesn't really change anything we know. Furthermore, ICU does not mesh with the "true" alternate history mentality either (and that's actually why the Alternate History Channel became ICU). True alternate histories, in novels or movies or on the television, show you how the world would be different if Chiang Kai-shek had defeated the communists in China, or if England and France had listened to Woodrow Wilson and not blamed Germany for World War One, or if Rome had never defeated Carthage, and so on. ICU deals with parallel worlds. Everything that can happen, has happened, and will continue happening. The world that we know can change radically at any time. ICU never asks, "What would it be like if the Nazis used World War Two as a red herring to distract attention away from their efforts to colonize the Hollow Earth and the moon?" Instead it says you live in the world where that happened, you just don't know it.

The Predicta sez: *While he was filming* Dr. Strangelove *(1965), the CIA approached Stanley Kubrick and asked him if he would like to make two science fiction pictures. One of them could be about anything he wanted, as long as there was a scene on the moon. The other would have a prewritten script that must be followed exactly, and to his dying day Kubrick could not take credit for it.*

The headset told them Captain Harry Anderson of the U.S. Army found Göring's salt mine, and that it was only a matter of time before the Allied forces were directed back to Miedl and then van Meegeren, who faced the following charges: fraud, aiding and abetting the enemy, and collaborating with the Nazis by plundering Dutch cultural property. Han van Meegeren, for his crimes, was therefore looking at extensive prison time and likely death at the hands of the other prisoners who would not look kindly on his involvement with the Germans.

If you were to watch ICU long enough, the woman had continued, you'd come to realize the station presents many different stories that couldn't possibly mesh. But that's a myopic view of reality. That's small town 1950s style thinking. Everything's stable? Newtonian? Fucking teleological? No. Your universe is separated from another, millions of others, by an infinitesimal space. And small changes, tiny changes would land you in a foreign world. Once you realize this, there's no more design, there are only events. To achieve this effect, sure, ICU has to depend on the psychology of the conspiracy theorist. None of the evidence can be conclusive. Everything must be suspicious. Nothing can be simple. There is always something more, something that's been covered up, something behind the scenes, something that's almost impossible to reach. Man, you have no idea. As an ICU viewer, you must question everything. That's why our narrators sound authoritative, though the subject matter seems laughable. That's why we choose experts who appear to be geniuses and lunatics simultaneously. That's why "facts" are delivered like pulp fiction cliffhangers. That's why no one in the office is allowed to say "as if."

The Predicta sez: *Having never made a science fiction movie before, why did Kubrick decide to make one now? The choice was not a coincidence. He was being funded by the United States government. Some people point out that the scenes on the moon in* 2001 *and the ones from* The Lunar Landing *look nothing alike. But isn't it obvious why? Plausible deniability.*

The headset told them that Han van Meegeren was left with a quandary: either accept his long prison term and be branded a Nazi collaborator for the rest of his life, or save himself by telling the truth about how he obtained Göring's Vermeer. The problem: telling the truth would involve admitting to more lies. To make his decision, van Meegeren spent three days incarcerated. Later, the Dutchman would remark that in Christianity the holiday Good Friday is celebrated, even though, according to the mythology, Jesus Christ himself spent that day and two more in Hell.

The man admitted, when the woman had finished her explanation of the "as if" rule, that ICU's argument was sound.

The woman had responded with the fact that her husband was dead.

Death… death surrounds us today, ladies and gentlemen. Maybe everyday. But the show must go on. A line, yes, very fitting, since it's a line from the circus.

Lost amongst the plastic flora, Edward R. Murrow, lit by the last quarter moon, lies rigid next to a stream staring up at the faux-jungle canopy. Madame Khryptymnyzhy has more…

KHRYPTYMNYZHY: Why… why… He sees… he sees a burning… a burning building. It is… it is the CNS headquarters. Why… am… why am I here? Why… why has this happened? Why… why aren't my problems more original? The… the burning building… "Senator" Maris stands outside… outside the

128

burning building…

"…just like the…" Senator Maris is nowhere to be seen, but his voice can be heard echoing through the hidden speakers.

"Why did you request me?" says Murrow.

"Wha was zat?" says Maris with a drunken sigh. It sounds, listeners, like he'd almost fallen asleep.

"Something tells me you requested me in particular. Why?"

"Liked your work, Ed. Mine if I call ya Ed, Ed?"

"You liked my work? I have never worked on a project even remotely similar to this one. Normally, the events I report are real, they make sense…"

"It's… uh… it's like dey almost happen."

"They…"

"Cept they didn't."

"You could've hired…! You could've hired someone like you."

"Arnchoo a narrator?"

"Of course I am."

"Whazza prollem? You speak. You speak from the script. In funny voices if ya gotta. My job… woh… almos' fell down air."

Murrow stands and begins walking through the jungle. In the past, P… Polly Semmy has said that our narrator requires logic, purpose, revelation, resolution. One day, she said, he would be required to display range. One day, he would be required to face the inexplicable. It would be his greatest test.

"It is my job to speak. And, yes, to speak in various voices, if need be. But when I speak, things happen. As soon as I start narrating your project, some unfortunate soul will come into being with no knowledge of himself at all, and the Gestapo will be interrogating him to boot. He will likely be accused of murder, a murder he didn't necessarily commit, though he might be convinced he did for Greta. Why are you going ahead with this absurd project? I have no idea. Yet you have purchased land and had an entire apartment complex built, a complex called the Hyperborean Arms! Where only one flat is being rented! You've corralled a man named Wallace Heath Orcuson in there, who for all I know you're going to claim was born at the age of twenty or thirty-something, he's going to be awakened by the Gestapo, and then he's going to find a dead body under his couch. Who is the dead body, even?"

"Uh, I dunno."

"Brilliant. And you want me to make all of this happen."

"Why'd you become a narrator?"

"I found I had the gift."

"Why not an accountant?"

"I was never any good at math."

"So here you are... you've ruined my buzz, you asshole... why can't you just do your job? lousy prima dona narr... you're a narrator. Could be anywhere else. Could be workin'... wooh... for anyone else. But CNS sent you to me. I knew you were the man for the job. Wall was sent to me too. And Greta. And I've decided what I'm gonna do with all a you. And you're gonna make it happen."

Murrow stumbling upon Maris now, leaning against a tree, looking pretty drunk, holding the manuscript like he forgot it was in his hand. The Senator glances at the cocktail shaker, raises it to his lips, stops, drops it to the ground.

"What a waste," says Maris.

"You understand, later, you and I, we'll be confused!"

"About what?"

"Not about what, but *for each other*."

Maris squints his eyes.

"You think so? I look like me, and you look nothing like me."

"Yes, but I will have spoken your words and made them come alive. People will assume I am *you*."

"Are you... are you the one who got drunk? You're not me, Ed."

"It's not that easy. I am complicit with you. I have no choice. Wherever CNS sends me, I have to go. And once I'm there, even if I'm working from the outside, I'm a part of the whole process. We may not resemble each other, but everyone will confuse us."

"First day on the job, Ed?"

"No."

"An' what was all 'at at the beginning where you were gonna leave?"

"If you let me go, I'd be free of the operation. I can't leave unless I'm dismissed."

"What if ya did?"

"I… I… I would never narrate again. Or… or worse…"

"Seems I gots ya right where I wants ya, Murrow," Maris says, picking up the stainless steel container.

"Yeah…"

"You ready ta… oh, Singapore Sling?" The Senator holds out the cocktail shaker that's mostly full of water and plastic leaves now.

"No thanks."

"Shoot yourself."

"I'd like to. So, I assume we'll begin with the Prologue?"

"Wrong again, Ed. Let's start with Part Two," says Maris, heading for the bar.

Edward R. Murrow, narrator from CNS, contractor to "Senator" Kipper Maris, sighs heavily.

There were many sighs between the man and the woman that day. If they had talked, the man and the woman probably would have admitted that coming to the Van Meegeren Gallery had been a mistake. The works did not show them fantasy worlds they could dream about, but instead solidified the fact that their problems were timeless and unsolvable.

The headset told them that Han van Meegeren decided against being branded a Nazi collaborator, but did so by accepting another brand. He informed the authorities that he had not sold Dutch cultural property to the Nazis because the painting, *Christ and the Adulteress*, was not a Vermeer. It was a forgery painted by himself, Han van Meegeren, in the style of the Dutch master.

The reason the museum did not help was because the works exhibited were generally viewed as a last desperate attempt not by many artists, but by one man. The painter, who had shown promise early in his career, was not interested in cubism, surrealism, or any of the other modern styles. Soon, he was ostracized for being a technician of the Renaissance school who lacked the major artistic virtue: originality. He copied classical styles with precision, but had none his own.

In response, the artist decided to fool his critics by creating works that belonged amongst the masters.

The Predicta sez: *On July 20, 1969, perhaps Stanley Kubrick's greatest triumph was released to the world. Until now, he has never received credit for it.*

The woman said that before her husband had been killed, the two of them were unable to be truly happy. There may have been some prurient excitement at first, but they had to live under the shadow of her spouse's likely response, when he would, with a simple gesture, sever them for good, and all joy would stop forever. Every minute she spent with her husband was torment, and every minute she spent with her beloved was marred by anxiety and depression. Her married life, she knew then, could not go on. But luckily, now, her husband had been killed.

When the man informed the woman that he had seen her husband earlier in the day, she said the man would make a lousy ICU employee.

She stood gazing at *Christ and the Adulteress,* and if there were an instance of movement that day, a moment that did not come from a montage of stills, a moment lacking the summarized conversations from the imagined narrator, it had to've been then, as she turned from the painting and looked over at the man, curling a lock of hair behind her ear, smiling, walking toward him, as if they were an innocent couple on a date. But even then there could be no happiness, for the man knew what he'd have to do, he'd have to plunge into the turbulence of the future where there would be constant and inexplicable movement, and this memory would be a painful reminder of a time that never existed, a time when they understood everything.

The man stood alone, save the guards in the background, in front of the last painting he would see that day, shaking pills into his hand, pills imprinted with a D, pills that he takes without water, that he chews, his body soon obviously racked with pain, but something about his face, the pain's made a masochist of him and somehow of everyone else too, making those tears of... of joy...?

The Predicta sez: *No one is quite sure how the Moon Landing Hoax affected its director. Some believe that the rest of his career was influenced by his uncredited work on this film, seeing a progression from rebellion in* A Clockwork Orange *to an attempt at acceptance in* Barry Lyndon *to a horrible guilt in* The Shining *to an exploration of government and military operations in* Full Metal Jacket *and finally to an escape into sex and banal conspiracy theories in* Eyes Wide Shut. *Others claim Kubrick thought the project was a lark, never attaching any significance to it whatsoever.*

The headset told him that in order to prove his claims to the Allied authorities, Han van Meegeren painted one last forgery. The work, *Jesus Among the Doctors,* portrays a young Christ instructing learned men. Although a shameful exposure in the eyes of the business end of the art world, one has to take this as the height of his career: van Meegeren showing his critics that he was right. After the trial was completed, the Dutch forger was no longer thought of as a traitor. He had foiled the Nazis. He had duped the Reichsmarschall. He was a hero. But van Meegeren said, "My triumph as a counterfeiter was my defeat as a creative artist." And yet, although a forger, he was not a plagiarist. Van Meegeren did not paint duplicates of already existing works, he created new pieces in old styles utilizing subtly ironic subject matter, all of which would become tropes in postmodern art. Somehow the Dutch, the Allied authorities, the artist himself missed this achievement, and instead reacted like the Reichsmarschall. For when Göring, before his execution, learned that his only Vermeer was not a Vermeer at all, he looked as if he had finally discovered that the world truly was made of melancholy.

And it is. We have here, ladies and gentlemen, the best decryption of Polly Semmy's final piece, her take on Narratol, though again, we are not positive it is from her, or if she is indeed dead. Without further ado, take it away, Polly Semmy.

SEMMY (*voice heavily modulated*): Those who disapprove of Narratol believe we can know ourselves through and through. But everyday we learn new things about ourselves, we forget things we used to know, and we dismiss that which we thought we knew. Much as we can never truly know anyone else, we can never truly know ourselves. A drug that gives our lives a narrative can hardly hinder our self-exploration because that exploration was doomed to failure from the beginning. The argument against Narratol sounds too Romantic for my taste. What is your true self? What is your authentic self? I do not know, nor will I ever. So if a narrative would alleviate my pain, should I be in pain, or boredom, should I be bored, why not take it? You will come no closer, nor slip further away from

133

your true identity than before the drug, since you were always to remain a stranger to yourself.

And to us too... That was Polly Semmy. Our former ambiguity expert. She will be... she will be mis...

Oh god! Oh god! What could... what could possibly come next?!

And... and now this:

§

ALGONQUIN: Greetings to all. What's this? Crickets? Worry not, for they are your true audience, Blaise. Where would you be without family Gryllidae? From them no vulgar standing ovation, but the more majestic hunched stridulation. Their appearance is my harbinger, my appearance theirs. Ha-HA! And what is this? Oh geist of liquor, you hang about the room like a fortnight house guest in his fifth week. You are the man on the couch, the cellar dweller, The Thing That Wouldn't Leave. And now... It appears our Station Manager is out cold. Will do him well, I suppose. He needs it. His sadness not only rends the heart, but renders the heart, bringing forth the throb and pulse of all human feeling. Expect not a dry eye in the house, especially when they turn you away with the firehose. What about the good doctor, Ben Blotto? Rising below his name, yes? Ne'er before has the essence, the spirit of gin been so fully encompassed by one man who lived to tell the tale. That means it is left to me, Blaise Algonquin, one-time actor, one-time dramaturge, full-time hack. When he stepped upon the boards the audience immediately rose! And then departed, requesting refunds on their tickets. I shall call my performance harrowing (for it distresses the mind), a tour de force not witnessed since the Tour de France (for only those on drugs can endure it). I could do this in my sleep, in my sleep, I tell you! And who knows but I am. Sound asleep and dreaming of you, you, my beautiful public. Do you sleep? Do you dream? Do you dream of me speaking to you? Hubris, hubris, all of this Shakespeare is hubris. A little touch of Blaise in the radio night is all. Though I must admit, I feel more like Fortinbras come onto the scene amongst a lot of corpses. Anyhow... Edward R. Murrow appears to be alive (if not well), though Senator Maris is currently toes up. (Bill W. himself would recommend a stiff drink looking upon these comatose sots!) Mr. Orcuson, or whatever he's being called now, is conscious, barely, lying on a couch as Greta observes Freud-like from the chair. The Gestapo are nowhere to be seen. Meaning they are likely in the last place we'd expect. So, we should check there first... Now where is the last place we would expect? I suppose we shall find it later. All present and accounted for, captain. Even that wretched Idiot Box goes on and on about Nazis on the... Look! Look outside! It is the new moon, meaning there is no moon. Darkness. Has the show begun? Has the curtain risen on our tale? How would we know? This is radio. Being the new moon, it is time for new beginnings, so let us not worry about what ought to happen, but what we want to happen and how we want to go about it. To you, my public, I say: what about an evening at the theatre? And now, if you'll allow me, right this way, your chariot awaits. A little music? Ah, what's this? A commercial:

"*What do you want to do?*"

"*I don't know. What do you want to do?*"

"*I don't know. That's why I asked you.*"

"*I don't know either. That's why I returned the question.*"

"*How many times have we had this conversation?*"

"*Maybe it's a rehearsal.*"

"*For what?*"

"*Nothing.*"

"*A rehearsal for nothing?*"

"*In case it ever happens.*"

"*Do we want nothing to happen?*"

"*Maybe it already is.*"

"*Will nothing ever happen?*"

"*No... But if it does, we'll be prepared. We will be stars.*"

"*But I don't want to be the star of nothing, I want to be the star of something.*"

"*Then maybe Narratol is right for you.*"

"*Narratol?*"

Just when you thought there was no narrative at all...

"*We've done it! We're the stars of... something!*"

...Narratol.

Brought to you by...

Enough of the radio... I'm sure you've heard these commercials before. It seems lately we can't escape them. Narratol ads follow one about with the dogged persistence of zombies in a George A. Romero picture. Certainly we'll be safe in this abandoned farmhouse, since there aren't any radios or Idiot Boxes or computers in sight. But what's that, there, in the distance? Looks to be a mendicant unrolling a banner. Whatever does it say? Yes, give me the binoculars. Ah, "Just when you thought..." Nooooooooo! What of the drug itself? If you don't mind, I shall dissertate. The problem with Narratol is that it gives you a singular, coherent character. I demand this from a two or three hour play, not from a human being. As it was in the beginning, is now, and ever shall be: characters are not people. They are ideas. Gussied up to seem like people, perhaps. Yet I say, if you prick Shylock, he will not bleed, tickle him, he will never laugh, though not for the anti-Semitic reasons he's trying to refute, instead because he is a character. Characters are metaphors, models for various things human and even inhuman. And if we're thinking inside the box, George Box, that is, then we know: "All models are wrong; some are useful." Characters therefore have the same relation to people that words have to their referents. A rose is not a rose, my dear, nor is Hamlet–yes, even the Dane!–nor is Hamlet anything more or less than Hamlet – words on paper we briefly imagine among the rest of the *Homo sapiens.* People, though they may often tell themselves otherwise, are awful at living narratives. Think of the times when your life has no focus, no purpose, no arc. Put those moments into a script, and I would say, "It appears the playwright entered the labyrinth of this drama without a clew." Think of how we would sound if we were to record the lot of our conversations in any twenty-four hour period. Would it be dialogue? "The ums and uhs spoken throughout became so prevalent I believed they were a secret cipher, a Morse code, the three dots, three dashes, three dots of those who want to escape. I wished I could help them. Alas, I could only look on at the unfolding disaster." And what of the story? "To say this piece is full of tangents would be to imply it has a through-line, and Mrs. Algonquin raised no liars." Listen to me going on and on. I apologize. Anyway, we are here: The Glasgow City Showhall, though the kids call it the GCS. I agree, I can't think of a single town named Glasgow in the vicinity. And I hardly believe anyone expects to stimulate our dream-life by referencing Scotland. But allow me to tell you what you're in for. Entering the lobby, you will see, perhaps, the usual: bronze, brass, red velvet, plush carpet, marble, everything ornate, attendants who look like what we presume elevator operators used to look like in olden times: red pillbox hats, red military style coats, black pants with stripes, black polished shoes. Once your ticket is torn, however, the experience changes. The theatre itself is pitch dark. Not the kind of dark one might expect before a film or a play, but the kind of dark, I judge, that is utterly impervious to light. Inside that stygian domain there are no smells, no sounds, and the only other person you'll be aware of is your personal Charon, the usher, who directs you through the auditorium. You will doubt him, you will wonder what you are doing there, you will question why you decided to come, why this sounded like a good idea, but worry not. Regardless of your actions, the usher will reach his terminus, delivering you to the seat reserved in your honor. It is normal for neophytes to concoct byzantine fictions involving their invisible guides—I *don't remember how I met him, nor will I ever know why. He appeared as if we were on a blind date. He was intelligent, urbane. He seemed to have opinions on everything; he spoke as if he'd been speaking for all of eternity, it was only now I stopped to listen. And then he took me to The Glasgow. The best account I can give of that marvel is: it wouldn't surprise me at all if I drove to the GCS and found it had vanished, not because of Chapter 11 or rage or indifference, but out of pure improbability. How did he ever discover The Glasgow? Maybe he was connected to it. A visitor from some other place who'd chosen me, of all people!, to join him in this wonder. The darkness inside, I didn't feel as if I were dead, but I also wasn't certain that I was alive any longer. I panicked, yes. But he was always there, guiding me, the inky black no more a problem for him than a thin fog. And he kept talking, though his style did change slightly while he played my guard. Afterwards, believe it or not, we went for drinks, as if what had just happened were normal!* You can give him a name, a personality, an appearance, if you wish, though you will never know who it was. And as suddenly as he entered your life, ferrying you past unknown and unknowable dangers, he will be gone. Perhaps a part of you will miss him, like the earth misses the moon, but there will be little time to think on this. When the show itself begins, you will remain in the vacuum of the theatre, unaware of any sonic or visual stimulus except for that coming from the stage. You will be alone in a way you aren't while, say, watching the Idiot Box at home—for there you imagine next door or upstairs or downstairs neighbors. The isolation at The Glasgow is complete, but being so plenary, the show appears to be for a singular audience: you. There will be no indication as to how you're experiencing the program because you will be certain your five senses have nothing to do with it. Your focus on the performance will reach an intensity an order of magnitude greater than that which you accord dreams, and later you may be convinced it took place nowhere but in your own mind, an ephemeral phantasm slipping away as soon as you awaken from its thrall. It isn't uncommon for an entire audience to forget vast portions of the show, meeting afterwards in an attempt to reconstruct it all, unable to do so, returning to the GCS again in the hopes that this time, this time… But no two performances at The Glasgow are alike. Keep that in mind when the program has concluded, when you find yourself frantically attempting to recreate the experience, to describe it, to capture it whole and in its entirety, as your usher directs you away from the darkness therein and back to the world outside. Will your re-emergence be a relief? Will the world outside be the same one you left behind? Impossible to say. All you can do now is hand over your ticket and submit yourself to the Glasgow City Showhall.

A Night at The Glasgow

The stage is split in half: stage right is the tiki bar, stage left Wall's apartment, though the glass dome from "Senator" Maris' place covers both sides. In the tiki bar, Edward R. Murrow narrates, silently for now, while "Senator" Maris sleeps on the floor. In the apartment, Wallace Heath Orcuson lies on a couch, while Greta looks on from the chair.

MURROW: Right now, you feel that, buddy? That sensation you're not where you think you are, where you should be? The apartment, well, something tells you it ain't the apartment at all, more like a theatre, complete with an audience, people showing up late, looking on, wondering what you're gonna do next. Know what I mean, pal? But, sure, tough to keep thinking along those lines since Greta

138

just dropped her bomb on you. Didn't see that coming, huh? Or more likely, didn't want to see it coming. Though the signs were always there…

Predicta: Operation Highjump, an Antarctic expedition, was the first indicator that not all was right with the world. Upon returning to the United States, Admiral Richard E. Byrd delivered the news through this cryptic speech: "All those who hear this be warned: our country should adopt measures of protection against the likelihood of an invasion by hostile aircraft swarming in from the polar regions. Now, I am not trying to scare anyone, but the fact of the matter is not only the earth, but the universe itself is shrinking. We must protect ourselves on every conceivable front."

Greta: "It takes a brave man *not* to be a hero in the Red Army." Stalin said that. I'd always wondered what he meant. But with your situation, Wall, I believe I know now… While you think things over, I'll tell you a story. Uncle Joe, so we've learned, loved movies. Especially Westerns. Every evening, after waking up from his nap, Stalin would have Soviet politicians over to watch cowboy pictures with him at the Kremlin theatre. Afterward, didn't matter that it was normally around midnight, he'd have a large dinner served along with a great deal of Georgian wine, Russian vodka, and beer. Protected by the Molotov-Rippentrop Pact, Dear Father believed he had nothing to worry about; being the Josef Stalin we've come to know and love years later, a man who trusted no one at all, Uncle Joe still had a spy in Germany—codename "Ramsay." "Ramsay" was very good at his job. He accurately predicted that Hitler would break the Molotov-Rippentrop Pact, and he accurately predicted when Operation Barbarossa would start. But as history shows us, Dear Father did nothing to stop Der Führer. Why? Why did Stalin let Germany attack his own country? "Ramsay," if you would please phrase your answer in the form of a Western. Low budget, dubbed in English, the actors completely oblivious to the film's purpose (and to seemingly everything else under the sun). It was called *The Return of Fred Barber*. The night the movie was shown was like many others. Various members of Uncle Joe's entourage were there, as were various Soviet politicians, including the head of the NKVD: Lavrentiy Beria. As the celluloid was fed into the projector, Ivan took his place next to the screen. Ivan was rather like a court jester. He claimed to know English (which he may well have believed, though it certainly wasn't true), so his job was to translate. Never mind that pretty much everyone in attendance could speak English, Ivan translated anyway. Stalin thought it was a scream, especially when drunken politicos started translating Ivan's translations. Sitting quietly, watching and listening, not the experience you get at the Kremlin Cineplex... Anyway, the movie, it's about this family, the Barbers, who want to purchase a large tract of land in order to reap the benefits from the available farming and mining, not to mention the railroad profits likely to roll in when the Union Pacific does. There's a problem, though. Not just one family, but a group of families own the land the Barbers desire, and whereas this commune (yuck yuck yuck) isn't using the land to its full potential, as the elder Barber, Floyd, is informed by his advisors, it'd be impossible to oust them. Well, I'm sure you can imagine what would happen in a run-of-the-mill Western from here, but that's not the case with *The Return of Fred Barber*. For one thing, the movie's told in flashback after the Barbers have already been defeated. And the narrator, she's the matriarch, Anita Barber, her constant promise that the legendary Fred Barber will return and revive the clan doesn't just come off as classic Southern-style romanticism (Dixie will rise again... yeah, yeah, whatever), it makes her seem as crazy as good old Floyd. After all, turns out Floyd Barber's strategy, having been told he'd lose if he went after the commune, is to *lose on purpose*, disappear, and come back at some unknown time in the future with the necessary resources to capture not only the farms, mines, and railroad money, but much, much more. Floyd also claims, just like Anita Barber, that Fredrick Barber, the probably mythological progenitor of the family, is going to help with this master plan, though how exactly is left ambiguous, otherworldly powers hinted at but never quite defined. Sounds crazy. And the rest of the clan isn't exactly excited about the idea, until, that is, the name *Fred Barber* registers. Works like abracadabra. Then, then, they're all on-board, suddenly unable to see through the nonsense. One of the major parts of this hilariously complex plan is to sign an agreement with the largest of the landowners, and then break this agreement as soon as possible to ensure a quick defeat. Most of Stalin's guests thought they were watching a (lousy) Western and nothing more. And, as usual, with Ivan translating, and with any number of film fans interpreting Ivan's "English," most thought it was hilarious, incompetent, incomprehensible. Uncle Joe, however, he recognized an actor in the film. Hell, Dear Father was one of two people who *could* recognize him, and right as this thespian appeared on screen, Stalin turned to Beria, also in the know, and they exchanged a nod. It was "Ramsay." "Ramsay" was playing the part Stalin himself would play in history: the dupe of the Molotov-Rippentrop Pact. Straight away the Premier of the Soviet Union interpreted the movie correctly: Der Führer was going to break the treaty on purpose to expedite his loss. After the picture was over, a great feast was served (unfortunately, Marshal Beria couldn't attend), and Uncle Joe encouraged his guests to drink the wine, the vodka, the beer, for tonight, tonight is a night worth celebrating. No one knew why, but everyone knew better than to ask. When all had eaten and drunk their fill, the party left, Dear Father, as usual, detaining Ivan to thank him for his wonderful translations, they always fill everyone with mirth and good cheer, and then the Premier sent his buffoon away, no no, that door's locked now, take the front. Even Ivan understood not to wonder, out loud anyhow, what that exploding sound was as he left.

PREDICTA: Armed with the fallacious notion that they had defeated the Nazis once, and so could do it again, the American-Soviet lunar mission was launched, using Flugkreisels designed by Renato Fregoli and Pseudo-Habermohl. Within seconds of entering the moon's vicinity, all but one of the American-Soviet discs were destroyed.

GRETA: Josef Stalin had no idea what Der Führer was up to, but he wasn't about to play into anyone's hands. He was the Steel Man, Teflon having not been invented yet. So if Der Führer wanted a swift defeat, that's exactly what Uncle Joe wouldn't give him. Luckily for Stalin, he'd already undermined his own military with the Purges. The next logical step, after eradicating most of the best strategists, was to make life even more miserable for the Red Army's rank and file. Here's what Dear Father did: First, he gave the NKVD the power to accuse and execute any soldier they wished. Second, he commanded that all POWs who failed to commit suicide were traitors. Third, he created a new punishment for those found guilty of treason, desertion, dereliction of duty, or fatalism. Anyone convicted of these crimes would be pressed into the new penal battalion: the Tramplers.

141

The Tramplers were stripped of all weaponry, forced to the frontlines, and when their unit came upon a minefield, the Tramplers' job was to activate the mines by running around in the area as quickly as possible, so that later tanks, artillery, and other soldiers could walk over the terrain without fear of being torn in half. In my opinion, Dear Father made being a Trampler even worse by limiting the sentence to three months. If you ran fast enough, you could get away from the explosions and the shrapnel. And how many minefields could there possibly be? Any villain has the capacity to invent the penal battalion, but only a legendary scourge would introduce hope into the scenario. With paranoia, despair, and abject fear firmly in place, Stalin watched his plan unfold. The NKVD did its job by arbitrarily accusing soldiers of desertion, isn't power fun?, and then pressing them into the Tramplers. But that's not all. Lacking strategic skill (thanks to the Purges), hordes of Red Army personnel were captured by the Axis, the Axis who invariably tried to starve the imprisoned Russians to death, the Russians who would later be "saved" by their countrymen, though their saviors would then force them into the penal battalions. So tell me, if you're a soldier in the Red Army, who's the enemy? If you answered everyone, you win a cigar. This confusion, then, gave Stalin exactly what he wanted—a good, long war. And he wanted it long because the Nazis wanted it short. Now, let's go back to that Stalin quote: "It takes a brave man not to be a hero in the Red Army." What does that mean? Think of the general troops. If you were contemplating cowardice in any form, your options were to fight and maybe get maimed, maybe die, or chicken out and absolutely die, living a horrific life right up to the point a mine aerated your body. After all, if you weren't performing your duties, you were saying, "I'll give the minefield a go." Think of how much easier it is in this situation to live the life of a soldier, to follow orders, to advance forward, to fire your rifle, and to maybe be killed or maimed by incoming ordnance. Granted, you still had the NKVD, but that was the Soviet Union all over. Anyway, compare that, living the life of the rank and file, to sprinting across minefield after minefield, knowing that each step could be your last, never sure which step that might be, secretly hoping you could run fast enough through three month's time to make it out alive. Only in Russia could such concepts take on opposite meanings: Bravery was Cowardice, Cowardice was Bravery. And now you have

142

your decision to make, Wall. I need a hero. Are you my hero? If you are, you'll follow your orders and kill my husband. Sure, maybe you'll get caught. Maybe you'll get the death penalty. But you'll die a hero ... Or, you can try to flee. He already suspects me of cheating on him. And sooner or later he'll get it out of me, he'll find out who I was with. And when he does, you'll wish he was only sending you through a minefield. You know this about me. You know this about him. So which one are you? Are you brave, or are you a coward?

PREDICTA: With no other alternative, and believing the Nazi Lunarians were content owning earth's only natural satellite, the Americans and the Soviets accepted the terms, and returned to earth prepared to launch the faux-Space Race, a diversion created to make it seem like only the coin flip winning Americans had ever been to the moon, that no one else was there. Over time, people would become bored with the space program, and later it would be phased out because of high costs and this very indifference. And on that day, July 21, 2011, the coverup was complete. In secret, the Nazis owned the moon and all of space.

MURROW: When Greta finished, Wall remained lying on the couch with an arm over his forehead. What *have* you gotten yourself into, Wall? Oh, Wall...

Greta stands and exits, switching the Predicta off as she goes.

"Senator" Maris rises from his stupor and sleepwalks into the apartment. He shuffles through the flat, not seeing the unoccupied couch move. From underneath, a figure, all in black with a white outline, slinks into view holding a 7.65mm Walther PPK.

Blackout.

A shot is fired.

When there is light again, the outlined figure is moving the couch back into place, then walks over to the door, exits.

MURROW: The phone rings, that terrible klaxon goes on and on. It

143

is time, Wall, to wake up. You can't hide any longer. Finally, he rises, stumbles around, picks up the receiver.

WALL: Jamais Vu, our special today's the red herring, how may I help you?

MR. E.: No thanks, I don't feel like a red herring.

WALL: I just talked to the folks in the kitchen and they said we're all out of red herring. Good thing you didn't come in. Woulda been a wild goose chase.

MR. E.: How are you?

WALL: Got a little trouble with the Gestapo. They think I'm a patsy, since I guess I fucked this guy's wife and now he's dead, murdered. But I can't complain. Who would listen?

MR. E.: You *have* been initiated into the order. These things happen. There's really no way out. Unless… Do you have a family?

WALL: Family?

MR. E.: Yes, family. A group of people who have been randomly selected to share certain features of yours, pass on debilitating and sometimes fatal diseases, not to mention habits and beliefs of a questionable nature, who brought you into this world regardless of your interest in the endeavor, who then treated you like a lowly subject in their mini-empire for eighteen or perhaps more years, and for this you are to be thankful and respect them.

WALL: No, I guess I don't have a family.

MR. E.: It's…

WALL: Unless we count you or the Gestapo. You guys seem like my family.

MR. E.: It's worse than I thought.

WALL: I love these little chats of ours. Always leave me feeling like, not a million bucks exactly, maybe more like a solid $19.42, but not a penny less. Not. A penny. Less.

MR. E.: Without any family…

WALL: No, I've changed my mind. You and the Gestapo *are* my family. All of you have expectations for me, things you want me to do whether or not I'm interested, and again and again I disappoint you. Perhaps one day, me, you, and

144

the Gestapo will realize that deep down on some pathetically sentimental level we're all the same, and we'll share a group hug and a good cry. "Oh, Major Freytag, you old Nazi, you, I know you just wanted the best for me. And Schmetterling, you always encouraged me to follow orders in your own quiet way." But lemme tell you, while that's going on, I'm gonna be hoping for the credits so this lousy show can end, and I can go home, wherever that is, and do whatever it is that I do when I'm there, which probably involves forgetting about this wretched sitcom—*My Family, the Gestapo.*

MR. E.: *Without any family!* you have no one to hide you. So what I want you to do is meet whatever demands the Gestapo have. There's no choice at this point.

WALL: Meet the Gestapo's demands. That's your plan. Gotta say, really outdone yourself on this one, Mr. E. Probably gonna wanna take some time off, go down to the islands, hop on a cruise, live it up, what after all the work you put in here. Meet the Gestapo's demands! Who does that?!

MURROW: But the phone, again with the racket, so Wall hangs it up, only to find the room hasn't so much gone dark, it's disappeared, a lone spotlight on you amongst the blackness.

FREYTAG (*unseen*): Vell hello, Herr Schtein.

WALL: Ah, yes. It's always nice to have the Gestapo over.

FREYTAG (*unseen*): Seeink ze Gestapo even vhen zey aren't zere, Herr Schtein? Not a gut Zeichen. Sign. You feel guilty, ja. Vhat is das Wort. Vord. Your Gewissen. Conscience. Ist gettink to you.

WALL: Strange, I haven't done anything.

FREYTAG (*unseen*): But you feel like you haff, ja.

WALL: I should. But when I take Diverticil, it's like I've built up this tolerance. It's supposed to remind me of what we did. It's supposed to remind me of World War Two. And it still does. Such scenes of tremendous pain. Only now, I dunno why, I feel nothing.

FREYTAG (*unseen*): Betäuben. Numb. You can't belief zis ist happenink to you. Narratol has told us much. You vere datink ze girl. Greta. Zen you vere schtuppink ze girl. Unt vhen she varned you about her Ehemann. Husband. He

145

turnt up Tod. Dead. Efen you sink you are der Mörder. The killer. Now!

WALL: I learn more about Mr. Stein every time you open your mouth. Please, go on. You got me on the edge of my seat. What happens next? I'll bet that girl, Greta, she ditches him for some other guy, or she sells him out, or she disappears, or…

MURROW: By an unseen force, likely Schmetterling, Wall is forced to his knees, arms wrenched behind his back, wrists attached as if handcuffs have been applied, though none are there.

WALL: Yeah, I guess it's time to haul my ass to jail. What with all the crimes I've committed. Shucks! It's a no-brainer.

FREYTAG (*unseen*): Herr Schtein, I vill tell you again, ve are not ze Polizei. Ve are ze Gestapo. Our concern ist not Justiz. It ist perturbation unt Katastrophe! Zo ve are not done vith you yet, nein! Zere ist much still missink. Zo much. Ve only haff… vhat ist ze phrase? …*ze bare bones*. But you haff, no Narratol zis Zeit. Time. You haff a choice.

WALL: Oboy, oboy.

FREYTAG (*unseen*): You zee, it ist not… unheard of for even Jude. Jews. Like you to infiltrate ze ranks unt play die Deutsche. Solomon Perel, for instance.

WALL: Right, because being Jewish, I'm snea…

FREYTAG (*unseen*): Zilence! Zo you can join us, or…

MURROW: There is a long pause. One of the Uncle Sam posters comes into view, towering above Wall.

WALL: Or what, exactly? I was waiting for you to finish, but that's all ya got? I guess I was supposed to imagine something awful in place of your ellipsis. "Zo you can join us, or you can be devourt by Hyänen. Hyenas. Herr Schtein!" Something like that. (Even though my name still isn't Mr. Stein.) Really, I don't think you had anything else. You're the Gestapo. You don't offer actual choices. You make commands and things happen. So do whatever you want with me. You were going to anyway. Just don't pretend I'm an active participant, huh? We're both smart enough to know who's running the show around here.

FREYTAG (*unseen*): I zee, Herr Schtein. Ve vill continue on as ve haff. Vith you in ze dark!

146

MURROW: Blackout. But this darkness doesn't feel like any darkness you've experienced before, though it may've been dark before, and you may've experienced it; in this benighted place you are cast adrift, your noctivagance insensate, an acherontic time that is older than humanity, that only the earth itself knows from the end of the Cretaceous Period when the K-T Extinction Event hit, when all went black, when plants and animals died in unknown and forever unknowable numbers, and here you are, floating along like Tasmantis, having broken away from Antarctica years ago, now having broken away from Australia, free at last, but free to what? free to sink, to sink into the deeps, into another blackout where you will be forgotten, darkness's darkness, where you will inspire zero prophetic visions, zero artistic images, the world turning to Atlantis, setting so many fantasies in that non-existent lost continent the materials used to invent it could've built a true physical manifestation. Oh, Atlantis—our land of dreams. But if Atlantis is our land of dreams, then Tasmantis is our coma world, nothingness, nothing for all, a void unprocessed, even though it actually was, it existed, and then descended beneath the waves, never to be referenced, exactly no one imagining what type of civilization the cities there might've represented, what artifacts would've been created, what the populace might've been like, no one so much as wondering what, on days when their minds were blank, unenlivened, the Tasmantians may've ordered after flagging down the bartender, on the hop, an amiable look in his eye, just how, in the name of all that is precious, would they have answered when he laid the usual line on them: "What'll ya have?"

ALGONQUIN: Singapore Sling! Yes, they do have a good one… Oh, this place? It's called Rancho Los Amigos. I often come here to rehabilitate myself after an evening of theatre analysis. And with this very drink… Ah, I feel it is the time for idle chatter. My favorite bartender, Furman Tayshawn, gave me this bit: did you know… *That* is the way idle chatter begins, by the way. And your job is to nod politely and ignore me while I speak, thinking of your own idle chatter to insert when I have finished. Ha-HA! So, did you know back when it was first invented, the Singapore Sling, called the Straits Sling then, was merely a modest member of the sling family? Not the prince, or the king, not even a significant acquaintance of the main players. Avaunt! Into obscurity you go. And it went.

147

Long gone. Never to be found. Not in this life, anyway. But its disappearance is our gain. The Singapore Sling, phoenix-like, rose from the ashes of the Straits Sling. Before a drink of minor note, now a chimeric cocktail built from a fantasy. The name, mellifluous, tells us it's from an exotic land, somewhere better than where we're from. If we could only visit that undiscovered country, wherever it may be, then... But we can't. Certainly you're not fatuous enough to believe the "Singapore" in the name is the one on the map! Ha-HA! *That* is a faux-Singapore. A pseudo-Singapore. As close to the real thing as Paradise, Michigan is to Paradise. No, if we left on the double, we would never arrive. Our lone connection to that other world is this mixed drink. Inconceivable: the very idea the Singapore Sling could be an insignificant libation no one quaffs anymore. And so, we have the red, fruity fantasia before us. Not a sling. Not the original, barely even based in the original, though superior in every way. I do suppose purists might not rejoice in this explanation. Yet should we be able to find that which was lost, what if it were inferior? What if, thanks to guilt by association, our narrative were tarnished, the one that floods our minds each time we take a sip? What if we couldn't go back? Would knowing the truth be better? No, I'm afraid I *am* a one and done man myself. It has been an evening to remember, that is certain. Though since we spent it at the Glasgow, I hardly know what I recall and what I have invented– which fills the night with grandeur. Ha-HA! But now I must leave you. Each day a performance, and this is closing night. I shall take my bow before you, my public. And, oh, listen, I couldn't... I said I wouldn't... the hunched stridulation, it warms my heart, almost as if it were telling me I would go on, that I haven't reached the end, that there's more to come, as if it were saying to me, to you, to us all–

And now this:

§

"The afterlife. That's the problem. So many people... even some supposed atheists... act like there's going to be an afterlife. A time of judgment. They pretend they're afraid of it. But they want it to come. They yearn for the reckoning. They crave the moment when it's their turn to say, 'Gaze upon all I have done and despair for you are nothing... in comparison.' And they fear... they dread... stepping before the congregation... all the collected souls the world has ever known... only to find they have nothing to say. Or worse, very little. Nothing at all... might have an excuse. Very little?... deplorable. Now here you are. Edward R. Murrow..."

"That's not actually..."

"*Do not interrupt me again.* You have come for help. You have come for help because you are a narrator who's unhappy with his current... assignment. Why should you care? It is your job to speak. To speak in the persona you are given. That is all. You are not a crusader. You are not a... detective. You are not an investigative journalist or documentarian. You are a narrator. Yet this project... you think... is beneath you. Or, you believe it to be immoral. Perhaps amoral, which for you would be worse. It could be that your religiosity runs deep. That this operation... you were chosen because of some Original Sin. You must make it right. You must atone. Only then will your god... whatever name it goes by... only then will your god shower you with... *light.* Count you amongst its flock. So you can bask in the sanctity of paradise. Or... maybe... your god is in your head. And you fear having to skulk before the assembly, an assembly made only of you, to confess, 'I worked for 'Senator' Kipper Maris.' ...I will tell you once... it will do no good... but I will tell you once: *there is no life after this.* Do your job. Then go home."

"Agent Asbestos, prior to the Senator, the world used to be real. There were events all in their causal chains. It made sense. Maybe it wasn't ideal, maybe horrible things happened all the time, but even those atrocities could be explained. Now, everything that came before is being negated. It's like history itself is being destroyed. There are only episodes, no context. And every time you try to bring order to a situation, more chaos emerges! He's already corrupted CNS, now he's trying to corrupt the world. This is the only path left. What else can I do?"

A deep, slow laugh.

"Very well... my son. Then allow me to be your... ecclesiast. You, dear novice, will go... to the Hyperborean Arms, and in Room 8 you will find a... situation. You will take care of this situation for me. And then you will leave. You,

149

my tyro, will drive. Where will you go? There will be a sign. You will know… when you are in the right place… the place where the story begins, though you are only the narrator, because there will be… a sign… at the top of a hill. The sign will ignite, will be a beacon for you, and when you read it… you will understand. This, Edward R. Murrow, is an important sign, yes, a sacred… sign. It will inform you what time it is, what it's time for, it will be the sign you have forever been seeking. Though your… life before may have been cast into the… chaos of the void, your existence from thereon out will… cohere… once again. Now there will be structure, form, order, real momentum that you can ride… to the holy land. And you will know you have reached your true destination when you see the neon that reads:

"Plot Now."

Pause.

"And you will…"

"Unlike you, Murrow, I understood what my job entailed. Did you know… tonight is the lunar eclipse? People used to believe the eclipse caused… moon disease. Lunacy. Wells had to be covered. Utensils turned down. Windows shuttered. Because… if you were infected, rage would consume you. You would become violent, vicious, savage, maniacal. Even… homicidal. The dragon that devoured our satellite would possess you. And whether you wanted it or not, you would have your vengeance on the world. Your mission tonight will be shrouded by this pestilent… darkness… Now… here are the keys to the car you will use. Go… and serve your lord."

And there he goes, ladies and gentlemen, in the black 1942 De Soto, as the building he met C. Irving Asbestos in crumbles to dust. What will our man Edward R. Murrow do? To all of you out there in Radioland I say: I do not know. But our prophetic correspondent, C.U. Tomorrow, does:

Tomorrow: Through the wide open spaces where the sky goes on forever motors Eddie Murrow. Silence may rule out there in space, but in Ed's car the radio is on playin' a crazy show 'bout Don the Beachcomber and Trader Vic. A course Murrow's disgusted cuz the narrator's three sheets, but it's Happy Hour, aight? The show: what it is is them two tiki founders are on a voyage. Good ol' Ngiam Dee Suan, maybe you could see him as the Dr. Fu Manchu of this tale, he reeled our two heroic suckers in by sayin', get this, that granddad left his recipe books somewheres, only got a bit of an old map here, but I couldn't be asked to part with it for any amount of money, what with the sentimental value and all, and oh by the way, did I mention those books have the original receipt for the Straits Sling? Figuring this was the Grail Quest for tiki bar owners, Don and Vic found out that any amount wouldn't do, oh how I wish granddad were still here, and what's become of the world, and I remember sittin' on his knee, the usual brand a buhloney, until the price got high enough that, though it pained his heart, Dee Suan let the map go. And out onto the high seas went our epic tandem, each time finding a chest with a book inside sayin', "Did my no good grandson send you on this wild goose chase? I apologize for my family. I was a respectable barman, but my brood a lot of swindlers. Listen: I didn't write my recipes down. I kept them in my head. So there is no treasure. I'm sorry. Go home. Unless, of course, this is where I left it," and then there'd be another map sendin' them to another uncharted isle where there'd be another chest with another book that'd have another map. You can imagine how this story might lead most people, even those who fancy themselves respectable, to strong drink, but since the guy on the radio started off blotto, he just kept goin', stickin' it out, makin' sure to leave nothing untold, audience picturing that Dee Suan laughin' his head off somewhere, countin' his money, servin' up them Singapore Slings. Absolutely, the original recipe passed down to me from my dear ol' granddad, how I wish, and so on. The yarn won't go on forever, though. Comes to an end. Here's the hook: the last map takes Don and Vic back to, yuck yuck, Dee Suan's office, only this time our dynamic duo ain't so interested in paying, *this time* they'd be perfectly fine with beatin' the info outta Dr. Barmanchu, who directly saves his own ass by tellin' a likely story 'bout how the book was taken by a, what was that jerk's name? Fregoli!, said he could decipher what was inside, the whole damn thing being written in code don'tcha know, and after droppin' not just a king's ransom, but an entire royal family's complete with gratuity, Mr. Fregoli fucked off to, well some people think it was Wainiwidiwiki Island. Yeah, that's a real place. Don and Vic, not interested in being duped again, hauled Dee Suan's sorry butt out of Singapore and off to

151

this island with its, scuse me, bullshit name (just look at it, ya gotta know it's bullshit), but what happened there, friends, no one's sure. Ngiam Dee Suan went to his grave sayin' the whole shootin' match was dreamed up by a swarm a souses, a flamboyance a fops. Vic told so many different versions of the story back in San Francisco that schools of interpretation have been formed to explain what they *really* mean in general, in specific, in chronological order, in reverse chronological order, and in orders more abstruse and esoteric, the orders themselves requiring *their* own schools of interpretation. Don, he moved off to Hawaii, where I hear he spent the rest of his days starin' up at the stars, warnin' people 'bout the end of the world, so paranoid he changed his name on a daily basis, though normally he still answered to Don. But there's one version I give credence to, one version I do believe can be believed, and that's that Don, Vic, and Dee Suan made it out to Wainiwidiwiki, where they met Fregoli, who gave them each a portion of the deciphered code book, savin' the fourth for his own brood, and then sent them on their way. Now, foax, I hope you aren't disappointed, but there are things even us prophets can't see. We're not infallible. We have our blind spots. So I can tell you that Eddie, he makes it to the Hyperborean. And I can tell you that as he stands outside room #8, there's a booming TV on in one a them thar apartments that says, ...*goli disappeared, though at different times it has been thought he was hiding under the names Richardson, Kubek, Maris, Mantle, Berra, Skowron, Howard, Boyer.* But when he enters, what he finds on the other side of that fateful door, I just can't tell you. Welp, that's all for me: C.U. Tomorrow.

KHRYPTYMNYZHY: The door. The memory... the event inside... unfolds again and again... with parts missing as if they were... edited out. Redacted. The door. He stands in front of the door. It is... it's Edward R. Murrow. He stands in front of the... of the door. No. It is... it's Wallace Orcuson. Wall. He stands in front of the door. Impossible to tell. It could be... be one, or it could be... could be the other. Murrow... Ed Murrow narrating from... from behind Orcuson. Murrow alone. Orcuson alone. Tracers of others who... who may've been there... who... who... at last... who opened the door... who went inside... who raised the silenced gun... who fired... Who... who indeed.

Wallace Heath Orcuson lies twitching on the floor in his now torn parodic Patton get-up surrounded by empty bottles of Diverticil, the Gestapo glaring down, the Uncle Sam poster glaring down too (though this version, strangely, looks like Vermeer painted it), as the Predicta plays the restored cut of *The Return of Fred Barber*, a joint venture between ICU and A. Parachroni, Inc.

The Predicta sez: *I got to interview Richard Walther Miethe just before he died, and he told me something astonishing. He said the reason Renato Fregoli was never pictured was because he didn't exist. Fregoli was a kind of joke the engineers made up because their work was so secret.*

"Feelink guilty, Herr Schtein?" sez Major Freytag.

In his throes, Wall manages to nod.

"You shoult."

"I… I told you. My family…"

"…started ze var. Ve know. But zat ist not vhy you shoult feel guilty…"

"No! When I take Diverticil now, the pain isn't real. A phantom limb. I can only think of World War Two *fiction*. It's like the war never even happened. It was only dreamed. A dream that's been placed at the center of *everything*. And it's all my fault. Because I took too much, too much…"

"No, Herr Schtein. Nonsense, zat, zat is vhat your story ist. You shoult feel guilty because you haff alvays known who der Mörder. Ze killer. Ist." Standing in the ill-placed coffee shop is Greta Zelle. The waiter finally arrives. "If you voult haff given to us ze information, it voult haff been better for you. But now, you von't be gettink off zo easily." As the major sez this, you see it's not a waiter at all, it's Schmetterling wheeling a stomach pump into the room.

"Really? Because you told me I knew nothing. If I'd sold her out, would anything be different?"

"Perhaps you know us too vell after all, Herr Schtein. Perhaps…"

Cresting the top of the roller coaster hill, you turn and, uh, yeah, over on the Predicta, the narrator is talking about the imminent arrival of Fred Barber. Do you have a savior, Wall? At this point, delusions might be your best bet. Along with putting up your arms. That's what the Gestapo's doing, and, really, Wall, you *should* follow suit…

Thank you, Mr. Tomorrow, Madame Khryptymnyzhy, and Ed Murrow.

Wise listeners of Radioland, if you recall, our own Polly Semmy was originally tasked with researching A. Parachroni, a corporation that's died and been resurrected many times over. Although, according to our sources, Ms. Semmy is no longer with us, one of her dizzying array of confederates is: physicist Norton Thales. Dr. Thales, thank you for joining us.

THALES: I would just like to say that I've never laid eyes on Polly Semmy in my entire life. That I know of. Well, that's not entirely true. I think I did see her once, but for some reason I don't remember...

Yes, yes, we all know how difficult it was to pin her down. But what have you learned about A. Parachroni?

THALES: It's not so much what we've learned about A. Parachroni, but what we've learned about the Hyperborean Arms. According to our sources, the apartment building sits atop the biggest untapped Explodium mine on earth.

Explodium? That sounds like a made-up element.

THALES: For a long time, it was, since it was merely theoretical, or actually hypothetical.

I'm afraid to ask, but what does Explodium do?

THALES: If you believe ICU...

Not for a second.

THALES: ...the Nazis used it to power their ships to fly to the moon. Otherwise, Explodium is hypothesized to be an element which, at certain extremely dramatic or climactic moments, merely explodes. Cars that are hit by trains, other cars, bullets, trees, power lines, newspapers, bicycles, etc. or automobiles in mid-air after flying off cliffs that immediately burst into flames are thought to be made of Explodium. Buildings powered by suspect generators, spacecraft that bloom into raging fires where there is no oxygen, horse-drawn carriages that lightly strike walls, sharks that are rammed with large pieces of wood, underground bunkers made completely of metal, when we see them torn to pieces by gargantuan infernos, we know that, once again, Explodium was involved.

Every single example you just gave came from a movie. I'm not convinced that something even remotely like Explodium exists.

THALES: And yet the largest remaining deposit of that nonexistent

154

substance is underneath the Hyperborean Arms. It's perhaps the very reason the Arms was built there. And if, at any point, someone connects a digital countdown to the Explodium, or a black-clad figure hooks up one of those plunging detonators, the Hyperborean just might go back to being a myth…

Are you even a physicist?

THALES: I am. I know I am. Because you said so.

Ladies and gentlemen, dead to me and I'm sure to us all: Norton Thales.

Back in the tiki, lit only by torches, the moon blotted out by Earth's shadow, Ed Murrow completes the narration, as the Senator, standing behind the bar, sets a Singapore Sling in front of him. Finally, the man from CNS picks up his glass and sips.

"So, what do you think?" says Maris, gesturing towards the manuscript and the cocktail, not specifying which one he means, as he knocks back his own.

"I think it has too many ingredients," says Murrow. "What about yours? Does it taste like the original?"

"Close enough, Murrow," says "Senator" Kipper Maris, flipping a switch behind the bar, and with a *click* the entire "glass" dome proves to be a projection, a planetarium, no window to the outside world, instead a simulation. "Close enough."

And now this:

Three

The Organization of The Organization

THERE ARE MANY TYPES OF ORDER. THERE IS ONLY ONE CHAOS. The enormous neon sign blinks in the distance, its legend topped by a distorted, sideways figure eight that appears to exist in more dimensions than we care to enumerate, a computer generated butterfly prepared to burst into the clouds. On second glance, ladies and gentlemen, the legend isn't there. Neither is the sign. Only the laser illuminated butterfly remains, coolly burning, strangely attractive, lights tracing every sinew, approachable, but unreachable.

From the room next door, the Predicta speaks: *Are you confused? Are you having trouble making sense of the world? Do you have the sneaking suspicion that a secret group governs all? Have you found that the word group is not right for you? Would you instead say network, a network of conspiracies? Or perhaps you are more interested in the operations of one particular cabal? You might even be unsatisfied with the existing secret syndicates, knowing that no one yet has been able to find the Truth. Do you believe that was why you were born? To find the Truth. No matter your reasoning, no matter what you are looking for, the Char Le Tannes Institute and Conspiratorium has the answers. The Char Le Tannes Institute and Conspiratorium. The truth is out there? No. The* Truth *is in here.*

"Kuzma, I... I have this feeling... this need to go... I don't know where. I don't know where, but I must go. I don't know where, but I'll know it when I see it. I have no idea why I want to go there. None. Except that this place... it *is* the place I've been seeking. Forever. Though, to tell you the truth, I don't know that I've been *seeking* anything. Before. I have been on no what I would call quests. My job has been to reveal the Truth through my narrating. But now I'm directed to go to the place where plots begin. I can't imagine where that might be..."

Agent Bezopasnosky sits smoking, barely listening. From underneath the couch a dead man's hand reaches out for mercy or assistance that never arrived.

"Soon, Kuzma, I'm going to leave, I'm going to embark on my first quest, I'm going to go in search of what I'm looking for, what I've been looking for my entire life... Though, honestly, I have no idea what this place is, where it could be, or why I would want to go there," says Edward R. Murrow. He sits at a table in the Hyperborean Arms. In front of him are a reel-to-reel, a microphone, and a slightly weathered *Vayss Uf Makink You Tock* which Agent Bezopasnosky collects and puts into a messenger bag along with an empty bottle of Milk of Amnesia–street name: Perma-Shave. Because it shaves part of your memory away... forever.

"What am I doing here?" Ed says, looking around. "Am I narrating something for you?"

"You are done," says Kuzma arranging his things.

"Oh. Strange. I don't remember a thing. All I can think about is where I need to be. Where I need to go. That's all I can think about, even though I can't think about it... because I don't... What's it all mean, Kuzma?"

Agent Bezopasnosky, now wearing an overcoat and a fedora, looks at Murrow. "Da. Dat ees question. Question maybe for Organization," shifting his weight from one foot to the other. "Eef you can find zem."

"*The* Organization?"

"Da."

"So now you direct me to myths. Just as likely these days, I suppose. Especially after Maris..." Ed points at the couch. "Are they the ones...? Is that who…?"

Kuzma shrugs.

"But why?!"

Agent Bezopasnosky glances down at the blood-stained carpet, the gun, the hand still reaching out from underneath, from beyond the void. Listeners in Radioland, Edward sees it too, so he slides the davenport forward, the body swallowed by the abyss.

"Answer ees on horizon."

"Right."

"Now, ees time for you to go."

"Where?"

"Place where plots begeen."

With that the Russian walks out the door as men, but who are they? And how did they get hired onto this operation? Put a bag over Edward R. Murrow's head, then lead him away. He goes quietly, as if his abduction were all a part of the plan, as if some semblance of a plan, any plan, were still intact, hearing in the background a door bang open, followed by: "What's it all about?" A different formulation of the same searing inquiry.

This uninterrupted portion of our radio play was written by "Senator" Kipper Maris, Kuzma Grigorovich & Feliks Semyonovich Bezopasnosky, Citronella Fogge, Uwen Farr Oarbytt, Anne T. Epifanik, C.U. Tomorrow, Norton Thales, Brahma Gupta, and others. It is made possible by Diplomatic Immunity Liquors, Narratol, Extra Strength Diverticil, Milk of Amnesia, the International Channel of Uchronie, Columbia Narratorial Services, the Char Le Tannes Institute and Conspiratorium, A. Parachroni, Inc., and listeners vaguely reminiscent of, though perhaps not exactly like YOU.

Now, take it way, Ed Murrow:

§

Somewhere in time a whirring descends, but where exactly? And just what is whirring? Impossible to tell, but if music were playing it'd probably be that

159

1950s sci-fi theremin–what's that?! Up in the clouds! Those lights! It could only be... Oh, the radio tower for KTUE, sure, blinking blinking blinking, the radio waves moving at the speed of light, transmitting, well, yes, it's about time for *The Unknown Empire Tonight*, and the signal has found its way out to the Arms–guess it's true what they say: neither by ship nor on foot will you find the marvelous road to the Hyperborean, where Wallace Heath Orcuson sits in the dark smoking, as the antique receiver comes to life in simultaneity with your old pal the Predicta.

The radio sez: *Yuh leavin' the planet's atmosphere. Soarin' beyon' the great beyon'. There's no turnin' back now, ya hear? Earth looks like a moon as ya circle it. Yeah! Yuh way out, way far out! And yuh locked into this far orbit with ya captain, Uwen Farr Oarbytt. Uwen, lay some knowledge down...*

Only, let's pause here for a moment, Wall. Freeze the entire world. And lemme ask you, do you get the feeling like there's something you ought to know, like there's some knowledge you're missing, there's something you should've done or, really, if you were honest with yourself, *ought* to be doing right this very instant? If you did what you were supposed to do, you'd know, you'd understand, you might even be, gasp, enlightened. But no matter how hard you try, you just can't figure out what that thing is. All the same, it keeps you up nights, pacing back and forth, and back and forth because you think, you believe, you hope that you're constantly on the verge of doing that which you need to be doing. At the same time, it's equally conceivable that the door leading to the knowledge you seek, as I speak these lines, is being slammed shut and locked and fused into place, with any available furniture jammed up against it for good measure so you can never, never get inside. Nothing you did wrong, it's just the way it is.

Or maybe you're more the paranoid type, and you think this knowledge that'll lead to your enlightenment, that'll lead to the transcendent meaning of, well, no, maybe not life, the universe and everything, but *the* transcendent meaning you need to move forward confidently, knowing you're doing what you should be doing, man, are you one of those who thinks it's being kept from you? Like, by malevolent, or at least powerful forces?

Yeah.

Bad news, Wall: both of these possibilities are true. There *is* something you ought to do; there *is* something you ought to know. But...

Oh sure, right now on the Predicta, it's ICU, by all accounts your favorite station, and they're showing the kind of fare you'd expect to find on the old Alternate History Channel: out-of-focus pictures of ever hazier flying saucers. Probably if we could turn the cameras around we'd see, uh huh, there they are, the rank amateur photographers, and behind them? Yep, folks using the time-honored tactic of throwing shit in the air to fool us, to make us think those are one hundred percent, Grade A++, gen-u-ine UFOs, look, I'm tellin' ya, this picture wasn't doctored, dude, course that's because what it really shows is a pie pan Uncle Bob whipped into the sky, bein' the Frisbee champeen round these parts for the past twenty-three years an' countin' an' all. But, hate to say it, Wall, there's another program airing at this very second on another station you should be watching instead. Only you're not. And right here–this is the thing you should do to gain enlightenment: turn the channel. And right here–this is the way They're hiding the knowledge from you: by sticking it in a poorly produced infomercial for the Char Le Tannes Institute and Conspiratorium.

Of all the services the Conspiratorium offers, the one for you, Wall, would've been the tailored abduction experience. On the screen the speaker, who is not so much a patient of plastic surgery, but possibly made of actual polymers, and who could be called a Valley Girl if the valley we're talking about is the Uncanny one, and who is only ever referred to as the SPOKESWOMAN, indicated as such by a medium shot and the word Spokeswoman underlined, and who stands and smiles not rigidly, but as if she were programmed to do so (looking a little too smooth to be natural), backed by what now appears to be the space station this infomercial was filmed on, the Spokeswoman explains:

"*According to our researchers, the folklorist Das of Yore and the ufologist Paisen DesGuise, the abductee goes through eight stages. They are:*

1) Anticipation

2) Capture

3) Examination

4) Conference

5) Journey

161

6) Loss of Time

7) Return

8) Aftermath

"Although the stages are the same for everyone, there are still choices to be made for each stage, choices that can alter the meaning of the entire experience for you. And whereas you cannot choose to be part of an event, by planning your experience with the Conspiratorium, you can sculpt the nature of your event should you ever have one. You can ensure that your experience is in the right hands: yours (with the help of our Abduction Artists).

"The first stage is the Anticipation stage. Here, you are filled with the strong feeling that you are about to embark upon something that is both familiar and unknown. You yearn to be at a certain place at a certain time, though you may not be certain about what place or what time. Here, the Conspiratorium can help select a pairing that is right for you. Would you prefer a well known landmark in the morning, a mysterious or ominous site in the great outdoors at midnight, maybe somewhere as goofy as a bowling alley, or as quirky as a donut shop? You can even have our staff select the location so it is an enjoyable surprise for you and not a traumatic one.

"'But why is the Anticipation stage important?' many of our clients ask. Those who are selected for abduction are like modern-day heroes and heroines. Legendary figures of the past always believed they were in the wrong place, that they belonged elsewhere, that they ought to be doing something more. The Anticipation stage helps set the scene for the important events to come. With the Conspiratorium, you will better understand this momentous experience because you, with the assistance of our Abduction Artists, will be the architect of the event. Yes, the Char Le Tannes Institute, bringing meaning to us all."

Will you ever see this infomercial? Impossible to tell. But that's not the real problem. The real problem here is if you do finally catch the Conspiratorium's ad, it'll be too late. You won't be able to use their services there in the future. You won't be able to benefit from their assistance. Instead it will be up to others to frame, order, interpret the episodes you experience. To learn lessons and deduce themes you never realized existed. Organized fully, we'll wonder if you can be said to've experienced anything at all, buddy, since you'll've missed all the important information. And then, perhaps, in some far-flung time, you'll see the informercial for the Char Le Tannes Institute, a curiosity, what a weird deal, and you'll never know how much it could've helped you.

Unpause.

The radio sez: *Thank you as always, Red Bluesman. And good evening, good morning, good afternoon, and hello to you, my listeners, wherever you may be in time and space. Welcome to* The Unknown Empire *Tonight. Recently, I was asked where we broadcast from, since I often say 'an undisclosed location in southeastern Nevada,' but it's difficult for me to get more specific than that. The area goes by many names. Home Base, believe it or not, is one of them. But as I'm sure all of you can imagine, a run-of-the-mill name like that could refer to anywhere, meaning it's as good as nowhere. Probably what They want you to think. Why They called it that. There's more than one way to make something Top Secret, don'tcha know? Paradise Ranch, that's another name. Sounds like a housing allotment, don't it? Full of McMansions made of brick and vinyl siding. Broad lawns and narrow minds. Doesn't really describe where we are. Groom Lake is my absolute favorite. Orbiters, this is the desert. There is no water. There are no lakes. But the name we use the most, the name the locals hang onto is Dreamland. Out here, I'm told, every last one of us has his head in the clouds…*

A light… now just where is that light coming from, Wall? seems like maybe, well is that the clouds? Naw, couldn't be. There aren't any little green… could be thin gray… Let's say an unknown source ignites dramatically revealing the only poster in the room. Hastily applied, as if by a friend who slapped it up before They got him, hauled his ass off to… hmm, are they up there right… you know, like with the probe? The poster shows a pair of eyes staring out from beneath a helmet, the rest of the face hidden by a bluish shadow (do you think of a far more sinister Marvin the Martian?), the legend proclaiming: HE'S WATCHING YOU. Indistinct flying saucers arc through the black & white sky on the Predicta. Then the mysterious light goes out, replaced by the normal electric ones we all know and love here on planet earth, only, as if that were a signal, the door creaks open, and standing there, standing ready for you, ready for you to bare all, sensing you've relented, understanding you can't fight this war all by yourself (resources depleted, options few), prepared for the flood of information you *will* provide (no more holding back, Wall), discerning that it could be no other way, detecting this weakness early on, and now here to take advantage, standing *right on the other side of the door*, knowing everything about you, everything, knowing, knowing, is…

The Predicta sez: *Some call the Roswell UFO Incident the most significant event that never happened in United States history.* An unambiguous flying saucer comes into view on the black & white screen, only is it out of an Ed Wood movie or something? *But it did happen. And the perpetrators were…*

"*The Organization,*" the radio seems to respond, though the Roman Saluting figures on rancher Mac Brazel's land might quibble about the name. "*That's our topic today. The Organization—the seemingly independent international intelligence agency few know anything about…*"

No one? No one. There's no one in the hallway. No one on the other side of the door. Door's just open. And the hallway's empty. Why? What's wrong? Feeling a little anxious, Wall? (If you'd seen the Conspiratorium's infomercial you'd remember the Spokeswoman, who doesn't blink and whose makeup looks like a physical mask and whose hair is not so much helmet-shaped as a helmet proper, and who's either standing in front of a green screen or is being teleported to various sites containing spacecraft, who would've told you that what you're feeling is perfectly normal, that history and myth teem with the unwilling—that, to be sure, this is the prime moment, as momentum builds, to contact the fine customer service representatives at the Char Le Tannes Institute.) Or were you expecting someone? You were? Then where are They? Where'd They go? What are They doing? What kinds of friends are you keeping, Wall, now really? They open the door and then run off? Who do They think They are?

The Predicta sez: *The Roswell UFO Incident, next on ICU.*

No one.

The history of this world…

No one.

…and others.

These your *invisible* friends, buddy? Are They gonna come in? Say, are They in already? Hard to tell. Well, are you going to look for Them? Go ahead. *Go ahead.* There's nothing to see here. Nothing to see. It appears you're a free man. The door's open. Come on now, baby bird, fly away! Spread your wings and fly! Oh... was it simpler when you were confined? Is your independence unnerving? Do you find yourself missing Them already? Their crazy accents. Their theatrical uniforms. Their diabolical plans. Or is it that you think you'll give up more information with complete freedom than you did while being interrogated, Herr Schtein? Ist zat it? Sure, probably best to stay in the apartment. Embrace your inner couch potato. And if They're watching, well They can go ahead and watch while you do nothing at all. Catching some TV. Listening to a crazy radio program. (Not watching the Char Le Tannes infomercial.) But really just sitting–in your apartment. Lit by... uh, yeah... it's back... an *unknown* source. Dramatically lit. Like, is this a Universal horror film or something?

The Predicta sez: *On July 7, 1947, debris fell from the sky onto rancher Mac Brazel's land in New Mexico...*

What would you see out there? Out there in the world. Nothing strange, right? You've been outside before, haven't you, Wall? You know the place don't you? *Oh my God, it's full of...* well, no, not stars. That's the final frontier. The world's full of objects. Composed of matter, occupy space, they have a size, a shape, a smell, a taste, a color. And for the most part those objects are static. Whether you're around the stuff of the world or not, doesn't matter. It's there. Out there. For you to experience anytime you want. What's so scary about that, Wall? Oh, sure, sometimes you'll be off your game, senses not working at peak capacity, but how often does that happen? Wall, maybe this'll calm ya: if you go outside you'll see, as you've always seen, the things of the world as they really are. There are no mysteries left. Nothing to be afraid of. Physics governs all. So what could be that freaky, huh? Come on now. Though... there must be some problem here, some anxiety, what with all the basic level argumentation needed to get your ass out the goddamn door.

The Predicta sez: *Even if you're one of those who thinks humankind is the sum total of intelligent life in the universe, you know Roswell. Probably as the capital of conspiracy theories about aliens...*

Let's say you do leave, Wall. Left foot, right foot, left foot, right foot.

Come on, now. Up to the threshold. On the verge of the known world. Completely known. Utterly known. Not a single dark spot on the map. You are needed elsewhere. For what? You're not sure. Why you? You don't know that either. Nor will you ever. You might not even remember any of this later. But you gotta go. One step from salvation, Wall…

The Predicta sez: *For believers, well, Roswell is their Mecca.*

…or maybe damnation, but let's say salvation. And there you are. Moving in the direction you need to move. Locomotion provided by millions of years of evolution making it so you can go where you need to go. Serenity washes over you as you walk through the hallway, the lobby, a regular Ernest Shackleton, an explorer of the Hyperborean (and since everything's covered with dustcloths–what is this, some rich bastard's country house?–you kinda feel like you're walking through a snowscape), set to embark on an historic journey, no, an epic journey, yes, epic is the right word, perhaps you had to be lured into this narrative, abducted, *will you follow the yellow brick road already, for fuck's sake!*, but now you're on your way, Wall, and, finally, finally, outside, where the light intensifies and…

On the Predicta, on another channel, a channel you may never flip to, may as well be a secret channel, the Gnostic Channel (*There are many channels on the dial, but there's only one Gnostic Channel*), describable by what it isn't showing, instead of what it is, the Spokeswoman appears to be lit by the same light from above you're swathed in, Wall, chiaroscuro cinematography, her voice calm, preternaturally calm, almost, almost a robotic voice, the voice the starship captain on a sci-fi show hears when the computer speaks:

"*Heroes are frequently lured or carried away on their quests. They do not get to choose what kind of journey they will go on, nor how that journey will begin. But with the Conspiratorium, you do have a choice. You could be walking through a field when a flying saucer appears above, an intense light lancing down through the blackness, levitating you toward its inner sanctum. Or, perhaps you will be asleep, experiencing strange dreams of what is to come, and upon your arousal you discover yourself surrounded by Grays who lead you away from your home to their vessel, a hatch opening or already opened, a staircase extended. Or, you might be driving on a dark, lonely road when much to your surprise you are enveloped by mist lit by a powerful luminescence, the beam reflecting off the fog. Remember, this is about you and you alone. It is your journey, your experience. And if you need assistance, our Abduction Artists are always there to help you."*

Do you have a car, Wall? Let's say you have a car because you are driving. Or, at least later you'll remember driving, you'll think you remember driving down this, sure, dark, lonely road. Maybe you might even input other likely and, why not?, unlikely memories... yeah, seems to be some missing time here, driving, right, driving, radio on, sonic resonance bouncing off your eardrums as you cruise out into the night. What is it about those Amplitude Modulated waves, that old AM band, listening in the darkness out there on the open road, even when a dubious source isn't shining down on you, that lends an unsettling air to the situation? Like you're maybe being watched by a force incognito, like you're maybe receiving a transmission from parts of the world, the galaxy, the universe that aren't unknown, they're unknowable.

The radio sez: *"...but that's where I come from. What about The Organization? Some believe they're extraterrestrial. And now I see we have someone on the line, Frank in Los Angeles, you're in a far orbit..."*

"Uwen, that's just the problem. We don't seem to know anything about The Organization..."

"Frank, for now, let's stick to what we do know..."

"OK, Uwen."

"...for instance, have you visited The Organization's headquarters?"

"I've never been there, but I've seen pictures of it. Man, I don't even know how to describe that place."

"You know the story about the HQ, though, right?"

"Uh..."

"That it's bigger on the inside than it is on the outside."

"Oh, sure, Uwen."

"Of course, everyone's heard that one. And The Organization's home office isn't the first place in history that folks thought..."

"Yeah, I've heard that about the Pentagon."

"Exactly. And the Vatican, and various Masonic lodges. But, Frank, have you

heard about the time when they tried to measure the perimeter of the building?"

"No I haven't, Uwen."

"Frank, and all my fellow Orbiters tuning in, since there's been so much speculation about The Organization, conspiratorial, occult, ufological, and so on, a surveying team, they went by the unlikely moniker Waits & Measures, Mr. Waits and Ms. Measures, a surveying team decided to begin debunking the various outrageous claims by disproving what they saw as one of the most obvious: that The Organization's HQ is larger on the inside than it is on the outside…"

"Huh."

"Waits & Measures figured that once they proved The Organization's home office was just as real as any other building, then, then we'd begin to see all the past claims were ludicrous too. And so our valiant surveying team assessed the distance around the outside of the building. Being a diligent pair, they measured twice."

"Measure twice, cut once."

"That's right, Frank. Do you know what they found?"

"What, Uwen?"

"The two measurements were different."

"On the inside and the outside? So the building is bigger on the…"

"No, no, no, Frank. This was still the exterior. Two exterior measurements, two different numbers. And so Waits & Measures went at it again. And again. Each time they used better and better instruments, but the numbers never added up. How can we say that the HQ is bigger on the inside than it is on the outside if we, now listen here, Frank, if we cannot determine how big the outside even is?"

"Um…"

"The measurement debacle came to the attention of a mathematician, Brahma Gupta, who took an aerial photograph of the home office. He discovered something even more startling: the shape of the building, and like you said, Frank, who knows what shape that is? But the degrees of the angles present in that mysterious configuration, when you add them all together, are infinite."

"Infinite…"

"That's right, Frank. Then, after his aerial photograph, now you gotta listen to this, next Professor Gupta had a velvet rope stretched around the headquarters. Yep, like

168

it was a nightclub! I'm telling you, Frank, you can't make this stuff up. But why? What was the point of the velvet rope?"

"I dunno, Uwen."

"Here's what Brahma Gupta said: 'By stretching this velvet rope around The Organization's headquarters, I have shown that whereas the angles in its shape are infinite, they are containable in the finite.'"

"What the...?"

"Had to bleep you there, Frank."

"Sorry, Uwen."

"No problem. I said the same exact thing myself when I found out. Anyway, Waits & Measures, their goal was to prove The Organization was normal, but what they ended up doing was adding to the mystery."

"Is this when we found out that each room is, I don't know how to put it..."

"You guessed it, Frank. After Waits & Measures went home, defeated (the poor so-and-sos), Professor Gupta took a tour of the building where he found that at any magnification, whether you're looking at an aerial photograph, or whether you're standing in the john, the headquarters and each and every part of it is the same exact shape. He called this self-similarity."

"..."

"Frank?"

"..."

"I guess we lost you, Frank. But don't let us lose the rest of you out there, Orbiters. We will be right back."

By the way, Wall, where you going? Just out for a drive? Sure is dark out here. Wherever *here* is. Maybe that's why we get so nervous when we're lost. It's that sneaking suspicion that somehow we've fallen off the map. The middle of nowhere is, of course, a redundant phrase. If you're in Nowhere, then you're in the middle of it. Nowhere, by its very definition, is only middles. There are no edges, no borders, no landmarks. There is nothing to show you where you are. Because you're Nowhere.

In these situations, out on your own, out in the darkness, do you start to wonder who the hell you are? Feel like you aren't anyone, right? Like you could vanish from the face of the planet and no one would ever know or care because, follow along now, *you never really existed.* Or, maybe, when you finally come to realize how unlikely you are… well, when that happens, probably you'll need to be taken away for examination so we can learn just what in *the* hell you're supposed to be. Before that examination even starts, though, you could be someone else, anyone else, and it wouldn't make a damn bit of difference. Who are you, man? Are you really even driving right now? Or are you being taken somewhere?

Too much of that kind of thinking and your brain's gonna hurt (kinda got a headache anyway, don'tcha?). The road's here and you're driving on it. Of all the strips of asphalt and cement in the world, this is the one you're on. You must be going somewhere. And even if you don't know what that place is, you'll know when you arrive. It'll be your destined location, the place where your talents are needed, the part of the world (whatever world that may be) where you fit in.

Wall, what do you see, right there, yes, running alongside the, too small to be billboards, little signs, spaced evenly:

THOUGHT WE

INVITED EVERYONE

WE KNEW, BUT

HEY THERE BUDDY

WHO ARE YOU?

Perma-Shave

Sure, must be time for some donuts because you're standing outside a Pilgrim & Pagan, Wall. Little more missing time here. Gonna have to get used to it, pal. What's the last thing you remember? Yeah, a billboard right after the Perma-Shave. This was no advertisement, though. Actually, at first, it wasn't much of anything. A large, white sign. That's all. Nothing on it. The kind that usually advertises if you were a smart business owner, you could be advertising here. But this one, even though it displayed neither pictures, nor text, well it didn't seem blank. The white was like a radiance. A resplendence. Not the kind of light you hoped for, you prayed for when you were little and you found yourself in the dark, monsters closing in, how did I end up in this situation? Mommy? Daddy? Where are you? Oh why did this have to happen to me? No, not that kind of light at all. This is the light that dazzles, that awes, that horrifies. An Old Testament-style divine effulgence that lances out of the clouds and strikes you blind. After you've looked into it, you'll never be able to see again. At least, not with your eyes.

And tell me, Wall, what sick fuck bought advertising space for *that*?

All right, all right, why not roll in and, sure, grab some donuts, maybe some coffee. No. On second thought, no coffee. Right now, Wall, coffee's a bad idea. Bad to the last drop. And that drop's bad too.

"Wait for the cue."

"Huh?"

Hold on, hold on. What's going on here? When you walked in, do you remember walking through the door of the Pilgrim & Pagan, Wall? Yeah, that door, right behind you, which is closing, has closed, and was obviously designed by someone or some*thing* that never quite took to the idea that fewer moving parts equals better. Turn back around and, as expected, or possibly contrary to your expectations, everything's there. Or here. It's a donut shop. There's a customer off in the back booth drinking coffee (can even hear the porcelain scrape the table) and reading a newspaper. There are donuts in their trays. Smells of brewing beans, sugar, bacon. Hell, the sun's up "outside," it's "daytime," and here's this guy leaning against the counter, nametag sez Arty, seemingly ready to take your order, but who just a few seconds ago said, "Wait for the cue." Cue?

The Predicta sez: *The first report we get is from Walter Haut, public information officer for the Roswell Army Air Field (RAAF). He says that personnel from the 509th Operations Group had recovered a 'flying disc.'*

Hmm, sounds familiar… But are ya, are ya having a little trouble spinning your head to the left there, buddy? Gosh, it doesn't seem hot, and yet there's this trickle of sweat running down the side of your… Ah, now you see it, Wall. And tell me, how exactly did that get here? Who knows, but it's the Philco Predicta from the Hyperborean. Your old pal. Standing there on its black pedestal. Is it reminding you of the monolith from *2001: A Space Odyssey*? And, yes, it's full of stars.

"How may I help you, sir or madam?" sez Arty.

Do you feel androgynous, Wall?

And, lemme ask, have you ever been to a play, not one of those on

171

Broadway or in Chicago, but, like, community theater, and one actor, the one who's on the ball, sez a line and then the other actor, who probably shouldn't be up in front of an audience in the first place, just stands there? You know that feeling, call it anxiety, that everyone else gets, and, sure, the lackluster actor, maybe he or she gets it too? Eventually, anyway. You know how this pressure, sooner or later, it fills a person up, distending their guts with anticipatory air, until the audience members, well they're ready to shout the goddamn line out themselves to dispel this horrible internal pressure everyone's got building inside of them? Do you know that sensation, Wall? Do you have it right now? Do you think, like, maybe you should?

The Predicta sez: *Later on July 8, 1947, the Eighth Air Force's Commanding General, Roger Ramey, stated that a weather balloon was retrieved by the RAAF personnel. At this same press conference, foil, rubber, and wood said to be from the crashed "weather balloon" were displayed.*

And then, as if someone's speaking through you: "I'll have the Mystery Donut."

Collective fart of everyone in the house as they all deflate, none more so than Arty, who smiles, not quite proud of you, Wall, but definitely relieved.

"Ahh, the Mystery Donut, sir or madam? No one's, like, ordered that in ages, right? And anyway, I dunno how to make it. I keep asking people, you know?, 'How do you make the Mystery Donut?' but all they say, man, is, 'It's a mystery.' Slike that one, you heard this, about the woman who like walks up to the donut and sez, 'I can see right through you.'"

"You, uh, you going to be here all week?"

Arty gives you a look, and then you're alone in the donut shop, well, uh, except for about a million pieces of copper floating before your eyes, pennies from heaven?, and when they fall to the floor, yeah, they don't actually fall, just sorta seem to be on the floor now, or, right, on the counter, a roll busted open by good ol' Arty.

"That'd be, like, you know, a good one, sir or madam, but sure that ain't it. Funny, though. Get this. This one's like a classic. Me and my brother, right?, we used to, you know, play this game, sure, to pass the time. We'd pick a… we'd pick like a historical figure, game was called *History,* right?, we'd pick this historical figure and tell each other not to, you know, think about him. Think about him and, sure, you'd lose. For the game to like work you had to, right?, be honest about when you lost. But you wouldn't just *say* you lost, ya know? There was like a final gambit for the... for the loser. What you'd do, get this, what you'd do is like tell some long, ridiculous story, ya know?, and whoever thought of the repeated closing line first, man, lost that round. We played that game. And me and my bro, right, we had, ya know?, tricky ways to make the other one lose. Hide pictures of the person in like places we knew the other'd look. Drop hints that'd like send the other off on sure a doomed train of, right?, thought. Pretty soon, man, we could just like leave little notes that, get this, that just said, 'you lost'. Turns out, sure, when you like tell yourself not to, you know, think about something, right?, it's the only thing you can think about. It's like this historical figure, man, he created, ya know?, the reality you live in. He's real, he like made reality, and you, right?, you're just a reflection.

"Like you, sir or madam. We're all not ourselves sometimes, right? Right. Just like, uh, yeah! Stop me if you heard this one..."

The Predicta sez: *Even at this early stage, less than a day after the event, we have conflicting stories. Haut said there was a flying disc, General Ramey a weather balloon. And then the evidence is brought out. Even more suspicious. Why wouldn't the army just throw it away if it were a weather balloon?*

Is that...? Woh. Wait a minute. Even before he's started, Arty appears to be done. Think, Wall. Remember.

"You're ready to go."

Remember. What did he say? Remember. It was a story, yes. And it went a little something like this:

At the beginning, a child is born. But wait. Where does the story take place? It seems like one of the Carolinas. Or maybe Kentucky. He might've just beamed out of the sky. You do remember that later, people would call the child a self-made man. At the beginning, they don't say that, though. At the beginning, yes, there's a problem. A big problem. But what was the child's name? And what was the problem? Wait. "Prollem was, this kid wasn't anyone in particular." That line is crystal in your memory, Wall. That was the problem. There's no name to recall. "He didn't look like anyone. Didn't sound like anyone. Didn't feel or smell or taste like anyone. Hell, the parents didn't even give the kid a name. What could they do? Names are for particular people. But when they looked at this pipsqueak, they saw no one." Wall, it's OK, Arty sounds a little different. Don't worry about it. "And who in their right goddamn mind gives a name to no one, ya know? I mean, like, who *is* this little jerk?"

The Predicta sez: *Lacking any other evidence, the weather balloon story was generally accepted until 1978, when ufologist Stanton T. Friedman interviewed one Major Jesse Marcel, formerly of the 509th Operations Group. Marcel claimed the wreckage was not of this earth.*

In the story, if you can trust your memory, Wall, time passed and things didn't get much better for the Nobody. "People'd come to town and, right?, they'd look at the kid and they'd know. They'd know all too well. This bastard's no one in particular. Slike a minor, unnamed character was born right into the goddamn world. An extra. Just there to fill up the scene, ya know? Only there ain't any actual minor, unnamed, like, characters in the world. Aren't supposed to be, anyway." Did Arty really get this deep with the story? Seems implausible, but what else do you have to go on, Wall? "This kid drove everyone to distraction." Not a chance in hell he said that. "'Drove everyone to distraction,' that's the way, ya know?, people talked back then." Although, maybe he did. "It is. 's how they talked. Back when this story takes place, right? I dunno when." Sounds more like good old Arty now. Only, you don't remember how he said the next part. You do recall that people, when they met the Nobody, would yell at him, something like: "You can't go around like that, kid! You have to be somebody. It's not right, you not being anybody!" The Nobody, it's like he was blurry. Your eyes could never hone in on him. "Like he was his own Bigfoot photo, ya know?" Or even, as if he were this very story. Out of focus. Your memory, Wall, changing it.

And now you realize that you do remember the end, though you have no idea how Arty got there:

"That's right, one day, just like that, he, ya know?, snapped out of it. He wasn't an extra anymore. He was memorable. He was in focus. He was someone in particular. He even got himself a name, this kid who wasn't anyone. And that boy grew up to be… Abraham Lincoln."

The Predicta sez: *Major Marcel said: "It is my belief the military covered up the fact that they'd found an alien spacecraft."*

"You're ready to go."

"Where's your brother now?" you say.

"Brother?" Arty looks confused for a second, recovers. "Sure. My brother. I've got like a story about that…"

"And that boy grew up to be… Abraham Lincoln?"

"You lost, right? Right. But sir or madam, we won't like, ya know?, send ya home empty-handed," sez Arty as he hands you a rose, Wall, with a small square of paper attached to the bottom.

The Predicta sez: *From here we know the drill: the flying saucer was taken to Area 51 in Nevada, Majestic-12 physicists began reverse engineering the spaceship, while MJ-12 doctors performed an autopsy on the dead aliens. Any number of even wilder, and more baseless assertions followed…*

"What about the Mystery Donut?"

Only Arty appears to be done talking. There's a scrape of porcelain as the lone customer picks up his coffee cup, are we holding for editing or something? And then… you're back in the car. Driving. Best not to worry too much about it, Wall. Sit back, relax, let cruise control… oh, well, right. This car's too old for cruise. So you actually have to operate your machine while you listen to the radio:

"…in my recent interview with Citronella Fogge, she's a former counterespionage agent and now a freelance expert on the subject, well Fogge had this to say…"

"The Organization, unlike all the other intelligence agencies, is an open book. Every piece of correspondence, every plan, every agent, every meeting, even details on every operation are available to the public. The reason The Organization remains mysterious: the sheer amount of information it generates. Each time a country has tried to investigate this elusive agency, officials have been sent in, directed to their various areas of interest, granted access to all databanks, reports, documents, they've always been given carte blanche to carry out their inquest, and yet nothing has ever been learned."

175

"Maybe there's corruption, payoffs, misdirection."

"There may be, but if that's true there's no evidence of it. Instead, each team of inspectors has marveled at how smoothly The Organization runs. Being larger than many of our own bureaucracies, you would expect the usual problems. The Organization, according to everyone who has gone inside, has none of them."

"It always works at maximum efficiency? I find that hard to believe."

"I did too. But take the most recent inquest into The Organization, the Tamam Shud operation. We picked this operation at random so we wouldn't get caught up in the details. We only wanted to learn how The Organization runs. Tamam Shud piqued our interest right away, being about the mysterious death of an unknown man who happened to be carrying a slip of paper in a secret pocket that said Tamam Shud. At first it read like any other unsolved mystery, except that, in the end, no one seemed to know who he was or why he was killed."

"That's interesting in itself, isn't it?"

"Of course, but also problematic. We were drawn in. We weren't thinking about The Organization anymore; we were thinking about Tamam Shud. So we stepped back and soon found there were not only connections between Tamam Shud and other operations, there were connections to everything The Organization was doing. Finding it everywhere, we began to question whether Tamam Shud was a separate case. In this way, it appears, at all times, The Organization operates as a unified whole. An enormous, unified whole. But even if a lone person could isolate a single operation, and that has never been done, the information generated by just one operation would be so vast the lone official could never leave his observation post without completely losing the thread of the clew. So we're left with this question: how can it be that we always move from the smoothness of a completely open agency to this turbulence?"

"We leave it to you, Orbiters, for we're entering the portion of our program, no, we're not being interrupted, we operate like The Organization now, so we're entering the portion of the show where other people talk, some of them trying to sell you things."

Do you still think you're out driving on your own, Wall? Sure, sure, it seems like you are. Stars. Night sky. Occasional billboards. Lights. Radio.

But how do you know this is your chosen road? What if this is just the road you're on? You can only go where it takes you. And later you'll have to tell us how you feel about this: there's the distinct possibility you're motoring along and you're sitting at a lengthy wooden table, every seat taken save the one at the head, as if you were some office drone waiting for a meeting to start. And now you notice, instead of looking at the director's chair, everyone's looking at you, Wall. You. Asking you a question with their expressionless eyes. Demanding an answer. So, do you really believe there's a destination ahead? Or is it more likely you're on this road and that's that? They say if you don't know, best to guess. And, really, do you want to find out what happens if you fail this exam? Right before the silence becomes damning there's an explosion behind you, an explosion of … is that, like, a cocktail shaker? Man, *what* is going on here? When will this meeting start already? And just who the fuck is running the show?

Does the Conspiratorium have that information? Alas, even with its vast resources, the Char Le Tannes Institute *still* does not know which conspiracy leads to the omnipotent meta-conspiracy. Not yet, anyway. On the screen, for a moment, the SPOKESWOMAN's plastic mask slips, proving even she is daunted by the sheer improbability of attaining such knowledge. But after that instance of discomposure, the infomercial continues. *"Once the mythological hero has left home, he or she must undergo a supreme ordeal. The ordeal the experiencer must endure is the examination. At the Conspiratorium, you choose what areas the interstellar scientists focus on. Just ask if you would like a diffuse array of colored lights to flash while the examination takes place. One piece of bad news: I am afraid at this time we no longer have the anal probe, but subscribe to our newsletter and you will find our options are constantly being updated. For the mental examination, you will see a series of images intended to bring about an emotional response. Although you certainly have the option to select the images yourself, we have found our clients enjoy the experience more when they do not know which ones will be displayed beforehand. And do not worry. We at the Conspiratorium will prepare you for your ordeal. You will be given a thorough physical examination to ensure your well-being. Here, we will test your blood for fluoride, extract tracking devices from your person, neutralize all disease-causing agents, and remove microchips from your brain. Now you will be pure, free, healthy. Now your thoughts will be safe and private. Now you will no longer need that tinfoil hat, though you may be interested in our museum dedicated to tinfoil headwear designs of the past."* The kaleidoscopic light from the headgear is…

Wall? At this point what ya might be saying to yourself is: "Why does this boardroom have a disco ball?" Perfectly logical question. No one would fault you for asking it. But, buddy, if you're asking only that question, then you've missed the important ones like: "What am I doing lying on the conference table?" or "Who or what are all these beings around me?" or "What are they doing to me?" or "What are they saying?" or, and perhaps most importantly, "Why does it sound like someone's making cocktails?" Instead, for you, colored lights, road, and, later, ya really gotta tell us how this makes you feel, I mean there's this guy on the billboards, he's carrying a pistol, and, ohhh interesting, he doesn't appear to be the least bit hesitant, no, almost seems if the billboard had focused a little lower we'd see his other weapon, mmmm interesting response, cocked and ready for action. But it's not like there's only one billboard repeated. Boring. *You* get to see the same model holding a different weapon on each… Would you call this massive art installation *Murder Fantasy*? Interesting. When the billboards change and become flipbooks of the victims, do you speed up because, hmm, I see, because you hope to change the tenor of the scenes, figuring the double cranked hijinks of the Keystone Kops will trick you into believing this is all just a lost Grand Guignol directed by Mack Sennet, or because you already thought it was funny and, hell, it could only get funnier by adding an old-timey silent film aspect? Tell us how this makes you feel, Wall. Interesting. Supremely interesting. Is that nervous laughter? Who is that butcher in the pictures flying by? Are you really surprised to learn the killer on the billboards is you? Tell us how this makes you feel. Leave out no details…

Oh my.

You *are* quite a subject.

Tell us more…

On second thought, Wall, never mind. We already know.

And then, on the side of the road, you see little signs spaced evenly that say:

YOU'RE DRIVING

LIKE YOU'RE IN

A RACE, WHEN

YOU COULD BE

LOST IN SPACE

PERMA-SHAVE

There's no ignoring it. There's no repressing it. Was a white sign. Piercing light. Blazing forth from the unknown. And the light gave birth. A silhouette. At the center of the billboard. What could survive in that refulgence? An avatar of shadow. Impossible to recognize. To comprehend. You wished your eyes had never seen it. You wanted to turn away. Restrained. Metal bars and straps. Force field. You, Wall, on a table, eyelids refusing to close, unable to close. You *must* see. Afraid that if this thing becomes aware of you… And with that image drilled into your head, wound cauterized, smells like burning hair, nose bleeding, yes, you *will* see…

Wall! In the window glass! Are you seeing it again?!

Well, no. This is ICU. Their offices, anyhow. And it appears to be test day. Everyone silent. Eyes on their own papers. The monitor sees all, as do the hidden cameras. What you don't know is that exams at the Alternate History Channel are less about the number of correct answers, and more about how you justify your answers later on. The frosh are always terrified after their first test because the questions never make much sense, being as they're about abstruse historical concepts from dimensions so far along the pitchfork bifurcations even seasoned ICU veterans barely know which timeline we're talking about. The test is followed by one of the finest Alternate History Channel traditions, namely getting bombed at a nearby bar called The Conference Room, though no one has ever acknowledged this as a tradition, the rookies getting together, complaining about how unfair, I mean could

179

you even begin to unravel question number, until someone gets the idea, normally around last call, to walk into the offices the next day still drunk and in last night's clothes, and demand that all those answers, yes, even that *one*, I doan give a googadam wha you think, 's right, at which point the freshman in question is immediately promoted and sent home to sleep off the hangover.

No need to worry, though, Wall. This exam isn't yours to take. Employees only. Speaking of employees, isn't there kind of a lot of security here for a zany TV station? And even though you can't see the guards' eyes behind their shades, Wall, you get the idea they're waiting for you to explain your presence, and every second that passes, it's like those standardized tests where each time you get one wrong, you not only lose points, you end up with a batch of lightweight questions afterwards, making it so no matter what you do... And I hate to tell ya this, but based on their expressionless faces, you've already missed so many, I mean, did you even get your name right?

"Ima Fre..." Oooh, that's not it, is it, Wall? But Gene, tell the man what he's won! A lifetime supply of Nada! Gosh, ya need help carrying that to the car?

"Where's your gun?" sez one Bureau member. When you give him that confused look, he sez: "This is America. Everyone has guns."

"What is your purpose here?" sez another Bureau member.

Do you really have a purpose anywhere, Wall?

The Predicta sez: *There is another theory on what fell out of the sky in New Mexico on that summer day, and its name is Project Mogul.*

Of course it's not exactly surprising to hear an ICU broadcast when you're standing in their headquarters. But instead of hearing it from, say, all around you, Wall, seems to be coming from one direction.

The Predicta sez: *Project Mogul was a high altitude surveillance balloon designed to detect shockwaves and radioactivity from Soviet atomic bomb tests...*

And, yeah, there it is. Your Predicta. On the black pedestal. Maybe if you took it out for a walk now and then it wouldn't follow you around like this?

"*What* is your purpose here, sir or madam?" sez security. Again with the androgynous stuff?

The Predicta sez: *For the Cold War, this sounds like a perfectly acceptable form of espionage. Project Mogul is just another U-2...*

"Greta Zelle," you say, but just like back at the donut shop, Wall, you wonder who's doing the talking. Best possible answer, though, because you no longer think you're watching someone about to be eighty-sixed. Instead, it feels like you're supposed to be here, like you belong. It's a nice feeling.

"Please sign in," sez security, and you do, still with that autopilot sensation. That doesn't...! that's not your name! Wall, what's going on? "Right this way."

The Predicta sez: *...unlike the U-2, however, Project Mogul was a complete failure.*

Somehow Greta's office is full of clothes, more like she's a costume designer than an ICU writer, and you find yourself winding your way through the maze, wishing you had a machete to hack into this dense fashion show, coming out on the other end wearing a feather boa, bowl of fruit hat, and about a dozen sequined nightmares (it's a good look for you, Wall, really) which do a better job of impeding your progress than the security guards. On the other side you see, well, nothing. It's pitch black. Throwing money at problems helps some people, but a five dollar bill, you think they're gonna put on a special performance for that? Hold on. Is this the end or the beginning? Maybe there's another showing? A good guess, because, as you watch, you're not sure if this is the first time you're seeing it, or the second, or the tenth, or if you only ever saw it once, and now it's playing in your memory. Doesn't matter. A cigarette lighter ignites, seems to be brighter than it ought to be, is there, like, a spotlight on in here? And the performance begins:

"Let me ask you a question. Did I ever tell you," sez Greta, "that my mom used to accuse me of being pregnant, years before I even kissed a boy? From my twelfth birthday until I ran away when I was eighteen? Did I ever tell you about this? Did I tell you what I said to her before I finally left?

181

Did I tell you what I did?" She inhales on the cigarette and broods. "Did I tell you that, as I was about to leave her sight forever, did I tell you I let her know she was right?" Greta leans forward. "That she'd been right for the past six years? That I'd been knocked up exactly as she suspected and on that final night, I told her as I was preparing to go, that, at long last, I'd given birth to the baby that'd been inside me for over half a decade? Did you know? Have you heard this before?" Greta stands and begins pacing, waving the cigarette about creating a red cherry tracer. "Would you believe me if I told you that, true to form, my mother, enraged, demanded to know who the father was? Would it seem like just another performance, and I know I can be dramatic, if I told you that I looked to the sky and said, 'Mother, I do not know which of them impregnated me, but they have been beaming me into their ship for the past six years, and they have informed me now that my child will be the leader the world has been waiting for,' I mean, if I said that, would you believe it?" Greta, pleading, then stubbing out the cigarette, plucking another from the pack. "And furthermore, would you believe I then handed her an infant wrapped in a blanket that was of human and extraterrestrial origin? Would you believe I said, 'Now take this child and raise it as your own, for I have been but the incubator; it is your job to be the true mother,' tell me, is that outside the realm of acceptability? Or would you assume (justifiably, granted) I handed her a doll whose arms and legs I'd ripped off and replaced with tentacles from an octopus bought at an Asian market the day before? And tell me, which version are you more likely to think is the truth when you learn that my mother held what I handed her and immediately said, in a grave tone, 'I accept this responsibility'? Would it be worse or, well, maybe not better, but more in tune with the rest of the story if you found out that she raised a baby doll with tentacle arms and tentacle legs as if it were her own child? Or, do you find that, for reasons you can't explain to yourself, and perhaps to your future consternation, you've immediately accepted my story, and the proof is in the fact that you question nothing at all, and now your one and only hope is to learn who my child went on to be?"

The Predicta sez: *Being a Top Secret project that failed catastrophically, the United States government had to cover up their failure so the Soviets wouldn't know what we were trying, and so the American people didn't lose faith in the CIA and in their own military.*

Ending her speech by turning toward the audience (you, Wall), lighting her cigarette, and do you get the feeling, yeah, like this is the end of one of those old VCR murder mysteries? I know who the killer is, do you...?

"No," you say, though you probably meant yes, Wall, or maybe nothing, since the words continue flowing of their own accord. "I don't wonder who your child went on to be."

"You don't?!"

"No. Because I already know."

Greta smokes incredulously.

"Your story ends: And that boy grew up to be... Abraham Lincoln."

Pause.

"Lincoln County? Area 51? Why does he want to see me?"

"I don't know," you (or someone) says, and that's the lord's truth. But you manage to hand her the rose Arty gave you earlier.

The Predicta sez: *But this still does not explain why Walter Haut described what the military had found as a 'flying disc,' or why Major Marcel described the aircraft as being "not of this earth."*

"I guess you wouldn't," she sez, taking the flower. The spotlight, or whatever light, continues to radiate down on her, surrounded by the smoke from the various cigarettes, and soon the mist and the glare are so powerful it's like driving through fog with your bright lights...

...Lights. The lights, the headlights, shining on and on, illuminating, reflecting as you move through a thin fog, listening to the radio.

"As Citronella Fogge informed us, The Organization does appear to operate as a whole. But then what is it made up of? Normally there'd be departments. Go to any government office and you'll find plenty of departments, maybe too many departments. But at The Organization, none. There's only work, Orbiters. An unfathomable amount of work with no divisions whatsoever. None. Except... that isn't entirely true. There is one division. The Counterclockwise

183

Department, headed by General Archibald Kayahs. Yep, that's right. General Kayahs... But let's back up a bit. The earliest theory on The Organization: it was a discordian society. Simple enough... until The Counterclockwise Department was discovered. Then, suddenly, no one knew what to do with The Organization. This one coherent structure drove everyone to the brink. A comprehensible segment, as obvious as the Great Red Spot on Jupiter, on the face of all that insanity. What keeps us talking about The Organization, I think, is the existence and persistence of The Counterclockwise Department. Amidst what we assume is disorder, there's an office with a title placard and a director (even if his name is unlikely). The only explanation we've come up with, Orbiters, for why so many people remain obsessed with The Organization is the fact that we're used to chaos breeding more chaos, and we're used to order descending into wild disorder, but without self-conscious, pointed assistance and planning, we're not used to orderly structures arising of their own volition from pandemonium. Orbiters, steer your thinking this way: when we see something like The Organization, we may be confused, but we've learned to accept chaos. When we see something like The Counterclockwise Department? Honestly, we wish, we hope, perhaps we even pray that someone who knows, who really knows will come along and give us the answers..."

"You're probably wondering why I've called you all here," sez a man walking to the head of the long wooden table. He tosses a binder into the air which traces a slow-motion arc (how'd he do that?) attracting the attention of everyone, almost like the thing's hovering, and what a surprise when it lands directly in front of him, already seated, sure, been there the whole time, impatient, waiting for touchdown. "I've called you to this place because it has grown late, the time having moved beyond beer o'clock and progressed directly into the cocktail hour, when all of the answers will be given to you. Yet we must be swift. For soon what shall descend upon us but shot thirty, oh shot thirty! That dreaded span when our minds will be scrubbed clean and we will forget all we've learned."

Can things get more confusing, Wall? And this probably won't help any: it turns out (tell yourself it's a hallucination if that makes you feel better) the office with the long wooden table is, um, yeah, a watering hole called, you

184

guessed it, The Conference Room. You're also driving, listening to the radio. Maybe at one point you thought you were on the road of destiny, Wall, or if not, at least you were on a road, but now, see, do you find yourself getting a little suspicious of the car? When did you buy it? And from where? How much did it cost? What were you thinking when you went with the '42 De Soto? If you answered, "Uh...?" to all of those questions you might wanta, not now, don't rush yourself, Wall, but maybe in the near future you should, let's say, explore the idea that you're not in control of your automobile at all. If that's true, um, where's it taking you? Hell, where are you now? Maybe if you close your eyes and click your heels together you'll find yourself back in Kansas, maybe you'll find you never left, maybe you'll find it was all a dream. And you were there, and you were there, and you were there, but you, you weren't there. Nope. Fuck if I know where you were. Wasn't my turn to watch you...

What you need is a drink. Cheers? Men in white shirts and black pants are rattling shakers and appropriately serving a creamy concoction, Painkillers, them's the cocktails, which seem pretty necessary after whatever it was these assholes did to you when you were out on the table staring at the disco ball. Speaking of, if you were to put a bar in a corporate setting, turn on some jams, spin a mirrored orb on the ceiling, invite girls clad in highly improper office attire, and cover the place in TVs, you'd have The Conference Room.

And as it turns out, the director is walking toward you. Over his shoulder you see, sure, the Predicta...

The Predicta sez: *We always hear about the weather balloon and then the spy balloon (Project Mogul), but what really fell to earth is far more unnerving...*

Over your shoulder, Wall, buddy, the director sees the Conspiratorium's infomercial. It does him no good whatsoever. Why couldn't you turn around right now and demand that they crank the volume? Why is salvation, for some, so difficult to come by, while others stumble into it blindly? Why can't this be the point where it's all revealed to you? But, no...

185

The Predicta sez: ...*because what we did find was a flying disc, only it wasn't extraterrestrial...*

Instead, out here, either out here in space or out here in your car (or someone's car, anyway) or out here in The Conference Room or out here in the middle of nowhere (har dee har har), you sit and drink, as the director joins you.

"You ever go to a movie," sez the director, only looking at you out of the corner of his eye, "where the characters, when they talk, give each other far too much information? They say things everyone in that film world should already know. Each bit of dialogue is overblown. For instance, let's say you have a brother named Iam, and I have to inform you what's happening with him; I'd say: 'Your brother and sibling rival, Iam, who is always embroiled in some sort of intrigue, normally with you, but also with others, has really gotten himself into trouble this time because he wants to expose our secret plan, and...' As if you wouldn't know your own brother's name or his predilections or that the two of you have a rivalry. In another case, a character might detail a large portion of the plot instead of letting it unfold on screen: 'Although Iam is no micro-manager, he can't stand the fact that his sister's chaos incarnate. She's uncertainty, Iam is relativity. She foils all of his plans, not because she doesn't love him, but because she thinks his methods are ineffective...' It's called Expository Dialogue, and it's considered weak. Poor writing. But the next time you're sitting in the dark down at the local megaplex, crunching on your popcorn and sucking down that gallon of soda pop, when you hear Expository Dialogue, I want you to get suspicious. For it's my belief that *that* character, or those characters even, realize they're being watched. They're well aware. Of course, they don't let on physically. There's no waving, nodding, pointing. But they know you're out there. And they're talking for you, to you. Think about this, though: what motives could they possibly have for being so obvious? What might they be covering up with all that noise?"

The director, finally, turns in your direction, Wall, and frowns, as if he hadn't quite noticed you before, as if he were talking to himself, or to an assumed audience. He dusts you off, like he's your dad or something, and tries

186

to help you recover from your recent ordeal.

The Predicta sez: *The flying disc was an American-made saucer programmed to spy on the citizens of this country. Our government was so paranoid at the time, they were willing to take extreme measures to ensure we weren't becoming commies.*

"Sorry about my associates. They're overzealous. That might be why we hire them. Good at their jobs? Absolutely. Too good? Can you be too good at something? Ted Williams tried to tell people to look for the president's signature on the ball. That's the way you hit. Look for the signature on the ball. And the ball's moving ninety-five miles an hour! Maybe that's too good… You look like you need a drink. Already have one? Well, in your condition, my friend, two wouldn't be out of the question. Let's be honest: two might not even begin to take the edge off…"

The director flags down one of the waiters, orders you another Painkiller.

The Predicta sez: *You can imagine how happy our government was when they realized their botched program made it look like extraterrestrial evidence was being hidden! They couldn't possibly have invented a better cover story themselves.*

"What were we talking about? Time. It's one damn thing after another. Am I right? I think I am. One second, one minute, one hour, one day, and then there's another. How much time do we have, and what are we going to do with it, Wall? Your name's Wall, right? You look like a Wall. The idea is to save time. Yes. That's why we think Expository Dialogue is phony. We don't say what's obvious. We don't say what everyone already knows. And the hell with unnecessary explanations. We only have so much time, and we aren't going to waste it. But I'm going to stop myself right there. Because I'm the one who'll tell you: that's why movies aren't realistic. One of the reasons, anyway. Because we do say what everyone already knows. We give way too much information. Even irrelevant information. We repeat ourselves. We explain and explain and explain. Even when there's no question about what's going on. Maybe we do it for those who are watching us. Those who

187

are listening in. Whoever They may be. Let 'em know we know. Wear 'em down so They'll get sick of it and go away. Or, perhaps, we're just waiting for someone to come along and tell us what is happening and what we ought to do about it."

Your drink arrives, Wall.

"Speak of the devil…" the director nods to the waiter. "Wall, I'm glad to've met you. Sorry the circumstances couldn't be better. Too bad we don't have longer to get to know each other. That's just the thing, isn't it? Our time is supposed to be short, so we don't want long explanations, we don't want to hear what we already know. But it's not as short as all that. When we don't know what's going on, when we don't know what to do next, we tend to do nothing. The seconds, minutes, hours, days expand. At least, it feels that way. That's been your problem, hasn't it, Wall? You don't know what's happening. And you don't know what to do next, or even now. But you're lucky. That's where we come in. You see, if my associates were a bit rough with you, it's only because we had to make sure you were up to the task at hand. Our educated opinion is that you're not merely capable, you were born to do it. You, my friend, are going to play a killer. Afterwards, it'll be assumed you're the culprit, though not right away, and even then evidence will be scarce. When the usual suspicion comes down on you, show no signs that you're guilty, or that you even care about what happened. You should appear divorced, completely, from the proceedings. With this performance, everyone will finally see the real you and they will be awestruck. Confusion is the desired effect. Believe me, this is the role of your life. And don't worry about where you need to be or any of that logistical crap. We will direct you. If this seems blunt, forced, unnatural, overly expository, remember – maybe I'm talking for Them. Letting Them know. But… what *are* my motives? And *what* am I covering up?

"Honestly, Wall, after a lifetime of nothingness, I don't think you'll have a problem with this business proposition. Before, it was as if you didn't exist. You've been waiting for us off in the ether, waiting for us to come along, waiting for us to tell you what's happening, waiting for us to tell you what to do next. Now, I've spoken the word, you can go forth. Yes, I believe you understand your role and the importance of this assignment. I believe you understand your own importance. And even if you didn't before, you do now. Because I've explained it to you."

The Predicta sez: *Government officials purposely botched explanations that probably would've dispelled any belief in alien activity in order to keep the truth away from everyone. The truth that the CIA and the military were expending more effort spying on their own people than they were on the Soviets.*

"Just in case, here's a picture of your contact. He'll help you out when necessary. Now it's time to get lit. And drinks are on the house!"

Contact?

Meanwhile, behind you, Wall, if only you would turn around, if only... But what would be different if you'd watched the Conspiratorium's infomercial before your experience? Let's say, for instance, you saw the damn thing, thought it was a hoot, and that's that. Nothing else. You didn't call them up. You didn't go into their offices for a consultation. Naw. *You* did the same thing people the world over do when they see lengthy ads for weight loss supplements, cock inflation pills, get rich quick schemes, miracle inventions, and the like. You had a laugh, drank another beer, scratched your ass. So, sure, Wall, you're probably wondering: "Just what would change if I'd seen the Char Le Tannes Institute infomercial on the Predicta?" The answer is: *you* would, Wall. You would change. "*There are an untold number of alien abductions every year*," says the Spokeswoman on the program you may never see, that you certainly didn't catch in time. "*But only those who come to the Conspiratorium are prepared for their experience. The unprepared are often driven mad, wracked with pain from the physical ordeal, left with a vague recollection of the events the mind can only translate as terror.*" Seeing the commercial, though, well, you'd at least be primed, an autonomous agent, if only mentally, ready for your transformation. Instead, you're like some lucky (or unlucky, depending on how you take it) bastard who stumbled past the gargoyles at the entrance to the secret temple and inside found bupkis. The Great Bejeweled Bupkis. And the bupkis eliminator, the bringer of the great whatever the opposite of bupkis might be is right behind you, Wall. But you aren't turning around. You won't turn around. Even if you did, in this here situation, you likely wouldn't know what you were looking at. Its import wouldn't strike you. Wouldn't stick.

The SPOKESWOMAN, now walking through the poorly generated image of a space station, sez: *"After surviving the supreme ordeal, the examination, the experiencer gains a boon delivered through a conference. At this time you will find your abductors to be warmer, kinder, more open. Here you can ask questions about the visitors, answer questions about life on earth, accept apologies for the forced medical procedures and kidnapping, listen to explanations of why you were chosen (a very popular segment), listen to plans for future mass communication with earth or future conquest, attend lectures on what we (as earthlings) are doing incorrectly in the political, environmental, social, or ethical spheres. Often, the visitors want to talk about time, lifespan, and individuality. If you are so inclined, the Conspiratorium can help design your experience so you focus on what you want to know, what you want to discuss. Sadly, remember that, thanks to the required Lost Time portion of your abduction, you will not immediately recall much of what is said. But at the end of the conference, if you so choose, you can be assigned a task to perform when you are returned to earth. What would you like your mission to be? With the Conspiratorium, the sky is not the limit. With the Conspiratorium, there are no limits."*

Now's as good a time as any: what if you aren't in control of the car, Wall? It does seem to be taking you to where it wants to go. And, yeah, buddy, there's really only one way to test this hypothesis: slam on the motherfucking brakes.

The De Soto slides to a squealing stop.

It actually does.

Maybe you *are* in control of this machine?

Outside, walking around the De Soto, engine still running, do you wonder? Where are you, exactly? What are you doing here? In the darkness. Like you're light years away from anywhere. As if you've been taken from earth against your will, everything against your will, briefly placated by the fact that you were able to express autonomy.

The Predicta sez: *A new idea, by author Annie Jacobsen, combines both the Cold War and the alien flying disc theories into one.* A saucer crashes into a ranch on the screen, and as the camera gets closer writing can be seen on the ship. Writing in Cyrillic.

Oh, Wall...

Maybe you saw this coming. What with the Predicta directly in front of the car. Looking like, well, you would've smashed into it if you hadn't've hit the brakes exactly when you did. Heh heh heh, lucky that, hey? No... preordained. And there it is. Sitting right where you were supposed to stop. In all its glory. Shining away. It's illusions showing you once again that free will is a delusion.

The Predicta sez: *It is widely known that Josef Stalin was obsessed with the Orson Welles broadcast* War of the Worlds *(1938). According to Jacobsen, he planned to use a* War of the Worlds-*like plan to terrorize the American public...*

"*Why did you have me sleep with him?*" comes from the De Soto's radio. Wouldn't be too surprising, now, since you left the car running, Wall, but that's not *The Unknown Empire Tonight*. It sounds like... Greta Zelle?

"*Did you know this stamp on your rose is the... oldest usable stamp in...*"

"*Why did you have me sleep with him?*"

"*Fine, Ms... Zelle. Fine... Do you know why... novels, as they were... developing often centered on adultery?*"

But who is she talking to?

"*Would you answer me...?*"

"*Adultery was used... Ms. Zelle, because the novel was a middle class form of... entertainment. People could... identify with plots stemming from... copulation... because in general sex leads to drama. The middle class knew that; they saw it all the time. A love interest is... never included to soften the story arc. A love interest, Ms. Zelle, amps up the drama. If people... approached sex the way they... do most of their pleasures, it would be different. We are told that in the... 1960s people fucked whomever without worrying about... it. Hard to imagine. We've always put... a great deal of... stock in whom we sleep with. And we also... put a lot of stock in whether or not... we're sleeping with anyone at all. Throughout the... ages we've ascribed... morality to sex and sexuality, we've... fought wars over it, we've been... tortured by it, we've yearned for... it, we've even given it the euphemism... it. The most... abstract word possible in our language, but everyone... knows what you're talking about when you're talking about... it. As if speaking its... name would summon our dread overlords. And all for what ought to be... a pleasurable pastime."*

    "You still haven't..."

    "I often... wonder... if people don't actually enjoy... sex very much. They only... think they're supposed to. Now, when you want... a good meal, you go and eat that meal. When you want... to gamble, you go to a casino. But if we did... everything the way we go about... fucking... Imagine a bar where... to get inside you had to go through... an elaborate performance... and if you were... unsuccessful... they wouldn't let you in. Since boozing establishments aren't... accorded the same rank as sex, no one would put up with this... bullshit. They'd find another pub. And so, because we have come to... accept the morality of sex, because we have come to accept the... social institution of sex, we also accept the inherent... drama surrounding sex. If the thing itself were... good enough, we wouldn't need to... form narratives around it. Obviously... it's not good enough. So a mystique must be... built. And that mystique... felt by almost everyone... entices the largest possible crowd. Now, to carry that mystique even... further, we include the entire history of... infidelity–a scandalous act made even... more so. Therefore, in order to... ensnare Mr. Orcuson... in a trap impossible to... escape... in order to entice him on to action... in order to transform him into an... agent others would understand... in order to convince any prying... eyes afterwards, in short, in order to... create of him a character worthy of... scrutiny... you had to fuck him. You made him a man... before... he was only a child."

    "And that boy grew up to be... Abraham Lincoln."

    The Predicta sez: *Stalin's plan, according to Jacobsen, was to send a flying disc down the West Coast, and to have this disc land in Southern California. There, the pilots of the saucer, unearthly-looking beings who were actually genetically engineered humans developed by Nazi Dr. Josef Mengele, were to*

192

disembark from the craft where they would be mistaken for Martians. Martians clearly in league with the Soviets.

Are you trying to lose, Wall?

"Why are you... here?"

"You sent for me."

"I sent for you. I see. And where did you get... this flower?"

"From..."

"As I... suspected. You see, I did not... send for you. And this flower..."

Feedback pierces through the speakers until it becomes static.

The Predicta sez: *According to Stalin, the event would be "something that could sow terror in the hearts of the fearful imperialists and send panic-stricken Americans running into the streets." But on July 7, 1947, Stalin's botched plan crashed outside of Roswell, New Mexico.*

Back in the car you look ahead at the Predicta as if this were a drive-in with the world's smallest screen. It's you, Wall, so none of us are surprised that at this stage you've chosen to do nothing. You aren't starting the car, though it starts. You aren't easing the whale into reverse and then into drive to get around the Predicta, though that happens too. You haven't even put your feet on the pedals, your hands on the wheel, any driving instructor would be docking you major points right now, buddy. But the car is moving. And coming into view are the Perma-Shave ads,

NEVER FEAR,

NEVER WORRY,

YOU'LL FORGET

EVERYTHING

IN A HURRY

PERMA-SHAVE

What to do? Um, right, maybe that's best, lying down across the front seats so you can't see the road anymore. Only unnerving, unsettling things out there anyway. But as you lean back, something falls from your pocket, hits you square in the face, Wall. It's a picture. A picture of your contact, whoever he or whatever *it* may be. And you get the idea from this photo that, really, there's no escape.

The radio sez:

"*Orbiters, a while back we had Brahma Gupta on the show, the mathematician who worked on The Organization's headquarters. He wasn't here to talk about our mysterious intelligence agency per se, but what he said does apply, so I'm going to replay it here:*

"'*Uwen, you took geometry in school, yes?*'

"'*Sure. But I'd bet your grades were far better than mine.*'

"'*The geometry you take in your grade school, high school, yes, it is Euclid's geometry. It is based on straight lines and planes, triangles and pyramids and cones, circles and spheres, shapes that are coherent. But how often do we see such things in nature? Our universe is not smooth, flat, straight. Our universe is rough, asymmetrical. Euclid gave to us a good map. It is a map, all the same.*'

"*A map, Orbiters, or we could also say a metaphor. I believe one of our problems with The Organization is that we try to use Euclid's metaphor to understand it. I know that sounds too academic, so let's give this explanation a go: we try to say a tree is a circle on top of a rectangle, when really it isn't. A tree's shape is far more complex than that. It isn't smooth or straight, no matter how much we wish it were. Along these same lines, I'm going to play for you what Theo Reticle had to say about The Organization at the Association of Espionage and Intelligence Organizations United Conference (normally just called the AEIOU Conference).*

"'*There are those who believe that if we could go back to when The Organization began, whenever that was since we have evidence for its existence in the earliest eras of man, we could understand this agency better because we could observe its evolution. And so we spend a great deal of time trying to model the development of The Organization. There are so many people who say, these are the conditions, now what? It's become a kind of parlor game amongst mathematicians and theorists. But the problem is that each and every one of the conditions is important, and through the very act of giving conditions, you end up excluding other equally important conditions. You end up with a map, and not a particularly accurate one. The frustrated often throw up their hands and say, if only we could go back to the beginning, we could transform The Organization into something we understand. Maybe we could, but then we'd never know what it would have been. We wouldn't understand The Organization; we'd understand this new thing we created instead…'"*

The photograph: Hands about chest high pushing against the picture. Trying to break out of the billboard world. Trying to break into your world. The world you *live* in, Wall. Looked vaguely human, but not quite human. Not merely human. This shadow figure which can withstand the searing white. Sooner or later it *will* push into this world. It will. It will get loose. It will. Who knows but that it might come for you?

Actually, the only figure you're looking at Wall is the one standing behind The Conference Room bar: Furman Tayshawn, whom you've inexplicably (or, after all those Painkillers, maybe quite explicably) taken to calling Lloyd. He looks like a Lloyd. Maybe to dissuade you from drinking anymore right now, Lloyd's showing you his wall of what appear to be mini-washing machines, which he calls rotors, that constantly mix all of the slushy drinks The Conference Room serves up. Each washing machine is labeled, but the language, it appears to be multi-dimensional, having trouble wrapping your brain around it, sure, even kinda tough to make out the alphabet, and closing one eye doesn't help any. You do, however, get the distinct impression that if you drank every last drop from these rotors, you'd not only be able to comprehend this language, you might become its Shakespeare. Only one way to find out…

But Lloyd interrupts your experiment:

"Let's check out the engine room," he sez, and whisks you away, how you're mobile you're not entirely sure, seeing as how you can't imagine walking right now, let alone moving quite this quickly. Behind the wall of rotors is a bank of blinking lights the like of which would make any Xmas enthusiast seem like a regular Scrooge. In another state you'd be awed by all this twinkling, but the Painkillers don't seem to approve of the season of Santa Claus, and soon you're on the ground adding your own flurry of colors.

"Aww, boy, you need to get in the tank," sez Lloyd, and maybe he's a weightlifter or something because, effortlessly, he lifts you into an aquarium full of some kind of thick, viscous liquid. You'd think it was one of the drinks they serve here, except much to your surprise it's like a womb, amniotic, not cold, though once you're enclosed, uh, yeah, everything's moving, and that's when you end up back in the car. Sure. Why not? I mean, maybe it's the car. But how did you end up in the passenger seat? You're not out for a drive anymore, pal, you're out for a ride. Motoring through a desert toward a city made entirely of what appears to be neon, until the autopiloted automobile deposits you next to, what's that burned out sign? Oh, Another World Motel. (And if you were reading the reviews, Wall, you'd find someone had this to say: "There is a world where motels have clean blankets, clean towels, delicious room service, pleasant help, where cockroaches and even more undesirable critters do not thrive, where bodily fluids are not congealed throughout, where screaming bouts and gunshots are not the norm. But you aren't in that world, no, you're in Another World.")

Where in the hell are you?

"Vall ees in apartment vaiting," sez the big Russian standing next to a projector projecting an, oof, unfortunate picture of you up on the screen, buddy. Wait a minute here. What happened? You were in the car outside of a fleabag motel, and now you're looking at slides with a gigantic Kuzma (or, so sez his luggage tag). The room, a hellhole, sure, but it doesn't encourage much information gathering, except there is some information to be gathered from one feature: a mirror. Why does a place like this even have a mirror? Who in Another World would care what they looked like? By now, well shit, it's just inconceivable that no one's ever said, "Seven years bad luck? Ha! How could it get any worse?" Sure you agree, buddy, since what you see reflected: Kuzma, no surprise there, and then a person of unknown gender. Sir or madam. Who is it? What is he… or she doing here? As for you, Wall, looking at the glass, it's like those folks who couldn't show up when the photos were being taken for the yearbook: PICTURE UNAVAILABLE. With us in spirit…

Believe it or not, buddy, next door there's a gal who's watching the Conspiratorium's infomercial. She just dropped out of art school. She just dropped out of everything. But this ad, it reminds her of Salvador Dalí (goddamn art students, but what are ya gonna do?). It reminds her of *The Phantom of Vermeer of Delft Which Can Be Used As a Table* and *Enigmatic Elements in a Landscape*. It reminds her of a paper she wrote about the paranoiac-critical method where she talked about how paranoia's goal is the domination of the physical world by our own internal worlds, and that the masters of reality are those who get the most people to believe them; *They* write the narrative(s) of the world. Originally, having sickened of these narratives and unable to see any way to add her own, she'd come to Another World to kill herself. But don't worry. She's not gonna do it. When the commercial's over, she'll call the Char Le Tannes Institute and make an appointment. Her life will be changed. And you know what? She does get abducted later on. And, because of her time at the Conspiratorium, she not only understands all of the events, she even understands the meaning of the events. Maybe we should follow her instead. She's informed. Her story is coherent. Her responses make sense. Even when something out of the ordinary happens, she knows it's out of the ordinary. There is form. There is structure. There's emotion. There is meaning. She plays her part and she plays it well.

But instead we're stuck with you, Wall.

No, actually, you're stuck with us. Our zombie. You got out of the car because we wanted you to get out of the car (the camera in the Conspiratorium's ad moving through a spaceship, the budget apparently having gone up… uh, no, actually it's just a clip from *2001*), you walked through that anonymous vacuum of a parking lot because you were supposed to (the camera glides through space: planets, stars, comets, asteroids), you stopped in front of room 083 because it was part of the plan (the Spokeswoman as plastic and placating as ever), and you couldn't understand what the television next door was saying, even though it was loud enough to reach the very verge of the final frontier, because what would be the goddamned point?

"*After the conference, you will want to unwind, and what better way to do so than by seeing the entirety of the ship? Now your tour can be official or unofficial. If you choose an official tour, you will be shown around by a group of*

197

visitors. *If you select an unofficial tour, you will either be guided along by a rogue crewmember, or you will be on your own. No matter what, you should take in the sights. See the engine room, or the command center. See where the visitors live and relax. Maybe you would like a different kind of tour, one that has very little to do with the vessel itself. Perhaps you wish to journey to a distant world, or to a hidden portion of earth. Will your voyage take you underwater, through vast extraterrestrial oceans? Will you travel underground to the center of this or some other planet? Will you cross a desert? Will you visit a futuristic city made of alien technology? Or will you trek through a jungle populated by unidentifiable beasts? Will you, much to your surprise, find other humans on these far-flung worlds? Or will you opt for an Out of Body Experience? With the help of the Conspiratorium, the choice is yours!"*

When the hour struck, someone on the inside of room 083 started knocking. Maybe he wanted to see if anyone was home in the world, Wall. And when you were finally pulled through the doorway, that's right, pal, nothing you could do about it, Kuzma, that big Russian, kissing you passionately, with tongue, and you powerless to get away.

The Predicta sez: *There is one problem with Jacobsen's Stalin/Mengele theory. Not a single reputable source agrees with her recount. It even defies logic. If we learned that the Soviets were in league with someone like Mengele, why wouldn't we tell the world about it?*

If nothing else, the Predicta classes the place up a bit…

The big Russian, after finally letting you go, moved to set up a projector.

"I'm wondering why you've called me here," sez the man or woman in the mirror.

"I have put together dots," sez Kuzma. "All dots."

All of them ever?

The Predicta sez: *For years, these were the major theories used to explain what happened at Roswell: the weather balloon, Project Mogul, aliens, even Stalin. But now a new culprit has been found.*

Roman saluting aviators stand around a flying saucer.

The projector's fan sounds like some futuristic engine.

"Here you see Renato Fregoli and Agent Pseudo-Habermohl vorking een my country. Een Soviet Union. They vere preesoners. Your papa got close and learnt about Explodium." A snowy mineshaft opening. "Nazis use Explodium for saucer fuel. Also secret veapon. Location of secret veapon…" The Hyperborean Arms' promotional rendering, drawn before it was built. "…under apartment buildeeng. Acteevation of veapon: vhen drama is at peak." An Asian bartender at the Long Bar at Raffles Hotel. "After Fregoli testify against Agent Pseudo-Habermohl, he escapet Soviet Union. No vun stop him. Vent to Seengapore vhere he met bartender Ngiam Tong Boon. Bartender goot to know. He hear seengs. Bartender Ngiam and Fregoli put eentelleegence together in recipe book." An ornate book: dark red and gold. "Book contains Nazi planz in Antarcteeca, Hollow Earth, Luna, and earth eenvasion. Also contains dreenks." A drink called a Zombie and then a host of pictures of obviously different people, though all are labeled "Renato Fregoli," on Wainiwidiwiki Island. "Fregoli moves to small island, draws up plans for A. Parachroni, deesappears or ees murrderred." Two children outside of a house with the outline of Canada superimposed on it. "Fregoli sends cheeldren to Canada… Oh, my Ima." Overtaken by passion, the Russian leans in for another kiss. Are you getting used to this, Wall? "Nannies raise cheeldren. Fregoli vorks on plan to expose Nazis. Seenks people eenterested een truth." The front page of the *Roswell Daily Record* from July 8, 1947.

The Predicta sez: *Jacobsen and the people who believe the Soviets were behind Roswell overlook the fact that both Russian and English were found on the spacecraft. And we know why. Roswell was the fallout of an American–Soviet attempt to fly a disc to the moon in 1947. Obviously, it failed.*

Do you notice, Wall, how in the mirror it looks as if the Predicta and its obelisk-like stand were superimposed onto your reality? Almost a trompe l'oeil kinda thing going on.

"After Rosvell, most people seenk of UFOs as fantasy. Not real. But dere are zose who leesten." A tall, thin man in a black suit. "Owen G. Asbestos. Vorks for American government. No known agency. Does not vant eenformation een book to get out. Hunts for Fregoli. Supposedly finds heem. Supposedly murrderrs heem. Can't locate book." Another bartender at the Long Bar in Singapore. "Before death, Fregoli broke book eento four parts, handed parts off to Donn Beach, Veector Bergeron, and Ngiam Tong Boon. Two parts for Tong Boon. Later hands parts off to son: Ngiam Dee Suan. Younger Ngiam ees smart. Keeps hees parts moveeng unteel Fregoli seeblings are old enough." The grown Iam Fregoli holding the book. "Last known photograph of brother unteel recently. Many disguises." The 1961 New York Yankees. "Hides under surnames of Bronx Bombers." Roger Maris hitting a weak grounder to Hoyt Wilhelm. "Last known alias, 'Kipper Maris.' No one quite sure what ees hees plan." The ICU home office. "It might eenvolve seelly TV station…" The so-called Edward R. Murrow sitting in front of a microphone with the initials CNS stenciled onto it. "…and radio. No one knows how." Another tall, thin man in a black suit. "C. Irving Asbestos takes up vhere father left off. He ees more conniving. Asbestos builds triangle between Iam, hees vife Greta Zelle…" A picture of Greta from her days as a stripper. "…and Vallace Orcuson. Patsy." Pretty unflattering picture of you there, buddy. Say, how many years have you had that hangover for? Come on, have you ever heard of a comb? And, uh, yeah, patsy. Never gets easier, does it? Never gets easier hearing that. Never gets easier playing your part, huh?

The Predicta sez: *But why did the Americans and the Soviets try to rush to the moon using technology they hadn't even grasped yet?*

"Everytheeng ees set up. Iam ees at hees Tiki bar and vill go to Hyperborean later. Zelle ees at ICU. Asbestos ees at library. Vall ees een apartment vaiting. Now, vhat do ve do?"

The Predicta sez: *The answer is: they thought they had their enemy on the run.*

A long pause.

"Thanks for briefing me so early in this operation," you say.

"Ima …"

"Are you even certain this 'Senator' Kipper Maris is my brother? He could be one of Iam's doubles. He could be in with Asbestos. Or with anyone else. I spent my day trying to find out what's been going on. Mostly, I learned they, or I should say you have a fall guy…"

"Ima…"

"A fall guy for my brother's murder."

"Ve can stop…"

"Shut up! I still don't know how Iam got the book together. He had my part. He stole my part before I could ever even see it. Where the hell did he find the Beach and Bergeron copies?"

"He vork een Tiki bars."

The Predicta sez: *Even in the 1950s, when the quote unquote successful mission to the moon lifted off, the two quote unquote superpowers thought they were dealing with wounded prey.*

"I have to see him."

"No, Ima. No," sez Kuzma putting his arm around you, trying to comfort you, to protect you. Doesn't feel too bad, does it, Wall? No one's been this nice, well… sir or madam in the mirror starts shaking, tears streaming down his or her face.

"I have to. You think I'm going to leave it up to you?!"

"Zen here. Take zees," sez Kuzma, handing you a 7.65mm Walther PPK.

"I'm not going to kill him! That's what…"

"He might keel you."

The Predicta sez: *When the Nazis decimated the American-Soviet attack, the two quote unquote superpowers finally saw their place in the universe.*

"You're… you're right… He might be fanatical enough now. I hope it isn't him. I hope this is all just another red…"

"Also, Organeezation might be eenvolved."

"*The* Organization?"

"Da."

"Then anything could happen."

"True, but I might have plan…"

You and Kuzma sit in Another World, his arm around you, Wall, holding you tight in front of the obelisk-like Predicta. And maybe he has a plan to save Iam, a plan to save you, a plan to save us all. It seems likely in that hellhole. Things can only get better from here, uh, right? Sure, maybe there's so much you want to say, so many questions you want to ask, but you feel warm and secure folded into the Russian, as if you've known him for years, and you fear words would shatter this newborn tranquil, fragile dimension, only silence can preserve it, stillness, the two of you staring ahead, the tears drying into salt on your cheeks, the saline blur replaced by a haze as your puffy eyes strain to make sense of the utterly nonsensical...

Speaking of, you're back in your place, Wall.

"Do you know where you are?" sez the voice on the phone. Your old pal Mr. E., maybe? Anyway, *back* might not've been the right word. You never left.

The radio sez: *Uwen, The Organization's agents, when we talk about them, are often split up into two categories: those who work linearly and those who work nonlinearly...*

"Do you know what's happened?" sez the voice on the phone. What, you don't believe this is your place? Look around, and, uh, sure, right, the Predicta's right where it always is, and there's that behemoth of a radio with the picture of Edward R. Murrow on top, but something doesn't seem quite right.

The Predicta sez: *Another theory is that the Nazis, recognizing the US and the USSR might be a threat in the outer space portion of the real World War Two, gave the Soviets, via Pseudo-Habermohl and Renato Fregoli, Flugkreisel technology.*

"This isn't your apartment," sez the voice, and then, what seems like way too quickly, the phone starts making that off-the-hook racket, only hanging it up doesn't solve anything. The sound continues, continues as you wonder where your World War Two propaganda poster is, continues as you look around again and notice a gigantic painting in its place, continues as you look at the car impaled on a tree, continues as your eyes avoid the foreground and so fall on the blasted landscape, on the imposing cliff-face, on the smooth desert, on the inexplicable dresser burping out underwear from its top drawer, continues as the town of Delft rises (for you) from the background (but the boats, the boats, where are the boats, their absence mutating into an ever more menacing presence), continues as a grating sound, can feel it in your teeth, in your fillings, joins the phone, oh, buddy, if you'd seen the Conspiratorium's infomercial, even if you'd laughed it off, you'd know what's going on, you in your white tux (uh, where'd that come from?), you'd fall back into your chair (is the cacophony from the handset ever gonna reach its crescendo?) and, hell, buddy, it'd be like the Spokeswoman had come into your room for a personal recording of the infomercial, in all of her uncanny, plastic glory, relating your realization moment to you, for you:

"Mr. Orcuson, it is true that the Conspiratorium, along with all abductees, must endure Missing Time. But it is the place of the chronicler, not of the hero, to remember. That is why the Char Le Tannes Institute employs only elite, triple certified hypnotherapists to assist in the reclamation of your memories. We will help you remember that long drive from Another World, for instance. You will even find that, through Trance Therapeutics (a treatment performed only at the Conspiratorium), you can recall far more than you ever thought possible: tastes, smells, physical sensations, even what was on the radio as you drove: *The problem with splitting The Organization's agents into linear and nonlinear is that, well, it's like splitting zoology into the study of elephants and non-elephants...*' and roadside signs:

TWINKLE, TWINKLE,

LITTLE CAR

DO YOU KNOW

JUST WHERE

YOU ARE?

PERMA-SHAVE

and billboards. Billboards. Billboards. Oh, Mr. Orcuson, it's not a billboard anymore. It's three dimensional now. And the shadow is pulling the light with it. Stronger than the light. The reason for the existence of the light. The face is blurry. Just out of focus. But coming into focus. The face slowly stretching through the membrane it's hardly trapped behind. The creature starting to press through. Testing its barrier. Gaining confidence. Determined to emerge, to erupt from the conquered billboard world. Determined to enter your world, Mr. Orcuson. We will then help you remember arriving at 'Senator' Kipper Maris' tiki bar office. What were you doing there? The Abduction Artists and Trance Therapists at the Conspiratorium are nonjudgmental. Your reasons are your own. Our only goal is to retrieve the information from your mind. For example, when you followed 'Senator' Maris to the Hyperborean Arms, keeping your distance so he could not tell that you were tailing him. I am now obligated to remind you that the Char Le Tannes Institute is not responsible for your actions. We only shine a light on what is already there. *'Just who works for The Organization, then? Being so vast, there are those who believe everyone works for them. This couldn't possibly be true...'* Were you surprised that 'Senator' Maris drove to your building? During our sessions, we have found nothing that sez so. How did you know to go to room #8? Why did you trace the number with your finger? And where did you get the gun? The Conspiratorium, though we seek out cabalistic secrets everywhere so the public may be truly informed, still supports the Constitution and its Amendments. Your gun ownership is a personal choice. One service the institute does provide: if a memory seems too harmful, we will protect you from it by reinducing amnesia through the use of Perm..."

But there will be no realization moment for you, Wall. Instead, you sit in this room in front of the Predicta near the radio beside the painting, completely ignorant, the racket getting louder and louder.

The radio sez: *Another theory is that none of The Organization's agents know they work for The Organization. Of course, it's likely the case that, occasionally, operatives do not know just who they are working for. But that could hardly always be the case...*

The Predicta sez: *It is believed, however, that Fregoli was against the plan. He therefore botched the construction of the disc so the Americans would know what the Nazis were up to. Fregoli would later escape to Singapore and then disappear, some say to an uncharted island, others claim he was never heard from again.*

Wall, how come the Predicta and the radio are set to stadium-level volume? Like a World Series, top of the ninth, home team one out from the championship kinda loud? Nope, there aren't any other sounds. And what's that light coming from underneath the couch? So bright, that intensity's normally only reserved for stars.

"USE PERMA-SHAVE IN / LIQUID OR PILL / THEN LET / SOMEONE ELSE / PICK UP THE BILL."

So, uh, did you get a job as a copywriter, Wall?

The couch moves back and beneath is the rectangle of searing light. The refulgence burns into your brain, Wall. Burns through your eyes. You believe you are blind. You are not blind. Blindness would be an escape. There is no escape. The figure pushes out against the membrane until the shadow and the membrane are one. It rises, the resplendence tracing an outline that's both human and not human. Its movements are erratic. Double-jointed. It is once again two-dimensional. It does not appear superimposed onto your reality. Reality is a green-screen projection behind this figure. The world is special effects. It is real. Its substance is darkness.

Kin to the figures in the foreground of the painting. *Apparition of the Town of Delft* by Salvador Dalí, as it turns out.

Um...

The radio sez: *My favorite hypothesis is that everyone is always both working for and against The Organization. To determine which, however, is almost impossible because if you try to prove someone is, say, working for The Organization, you'll find that you're right. But now test to see if that same person is working against The Organization, and you'll find you're right again...*

The Predicta sez: *But there is a far simpler explanation for what happened. Two years after World War Two supposedly ended, no one wanted to hear that the Nazis were stronger than ever...*

"*You*," you say, Wall.

"Close. Try again," sez Mr. E.

"Right..."

205

"Are you ready?"

"What's *ready*? Am I supposed to be ready?"

"No."

"Then I guess I am. I'm ready to be unprepared for anything and everything."

"Perfect. You are a credit to your Order." And you realize where you are. It's the Puppet Regime's chapter room at Jamais Vu. Some reason, feels like your apartment too, doesn't it, Wall? Yeah...

"It makes me all warm and fuzzy inside to hear you say that. Seriously. When I croak, they'll pull more warm fuzz out of my corpse than guts or veins. Probably'll go down as the cause of death even. 'Worst case of the warm and fuzzies I've ever seen.'"

"Can't you feel it?"

"Feel what?"

"The building of events, the tension."

"No. I'm not used to this. Normally, I don't show up until the action's over..."

"I am the same."

"...if you see me enter, you know the excitement has passed."

"That's how it is with my race. Usually..."

"Oh?"

"But this time was different. I was early. I was not a momento mori. I was a prediction. Accurate, as it turned out."

"What happens now?" sez you.

"We wait," sez Mr. E.

"For what?"

"For the events that follow."

"I guess I've met the members of the Puppet Regime. The Gestapo, right? But what about the higher ups?"

"They've been watching from the beginning; you will never meet them."

"For all those listening in, if it matters, I didn't kill anyone."

"It doesn't matter."

"Somehow, I knew you'd say that. None of this feels real."

"You need to embrace reality."

"Reality?"

"Reality. That which everyone experiences differently, though we all claim it's the same, and anyone who sez otherwise is considered a lunatic. It's made up of random occurrences we think happen for a reason, coincidences we find meaningful, and blank spaces our minds edit out for rhythm. It is made up of solids and liquids and gasses, a mélange of verifiable evidence, but it is supported by, rests on another world we can barely comprehend and often pretend doesn't exist. Reality."

The radio sez: *Orbiters, there is one final piece about The Organization I want to bring up: their insignia. There are those who claim The Organization has no insignia of its own. Instead, supposedly, our mysterious intelligence agency uses other agencies' insignias, sometimes changing them in small ways, sometimes in quite obvious, dramatic ways. If this were true, it'd be fairly simple to learn who worked for The Organization. But it's only true sometimes. I've heard those who believe that the spiral should be The Organization's insignia. But the spiral is a normal attractor that moves toward a single point. Others say, why not the infinity symbol? Better, certainly. However, I would like to propose the multi-dimensional strange attractor. That bizarre shape you used to see on computer screensavers. So, if anyone out there works for The Organization, or knows someone who works for them, my idea is free of charge...*

"I'd say I'm getting tired of this, but I was tired when it started," you say.

"You might as well take a nap," sez Mr. E.

"Earlier you said I'm a credit to my Order. Is there anything I could do to get discredited?"

"Suicide."

"You ever think about starting a hotline? Anyone who called in could tell you their problems after they'd already decided what they were gonna do. If what they decided matches what you say, they'd know it's the

207

worst possible choice."

"It may be that in the past you were no one, nothing, like me. But now you will be someone, you will be something."

"But I want nothing to do with this."

"Unfortunately, this wants everything to do with you."

The Predicta sez: *So when a Flugkreisel crashed into New Mexico, a host of rational and outrageous theories were given. The Roswell Propaganda Industry is even alive and kicking to this very day. Movies, books, TV shows. All to cover up the fact that the Nazis are still around, biding their time, waiting to attack.*

And with another blip, Wall, you're asleep on the couch, your couch, in your apartment, sawing logs, Mr. E. nowhere to be seen, the radio and the Predicta still broadcasting, but their transmissions fall on dead ears.

The radio sez: *The Organization is still out there. And even after this show, I'm not sure how much closer we are to understanding them. Perhaps forever and always this mysterious intelligence agency will serve the Unknown Empire, performing its incomprehensible espionage. Thank you for tuning in, everyone. I'm going to send you back to your own orbit now. Wherever that may be...*

The Predicta sez: *World War Two didn't end in 1945. It had hardly even begun. And the proof fell to earth outside of a small desert town in New Mexico two years after victory had been prematurely declared.*

Somewhere the Conspiratorium's infomercial sez: *Being abducted is an ordeal few are able to handle, but with the Char Le Tannes Institute, you can cope. We can guide you through the steps. We can prepare you for your experience. We can design your ordeal so it is as beneficial as possible. We are here for you. The Char Le Tannes Institute and Conspiratorium. Call us now.* A spotlight comes out of the sky, focuses on the SPOKESWOMAN. *Before... it is too late.*

And then, for whatever reason, it sez this on the screen: You Lose. What game were you playing?

A whirring sound, Wall, even that sci-fi theremin, the stage lights turned toward you (what theatre is this again?), only those aren't the stage lights, those've been turned off, this new luminescence comes from above, still lets you see the performer, though, a rumpled looking man who must be hilarious because everyone in the house is on the verge of laughter, you too, until you realize they're all frozen in time, an audience sculpture. This otherworldly light lifts you from your seat, lifts you out of the theatre, and sets you on the ground outside. Uh, what're you supposed to do now? Go for a walk? Why not? Your legs are long, so the ground speeds by underneath, granted, you're still wondering if maybe that light from above has anything to do with it, and if it has anything to do with the fact that you seem to be getting shorter, growing younger, but no slower. It's not just the ground that speeds by, maybe time does too, are we headed to the future? You arrive in a vast desert, a place that doesn't exist, a place with many names, a place with no name, and here you are confronted by a colossus, with the other colossi it'd be a beanpole, sure, but to you it's mammoth, the upper portion covered by clouds, its shadow extending not just to the horizon, but through dimensions, throughout history, a shadow you think created history, bent the light of time around itself, erasing everything else. The legend at the base of the colossus reads: THE GREAT MAN, and as the clouds move away, you turn, terrified to look upon that fierce visage, a god that threatens to awaken, that will awaken, that will devour the lesser… sure, right, a narrative absolutely no one should buy into, but pretty much everyone believes. The surrounding terrain is no better, though. Laid out underneath THE GREAT MAN is what appears to be sand and salt stretching in all directions, only your eyes are suddenly stronger, and you can see infinitesimal structures, spreading rhizomatically, tiny, but no less awful in their power, giving you the impression that they don't reflect the sun, no no no, they *generate* light, a sparkling, hypnotic light like you find in the casino town to the south that was originally in this very county, a light that illuminates nothing, that dazzles everyone, old Sol blotted out ages ago, a light so bright you can't see how dark the world actually is, can't see that shadow isn't about to engulf the entire planet, naw, it already has, and thanks to this boundless, though miniscule organization, you can't see the penumbra unless you know how to look for it. Believe me, you have no idea, man. And so you turn back, stare into the face of THE GREAT MAN, top hat, beard with no mustache, lazy eyes, mole, beak of a schnozz, messy hair, his shadow threatening to obliterate you (it will not), while the light from below threatens to beguile you (it cannot), before you accept who you are, before you take to ambling eastward, much slower this time, your young legs unafraid to stroll through the… well… yeah!, *shade* cast by the statue, unafraid to reveal the darkness the light covers up, this *child* just confronted THE GREAT MAN, this *child* confronted the nameless desert, and now, whoever he is, he treks for home.

Out of a spinning saucer, a group of grays beams onto the sand, watching you walk to your destiny, saying:

"And that boy grew up to be… Abraham Lincoln."

§

Ladies and gentlemen, Edward R. Murrow sits catatonic in the Hyperborean Arms. He holds a gun.

"Here," says Kuzma, handing Murrow a bottle from which he drinks without thinking.

"I found him…" motioning to the dead man in front of the couch.

"Da. Dreenk. Dreenk. All done?"

Murrow hands the bottle of Milk of Amnesia back to Kuzma.

"I found him here. He's dead. I think… I think Orcuson killed him. But…"

"Nyet. You deed."

"Wha…?"

"You deed."

"I didn't…" Murrow looks down and sees… "Oh no," he drops the gun to the ground.

"Da. Now ve build cover up," sez Agent Bezopasnosky, pulling *Vayss Uf Makink You Tock* from a messenger bag. "Orcuson is murrderrerr. Narrate."

"But…"

"Vhat?"

Pause. A blank look on Murrow's face. He appears lost, confused as to how he got there.

"Nothing."

While he prepares to narrate, ladies and gentlemen, you should know there is an omission in the manuscript. One portion of the Uwen Farr Oarbytt show informs us that whenever The Organization's plans appear to be the most coherent, those plans are either red herrings or they don't actually come from The Organization at all. This has been the problem in the past. The fact that so many intelligence agencies think they can understand what The Organization is doing, when no one has ever been able to comprehend anything until the operation is concluded. And sometimes not even then.

DesGuise: The Organization sounds like it influenced A. Parachroni.

Surprised listeners of Radioland, joining us now is ufologist Paisen DesGuise. Do you have some credible evidence about A. Parachroni? So far, we've only gotten wild conjecture and nonsensical movie references...

DesGuise: I suppose you'll have to be the judge. Our task force started with the idea that A. Parachroni, Inc. is a front, and therefore went looking for its real owner. But we couldn't find one. Actually, if our information is correct, A. Parachroni operates a number of fronts itself. Some of them are even in competition with other A. Parachroni fronts. Let's take the constant reports from ICU in your *Vayss Uf Makink You Tock* for an aggregate example, alright? First, we know, there's a group whose goal is to expose the Moon Nazi coverup (they're called Nazi Hunters on the Moon). Fair enough. Next, as is always the case in conspiracist circles, there's another group that claims Nazi Hunters on the Moon is wrong, that no humans live on our only satellite, but there are aliens (this group's called The Lunarians Live!). Yet another group claims that the United States and the Soviet Union destroyed Luna by testing Top Secret weapons there in the 1950s, and that what we now see in the sky at night-time is a powerful projection (this cell's called The Moon's Forever New). And, as is also always the case, each one of these organizations (and

211

there are many, many more) infiltrate each other, spy on each other, convert members so they now believe whatever, instead of believing whatever they did before...

What do these fringe crazies have to do with A. Parachroni?

DesGuise: They're all fronts for A. Parachroni. A. Parachroni has a hand in each and every one of them.

But they don't agree. In fact, they don't even agree with Renato Fregoli, the founder...

DesGuise: I'm well aware. But then we don't have verifiable evidence that there really ever was a Renato Fregoli.

Except that he had kids.

DesGuise: Or two people are using his name, anyhow. Think about it like this, all of these fronts that A. Parachroni operates use astroturfing to spread their ideas. And the term astroturfing comes from AstroTurf, so named for the first team to play on that artificial surface: the Houston Astros. But the Houston Astros' home stadium no longer has any AstroTurf. The name is historical, but no longer accurate. Perhaps we can see Renato Fregoli's connection with A. Parachroni in the same way. Once, A. Parachroni operated Nazi Hunters on the Moon because that was the founder's passion. But now, as corporations will, A. Parachroni's expanded beyond its original scope. AstroTurf no longer references the team that plays on it.

What could the purpose possibly be?

DesGuise: Isn't it obvious? Renato Fregoli, if there ever were such a person, supposedly wanted to expose the Moon Nazi Conspiracy, but he knew that wasn't going to be easy. He claims the Explodium on Wainiwidiwiki Island (that argument about it being covered in fertilizer is all fertilizer itself), he claims the Explodium in Nevada, so there'll be fuel for the flying discs. But he needs people to be skeptical about the history they've been given. The more conspiracy theories there are, the more skeptical people get. And this tactic, it's working. People in general are convinced that the real story never sees the light of day, the real story about anything. Or, at least, that's the way it seems. We don't actually know any of A. Parachroni's motives.

At least you were a bit more coherent than our other correpondents in talking about this baffling corporation, Mr. DesGuise. As for you, perplexed and persevering listeners of Radioland, thank you for tuning in today. And, if you can, please support our sponsor, Pilgrim & Pagan Donuts. I highly recommend the Mystery Donut. It's out of this world.

And now this...

Four

The Throwing of the Butterfly Ball

Are the saucers here already?

Does that explain the interference?

Last night, while the whole world was asleep, yes, *everyone at the same time*, somehow the entire planet having gone dark, no one thinking anything of it, huh, might as well get some shuteye, I mean I've been on the hunt for so long, it's about goddamn time I finally caught those ZZZs, well during that period of slumber, the known and even the unknown cabals (both terrestrial and extra) remained awake, alert, no rest for the wicked as it were, to discuss a pressing topic, something of the utmost import, the highest priority, namely that unaffiliated, uninitiated, "independent" humans (in other words, those who weren't in a cabal) all over the Earth believed, indeed truly believed that the assembled nefarious organizations had wired microphones to intercept personal conversations, had hidden cameras to film intimate and embarrassing moments, had planted bugs to capture telephonic exchanges, had launched and stabilized in orbit satellites that steal thoughts, had built radio towers and laid fiber optic lines to fill the public with mystifying impulses, and if any of these devices failed to work, the assorted conspirators always had surgeons at the ready to implant microchips and nanobots so the manifold devious syndicates would always know exactly what the public was thinking, saying, doing, and if the thoughts, words, actions were unacceptable, heh heh heh, well... behavior modification would not be a problem. For the lay populace, this covert intelligence collection and manipulation was as obvious as the black helicopters in the sky. The meeting therefore covered why, uh, um, you know, the secret cabals hadn't, right, gotten around to any of that stuff yet. Seems like we should've. Seems like, uh, a good idea... Silence, only disturbed by that cartoon blinking sound. Plink. Plink. A legion of forgetful school children shuffled their papers, looked at each other, confused. Then a flurry of activity, every single operative in on the hastily constructed, uh, *plan*? (word being used so loosely here it threatens to negate all definitions for all words, in turn almost destroying the very concept of language itself), until, still under the cloak of darkness, absolutely everything was covered with microphones, cameras, satellite uplinks, bugs, fiber optic cables, and myriad types of suppressed and otherwise hidden pieces of crypto-technology, better late than never. Now, every shred of metal and glass was a receiver and a speaker, every surface could record and transmit visuals, yes, a ubiquitous telecommunications network that could broadcast not only through space, but also through time.

Of course there was a glitch.

Actually, yeah, lots of glitches.

What was intended to be a ubiquitous telecommunications network became a worldwide white noise machine that soon jammed everything.

Static. On the Predicta, on the radio, static, nothing can be tuned in, nothing at all, just a universal call for silence which itself ensures there will be none:

shshshshshshshshshshshshshshshshshshshs
shshshshshshshshshshshshshshshshshshshs

216

shshshshshshshshshshshshshshshshshshshs

shshshshshshshshshshshshshshshshshshshs

shshshshshshshshshshshshshshshshshshshs

shshshshshshshshshshshshshshshshshshshs

The sound is so pervasive, you try to convince yourself it's playing in your brain when you're nowhere near a radio or TV, ignoring the fact that the forks and the windows and your filing cabinet and your wine glasses are all transmitting that noise. It's like a bad pop song or commercial jingle that's stuck in your head, you hear it everywhere, you think this sound will go on forever, will be the last thing you or anyone else ever... And then, *at long last*, reception. Sweet reception. Beautiful reception. The interference... or cosmic microwave background radiation ... well it's gone, though none of the appliances seem to work right, not even the toaster ... and it constantly sounds like a radio is on in the other room ...

EUCHRE: ...and it's a beee-utiful day for football. At a less than balmy forty-two degrees, we're ready to pile on the pads, strap on the helmets, and charge out onto the old gridiron...

...though when you walk into that room, yeah, you guessed it, it sounds like a radio is on in yet another room...

EUCHRE: ...But, foax, we're playing baseball. The last game of the season...

...and, sure, you see Predicta screens everywhere, brick walls, marble floors, hovering in mid-air, but there's no need to fear, technical difficulties is all, happens now and then, 's way it is. Look, hunker down, shrug your shoulders, grab yourself a beer (or twelve). Until further notice, all electrical communication systems are on the fritz...

Awakening without a hangover (for once), Wall again has the feeling he's never been here before. And this time, uh, yeah, he's probably right, since surrounding our persecuted protagonist is... um... sand. Sand and salt. The kitchen's gone, the bathroom's gone, the bed's gone, the door's gone, the telephone's gone, all of the propaganda posters are gone, as are

217

the two couches and the chair, though everything has been chalk outlined and labeled, as if the blueprints for the Hyperborean weren't filed in some government office somewhere, naw, they're right here on the ground in one-to-one scale. A Predicta screen does appear over the space marked Predicta, showing a swarm of Flugkreisels bedecked with that new Nazi insignia descending from the sky as *Flight of the Valkyries* plays. The chalk radio, not to be outdone, though, well, I'd say it sounds like it's coming from next door, except from what you can see, Wall, there aren't any doors for miles around…

EUCHRE: *And foax this one's for, you guessed it, absolutely none of the marbles. Both the Minnesota Twins and the Texas Rangers have been eliminated from playoff contention, the Twinkies standing at 80-81, while the Lone Star State representatives come in at 81-80. Just for fun, today's a throwback game, both clubs wearing uniforms from 1942, meaning it looks like we only have one team playing out there, and that team's called the Senators, half the club in their home pinstripes, the other half in their road grays, everyone sporting a blue W. Of course, both the Minnesota and Texas franchises originally played in our nation's capital before they moved to their current locales. Trotting in from the bullpen is Senators' knuckleballer Arthur Magam, Arty Magam, foax. This meeting of also-rans should be an interesting one, since in this kind of weather that dry spitter can really dance…*

To everyone out there in Radioland, the pre-game's over and Arty Magam, our donut clerk, has taken the mound in front of the Pilgrim & Pagan counter. He's toed the rubber. And here's the first pitch! For all anyone knows, ladies and gentlemen, it might be a strike. Next to the cash register, before our knuckleheaded knuckleballer, are nine mangled stacks of what appears to be, or, perhaps, what used to be the manuscript for *Vayss Uf Makink You Tock*, each pile labeled with a card covered in a chicken scratch so illegible, it was likely inspired by the entire hen house. But thanks to handwriting expert Otto Graff, we know what each card says: Greta Zelle, Kuzma Grigorovich Bezopasnosky, Myself, C. Irving Asbestos, Mr. E., Ima Fregoli, Wallace Heath Orcuson, Some Guy, Iam Fregoli. According to

218

Loman Drab, our reviewer of the airwaves, however, there's nothing that says this is the correct order, or, judging by the condition of the various pages, that a proper order even exists. Seated at his normal booth is Edward R. Murrow. Covered in sweat, hands shaking, red-cracked eyes darting, it appears that our narrator has had entirely too much coffee. The jitters won't stop him, though, as he pops some aspirin, gets up, and retrieves the first stack of the... what's left of the manuscript.

On the way to his booth, he stops. He stops and stares.

"Arty? Arty, does it ever seem like none of this is actually happening?" says Murrow.

"What?" says Arty.

"Never mind. Can I get some more coffee?" says Murrow, returning to his booth.

A radio somewhere sez:

EUCHRE: ...stee-rike three! Magam sends down his second batter. That butterfly ball is really fluttering. Now, joining us in the booth today, foax, is baseball historian and knuckleball expert Count O.N. Tu. Count O.N. Tu, everyone. By the way, how'd you become a count?

TU: Actually, that's...

EUCHRE: Is it because you love to count?

TU: Hilarious. No. That's actually my given name.

EUCHRE: One, one man who lacks a sense of humor. Ah ah ah! Anyway, give us a quick one: why is a baseball game nine innings long?

TU: Very little is known about the early years of baseball, but one of the explanations is that it's because the number of players on a side is nine. Nine players on a side. [Long pause.] Ah. Ah. Ah!

EUCHRE: Maybe there's hope for you after all, Count. And with that line out, we've come to the bottom of the first. This is George Euchre, radio voice of, I guess, the Washington Senators...

Back through the one-way glass (which is somehow still there, hovering), sitting in the chalk outline of the Hyperborean Arms, well, there's nothing for poor old Wall to do but listen to the intermittent radio and

Predicta transmissions being blown in on the desert wind, stare at himself in the mysterious mirror, and check the mail. Because there's a mailbox. Outside of the chalk outline. It's a ways off, but clearly visible. Just turn your head a bit and you couldn't help but see it, Wall. It's right there. A mailbox. Even your lazy ass can't resist this one. Yeah…

The Predicta sez: *In 1947, two events coincided proving the recent world conflict hadn't been what it appeared to be. The events were Admiral Byrd's return from the Antarctic and the Roswell UFO Incident.*

At the mailbox, do you get the feeling, pal, that this is like it? Do you already hear yourself saying, futurewise, "Had I but known then what I know now…" even though then is now and now might never come? Are ya, and don't hold back, are ya already imagining various compounding and concatenated events that'll lead to some dark conclusion? And if you *are* thinking along those lines, do you also wonder why you're starting to narrate your own life as if it were a mystery novel? There's a reason, buddy. You're sick. You got it bad. Real bad. Condition's called Agathopathy, though it ought to be named Rinehart's Disease…

A puff of smoke wafts in from behind you, Wall, as you pull a coal-colored envelope out of the mailbox.

The Predicta sez: *Admiral Byrd saw Nazi discs over Antarctica. In Roswell, we actually captured a wrecked saucer.*

And you don't have to turn around to see whose smoking because big, powerful hands turn you around.

The Predicta sez: *After Antarctica. After Roswell… Look, we learn that in World War Two the Allies won and the Axis lost. We learn that the Nazis are no more. We learn that the global conflict was fought from 1939-1945. Wrong. That was all theatre. Fake. The real war hasn't even begun…*

And standing there in the sand, so happy to see you, dressed in their desert khaki best with the usual triangular armbands, mirrored goggles not so much protecting them from the ultraviolet rays, instead reflecting those rays right at you, Wall, as if they were themselves fiends of fire, avatars of flame…

...The Real *Second World War, an ICU exclusive...*

...yes, before you once again are, who else...

...ICU, the history of this world...

...the Gestapo...

...and others.

The Gestapo.

For dramatic effect, Major Freytag enjoys his cigarette a little longer. Schmetterling has no drama, since he's still a block of meat.

The Predicta sez: *In order to understand where we are now, we need a little history which probably would've been called crypto-history before...*

"Vhen ve met you, Herr Schtein, ve tolt you zat zomesink had just happent or vas about to happen. Unt now, look how right ve vere on boz accounts! I zee somevun ist even sendink to you die Erpressung. Blackmail."

"Nah, Major. I was..."

"Zilence! Ve haff had enough uf your tock. You haff tvisted sinks around, ja. Unt maybe it vas even entertainink... for avhile, Herr Schtein. No more! Now ve continue on. Unt vhere voult our Geschichte-story-be vithout your luffer unt former stripper, Greta Zelle?"

The Predicta sez: *On February 14, 1942, the Nazis landed on the moon where they found the ruins of an alien colony, obviously built by the same civilization that at one time resided below Antarctica. Amongst the ruins was a strange shrine composed of glass tubes containing books. Each tube had a button at the bottom.*

Schmetterling grabs you by the shoulders, Wall, spins you around, the mailbox gone now, instead there's a, yeah, table, as if the desert were an exclusive bistro, the most exclusive there is, since one table's it, probably need to make your reservations a couple decades in advance, and seated at that most sought after of dining surfaces are two men, one woman, and a speaker. That's right, a small audio device that's been given its own place as if it were gonna be sipping wine, eating Beluga caviar, and ordering the soufflet, as if this were *Charlie's Angels* or some damn thing, even has a name placard in front of it that sez MR. SPEAKER, and who knows who (or maybe what) is on the other end? But there it is, a speaker, and its three human ,companions, though frozen for now, don't seem to find this setup strange at all...

The Predicta sez: *When the Nazi exploring party pushed one of the buttons, the tube opened and the commanding officer removed the book. But a strange thing happened at the same time: all of the other books were immediately turned to dust.*

The tableau goes live when Mr. Speaker starts giving off that slight hissing sound, normally lets you know the stereo's on, but here calls to mind poisonous snakes. From the look of things, well, if these folks were sitting inside, we could say the air's just been sucked out of the room. Since they're outside, maybe the air's been sucked out of the entire planet and a couple other planets for good measure, seeing as how the two men aren't staring daggers at the woman because daggers aren't nearly deadly enough. Oh no. Entirely too tame. Can one stare nuclear weapons?

"Say, Gestapo agents, who are these folks?" sez Wall.

"Allow me to introduce Agent C. Irvink Asbestos, Agent Kuzma Grigorovich Bezopasnosky, unt Ms. Greta Zelle."

"Um, that's not Greta."

"Ve sought you didn't know Greta, Herr Schtein! Too many lies to keep straight, hmm?"

"You've certainly introduced me to her since..."

The Predicta sez: *Reading the book, the Nazis realized it was the entire history and future of earth. This was 1942. The Antarctic expedition had been successful and the German elite had never believed they could win an armed conflict against the rest of the world. This alien book proved they were right.*

Ladies and gentlemen, we understand that our narrative has knotted up a bit, so let us untie it for you. First, what Wall doesn't realize is that the radio program he's in, *Vayss Uf Makink You Tock*, has merged with the television program *Youdunnit*. Our own TV critic, Davenport Starch, has more...

STARCH: The premise of the show *Youdunnit* is simple–the producers take a murderer who claims he doesn't remember his crime and they put him into a situation where he can kill his victim or victims again, the idea being that at the moment he commits the *second* murder, the first, as if by magic, will re-emerge from the depths of his clouded memory. What if he forgets the second murder too? All the better! Then there could be a spinoff called *Youdunnit... Again!* But I'm getting ahead of myself. The reason the show is called Youdunnit is not only because it's a high-larious play on whodunit, but also because the entire farce unfolds in an English Country House, the locus of the murder mystery genre. Why doesn't the forgetful felon shout, "Hey, what the deuce am I doing in an English Country House?" Because he's been infected with Agathopathy...

Excuse me, Mr. Starch, but *Agathopathy* is one of the knots we're trying to deal with. Dr. DeMent, could you give us the diagnosis?

DeMent: Agathopathy is a disorder wherein the afflicted develops the irrational belief that he or she is a character in an English Country House Murder Mystery. Symptoms of Agathopathy include hearing people speak in accents they don't actually have, summoning servants that don't exist, being scandalized by behavior that is commonplace in our current century, receiving and/or making vague threats (or interpreting almost any statement as a vague threat), eating British food voluntarily, using dry humor to humiliate anyone at all (present company excluded, of course), acting melodramatically, referencing the contents of your or someone else's last will and testament, and being constantly suspicious of everyone. In short, those with Agathopathy will see the events of their lives as if they were all taking place in an Agatha Christie novel. If this were all, Agathopathy could likely be seen as a benign, perhaps even entertaining psychosis. But as the condition worsens, the afflicted doesn't just see himself as any old character in a murder mystery–*he comes to see himself as the murderer.* And a murderer will do absolutely anything to cover up his crimes...

How could anyone be infected with this disease? It's a psychosis, not a virus or pathogen or...

DeMent: In this case, very easily. Acute Agathopathy is a side effect of Narratol addiction and/or overdose.

Acute Agathopathy?

DeMent: Yes. Meaning your Mr. Orcuson is going to have one wild ride.

Starch: Then I stand corrected. This show sounds like it'll be a real humdinger. Four stars!

But why does Greta look different?

Starch: Although the principal player suffers from Agathopathy, the viewing audience doesn't. Actors are therefore used. Also, as much as possible is done to instill the same creepy sensation the main character is feeling into the audience. In this case, there will be scenes that begin in tableau, followed by what will appear to be private performances, the import of which should be immediately apparent to the protagonist, though he swears none of this happened before (the whole denial thing).

Thank you, Mr. Starch and Dr. DeMent, but we must now send the good people of Radioland back to the desert. Take it away, Ed Murrow…

Euchre: Count, we've gotten to see a little bit of Arty Magam's knuckleball, can you tell us something about the pitch?

Tu: George, most pitches are about power or precision, sometimes both. When we hear a fastball went 100 miles per hour, we are awed. When we see a batter flailing away at a change-up, we are impressed. When we observe the arc of a curveball or the break of a slider, we are amazed. Even when sinkers are pounded into the dirt again and again, we understand. Or think we do, anyway.

Euchre: Oh, I get it alright. I spent most of my career being awed, impressed, and amazed by the pitches I saw… But whattaya mean we think we understand?

Tu: Actually, there's a great deal of physics involved with every pitch in baseball. But, as fans, we don't bother with the science. By watching we think we know. Except with the knuckleball. The knuckleball is a pitch so confounding, so baffling, we want an explanation. The knuckleball is perhaps the only pitch that demands an answer…

EUCHRE: *Sounds like my second wife…*

TU: *…only, when your answer involves the Magnus effect, Bernoulli's principle, Prandtl's boundary-layer theory, wake, drag, and aerodynamic regime changes, it no longer sounds like you're talking about sports. And yet you are.*

EUCHRE: *Remember, foax, all this will be on the test. But for now, we interrupt this episode of* Mr. Wizard *to begin the bottom of the first…*

Excuse me, that was not Ed Murrow, that was the radio voice of the Washington Senators, George Euchre. Without further ado…

"What… are you telling us?" sez Agent Asbestos, finally breaking the awkward silence before filled only by Mr. Speaker's slight hissing.

"Who are you vorking veeth?" sez Agent Bezopasnosky.

The Predicta sez: *But how were these alien visitors able to see into the future so clearly? None of the Nazis knew. Years and years later, though, they'd finally find out.*

"My husband. Kip. Kipper Maris. Everyone calls him 'Senator.'"

"Maris," sez Asbestos.

"Senator," sez Bezopasnosky.

"Kipper," sez Wall. "I could go for a tin of sardines right now. You want me to pick something up for you boys while I'm out? Sauerkraut balls or…"

But Major Freytag looks into the distance, only as an afterthought saying, "You are goink novhere, Herr Schtein," then snapping his fingers, and it's like the place went from bright, daytime lighting to dim, mood lighting, the kinda change you see at restaurants and bars, only this is, you know, a desert. Sure, there's the one table. Or, uh, there are two. The other one, a little ways away from the agents', from Mr. Speaker's, from… well, not Greta's anymore, she's walking toward the new table that happens to be occupied by a man in a Hawaiian shirt, sunglasses, drinking a tall, red drink and smoking a cigarette out of a longish holder. Asbestos and Bezopasnosky look on, coolly calm, though you're not really sure if they're seeing what you're seeing, Wall, or if they're frozen again.

225

"You know, I don't think you've ever told me the truth. I don't think you were born on some island in the Pacific, I don't think you grew up in Canada, I don't think your dad was an engineer with the Axis during World War Two or a spy in the Soviet Union after, I don't believe you're a… well, I don't know what you are, what jobs you may've had, because everything you describe sounds like something out of a book or a movie, and I definitely don't believe your name is 'Senator' Kipper Maris."

The Predicta sez: *The aliens had two special abilities–they could see into the future and they could see transdimensionally…*

The Senator looks at Greta nonplussed, slowly sipping his drink, when all in one motion she slides into his lap.

"And here's the thing: I don't ever want you to tell me the truth. Never. When we're married, we'll have to put our actual names on the license, but I won't look at yours. You can have a new name everyday, as long as you never tell me the real one. I've worked here for a few years, it *seems* like forever, and all of the lies, they've been so boring. Transparent. The liars, too often, ready and willing to admit… But I've just scored a great gig at the Alternate History Channel (they changed it to the International Channel of Uchronie, you know, ICU) and… and I've met you. Now, nothing will be boring. Everything will have a play, an angle… Remind me to tell you about the rules at ICU sometime…"

The Senator smokes his cigarette, doesn't really even seem to notice Greta, who stands up and grabs his chin, looking directly into his eyes.

"But listen here, *'Senator'* Kipper Maris. Kip. I'll know if you stop loving me. I will know. Because I'll find out you've told me the truth. Oh, sure, sometimes, to keep me guessing, you'll have to throw in a little truth. That's not a problem. This… This'll be different, though. It'll be big. And if that happens… if that *ever* happens… don't … don't let it happen… Kill me first…"

Greta tears up, then, collecting herself, smiles, turns around, and begins walking back to the agents' table, MR. SPEAKER's table, her table. The Senator picks up his cocktail, pauses, and then drinks.

"Now, I'm going to take your manuscript to ICU. I think it's fantastic," she says, turning back again, beaming, waving, glassy-eyed, childlike. "They're gonna love it. And this, well I couldn't use these words in the office, but this *fiction* is what I'll always think of when I think of us, of how we met. Everyone else always goes on about how the strongest relationships are based on truth. What a solid foundation! We're more honest. Ours is based on a big, fat lie," Greta arching an eyebrow, sexy. "I wouldn't have it any other way." At her original table, Major Freytag snaps his fingers, the light returns to that brutal desert sun glare, and...

The Predicta sez: *These two gifts actually don't play very well together. After all, how do you know if you're seeing the future of the dimension you live in or if you're seeing the future of some other dimension? You don't. The aliens invented a pastime, then, out of gambling on whose prediction was right.*

"You... were right to come to us with this," sez Asbestos.

"I... I was? I thought I was just..." sez Greta.

"You deed right seeng," sez Bezopasnosky.

"...telling you about a script from..."

"He came to you... Maris came to you... with this idea?" sez Asbestos.

"...uh... Yeah. I helped him organize it a little, but he brought the idea to me. World War Two a red herring, Nazis on the moon ready to..."

"Please," sez Asbestos.

The Predicta sez: *The Nazi explorers did not realize that when they pressed one of the buttons, they had inadvertently selected the "winner" and consigned the rest of the predictions to perdition.*

"It'll run great on ICU," sez Greta, hopeful.

"Yes... it will. But..."

"Unless you don't think..."

"Kooky TV station eesn't..."

"No, no, Kuzma. It will do very well... on ICU."

Bezopasnosky doesn't look so sure.

"No offense to Ms. Zelle, who takes her job very... seriously, but

227

no one else takes that channel… seriously. It might even help…"

"You know," sez Greta, paranoid, too confused to be offended, too bewildered even to follow her own rules, the rules she's hammered into every incoming ICU employee since she started working there, "you know, this is just a TV show. It isn't real. It's fiction. It's all *as if.* Right?"

The Predicta sez: *The Nazis believed they'd found the gospel of the future. So from 1942-1945 they followed it. And what we erroneously call World War Two played out the way it does in our greatest works of fiction: the history books.*

But the agents aren't paying attention to her anymore.

"My interest is not… in ICU's programming, Kuzma. It'll likely help us. I'm interested in the potential… threat 'Senator' Maris himself poses."

"No one een FSB veell help. Few even know of seetuation."

"Hold on, this is real? Actually *real?* As in *the truth?*"

"We need someone we can trust."

"Someone ve can count on."

"Someone efficient, unnoticeable…"

"Someone no one vould suspect. Da," sez Kuzma, as Greta retreats into herself, bewildered.

"We need a butler," sez MR. SPEAKER, finally breaking his hissing silence. "A butler."

And now, ladies and gentlemen, please welcome to the studio our station butler, Pierce Wryly. Wryly, welcome.

WRYLY: Mmmm-yes, thank you, sir. I wish to say that the pleasure is all mine…

Why thank you, Wryly.

WRYLY: But I'm afraid I can't find it in me.

Very droll. We'd expect nothing less. Wryly, maybe you could start us off with a little history of butlers.

WRYLY: Originally, butlers were like personal bartenders. They cared for and served alcoholic beverages which you appear to indulge in

228

quite liberally, sir.

A bottle now and then is not uncommon.

WRYLY: Indeed, sir, and *butler* comes from the Gallo-Romance word buticula, which means bottle. Wine being the inebriate of choice for the wealthy, the original butlers were rather like contemporary sommeliers. Oscar Wilde may have referred to the working class as the drinking class, but my own experience, sir, proves drinking is classless. It crosses all divides. Now, priests may handle your soul, but you likely don't keep one at home. Whoever handles your spirits, however, will be your most trusted advisor and will be kept in the highest regard.

What traits should a butler have?

WRYLY: I believe, sir, that the eminent Steven M. Ferry put it best. He said, "An attitude of devoted service to others, deference, and the keeping of confidences are the three most important traits a butler can have." Mary Louise Starkey has commented that she does not believe an American can truly ever display the "butler mindset." I am certain, however, that you, sir, will find a vocation someday.

Radio announcer?

WRYLY: Hmm, it is a difficult field, sir. Many fail. Even those who are currently employed.

Devoted service, deference, what about snide and sarcastic comments?

WRYLY: Those are provided free of charge, sir.

"But where can we find a butler?" sez Greta, her lips barely moving, her voice the ventriloquist version, mumbling: "How could he? How could he do this? It was all a…"

"To hire butler, ve need manor house, no?" sez Bezopasnosky.

"True. It's not like you see people just walking around… with butlers," sez Asbestos.

"No, you don't."

"Or mansion. Ve need mansion. And member of family needs to be colonel or admeeral. Lots of marriage eentreegue. And eef no vun vears monocle, ve're lost."

"We need to build a house, at least."

"Where can we build this house?"

"The United States government has land not too… far from here."

"But ve steell need ozzer servants. Butler ees head servant."

"Really? I thought butlers…"

"What exactly do butlers… do?"

WRYLY: Mmmm-yes, butlers are the head servant, as your Agent Bezopasnosky says. Everyone, the footmen, valets, housekeepers, answer to the butler, and he, in turn, answers to the lady of the house, not the master (the master hires, the lady fires). Although they are the servants-in-chief, butlers are specifically in charge of the dining room, wine cellar, pantry, and sometimes the entire main floor. The butler announces guests when they arrive, but the guests themselves are waited upon by footmen…

"But how can we be sure our butler will know how to do the job we need him to do?" sez Greta, flinty now. Focused. "The job he must do."

"Da. Real butlers not actually trained to…"

"Take care of the business we… require?" sez Asbestos.

Wryly, tell us, when was the first murderous butler visited upon the public.

WRYLY: The first murderous butler, sir, can be found in Herbert Jenkins' short story, "The Strange Case of Mr. Challoner." Mr. Jenkins, and with good reason, was not known for his writing; he was known for his publishing endeavors–the inestimable Wodehouse being the prime example. The most famous use of the murderous butler, then, is in Mary Roberts Rinehart's *The Door* (1930). Thanks to this, excuse me, forgettable novel, Mrs. Rinehart is credited with inventing the line, "The butler did it." The reason Mrs. Rinehart had such sway was because her second book, *The Circular Staircase* (1908), a solid beginning to the Had-I-But-Known style of mystery (if you go in for that sort of thing), sold over one million copies. Subsequent works did as well, if not better. She is even referred to as the American Agatha Christie. Strange, since Mrs. Christie's first book was published over a decade after Mrs. Rinehart's, but why should we bother with being accurate? It *is* such a chore.

"We will need a SASSY butler," sez Mr. Speaker. "A SASSY butler, that is right."

The trio stare at Mr. Speaker as a screen appears out of nowhere:

Montage: a collection of obviously rich people standing awkwardly in a garden looking at each other with lemons and pitchers stacked nearby; a gathering in a lounge where the wealthy try to serve themselves drinks, but spill more of the alcohol on the floor than into their glasses; a dinner party where the food is scorched and slung about the table as if by children; an assembly of gentlemen who have lit the brandy on fire and have attempted to drink the cigars; a tumbleweed blowing in through the front door that hits the lady of the house square in the chest, while the rest of the entry hall is an advertisement for a desert episode of *Wild Kingdom*; a blackmailer gleefully taking an envelope from a man in a tuxedo.

"*It is* so *difficult to be wealthy these days.*" The various rich from the montage agree wholeheartedly, especially the blackmailed who hands over his Rolex. "*Even though you live in luxury, it fails to feel like luxury.*" The garden party tries to make lemonade by smashing the lemons with hammers; the floor of the lounge is being licked and lapped en masse; the food fight has become a war; the brandy fire is spreading; prehistoric-looking lizards have made the hall their home; the blackmailer points to a picture of his mark's wife. "*But what can be done? Gone is the time when a legion of footmen, valets, hall boys, housekeepers, cooks, and groomsmen graced your estate.*" The rich have all congregated in the hall with the terrifying lizards, looking lost. "*So who can you go to? Is there anyone who can help? Set your mind at ease. There is.*"

"*Who?*" say the rich.

"*Your butler.*"

"*Butler? Are there still butlers?*" say the rich, as one unfortunate soul begins wrestling with a lizard.

"*Yes, there are.*"

"But where do they come from?"

"The British Butler Institute, The International Institute of Modern Butlers, The Guild of Professional English Butlers, The International Guild of Butlers & Household Managers, Magnums Butlers, The Starkey International Institute for Household Management."

"But which one should we pick?" say the rich, as the blackmailer enters, rubbing his hands together.

"Each school has its own merits, but if you want a butler who truly does know it all, you need a SASSY butler."

"A sassy butler?"

"The Silent Assassin Servant School of Yarborough, or SASSY."

Montage: butlers in full butler regalia serving drinks, welcoming guests, assisting their masters, while also performing ninjutsu on a military training ground.

"A SASSY butler is trained in unobtrusive and lethal combat. A SASSY butler can run your household, help you out of a jam, and remove unwanted houseguests and lifelong nemeses... forever." The garden party has lemonade; the gathering in the lounge has whiskey sours; the dinner party is going off without a hitch; there is so much laughing and brandy drinking and cigar smoking; the entryway is decorated with exotic lizard-inspired art. *"The Silent Assassin Servant School of Yarborough. If you merely need someone to manage your home, you do not need our service."* A butler delivers a drink to the blackmailer. *"But for those who want it all, who need it all, your butler must be trained in the fine art of murder; your butler must be a SASSY butler."* The blackmailer clutches his throat, looks incredulously at the glass, falls to the floor.

"Yes, the Silent Assassin Servant School of Yarborough. You think the butler did it?" A butler performs five consecutive handsprings down a hallway, kills a new blackmailer with a penknife, turns a corner, and announces a guest without anyone noticing the murder. *"Come on, now. That's a cliché."*

"Oh. A SASSY butler," sez Greta.

"You know, a fall guy would be... easier," sez Asbestos.

"Da. Someone ve could eleeminate aftervards," sez Bezopasnosky.

"And I believe I know just the... guy. His name... is Wall," sez Asbestos.

"Look. They're setting me up. They're planning to frame me, to kill me. Stop them," sez Wall, though, buddy, shouldn't you try to be a bit more passionate here?

"Vhy voult ve do zat, Herr Schtein? Perhaps killink you voult be ze best sink for you," sez Major Freytag. "Maybe it shoult haff been done lonk ago."

The Predicta sez: *There's an interesting omission in the Lunarian Manuscript—nowhere does it mention Antarctica or the moon...*

"The butler has been contracted," sez Mr. Speaker.

As the players disperse, Wall is turned around by Schmetterling, and what is standing there once again? Your old pal, the Hyperborean Arms, of course. The country house where our drama will play itself out. You can tell, Wall, because the Gestapo are forcing you in that direction.

Later, according to C.U. Tomorrow, our prophetic correspondent, when the real Greta Zelle walks onto the set of *Youdunnit,* she will recall a bit of voice-over work she did for ICU:

"It was on a Friday when I sat in the library reading a tome by one Mr. P. G. Wodehouse, a collection of tales about his excellent valet Jeeves and Jeeves's employer, the idle ne'er-do-well Bertie Wooster, that my chef entered wearing less than his full uniform, lacking a jacket. When I inquired as to why he was not fully dressed, remarking upon the absent item of required clothing, the man, who already appeared to be in the grip of some mental malady, evidenced by the fact that his eyes protruded grotesquely from his face, proclaimed in a shrill, inhuman voice, 'Here is my coat,' and with celerity he procured a handgun from his pocket which he instantly fired. I knew not what happened, and to this day, so help me God, I still do not, but I have it on good authority that the pistol jammed. When the shock of the incident finally left my person, and when I came to understand that I was not amongst the angels and saints, I looked up and saw the chef, whom I had passed over for promotion, lying on the floor, trussed up like a Thanksgiving turkey, subdued by a person I had never before seen. I asked him his name; he replied: 'Butler.' And so I made him my butler."

It's normal for ICU employees to pull double, sometimes triple duty, ladies and gentlemen, everyone helping everyone else out, often not even knowing which historical permutation is being manipulated. This was the case when Greta Zelle logged her voice over: she came into the office, punched the clock, recorded the piece for whomever needed it, and returned to her own projects. All in a day's work…

TOMORROW: But get this, futurewise, when our sexy smart Greta saunters onto the set of *Youdunnit*, all the heads mounted on swivels as they always are, oh yes she will, she'll hear an audience member, like this was the end of some snooty British whodunit, m'lud with a knife in his back, and all the high society foax lookin' just scandalized, scandalized I say! Greta Zelle will have this here madness bouncin' off her eardrums, hers and everyone else's, I mean it'll be ringing from the Peanut Gallery right after the firing squad fires and a body slumps to the ground, a long silence as everyone stares at the corpse, sure, and then: "But it wasn't him! The butler did it!" The butler. And she'll wonder, foax, if maybe that bit of voice-over copy, maybe it weren't for any flick at all. Maybe it was a warning. And I don't mind tellin' you: it sure as hell was…

Radio waves from somewhere in the desert say:

EUCHRE: *At the end of the first inning, no runs, no hits, no errors, not even a walk. But don't touch that dial. There's still plenty more baseball to play…*

And now this…

§

Z'DROPPE: Out in Another World, Kuzma Grigorovich Bezopasnosky pauses. Pauses. Pauses from what or for what, I'm not sure.

234

He looks like, yes, he looks like he's about to begin a routine. Contemplative. Placid. Prepared. An Olympic gymnast or figure skater or diver set to attempt his gold medal trial. Even the radio from next door doesn't shake his concentration...

TU: *Let's start with the myth of the knuckleball. It's generally believed that the dry spitter doesn't follow a smooth trajectory. Instead, according to batters and catchers and umpires and managers, the ball changes direction abruptly like UFOs darting through the sky. The usual description: at first it floats, enticingly, toward the plate. It looks so easy to hit. Isn't this the Major Leagues? But then the pitch flutters, shakes, shimmies, dances, wobbles, zigs, and zags. The ball's movement is so difficult to sum up, most people resort to a beautiful tautology: the knuckleball knuckles. It knuckles...*

EUCHRE: *Well, it is a knuckleball, right?*

TU: *It is, George. But there's only ever been one pitcher who actually held the ball with his knuckles: Eddie Cicotte of the Chicago White Sox. Though that just may be a myth. Every other knuckleballer has used his fingertips, his fingernails, a talon-like grip. So the pitch, for most of its practitioners, has nothing to do with the knuckles at all...*

Z'DROPPE: At long last, Agent Bezopasnosky reaches down and turns a Mr. Mxyzptlk action figure toward the wall; it had been facing him from atop a dresser. Yes, Mr. Mxyzptlk, that zany Superman villain. And now Kuzma's off! Walking in a deliberate manner as if he were measuring his steps, and, yes, maybe that's necessary because, and I have no idea why, he's moving backwards. You heard me right. He's moving backwards. Walking backwards. One foot behind the other. Scanning over notes in his planner from bottom to top and working toward the front of the notebook, then replacing it in his messenger bag, there's even a commercial playing on his television and *it's* running in reverse...

Our investigative reporter, Eve Z'droppe, filed this report yesterday evening. Madame Khryptymnyzhy was also on hand to tell us what Agent Bezopasnosky was thinking.

KHRYPTYMNYZHY: He's... he's thinking of a few different things...

235

at the same time. One of them… one of them is a man he knew… he knew in the Soviet Union. Haber. Mohl. Habermohl. That's… that's a name. A German name. But… I don't know why… there appear to be two of them. Habermohls. Or… maybe not. I can't be sure. Klaus Otto Habermohl. That's… I think that's his full name. It is. Yes, it is. Kuzma is also… hmm… perhaps another… no, this could not be… Ah! I see. Kuzma is maybe thinking about… about an historical figure. Iacomus Occasus Lacio. A Roman? A Roman. Not someone he knew. Like Habermohl. Or maybe… maybe he didn't know Habermohl… at all. Maybe Kuzma only knew of Habermohl. Or perhaps… perhaps Habermohl was not… not a person. Didn't exist… didn't exist… except on… on paper… Or someone connected to him… only… only existed on paper. There are two more… two… yes… very clear. Two more things Kuzma is thinking about… though I'm not sure how they're connected. A school of reverse engineering and… hmm… odd… I'm not having a joke… it's something called Daylight *Wastings* Time. That… that is all.

Madame Khryptymnyzhy from last night, ladies and gentlemen. To tell us a little about this Iacomus Occasus Lacio, Dr. Dusty Buchs, our classics correspondent, has joined us. Dr. Buchs, take it away…

BUCHS: Iacomus Occasus Lacio, later called Retrorsus, was a Renaissance man before the Renaissance: an inventor, a scientist, a sculptor, a statesman, a philosopher, a mathematician. Occasus, which is what he was called before he was given his agnomen, had a real lust for knowledge. He wanted to learn how everything worked. Absolutely everything. And he was convinced that most people, even those who supposedly knew how things operated, were wrong, that they acted on preconceived notions instead of the truth.

Was he like Socrates, then?

BUCHS: No, Occasus didn't necessarily want to change the world, or change how people thought. And he didn't want to expose anyone as a hypocrite or a fool. I guess you could call him an engineer of everything. It didn't matter what it was: a simple machine, a marriage proposal, a political debate, a math problem. He wanted to know how it worked. Over time he developed the theory, and this led to his eventual agnomen "Retrorsus," that to truly comprehend anything, you had to know it forwards and backwards. For Retrorsus, however, the reverse told us much, much more because our brains are accustomed to progressive motion in time. A then B then C then D. It's so predictable, so obvious, so comfortable, that we're not able, or hardly able, to think analytically about whatever forward action we're talking about here. In fact, Retrorsus said the majority of the people in the world barely saw anything at all.

We're speaking a bit abstractly. How about an example?

BUCHS: One time, Retrorsus asked an artist to make a fairly simple, marble sculpture of a man. Retrorsus specified, however, that this sculpture had to be made in public, that the sculptor could not discard anything he used, and when the artist finished, Retrorsus could do whatever he wanted with the final product, even crediting whatever became of it to the artist himself. The test subject agreed and made the figure. When he was done, Retrorsus went to work. Those who watched the original sculptor saw an artist, but many of them had seen artists at work before. Those who watched Retrorsus, however, would later claim they'd never seen anything like what *he'd* done before.

What was it?

BUCHS: Oh, for all intents and purposes, Retrorsus looked like he was sculpting. He used a chisel, a hammer, the usual implements. But instead of bringing the figure of a man out of a cube of marble, he obscured the figure of a man in the marble. Later, he installed the block in his garden. Whenever anyone asked him what it was, he said one of two things: "Man" or "Art." And then he would say, "It is the only work I own by…"

Was this Retrorsus a bit… touched?

BUCHS: No, he wasn't crazy. Although the journals from later in his life are difficult to read, having been written in reverse, still, it's apparent that he explored his philosophy with a clear mind. He knew what he was doing. For instance, he accepted, though it frustrated him a bit, that you couldn't eat or drink in reverse, since vomiting is not ingesting done backwards. On the other hand, it pleased him that breathing is a constant back and forth. Blood pumping, too. But he could write backwards, walk backwards, speak backwards (which the other statesmen thought was hilarious). There were those who were afraid of him. Most just thought he was a quirky fellow. He *had* followers, though he called them Leaders since he walked behind them. Later in his life…

I'm sorry, Dr. Buchs, we'll return to this fascinating story as soon as we can. But right now, listeners of Radioland, we're going to send you out to the Hyperborean, well, Country House, I suppose, where *Vayss Uf Makink You Tock* and *Youdunnit* continue. So, take it away, Ed Murrow…

The Predicta sez: *After Antarctica and Roswell, the Americans and the Soviets met in secret to discuss their situation. They agreed on an alliance. The American-Soviet Alliance, or ASA.*

At the front door of the Hyperborean Country House, Major Freytag looks especially excited, and that likely doesn't spell good news for you, Wall. Schmetterling bangs on the door and, yeah, is that Agathopathy kicking in now, buddy? Sure seems to be a footman in the entryway. Have you ever seen a live footman before? Tell the truth, when you've heard the word "footman" in the past, Wall, you've thought of a guy who enjoyed feet far more than you do, right?

"Your invitation, please," sez the footman.

"What invitation?" sez Wall.

Schmetterling sighs. Major Freytag, surprisingly, seems distracted. Like he's focused on something you can't quite see…

The Predicta sez: *Having drafted Flugkreisel engineers from amongst the "defeated" Nazis, and with the aid of their industrial might, the ASA believed it would have an unstoppable fleet of flying discs by 1950.*

"Your invitation, sir. To the ball."

Maybe it's asking a bit much, Wall… then maybe asking *anything at all* is asking a bit much of you, but I mean, sheesh, the mailbox! Remember the mailbox?! How could you forget it? Middle of nowhere,

238

surrounded by nothing but sand and a little more sand and then, yes, a lot more sand, and *Alakazam!* a mailbox just happened to be there. You opened it. Remember that? And when you opened the mailbox, and if I'm going too fast here speak up cuz I wouldn't want to leave you in the dust, when… you… opened… the mailbox… there was… an envelope… with… *your name on it!*

"What ball?"

"The Butterfly Ball. You need an invitation to enter."

Freytag, still distracted, wanders away like a somnambulist, even the Oberschütze looks confused, until the major pulls him in and forms a two-man football huddle. What are they up to, Wall? Being the Gestapo, well, the odds on "No Good" won't win you much at the track. Come on. Put a bet on "Making Their Organization More Transparent." Sure, it's a long shot, but just think what you could do with all that money if your ticket hits!

The Predicta sez: *No one's exactly sure what went wrong. Although the ASA existed, the Americans and Soviets weren't always completely open and honest with each other. So stories about Habermohl and Pseudo-Habermohl, about Renato Fregoli, they add to the mystique, but ultimately they don't tell us what happened.*

"I don't have one," you say.

The footman, as stoic and unflappable as you'd expect, especially with that Agathopathy in you, doesn't so much pretend you're no longer there, but gives off the air that *you never existed in the first place.* This isn't a weakness on his part, some kind of delusion or something, no. It's a *grave error* on yours. If you'd tried harder, Wall, you'd be there, you'd be corporeal, but you fucked it up, so you're nothing, ethereal.

The Predicta sez: *In the end, what we do know is that the Nazis destroyed all but one of the ASA's flying discs.*

Finally, the Gestapo break their huddle, start hoofing it in your direction, back to their old purposive style, no more wandering, and, huh, what?, it looks like they've recruited a new member. And they did. Joining

239

the SS is none other than Mr. E. That's right. The chalk fairy. The walking, talking chalk fairy. The trio surround you, Wall, flanked by Freytag and Schmetterling, while Mr. E. takes his position in front, reaching back, his "arm" able to extend and twist in inhuman ways, "fingers" slipping inside your jacket, swiping the envelope, then brandishing it before the footman.

"Here's my invitation," sez Mr. E. in your voice, Wall.

The Predicta sez: *What followed was a conference between the Nazis and the ASA. Both sides agreed that whereas the Germans were space's superpower, the Americans and the Soviets were still earth's superpowers.*

Heh heh heh. That's right, buddy, you've been replaced. No more of your antics, your petty rebellion, your stonewalling. We have someone who can play your part better than you can. Someone who isn't so much like *you*. Not a copy, or a sad, sad remix. Not even a lame impostor, no. We now have the revised, the perfected, the new and improved, the model that came back from the dealership after the recall.

Yeah, Mr. E.'s all of these things and *he's* made out of chalk.

As the footman leads you into the country house, Mr. E. turns around.

"*Now...* I'm you," he sez, and if he had a face, he'd probably be grinning...

The Predicta sez: *And so a pact was signed. The Germans and the ASA would not engage each other in combat until the general civilians of earth knew, without a doubt, that 1939-1945 had been the most horrific ruse in history, and that Nazis lived on the moon.*

Standing in the entryway, well, I mean, is there a radio on in the other room?

EUCHRE: *Magam sends down another batter. That knuckler is really dancing! Count, earlier you were talking about the myth of the knuckleball. That must mean there's a reality.*

TU: *There is. The knuckleball actually follows a smooth trajectory just like any other pitch.*

EUCHRE: *What? Have you seen what Magam's been throwing so far?*

TU: *George, no blunt object obeying the laws of physics can execute a sharp turn during flight. That's one of the reasons why the flying saucer myths are so laughable.*

EUCHRE: *Is that how you got to the park today, Count? You sure like talking about 'em.*

TU: *I'm telling you, George, the dry spitter follows the same trajectory as any other pitch, you just don't know what that trajectory will be until it's already gone through it. Even the pitcher doesn't know for certain. Charlie Hough, a longtime knuckleball thrower, went so far as to describe the pitch this way: "Butterflies aren't bullets. You can't aim 'em – you just let 'em go." But once it's in flight, there's nothing scientifically impossible about the butterfly ball.*

"Major Gustav Freytag and Mr. Wallace Heath Orcuson." It's no surprise the butler has announced you. This is a country house, there *are* servants. What's surprising, however, is *who* made the announcement: Oberschütze Lorenz Schmetterling. Maybe the cat that had his tongue was finally paid off. And unlike Freytag, who sounds like he picked up his accent from a bunch of old B movies, Schmetterling sounds downright British, with the usual dogged mispronunciations of other languages, making any word or name sound like an *English* word or name (hey, they didn't almost conquer the world by caring about other people's cultures, now did they?). Oh, and gone is his Gestapo uniform, having replaced it with... well, he's the mesomorphic version of Lurch now...

To all of you out there in Radioland, our own Davenport Starch, TV critic, has more on this strange transformation. Mr. Starch...

STARCH: Here's the story they're sticking with: there were too many characters–Major Freytag, Mr. E. as Wall, Mr. Orcuson himself, and Schmetterling, so the Oberschütze was recast. A very nice explanation, that. Sounds plausible. But it has one weakness: it isn't true at all. Here's what really happened: the actor who was supposed to play the butler didn't show up, and with no one else available on such short notice, Schmetterling had to take the role. Not exactly a big budget affair we're dealing with here. It plays on Friday nights between some sleazy dating show that answers the age old question, "Do young, stupid, attractive people like to get it on?" (SPOILER ALERT: they do!) and an educational program that informs us, authoritatively, though using nothing but uncertain terms, ambiguous phrasing, and (my personal favorite) "overwhelming circumstantial evidence" that aliens built the pyramids. I mean, sure, the ones in Memphis, Tennessee, and Las Vegas, Nevada were *obviously* built by aliens, but that's…

"Good evening, honored guests," sez Schmetterling, standing in the study. The guests themselves turn and, wow, really? look like they're posing for the cover of some future version of the board game *Clue*. Major Freytag, smoking a cigarette from a holder, leaning against the fireplace; Greta Zelle in a red dress, lounging on a chaise; "Senator" Kipper Maris, eyebrow arched, puffing on a pipe, making like he'd been reading for hours when interrupted; Ima Fregoli, vanity cane in hand, not just playing the matriarchal card from her wingback chair, but playing it in every suit and with wilds; Agents C. Irving Asbestos and Kuzma Grigorovich Bezopasnosky, both with cigars, conspiratorial at the edge of the room, letting on they know more than they actually do, ready to slip out secret passages that may or may not exist whenever necessary; and Mr. E., having a bit of fun perhaps, lying on the rug in the center of the room, a chalk fairy signifying some poor sap's past or possibly future demise. And what about you, Wall? Well, servants aren't supposed to be seen. How anyone could miss you in that maid's getup is beyond me, though.

The Predicta sez: *There was one question: how could the ASA coverup something as earth-shattering and monumental as Nazis on the moon?*

"You have been invited here by my master, a Mr. Iam Fregoli," sez Schmetterling, "because each one of you is in some way connected to a conspiracy. You may be a major or a minor player, you may know a great deal or almost nothing, but all of you, as they say, are in on it. Well, all of you save one."

Confused grumbling, eyebrow raising, throat clearing, suspicious glancing, coughing, harrumphing, indeeding, eyeglasses being torn off in shock-ing, oh my-ing, I saying, and so many these accusations are an outrage-ing it is, for sure, an outrage. But, yeah, there are more people here than just the main players. In fact, whoever put this soiree together doesn't go in for that "less is more" nonsense, oh no, "more is more" being the idea here, or maybe "more isn't nearly enough." After all, above our familiar characters on a vast network of catwalks, we could even say *lording over* our familiar characters, are an ungodly number of, uh, yeah, detectives: an entire old folks' home full of Miss Marples; more Spades (that's Sam) than can be found in a canasta deck; enough Nancy Drews and Hardy Boys to make, no, not a Scout troop, but an entire Scout division (who's gonna buy all those cookies, all that popcorn?); so many Philip Marlowes none of them could ever be solo, though they all likely think of themselves as lone wolves; an indeducible number of Sherlock Holmeses with Dr. Watsons sufficient to staff hospitals all over the world; a population of Charlie Chans that couldn't be determined for all the tea in China; enough Hercule Poirots to warrant immediately buying stock in any company that manufactures mustache wax (and not just a few shares either); a group of Ja'far ibn Yahyas, all of whom would rather be somewhere else ("Not again," they say in deep-sighing simultaneity); a plethora of limping Oedipi who apparently refuse to learn their lesson; and, last but not least, a mere handful of C. Auguste Dupins, all talking to the same invisible friend. It's even likely there are more hidden by the mob. Lew Archer? V.I. Warshawski? The Continental Op? Dan Fortune? Judges Dee or Bao? Franklin Blake? If only someone could find them for us…

The Predicta sez: *The Germans themselves had the answer: the Lunarian Manuscript.*

"My god!" sez Wall. "Have you thought about, I dunno, spraying for these detectives? This is the worst infestation I've ever seen. I know a guy, never mind how I met him, he can take care of this problem for ya. Might set you back a bit, but, seriously, there are so many gumshoes here, I mean, fuck, who chewed all that gum? What we need to do, get ourselves a time machine, fill it with nuns…"

Schmetterling continues: "One of you, one of you is not part of the conspiracy because one of you is my master–the person who seeks to expose this, as he would say, treachery."

"That eliminates Ms. Zelle and myself," sez Ima Fregoli.

"Not necessarily. My employer is a master of disguise, so it could be any one of you."

"How could you not know boss?" sez Bezopasnosky.

"The alphabet soup that makes up the Soviet or Russian intelligence community leads me to believe that you, of all people, agent, would understand."

"Da."

"Fair… enough. But why would… Iam Fregoli put himself at risk like this?" sez Asbestos.

"Since I do not know him, sir, I am sure that I do not know."

"He's my brother. Sure, he's been working to expose this conspiracy for a long time, but he'd never pass up the chance to throw a ridiculous spectacle for his own amusement. A spectacle, I promise you, he thinks he has complete control over, no matter how chaotic it may appear," sez Ima Fregoli.

The Predicta sez: *The Lunarian Manuscript itself outlines the history we know: the Space Race and the Cold War. What we didn't know until recently was that it was all like Ragnarök. The higher-ups in the US and USSR knew how it was going to play out from the beginning.*

A small safe is wheeled out by a footman, as the detectives above take copious notes, begin to put the puzzle together even before anything has happened, and act ignorant, though later remarking how Greta looked at Maris, how Mr. E. looked at Greta, how Bezopasnosky looked at Asbestos, in short how everyone looked at everyone else as if they were all about to murder each other in a Battle Royale.

"You are, perhaps, right, Ms. Fregoli, since I have been instructed to distribute these," Schmetterling sez as he opens the safe, revealing a brace of 7.65mm Walther PPKs, handing one to each character, except you, Wall, seeing as how you've been demoted. Same thing probably happened when they were handing out brains, eh buddy? "My instructions are as follows: once you are all armed, you are to pair off and explore the house…"

"Since he's your brother, how do we know you're not working with him right now?" sez Mr. E. to Ima.

"I haven't seen my brother in over a decade. And he and I didn't exactly part on amicable terms. I think he's a fool just like my father was a fool. I'd do anything to stop him. I won't lie, I'd rather not see him dead, but…"

"You don't know your own brother?" sez Greta.

"His reputation as a master of disguise isn't a legend. It's absolutely true."

"How do we know it isn't you?" sez Greta, cocking her gun and pointing it at Ima. Kuzma reacts immediately, pointing his own gun at Zelle, the detectives surprised, unsurprised, apprehensive, nonplussed.

The Predicta sez: *The constantly increasing paranoia during the Cold War wasn't fueled by capitalism and socialism or democracy and communism, it was fueled by the conspirators' fear that people would stop believing in the Cold War.*

"Point gun somevhere else, Greta. She is not murderer," sez Agent Bezopasnosky.

"So you say, Russky," and Greta backs down.

"If you don't know who the fuck you work for, Jeeves, then how in the hell will we know if we've killed or captured him?" sez "Senator" Maris.

"This production won't go on forever. My master has informed me that at the end of the evening, at midnight, we will learn who is alive, who is dead, who committed the murder, and who was murdered," sez Schmetterling.

"What if we decide not to shoot anyone?" sez Mr. E.

"Then you will have missed your chance to stop my employer from exposing your conspiracy," sez Schmetterling, the detectives nodding in agreement, giddy at the prospect of murder, children who see an entire table of unguarded candy, for only if there are murders can murders be

245

solved.

"Unt zere must be ein killink! Zo many gunz haff been introduced, ze rules zay zat somevun must die! Now, pair off unt explore das Haus! How can anyvun be shot vith all uf us standink here all togezzer?!" sez Major Freytag.

STARCH: When the plot starts to lag, you can always count on the Nazis to move things along.

"Ladies and gentlemen, this is the Butterfly Ball," sez Schmetterling, just as a radio somewhere chimes in:

TU: ...the butterfly ball's strange characteristics come from the stitches.

EUCHRE: Hate to tell ya, pal, but we use the same ball no matter who's up on the mound.

TU: Of course. But every other pitch is thrown with so much spin, the ball's movement negates the stitches. The spin makes the ball, effectively, a perfect sphere. The knuckler, on the other hand, since it's thrown with very little spin (one-quarter to one-half turn on its trip to the plate), doesn't act like a perfect sphere. And so the stitches create turbulence.

EUCHRE: There's some turbulence out on the field as the Senators' manager did not like that call.

TU: So here's what happens as the pitch moves toward the plate: it presents a different seam pattern to the flow of air in its immediate vicinity. What does that mean? Imagine if the stitches stuck out three inches from the ball. It wouldn't surprise anyone when the "ball" moved strangely. It's not even round! It's all bumpy! Who knows where that thing's going? But the seams don't have to stick out that far. Even as small as they are, the wind generated by the pitch reacts to them, consequently changing the direction of the ball. If a baseball had no seams, the knuckler would be impossible. The air would flow smoothly around that perfect sphere. But it does have stitches, and those stitches create a nonsymmetrical lateral force. Depending on where the seams end up during their flight, then, the ball could move in absolutely any reasonable, physically possible direction...

It seems that Agent Bezopasnosky is into women who look like men, or perhaps men who might be vaguely construed as women, because as he leaves the study, he puts his arm around you, Wall, and soon you're alone with the big Russian, all alone, or so you think, as the detectives look on from above, trying to preserve your isolation, not exactly doing the best job...

Excuse me patient listeners out there in Radioland, but to better understand Agathopathy and the *Youdunnit* show, we are now joined once again by Dr. DeMent. Dr. DeMent, could you tell us what Wall is likely seeing right now?

DeMent: This mansion, which was once Mr. Orcuson's apartment building (or so he thinks, for him there's no way to be sure), really *does* look every bit the country house. Of course, thanks to the *Youdunnit* show, it mostly resembles a country house to us, too, but even more so for Wall. We can see the evidence of the low budget–statues that don't quite appear to be marble, vases that look like they couldn't hold anything, furniture unsuitable for human use, the set swaying slightly, etc. Mr. Orcuson, however, he feels like there should've been a map of this place at the entrance, each room with its own name, its own décor, funded by donations from folks so wealthy their blood is that navy blue color indecipherable from black (until it's far too late). In other words, no one could possibly live in a building like this. It must be a museum. But, so goes Mr. Orcuson's thinking, it's not a museum. People live here. And people are going to die here. Being the archetypal location for murder mysteries, Wall will soon see shadows as potential killers, killers will be hiding everywhere, in every corner, behind every door. Once his paranoia reaches its peak, he'll decide that he must kill them before they kill him. *That* is what it's like to have Agathopathy.

Thank you, Dr. DeMent...

Wall, as you walk these hallways with your new companion, hallways that're supposedly foreign to the big Russian, tell us, does it bother you that Kuzma, uh, yeah, seems like he knows exactly where he's going? And don't let the detectives scare you, the detectives who are taking an interest in this very fact, who could be following any of the other couples, who could be researching the owner of the house, who could be doing background checks, contacting important and knowledgeable connections, running interference, who could be doing anything else. Don't worry about it. Just your turn is all. They'll get to the others later. Right?

Sure.

Keep telling yourself that.

While you're at it, keep telling yourself that Predicta screens totally aren't popping up all over the place...

The Predicta sez: *Because the ASA knew how it would all turn out, the point of the Space Race became 'there's no reason to explore outer space,' the point of the Cold War became 'there's no reason to engage in politics.' With this plan, the ASA believed it could hold off the real World War Two forever.*

Since he's got the floor plan down pat, uh, where's Bezopasnosky taking you? Can't say you've ever been pulled along by a KGB agent, can you, Wall? Hmm. How would you break his grip? And where would you go even if you got away? No, Wall, you're going where he's going, which appears to be this here room on the left...

Perplexed listeners of Radioland, I'm not quite sure what's happened, but Edward R. Murrow has broken off from the narration. He stares at the one-way mirror, obviously pained. Nearby, Arty Magam throws pitches to no one. Our own Madame Khryptymnyzhy has more...

KHRYPTYMNYZHY: Your Mr. Murrow... Murrow... feels that the world is... suffering from an increasing... increasing unreality... unreality... that everything that happens seems... seems less and less... real everyday. And... and Murrow believes that the... the catalyst for this... increasing unreality is the... the manuscript he's currently... narrating. That even from... from beyond the grave... "Senator" Kipper Maris... Maris... is corrupting the world... and if Murrow... Murrow... Murrow doesn't figure out what to... do... there will be an... an... an... entropy of explanations? Yes, entropy of explanations, where any and all narratives will become... equal... equal... whether factual or... or fictional. History... actual history... will be no... will be no different than... than conspiracy theories... no different... no different... And then nothing... nothing will be... will be real... any longer...

We thank you, Madame Khryptymnyzhy. For now, however, slowly, there in the Pilgrim & Pagan, Ed Murrow turns away from the mirror. He looks at his manuscript. He appears ready to continue. Nearby, Arty Magam throws pitches to no one...

A radio studio. Huh? Yeah, it's true. The room you're standing in, Wall, is small and has a big glass window that looks out onto other booths. The other booths are smaller and have microphones. Before you, frozen in time, is a man at a soundboard with his own microphone. He's so still he could be a mannequin, or part of a wax diorama. Except for this engineer dummy, you're alone. No more Agent Bezopasnosky. Which is too bad, really. He might've gotten a kick out of the fact that this tableau is a mock up of the Soviet All-Union Radio of yesteryear, though that logo can't be right, looking a bit like Major Freytag's armband with waves radiating from it.

Since no one's holding you against your will any longer, buddy, you figure you could just leave, but when you turn around Agent Bezopasnosky's... uh... son? walks in, almost knocking you over, my, what a nice move, Wall, what with the dive in the nick of time into the expected pile of boxes. When you get up and dust yourself off, the diorama has come to life: the engineer checking various levels, voice actors filing into their respective booths, Son-of-Kuzma donning a set of earphones.

"I seenk zere ees meestake een manuscreept," sez the engineer.

"Vhat?" sez... could that just be a younger version of Kuzma himself?

"Who ees Fregoli? Should be Schriever, da?"

"Nyet. Fregoli. Schriever's been dead for long time. No meestake."

"Oh. Zen ve proceed."

And really, if you want, Wall, you could put on a tap dancing routine. No one even knows you're there.

"Begeen," sez the engineer.

NARRATOR: At the conclusion of the Great Patriotic War, Nazi land, technology, and personnel were split between the Allies. With the new personnel, the Soviet Union sought to utilize each recruit's knowledge and skills, while also rehabilitating these men from their abhorrent political beliefs. It was and is our view that such beliefs were thrust upon them by an oppressive regime–an oppressive regime inevitably conquered by communism. It is widely known that many fascists have been corrected by and integrated into Mother-Homeland. It is also known that former Nazi scientists worked on our rocket program. But only now can it be told that rehabilitated Nazis also worked on a Top Secret project even grander than the rocket program: the flying discs…

We interrupt *Vayss Uf Makink You Tock/Youdunnit* to speak with station butler, Pierce Wryly. To be brief, Wryly, what's going on?

WRYLY: Mmmm-if I may, sir. I cannot speak with authority about Narratol or Agathopathy, but I *do* know the genre that's unfolding here. Flashbacks are quite common in country house mysteries. They slowly reveal pertinent information about the characters that advance the plot. This information may contain a vital clue or clues to solving the murder; it may also be full of red herrings. The audience only finds out once the game is afoot. And so, it appears your Mr. Orcuson has wandered into a flashback, presumably Agent Bezopasnosky's, sir.

But that's not the real Kuzma! He's an actor! Wall barely knows the big Russian.

WRYLY: Mmmm-very astute, sir. Always on top of things. Perhaps you might become a detective someday. Or at least a bobby. I think the helmet would do you some…

Very well, Wryly, but how are we getting this flashback if it's supposed to be Agent Bezopasnosky's and he's still at the Another World Motel? Well, ladies and gentlemen, it appears our butler's sassy comments have dried up for the moment, so we return you to the… All-Union Radio program?

NARRATOR: …This, comrades, is the trial of a treacherous spy

250

who refused his just rehabilitation. The Trial of Pseudo-Habermohl, on All-Union Radio.

PROSECUTOR: Can you state your name for the record, please?

?: My name is Renato Fregoli.

PROSECUTOR: Please state where you are employed and the nature of your employment.

R. FREGOLI: I am an engineer at the Top Secret, well, until recently it was Top Secret, Zhitkur Underground Base at Kapustin Yar.

PROSECUTOR: Please be more specific. What do you engineer, Comrade Fregoli?

R. FREGOLI: I work on flying discs, called UFOs by other comrades. Originally, in Nazi Germany, they were called Flugkreisels.

PROSECUTOR: What is your, or I should say what was your relationship with Klaus Otto Habermohl?

R. FREGOLI: Well, sir, we were friends. Or, so I thought...

PROSECUTOR: You will have more time to elaborate later. Were you integral in bringing Dr. Habermohl to the Soviet Union?

R. FREGOLI: ...

PROSECUTOR: Answer the question, Comrade Fregoli.

R. FREGOLI: Yes, I was.

PROSECUTOR: Considering what we know now, that this man who sits before us today is not Klaus Otto Habermohl the flying disc engineer, but an impostor and a spy without a name, why should we believe a single thing you say? You facilitated a Nazi plan...

R. FREGOLI: Comrade, please. My intentions were pure. I just wanted to continue working with the man I, and I don't think this is too strong a word, *worshipped*. And this time we'd be working *against* the fascists, a system I stopped believing in some time before. Instead, he... this *spy* used me! Used me to bolster fascism! That I cannot and will not abide! Plus, comrade, I brought this information forward when no one knew about it, of my own free will. *That* is why you should believe me.

PROSECUTOR: Very well, Comrade Fregoli. When did you and

Klaus Otto Habermohl meet?

R. FREGOLI: He and I met in 1939. When the Italians and the Nazis formed the Axis, I was sent to Berlin, though later we moved our headquarters to Prague.

PROSECUTOR: What kind of man was Dr. Habermohl?

R. FREGOLI: He was a secretive fellow. Not really outgoing. The others, Richard, Georg, even Rudy, were amiable men…

PROSECUTOR: You are speaking of Richard Walter Miethe, Georg Klein, and Flugkaptain Rudolf Schriever?

R. FREGOLI: That's right. To show you what kind of person the Flugkaptain was, Rudy, along with a man from Bohemia whose name he never revealed, well they sold the Eiffel Tower for scrap. He was a magnificent con artist, the perfect man to cover up the Flugkreisel operation. That's why he was the captain. We were working in absolute secrecy. Only a few people knew what we were doing. And Rudy cloaked us with an amazing array of subterfuge. Richard and Georg, on the other hand, were good engineers and even better drinkers. Wine, women, and song? More like bock, babes, and ballads. I was never sure how they did it. They'd close the beer hall, continue till dawn at someone's house, and then show up to work the next day. Klaus, on the other hand… Klaus was different. Very withdrawn. Inward. Private. Remarkably, he had no remarkable characteristics. He wasn't short or tall. He wasn't thin or fat. His skin tone was neither dark nor light. His voice was neither grating nor melodious. You could sit in the same small room with him for hours and not even realize he was there. This wasn't stealth. It was Klaus. But he was the best… would you say "scientist" or "engineer" or…? No. He was an inventor. An artist. As it turns out, more an Edison than a Tesla, though.

PROSECUTOR: How did you befriend this recluse?

R. FREGOLI: Klaus and I were the odd men out. At our meetings, you'd never know he was the mastermind. Rudy seemed to be in charge. Richard and Georg appeared to be his first lieutenants. I was there because San Marino and Italy didn't know what to do with me and neither did the

Nazis. I had my engineering degrees, but I wasn't particularly gifted. Maybe that's why we worked so well together. Rudy performed his bureaucratic magic tricks so no one knew about us, Klaus was the wizard, Richard and Georg were his lieutenants, and I did what I was told. Maybe you could see me as Klaus' assistant. But being the social outcasts, while Richard, Georg, and sometimes Rudy lived it up at the beer hall? Klaus and I got along well. I suppose it didn't hurt that I constantly told him he was a genius.

PROSECUTOR: Although you were friends, the fact that the two of you ended up in the same place was a bit of a surprise.

R. FREGOLI: That's right. There weren't many who knew what we were doing. Even the grunts who built the Flugkreisels, they thought they were building a new Vengeance Weapon like the V-1 and V-2. The secrecy was byzantine to say the least. That's why a con man had to lead us. Anyway, the few who knew about our work thought Rudy was the most important. The true architect. Flugkaptain. Richard and Georg were big names too. Me and Klaus were also-rans.

PROSECUTOR: But this hierarchy wasn't correct.

R. FREGOLI: No, of course not. Rudy wasn't even an engineer. Part of the cover. He faked his degrees. The idea was if anyone captured us, Rudy would come off as an opportunist who'd work on his baby, the Flugkreisel, for anyone who'd fund it. Being completely inept, though, he'd fail (and hopefully escape before anyone noticed).

PROSECUTOR: And as you've said, Habermohl was the true Flugkaptain.

R. FREGOLI: More like the Flugadmiral.

PROSECUTOR: How did we obtain this information, Comrade Fregoli?

R. FREGOLI: Can you be more specific, sir?

PROSECUTOR: We knew when we selected you and Habermohl that Mr. Schriever was only a figurehead. How did we come by this information?

R. FREGOLI: By that time Rudy was already dead...

PROSECUTOR: Answer the question please, Comrade Fregoli.

R. Fregoli: I... I volunteered the information. You got to me fir...

Prosecutor: Never mind. Were you ever suspicious of Dr. Habermohl?

R. Fregoli: After the flying discs were destroyed near the moon I...

Prosecutor: I said, "Were you ever suspicious of Dr. Habermohl?" Not whomever this man is.

R. Fregoli: Oh... Yeah. The Retrorsus School of Reverse Engineering...

We interrupt this flashback at the country house in order to bring to you, ladies and gentlemen of Radioland, more of Eve Z'droppe's report. Ms. Z'droppe...

Z'droppe: It's over now. For two hours, I watched Agent Bezopasnosky's... dance?... dance is what I'll call it. A performance, as far as I can tell, for no one. No one at all. Unless the audience is hidden like I am... This is what the routine consisted of: everything Kuzma did over the course of one hour, he did backwards over the course of the next hour. What does it mean? I have no idea. During the... what have you... a television in the background broadcasted a commercial for the Retrorsus School of Reverse Engineering. I have never heard of it before. I'm not even convinced it actually exists. But the advertisement, much like Kuzma's dance, played backwards when he moved backwards and then forwards when he moved forwards. I guess it was part of the show, though again, I have no idea...

That was Eve Z'droppe from last night. Joining us now, ladies and gentlemen, to talk about the Retrorsus School of Reverse Engineering is our engineering correspondent, Marmaduke Ekudamram. Mr. Ekudamram, what is this strange sounding ...

Ekudamram: It's a dream come to life.

Could you be more specific, Mr. Ekudamram?

Ekudamram: As a young engineering student, you hear about the Retrorsus School the same way you hear about any urban legend. You're sitting at a party, no one left is getting laid, everyone's kind of drunk, and then someone drops the name: Retrorsus School. The first time, likely, another clever jerk brings up Occasus, too. Weird. You don't say? Huh. He was one crazy cat… It all devolves into rambling and by the time you reach the diner to scarf down an omelet, no one's talking about anything so heady. Then nada for quite a while. Or maybe Occasus comes up again, briefly, somewhere down the road, and you wonder, "Now where did I hear that name before?" Later, at another party, you learn a little more about the school, that supposedly there are even branch campuses. Where are they? Area 51 and Kapustin Yar, of course. After that, only the chosen are able to collect more and more information, usually through the most unlikely sources …

I thank you, Mr. Ekudamram, we will get back to you shortly, but we must return to the Hyperborean for this…

PROSECUTOR: Please elaborate. What made you suspicious of Dr. Habermohl?

R. FREGOLI: Near the end of the war, Klaus and I were walking through the Flugkreisel factory. As we passed a line of completed discs, Klaus stopped me and said, "We! We have done this! We must celebrate!" It was strange. We didn't celebrate the first ship, the first flight, the first moon landing, or even the moment when there was no question: the lunar surface had been colonized because of our, well, really Klaus' efforts. Somehow, it finally hit him when we were strolling through the factory. Everything we'd achieved. Everything he *had* achieved. So we got a few bottles of schnapps… And… And… Honestly, I figured he was… was drunk. Never get drunk, that was one of the Bohemian's commandments, according to Rudy. Maybe Klaus just wanted me to think he was drunk. I don't know. At the time, he seemed tight, that's for sure… And I thought… I thought he was telling me he had a twin brother. He said, "There's a… you know?… there's a… it couldn't be, but it is… ja, it is. There's a man who looks exactly like me. Dop… doppa… el… Whatever. Whatever! Nothing… nothing like… me… up here." He tapped his temple. "The opposite. Reverse. I…

make. He… un… un… huh?… makes. And learns. And… learns. Never. No? Never. We're never… in… the same place. He steals… ha! I give freely. Freely… He steals my… what?… thoughts. Or… huh? I create his… One day… one… one day. We will meet! Ja. And what… what… what will… happen?" So I told him about Retrorsus and Prorsus. Before he passed out, he said a school of reverse engineering should be named for the backwards Roman. At that moment, I wondered if my friend had ulterior motives, if all this time, the entire time I'd known him, he'd been putting on a performance.

Excuse me again, ladies and gentlemen, but earlier we had to interrupt Dr. Buchs before she'd finished. Now, there's something more you were going to tell us about Iacomus Occasus Lacio, called Retrorsus.

Buchs: Yes, later in his life he theorized that since there was a Retrorsus, there must also be a Prorsus. Retrorsus, after all, lived to the ripe old age of 87, "a failing," he told his friends. "Against my better judgment, I've advanced forward for so many years!" Prorsus, on the other hand, would proceed forwards, always forwards, would do everything forwards, while getting younger and younger and younger, moving inexorably backwards in time. After inventing Prorsus, he feared that his dedication to reverse might not be enough, that backwards could become a kind of forwards after a while. He imagined his meeting with Prorsus. It would be his end. And it was. This was the last entry in his journals.

Thank you, Dr. Buchs.

"Enough," sez the young Kuzma back at the All-Union Radio station. "Enough for today."

"I steell doan understand. Who ees Fregoli? Ve had Habermohl and Schriever," sez the engineer. "Ve shot Schriever, Habermohl escaped. Who ees Fregoli?"

"You neet to learn to be quiet, comrade. Doan ask questions."

"Eet's only us…"

"*Doan ask questions.* Get you eento trouble, comrade."

"But Fregoli's not real," sez the engineer. "He can't be."

Pause.

"He ees now," sez Agent Bezopasnosky. "Ve've engineered heem een reverse."

Joining us, curious listeners of Radioland, is our counterespionage correspondent, Citronelle Fogge. Ms. Fogge, could you shed some light on this situation?

FOGGE: When the American-Soviet Alliance began planning for Operation Moonstone, the four Flugkreisel engineers were split between the United States and the USSR. The assumption was that since all four had worked on the flying discs, they could oversee factories in the two major countries. When Operation Moonstone was an utter failure, it was assumed that the loss of Flugkaptain Schriever was crucial. Now, even though the Cold War between the US and the Soviet Union was a red herring to cover up the Cold War between the Lunar Nazis and the forces of earth, well, Americans and Russians still weren't always open with each other. For instance, we didn't know Schriever was executed by the Russians, and we never even heard of Pseudo-Habermohl until we found pieces of this show trial transcript.

Pseudo-Habermohl? Show trial? Please explain, Ms. Fogge.

FOGGE: One of the engineers the Soviets drafted was Klaus Otto Habermohl. Or so they thought. Actually, the man they ended up with turned out to be a spy and a saboteur. No one ever learned his real name, so he was called Pseudo-Habermohl.

This was a show trial? How come?

LeBUSTRE: I believe I can help.

Thank you for joining us. Ladies and gentlemen, our legal correspondent, Phil LeBustre.

LeBUSTRE: I believe you were about to ask how this could be a show trial at all when everyone involved was an actor. Wouldn't this be a dramatization, instead? Normally, a show trial is comprised of various persons in the legal profession and the accused. And whereas the verdict has been determined beforehand, the legal persons involved appear to do their jobs. The Soviets, actually, are well known for the form, but there were frequently problems with the performances. Agents, experts, police, secret police, stenographers, lawyers, judges, "witnesses," at some point during the proceedings had trouble remembering their lines, their cues, their blocking, or they answered questions that hadn't been asked yet or that were supposed to be asked but weren't. Occasionally, the accused figured out it was a show trial and said as much, or the accused didn't react in a way that could lead to national catharsis. In a show trial, as our one-time colleague Blaise Algonquin would say, it's absolutely essential to keep the fourth wall up...

DRAB: But this show trial doesn't have any of those problems because everyone in it is a voice actor.

Loman Drab, our radio critic, ladies and gentlemen...

DRAB: Everyone was acting anyway, why not get people who are trained? Especially the accused. Being in a show trial, after all, is like being in a live action dramatization. Why not bring it on home?

But why has no one ever heard of this Soviet program?

DRAB: It never aired.

FOGGE: Before this flashback, there were a few theories as to what happened. One, Pseudo-Habermohl was never apprehended, so the Soviets planned to air this All-Union Radio program in case the failure of Operation Moonstone was discovered by the general populace. Two, the Soviets learned Lunar Nazi flying disc technology was just better because they'd had the Flugkaptain. So no sabotage, but they had to spin the story in their favor. Three, Habermohl was as inept as previously believed, Fregoli was the saboteur, and since Fregoli had escaped, the Soviets wanted to cover their collective butts. They planned to use a show trial (their favorite medium) for that purpose. Those who believed the last theory also believed Fregoli was blackmailing any number of important figures. Now, it seems like the Soviets drafted Schriever and Habermohl, shot Schriever for unknown reasons (maybe he was a con man, a bureaucrat), learned that Habermohl was a spy who had escaped, and created Fregoli to act in their show trial against this Pseudo-Habermohl.

Let me get this straight. Pseudo-Habermohl was never apprehended, Renato Fregoli (the star witness against Pseudo-Habermohl) may've never existed, and this flashback is a show trial, populated entirely by actors, a *show trial,* the sole purpose of which is to be *shown* in order to *show* the citizens that their country is effective at meting out justice (no matter how hypocritical that may be), and yet this *show trial* was never shown!

WRYLY: Mmmm-it was recorded for radio, sir. A medium you might have encountered at some point.

Very droll, Wryly. Very droll. What we are left with, ladies and gentlemen, are questions. Questions. The opposite of which is supposed to be the outcome of the show trial. Was there a Renato Fregoli? If there was, how did he escape being drafted by the Americans and the Soviets after World War Two? Where did he go? What did he wish to accomplish? And what does any of this have to do with the murder of "Senator" Kipper Maris? Perhaps the Hyperborean holds the answers. Ed Murrow, the airwaves are yours...

You find your way out of the radio studio, Wall, though you don't quite remember how, and the detectives can't help because they seem to've scurried elsewhere. Standing in the hallway, alone in your ridiculous maid's getup, that Russian is gone, so free will's returned (as much as can be expected, anyway). Now everything is calm, serene, and you're floating, as if a conveyor belt had been installed, they did say to explore the house, and so exploring you are. Where in the mansion are you? It doesn't matter. It doesn't matter at all. Such relaxation you've never felt before. Though, yes, you are tired of being between rooms (it's like someone got a case of hallitis when they designed this damn place). How's about ducking into...?

A gunshot.

The Predicta sez: *The Cold War itself began in 1947, the same year the ASA was formed.*

Standing in the doorway, Wall, you see a body on the floor, the detectives (where'd they come from?) almost leaping from their catwalks, though managing to remain calm.

Someone feels for a pulse.

"He ist tot, Herr Schtein," sez Major Freytag, obviously happy, lighting a cigarette. "Dead." Somehow everyone in the house is in this room (and what room is this again?). They all have guns but you, right? Uh...

The Predicta sez: *And on October 4, 1957, Sputnik 1 was launched into orbit a full fifteen years after the Space Race had been summarily won by the Nazis.*

Ladies and gentlemen... Good people of Radioland... Davenport Starch, I thought you said *Youdunnit* was a show that revealed to murderers that they had committed murder. Here, Mr. Orcuson doesn't even have a gun.

STARCH: The show's not over yet.

EKUDAMRAM: I know you're frustrated, but I believe I can clear one thing up.

Our engineering correspondent, Marmaduke Ekudamram. Go ahead...

EKUDAMRAM: We heard Eve Z'droppe describe the odd "dance" that Agent Bezopasnosky was doing in his motel room last night. What he's actually doing is the Daylight Wastings Time ritual. It's become a kind of sport, even. Like figure skating. It's a yearly deal at the Retrorsus School of Reverse Engineering for the students when the clock falls back into Standard Time.

But you said the Retrorsus School doesn't exist!

EKUDAMRAM: Did I? Well, I guess it's like reverse engineering. It exists, but you can't make that your major. You can't sign up for a class in reverse engineering. There aren't any reverse engineers. There are only engineers. So, really, every school of engineering is a school of reverse engineering. The Retrorsus itself doesn't exist, then, because it's everywhere.

What about Daylight Wastings Time?

EKUDAMRAM: Here's how it works: on the day of the time change the hour between 1:00am and 2:00am is repeated. The Daylight Wastings Time ritual, and it's almost impossible, is to do everything you did in that

260

previous hour backwards. There are official judges who make sure you're repeating in reverse what you did in the previous hour, and they rate the difficulty of your performance. For instance, some students sit perfectly still for an hour. You can do that, but you're not gonna score many points. Others make outrageous attempts: playing ping pong or shooting pool…

How do you think Agent Bezopasnosky is doing?

Z'DROPPE: Again, I have no idea what I'm seeing. I would describe it as ballet, but none of the moves are… It is perhaps its own dance, a dance of mundanity, all of the movements we normally make when no one is watching and then their opposite, a complete hour and then the erasure of that hour, the elimination of a small period of time no one else would've known about anyway. Even the baseball game continues on next door…

EUCHRE: *I've faced a knuckleball before, and I've seen it wobble.*

TU: *That's because of a phenomenon created by the speed of the ball and the slight rotation of the seams.*

EUCHRE: *Speed?! It's the slowest pitch in the game.*

TU: *That's true. But it moves just fast enough to trick you. The stitches rotate in and out of view slowly enough for the batter to see them, but the ball moves toward the plate too quickly for his brain to process and interpret what he sees. It's rather like a barber pole effect. The ball seems to flutter or jump when it actually doesn't.*

EUCHRE: *Two more goose eggs this inning, and more from our own egghead after…*

Z'DROPPE: …and at the end, or the beginning?, as he reaches down and turns the Mr. Mxyzptlk action figure away from the wall, I would like to call it a triumph, but I'm not sure that word applies at all…

EKUDAMRAM: From Eve's description, it sounds like Kuzma's a real competitor. But believe you me, he'll have to watch out for that East German judge.

East German judge? There hasn't been an East Germany in years!

EKUDAMRAM: Oh, I know. And there likely won't ever be again. But there will always be an East German judge. Always.

Ladies and gentlemen... Good people of Radioland...
And now this...

§

MANLEY: Welcome to beautiful Hawthorne Race Course in Cicero, Illinois, everyone. Just a hop, skip, and a jump from Chicago. Today we're here for the Wakefield Memorial Handicap. On the call, that's me, Chic Manley. Normally, we would tell you a little about the history of this run, but as you may know, the Wakefield Memorial's past, particularly the very existence of its founder, has been called into question. In fact, we're no longer certain there ever *was* a "Wakefield." It's as if, somehow, he woke up one day and decided to walk right out of his own story. A strange revelation. The race, now, might as well be named for the Boston Red Sox knuckleballer. When you think...

TU: ...about baseball, it appears to be orderly. It has form. There are nine innings. There are nine players in the field. Nine people in the batting order. Three outs in each half inning. Three strikes make an out. Four balls is a walk. The field, a diamond made of bases that are ninety feet apart, and you must visit them in sequential order. The game concludes after those nine innings are up and one team has more runs than the other. Simple. Oh, sure, there are intricacies. But in the end, it's like any other game. Isn't it? Of course. Until we look closer at Space and Time and see...

OARBYTT: ...the long-standing rivalry between Pilgrim & Pagan and Leader's, that's right, the two coffee and doughnut chains... when we look closer at their long-standing rivalry, a rivalry as fierce as Coke–Pepsi, Ford–Chevy, Nike–Reebok, IBM–Apple, even the American League and the National League, the kind of conflict where you're either for one or the other and never the twain shall... when we look closer, Orbiters, there's more than meets the eye, according to fearless journalist Colt Fuzhun, anyway. Fuzhun's article in *One Thousand and One Hours* (tag line: "The light of truth shines on and on"), Fuzhun's article, and it's a doozy, very intriguing, his article asserts that there's a connection between Leader's Doughnuts and the Nazi Party. You heard me right. And I don't mean those Neo-Nazis either, just a bunch of...

EUCHRE: ...slackers. Yes, foax, so many games are dedicated to the troops, fire fighters, police, doctors and nurses, teachers, the men and women who serve us, either nationally or locally. But today's game is dedicated to the slackers, couch potatoes, galoots, lugs, goldbricks, idlers, deadbeats, those, foax, who do little to nothing of note, yet somehow, somehow, find a way to continue on with their lives. Loafers of the world, we salute you! I was going to mention this earlier, but, well, I just didn't get around to it. Now, let's pause for station identification. This is the...

MAGAM: ...*Arthur Magam Show*, and I'm your host, Bootsy Snarkington. No, of course, I'm Arthur Magam, and with us today, ladies and germs, is none other than Edward R. Murrow. Edward R. Murrow on our program! Yes, indeed. We're going to ask him where he's been hiding out these past, oh, fifty years. Along with Edward R. Murrow, we'll have...

OARBYTT: ...the man who took over for Adolf Hitler. After Der Führer and his bride supposedly knocked back a couple cyanide cocktails, the Little Corporal following that with a Walther PPK chaser there in the Führerbunker (and we've had entire shows dedicated to whether or not Hitler actually *did* kill himself), anyway, after the suicide, well, the man who became the Nazi premier was the former head of the Kriegsmarine. Don't remember his name? Worry not. Few people do. And the reason for that is... Orbiters, the assumption was if Hitler were to die or get assassinated, then Reichsmarschall Hermann Göring would be the new leader. And why not? He was the highest ranking military official, he founded the Gestapo and put Himmler in charge, he'd been a member of the Nazi Party from the very beginning. Of course, of course the second most powerful man in Germany would become the new Führer if Hitler were no more. Obvious. Until you take into account...

TU: ...the dimensions of a baseball field. They aren't standardized. In every other sport, no matter where you go, the field is the same. Play

263

football in Hawaii, Kansas, England, on the moon and you'll be standing on a rectangle 120 yards long (including the end zones) by 53.3 yards wide. Soccer, basketball, volleyball, hockey (both on the ice and in the field), all have dimensions that've been set in stone, too. Not baseball. The infield, yes. But beyond that lies the undefined outfield. There have been cavernous centers and comically short left and right field walls. In the 1970s, parks were built that followed a generally accepted set of guidelines, a natural arc; they were derisively called "Cookie Cutter Stadiums," soon replaced by parks with irregular walls that have inexplicable indentations and severe angles creating, in turn, aberrant shapes. Houston's Minute Maid Park was perhaps the most notorious culprit. The center field wall stood at 436 feet. A long ways? Certainly. Still shorter than the old Polo Grounds, so there must be more. And there is. For in front of the fence was an absurd hill ninety feet wide with a thirty degree gradient that was topped by a flagpole in the field of play! It is…

EPIFANIK: …W.H. Auden's belief that mysteries makeup the most conservative genre. Violence enters our innocent world, which both frightens and excites us. Then we watch as the detective restores order through his or her masterful means. There are twists and turns along the way; there may even be a question as to whether or not justice will be served at the end. But even if justice is withheld, we know what happened and why. If the murderer is still alive and free, we know it's because jury-rigged society has failed the systematic and organized detective. If only our sleuth ran the world, then we'd live in perfection. Alas, no. And, anyway, who can expect…

EUCHRE: …to hit a pitch like that?! Wow! Magam's butterfly ball is moving! Three up, three down in the top of the third, foax. Maybe this is the beginning of a pitcher's duel. Then, things can fall apart quickly for the men of the knuckleball fraternity, though Magam really has it so far. Stay tuned. In the bottom of the third, we'll see…

MAGAM: …Edward R. Murrow. How are you? Are you feeling all right? You look a little pale.

MURROW: I'm fine, Arty.

MAGAM: Tell us, we have so many questions for you, so tell us, what's it like being dead, Mr. Murrow?

MURROW: You know, Edward R. Murrow isn't exactly my name. That's just what I'm going by for…

MAGAM: So there you have it. When we die, we don't even feel like ourselves anymore.

MURROW: That's not what I meant.

MAGAM: No one can understand you because you've forgotten who you were, who you are. A stranger to yourself. It's like a horse race where you aren't sure your horse is running. You aren't even sure he was signed up in the first place.

MANLEY: …they're off! On the inside It Beats Me, now One Of Those Horses goes for the lead as they move through the stretch. Up on the outside is I'm Not Entirely Sure, along the inside No One Knows, on the extreme outside is I Can't Say That On The Air and he's moving up. They move for the first turn with…

OARBYTT: …Göring on the extreme outside. There were stories. The Reichsmarschall asked to take power before Hitler offered it to him. Needless to say, the Little Corporal was furious. Not to mention Göring's brother Albert had a bad habit of rescuing people from the camps. Okay, then why not Heinrich Himmler? Ha! The Reichsführer of the SS went further than Göring. Good old Himmler tried to surrender to the Allies before Hitler was even dead. You can guess what Der Führer thought of that. No, the only member of the military who hadn't betrayed Adolf was the head of the Kriegsmarine. And so, as written in Hitler's final will and testament, the grand admiral was made Reichspräsident. Supposedly. If you believe that story. Oh, sure, it's plausible. Convincing. Hits all the right notes. But beyond that…

TU: …there are the stadiums themselves. The Oakland-Alameda County Coliseum shows us that not only are there no actual regulations for outfield configurations, there's also no set amount of foul territory. O.co, as it's now called, has so much foul territory, it produces twice as many foul ball outs as any other stadium. Then, there are the outfield walls themselves. Fenway is a veritable pinball machine. The Green Monster is thirty-seven feet tall in part because it's only 310 feet from the plate (when most are at least 325). The other walls sport garage doors, strange angles, and the Pesky Pole in right that's only 302 feet deep. The Metrodome's right field had a regular seven foot high wall capped by a sixteen foot high plastic extension called The Baggie. Elsewhere, there are walls with built in scoreboards, walls that were once chain-link, walls that were moved during the course of the season depending on who the opponent was. The crowning achievement in outfield walls, though, has to be Wrigley, where they are made of brick covered in ivy! Not to mention, baseball is, of course, played with a small, white ball, so you'd expect the general environs to be dark in color. Not so in the old Metrodome and in Tropicana Field, both of which have white domed ceilings. Tropicana even has catwalks directly above the field. No matter how these catwalks may interfere with the flight of the ball, they are in fair territory... And yet...

EPIFANIK: ...David Gordon disagrees with W.H. Auden. He says that Auden misses the fact that mystery readers are always moving on to new mysteries. When concatenated, a detective's solution is only a brief reprieve before we plunge back into the swirling maelstrom that is barely maintained even by the best gumshoes. The forces of chaos just...

EUCHRE: ...keep coming. Dizzy Egri has now thrown fifteen balls in a row here in the bottom of the third, the bases are loaded, and the pitch... Ball sixteen. That's a run and an RBI, our scoreless tie is broken, and there's no...

MAGAM: ...end in sight. Answer this—how did you die?

MURROW: How would I know that? It hasn't hap...

MAGAM: You don't remember that either.

MURROW: Okay. How about I was murdered?

MAGAM: Murdered? You say you were murdered.

MURROW: That's right.

MAGAM: Who killed you? Do you remember?

MURROW: I guess I don't.

MAGAM: When we die, we don't remember who or what killed us. It's an eternal mystery with no Sherlock Holmes or Hercule Poirot or Philip Marlowe or Lennie Briscoe to solve it for us. Do you even know how long you've been dead for?

MURROW: Since at least before this project.

MAGAM: Well, I'm glad, in the face of so much uncertainty, you haven't lost your sense of humor. Even though all you can say is...

MANLEY: ...Who Knows! Who Knows along the rail. Then it's I Can't Say That On The Air alongside I Can't Tell followed by Are You Serious and You've Got To Be Kidding. They're moving on the turns to...

OARBYTT: ...the German Antarctic Expedition of 1939. Who masterminded that project? And who, shocker of all shockers, took over after Hitler was dead? And who only served a ten year sentence following the Nuremberg Trials? And who supposedly spent the rest of his life in a quaint little village in Northern Germany where he whiled away the time by penning a couple memoirs until he died of natural causes? The Reichsprasident formerly known as Grand Admiral Dönitz, Karl Dönitz. That's right, according to Colt Fuzhun, Hitler was never the real Führer. He was the red herring. And what a red herring he was! No one needed to look any higher, did they? But then "higher" is the wrong word, isn't it? They should've looked lower. Because the *actual* Führer was busy building the *real* Third Reich under Antarctica. Now you might think I've gone far afield here, Orbiters, but listen up. Before Leader's Doughnuts was called "Leader's," it was called Grand Admiral Doughnuts. Ring a bell? Reichsprasident, it's for you. Their first location supposedly opened in 1939, but no one ever says where. Founded in 1939 is all. I bet it was under the South Pole. Probably it's still open. If you're hanging out with the penguins, you could stop by and get yourself some Nazi sinkers and an Aryan cup of coffee (plenty of cream in that now). Yes, Orbiters, in my opinion, Colt Fuzhun has given every one of you out there a good reason to go to Pilgrim & Pagan tonight. I know Arty Magam, he's manning the counter right now, ready to serve you up with…

Tu: …the coup de grâce. Having discussed Space, where the orderly infield leads to the mysterious outfield, the coup de grâce is Time. As time is concerned, there's no reason to think that any single baseball game will ever end. There isn't even a reason to believe that any half inning will end. Baseball is not bound by a clock. We can play…

Euchre: …forever. Egri has walked another four batters and no one's warming up in the bullpen. I guess the thinking is, well, he technically still has a no-hitter going. Pretty soon, they're going to be the Boys of Winter not the Boys of…

Tu: …summer. Baseball's relationship to time mirrors our own wishes for an eternal summer. Yes, summer will end. It can only last so long. Baseball, on the other hand, has the potential for infinity. Boundless. Amorphous. Ubiquitous. And yet, it is the game with the most statistics. More are added every season. It's as if we were constantly trying to give this sport a form, though that form is forever elusive. The knuckleball, the knuckleball reminds us of this ambiguity, this enigma we try to obfuscate with numbers. Everything else about baseball seeks to make the game comprehensible. Maybe the end…

Epifanik: …isn't the most important part of the genre, even though Mickey Spillane claims otherwise. It actually *is* the middle. If so, both Auden and Gordon have missed the point. It's the experience of the mystery, not the order of the solution or the constant threat of the next disturbance. One of the first works that fits the genre, *Oedipus the King*, does not have a violent beginning or a surprise ending. Every audience member or reader knows what happened and what's going to happen. Our viewing of the work is filtered through someone who is ignorant, though we are not. Why would anyone be there but to…

Euchre: …experience this mystery. Egri is still out there, foax. He's still throwing balls. I've lost count how many. You'd think he'd accidentally get one over the plate sooner or later. I hit a few dingers when

I played, and I don't have to tell you, I wasn't exactly a slugger. No one's up in the bullpen. How do you…

MAGAM: …think it will all end?

MURROW: What?

MAGAM: What's going on? What's happening?

MURROW: Behind the one-way mirror? Or here? I don't know what to say. None of it… Everything seems vague, dreamlike. I feel like there was a time when the world made sense, when what was real felt *real*. Really real. If only we could've stayed there. The further we move away from that point, the further we sink into unreality. So I can't tell you what's happening, and I can't predict what will come next.

MAGAM: You don't know who you are, who you were, or what's coming. All you know is that you were killed…

MURROW: I…

MAGAM: …but you don't know by who. When this is all over, when it's all behind us, at the…

MANLEY: …wire it's going to be–I Can't Tell, It Beats Me, I'm Not Entirely Sure, You've Got To Be Kidding, Are You Serious, Who Knows, No One Knows!

§

A radio somewhere:

EUCHRE: *It's the top of the fourth, the Senators lead 8-0, and…*

shshshshshshshshshshshshshshshshshshshshs
shshshshshshshshshshshshshshshshshshshshs
shshshshshshshshshshshshshshshshshshshshs

TU: *…inning I'll talk about the members of the Fraternal Order of Knuckleheads–the pitchers themselves…*

shshshshshshshshshshshshshshshshshshshshshs
shshshshshshshshshshshshshshshshshshshshshs
shshshshshshshshshshshshshshshshshshshshshs

Fact: Watt Gallman has a clear history of ethical behavior and steadfast leadership. A clear history.

Fact: Watt Gallman has a proven track record of fighting for more transparency. That's right, more transparency.

Fact: Watt Gallman has never been accused of insider trading, bribery, or corruption. Never even accused.

Fact: Watt Gallman... when you think about it, there are just too many solid facts about Watt Gallman.

Paid for by the Coalition to Elect Enke Hootz, Conspirator General.

shshshshshshshshshshshshshshshshshshshshshs
shshshshshshshshshshshshshshshshshshshshshs
shshshshshshshshshshshshshshshshshshshshshs

Perplexed listeners of Radioland, I am not sure what, just now, this transmission, I...

LE TANNES: I believe I can help.

Ladies and gentlemen, we are truly honored to have in the studio with us today the founder of the Conspiratorium, Charlotte Le Tannes. Char Le Tannes, everyone! Ms. Le Tannes, my first question is: how did you get in here? You appeared literally out of nowhere.

LE TANNES: I could tell you, but then...

Can you tell us about this, I want to say invasion by an alien signal, but I'll stick with interruption. It sounded like a political ad, but there aren't any elections scheduled for quite some time.

LE TANNES: No official elections, you mean. The Conspiratocracy holds its Conspirator General elections at arbitrary times and in secret...

The Conspiratocracy? The Conspirator General? What?

LE TANNES: The Conspirator General, as far as we can tell, is the highest position in the Conspiratocracy. As for the Conspiratocracy, itself, for want of a better term, we can call it a shadow government, though that might not be entirely acc...

This is very intriguing, Ms. Le Tannes, but we must interrupt you because things are really heating up in the Hyperborean. So take it away, Ed Murrow...

Standing in a clump in the center of the library is, well, everyone. Everyone, right, except the detectives who are spread out on the catwalks, each having found the ideal angle, the vantage point that will reveal, has probably *already* revealed the key to the mystery. Do you get the feeling, Wall, that their presence negates your own, makes any action you might take irrelevant, superfluous, so predictable, buddy, the bookies of the beyond aren't laying any odds on what you're gonna do because like everybody already knows? And now, as if in response to music only they can hear, the gumshoes begin moving, an extremely slow dance, every sleuth taking in the POV of every other sleuth, making it possible for each one of them to see how the others will solve the case, even though each detective is certain he or she solved it first, even though each detective is just waiting, waiting for enough evidence to mount so others may be made aware of what these nimble flatfeet already know...

The Predicta sez: *On July 20, 1969, the United States won the Space Race by successfully completing a manned mission to the moon. Soon after conspiracy theories arose claiming it was all a hoax.*

"Nein, nein, nein, nein! Vhat are you doink?! Zis vill not vork! No vun can zee anysink!" sez Major Freytag, who immediately begins reorganizing the scene, directing positions, choreographing movements, coaching reactions, orienting the corpse, until the tableau is set: "Senator" Maris, dead as a doornail (again), face down on the floor; Agent Asbestos, to the right of the corpse, glaring over his shoulder at Greta; Ms. Zelle, herself, slumped back in a chair, the embodiment of shock, though holding her pistol; Ima Fregoli, continuing with the matron deal, rushing to Greta's side (whether to console or disarm is unclear); Mr. E., to your left, nonchalantly smoking a cigarette, vaguely amused, glancing in your direction as you enter through the door, Wall; Schmetterling, in the back left corner, breaking character (probably why he only ever made Oberschütze), unable to hide his joy; Agent Bezopasnosky (how'd he get here so quickly?), checking the carcass's pulse from the left…

Wall… Wall… Why are you clapping, Wall?

The Predicta sez: *We should still look at the moon landing as one of the greatest accomplishments in human history, not because we were first (the Nazis made it there in 1942 and the ASA was there in 1950), but because keeping the conspiracy mostly intact for this long was more difficult than the mission itself.*

Everyone turns to you, Wall, their attention shifted…

"Really first rate, Freytag. Really first rate. I congratulate you. Such a beautiful triangle. It's so… natural? No, that's not the word I'm looking for. Not the right word at all. More like I walked in on a…"

"He's dead," sez Bezopasnosky.

"Ja," sez Major Freytag, rubbing his hands together. "Ve neet Körper. Bodies."

"What? What? What?" sez Greta.

"I think what Ms. Zelle is trying to ask is: what killed him?" sez Ima.

"Natural causes." Really, Wall? That's what you're going with?

"Obviously, he was shot. I heard the gun go off," sez Mr. E.

"Like I said, natural causes. English country house full of detectives, various government and honorary military personnel present, if he'd died of cancer that would be suspicious." Aren't you proud of yourself, Wall?

"Ms. Zelle has her… gun out. She points it… still," sez Asbestos.

Greta looks surprised to see the pistol in her hand. Ima pats her on the shoulder, lowering the gun arm as if it were on a mannequin.

"He ees dead," sez Agent Bezopasnosky to Greta as he moves away from the corpse. "You keeled husband; you keeled Iam Fregoli."

The Predicta sez: *The film of Neil Armstrong walking on the moon and speaking his immortal lines was pure Hollywood. Which is perfect when you think about the fact that everyone involved was putting on a performance anyway. Whether they knew it or not.*

"What?" sez Greta.

"Our friend Kuzma sez you've figured it out on the first try," sez Mr. E.

"I didn't kill anyone! I pulled my gun out when I heard the shot. Here, check to see if I'm lying," sez Greta handing her pistol to anyone who'll take it. Everyone but you, Wall, moves toward Ms. Zelle, but the Oberschütze butler stops them.

"Honored guests, this is the Butterfly Ball, not a murder mystery party where you are rewarded for solving crimes that take place," sez Schmetterling. "One of you has murdered 'Senator' Maris, who either was or wasn't Iam Fregoli. Honestly, I don't care which." The detectives disapprove, obviously, but they aren't surprised. "At midnight, we'll find out if you've kept your conspiracy covered up or not. For now, please accompany me to the dining room where dinner will be served."

"Who can eat at a time like this?!" sez Greta.

"Eef you can't, more for us. Da," sez Bezopasnosky.

The Predicta sez: *The performances did not stop there. Skylab and the space shuttle program continued the mock-exploration. But by the time Skylab fell back to earth, people were already tiring of the final frontier.*

Major Freytag and Schmetterling hustle you toward the dining room, leaving the corpse behind. In the mob, Wall, you end up next to Agent Asbestos, who whispers, "I have a... proposition for you. After we have dined, I will... find a way to slip out of the room. You should follow. It will be worth your... while."

A radio somewhere sez:

EUCHRE: *You know, people always comment on Magam's physique. He doesn't really have the look of an athlete, except maybe a bowler.*

TU: That is true. Most pitchers, like most athletes in general, live by the holy trinity of blood, sweat, and tears. They eat a specific diet, follow strenuous weight-lifting routines, and their cardiovascular regimens are unparalleled except maybe by soldiers. For the most part, ballplayers are young, impressive physical specimens who exert themselves to an almost superhuman degree even before the game starts. Then when they take the field, they make it all look so…

shshshshshshshshshshshshshshshshshshshshs
shshshshshshshshshshshshshshshshshshshshs
shshshshshshshshshshshshshshshshshshshshs

Who is Manny Masques really? He says he's a family man. He says he's a church-going man. He says he's a fair man. But can we trust him? YES.

Wolfe Cryer is also a family man. He has four of them; he's working on number five. Of course, they're all ignorant of each other. Wolfe Cryer is also a religious man. He has avowed his faith to every possible sect and denounced all of their rivals. Wolfe Cryer is also a fair man. It's fair to believe no one will ever expose Wolfe Cryer or his conspiracies.

Wolfe Cryer. Unethical. Duplicitous. Mendacious.

Paid for by the Association to Elect Ulysses R. Snookurd, Conspirator General.

shshshshshshshshshshshshshshshshshshshshs
shshshshshshshshshshshshshshshshshshshshs
shshshshshshshshshshshshshshshshshshshshs

TU: …knuckleballers, on the other hand, lift weights sparingly. They can throw for long periods of time because their pitch doesn't require great exertion. Tommy John surgery, rotator cuff injuries, shoulder problems, dead arms, early retirement, these are common with other hurlers, but not with those who focus on the butterfly ball. They can throw well into their later years. In fact, since the pitch is so difficult to control, usually it's the older lofters who dominate. Physical weakness is forgiven with the dry spitter…

Ladies and gentlemen, we are here with Char Le Tannes, founder of the Conspiratorium. You've told us that the Conspirator General is the highest ranking position in the Conspiratocracy…

LE TANNES: As far as we know, it is. I would like to stress right now, however, our intelligence is incomplete at best.

What can you tell us about the Conspiratocracy?

LE TANNES: Maybe it would help to discuss these campaign commercials a bit. Normal campaign ads operate in fairly obvious ways: they praise the candidate, deride the opponent, or do some combination of both. The spots might lie, make the candidate look better than he or she is, make the opponent look worse than he or she is, but in the end you have a general idea of what's going on—Smith and Jones are running for President. One is tough on crime, the other is against the death penalty. Jones calls Smith a fascist, Smith calls Jones a weakling. Whatever. Ads for Conspirator General, on the other hand, are made to conceal and reveal. Let's use the commercial we've heard most recently as an example. Manny Masques is derided and Wolfe Cryer is extolled.

Who are these people, even?

LE TANNES: We'll get to that. Anyway, in a normal ad, we'd know what's happening. But then you get that zinger at the end: "Paid for by the Association to Elect Ulysses R. Snookurd, Conspirator General." It's true that outside entities purchase campaign commercials even in our normal elections. However, this outside entity doesn't appear to be in favor of the derided candidate (Masques) or the extolled candidate (Cryer), instead it appears to be backing some other candidate (Snookurd). But don't be fooled, this ad isn't for Snookurd either.

Then who's it for? I feel like I'm falling down the rabbit hole.

LE TANNES: Exactly. Exactly! That's why I decided to use this advertisement to help explain the Conspiratocracy. But let's pause for a second to talk about what we supposedly want out of our government and our government officials. We always say we want representatives who are honest and ethical, we always say we want transparent operations, we always say we want policies that help those in need, we always say we want laws that are easy to interpret and that punish the guilty.

Power corrupts.

LE TANNES: Of course it does. But let's imagine for a second that we finally got what we supposedly want out of our elected representatives, out of our legal processes. Everyone was honest, everything was clear. Would anyone believe it? Not a chance. The Conspiratocracy, therefore, operates on the notion that any easily accessible information is either being used to cover up the Truth, or it's just plain worthless. And since it's so obvious that what people want is transparency, then it's obviously not true. If it were true, then it'd be the most closely guarded secret imaginable.

So the commercials are attempts to reveal other candidates? Because if we know their names, then they couldn't possibly be effective?

LE TANNES: We think. According to our best intelligence. But while trying to reveal other candidates, those purchasing the ad time have to keep themselves hidden. Consequently, those running for a position in the Conspiratocracy have to adopt multiple aliases and set up strawmen—names that have no conspirator at all behind them. In the end, any one commercial may be full of names that don't refer to anyone at all.

We certainly need to hear more about this... organization, but we must return you now to the Hyperborean where dinner is about to be served...

"Honored guests, this is tonight's menu: we will begin with a succulent red herring impaled on skewers, followed by a Bloody Caesar Salad and a split pea soup. Our main course is priest strangler pasta with head cheese and blood sausage. For dessert there will be spotted dick in bitter almond sauce and a delectable dead man's arm," sez Schmetterling.

The Predicta sez: *But at the beginning of the Space Race, both the United States and the Soviet Union appeared to be in an admirable rivalry. An admirable,* scientific *rivalry...*

"Wonderful, simply wonderful. It sounds like all the food's been brutally murdered. Just the way I like it," sez Wall.

The table is set with silverware and china, both of which gleam at an albedo normally associated with various heavenly bodies, making the otherwise lavish room a blare of white, even the detectives up on their catwalks, who've begun building a model of the crime scene for the purposes of collecting evidence, not being able to descend from their lofty realm, somehow duplicating the room exactly, perhaps too exactly, a model that surpasses the original, though who knows how it'll turn out in the end since it's still incomplete? Well the sleuths themselves wear sunglasses in defense of this offensive glare which continues on until the gourmands below take to tarnishing the plates and cutlery. Finally able to see, the party notices all of the seats are occupied except one: "Senator" Maris'. Everyone tries to not look at the vacant spot, but this labor proves Herculean, and none of the guests is a demigod.

The Predicta sez: *I like to imagine what if the Nazis picked a different Lunarian Manuscript, one that would've had the United States and the Soviet Union constantly vying for greater scientific progress? Instead, we ended up with the Ian Fleming and John le Carré version. Our bad luck.*

"Someone has been killed! My... my..." sez Greta, sobbing.

"Was it you?" sez Mr. E.

"No! Of course not! Why would I kill my own husband?!" sez Greta.

"He was your husband?" sez Ima.

"Yes. He... he was. I won't deny a certain fear of him, even though he never did anything violent. Or, nothing that I saw. I just... just always thought he had the capacity... oh, what does *that* matter now?" sez Greta.

Wryly, earlier we saw Greta Zelle furious with her husband, then we saw her spurring Wall onto murder, but now she's grieving as if she actually loved him. Can you explain?

WRYLY: Mmmm, yes, sir. It could be that Ms. Zelle never expected anyone to kill her husband. She was therefore playing some kind of game

277

with Mr. Orcuson. Or it could be that she killed "Senator" Maris and is now playing the widow to divert suspicion away from herself. Or she might be traumatized from seeing a dead body. Dead by murder.

It sounds like you already know who did it.

WRYLY: I *am* a butler, sir. We always know. Not to mention, this is the time when the red herring or red herrings appear...

They are being served, you are right.

WRYLY: Mmmm, yes. How perspicacious, sir. Nothing can be hidden from you. As I was saying, this is the time when the red herring appears, so whomever you think is the killer, is probably not. The least likely suspect is found guilty in the end, but not before an avalanche of accusations.

"Did you kill him?"

"No," sez Mr. E.

"Did you kill him?"

"No," sez Ima.

"Did you kill him?"

"Nyet," sez Kuzma.

"Did you kill him?"

"No," sez Asbestos.

"Did you kill him?"

"Nein," sez Major Freytag.

WRYLY: Mmmm, there are more elegant ways to go about it, though...

"All right, detectives, might as well go home. No killers here. Thanks for coming out. Sorry to waste your time. Unless... Unless... Unless Maris did die of cancer! A new type of projectile cancer! Detectives, detectives, come back! I know who the murderer is! It's..."

A gunshot goes off and, as if everyone had their getaways planned out beforehand (not a bad idea, what with the death that's already taken place), the room clears... well, except for you and Agent Asbestos, Wall.

The Predicta sez: *The problem with space is that it's just so big. You don't even need Nazis on the moon to dissuade you from exploring it. If we could travel at light speed, the second closest star to us is Proxima Centauri, and at light speed it'd take over four years to get there. The closest earth-like planet, Kepler 452b, is 1400 light years away. So once we lost our human rivals in the Space Race, our exploration out there lost its narrative.*

"Not exactly what I had in mind, but an... effective diversion, nonetheless," sez Asbestos, taking your arm and leading you, uh, where, exactly? You don't know, Wall. But perhaps, finally, it's to the room where that radio's playing:

EUCHRE: *A diving grab by the...*

shshshshshshshshshshshshshshshshshshshshs
shshshshshshshshshshshshshshshshshshshshs
shshshshshshshshshshshshshshshshshshshshs

EUCHRE: *...and it's three up and three down again, though Magam should be thanking his lucky...*

shshshshshshshshshshshshshshshshshshshshs
shshshshshshshshshshshshshshshshshshshshs
shshshshshshshshshshshshshshshshshshshshs

TU: *Thank you, George. The Fraternal Order of Knuckleheads is, we can say, a miniature culture, or maybe a subculture, possibly even a counterculture in baseball. For now, let's call it an exclusive club. They have a Grand Poobah (Phil Niekro, who took over after Hoyt Wilhelm's death), a uniform number (49, first worn by Wilhelm), a common handicap (finger cramps, thanks to the claw-like grip needed to throw a butterfly ball), and a common trait (alienation). Why alienation? Well, a Knucklehead can't ask other pitchers for help. As for pitching coaches, R.A. Dickey said this is the kind of advice they normally give: "Throw another one of those that floats and then drops so they can't hit it." So the only person a Knucklehead can turn to is*

279

another Knucklehead. But except for the 1945 Washington Senators, it's rare for a team to have more than one dry spitter. No matter what club they play for, then, the Knuckleheads cheer for each other, give tips to each other, and the older practitioners even feel they have a responsibility to assist the new initiates into the rites of this fraternal order, but almost always from a distance...

shshshshshshshshshshshshshshshshshshshshshs
shshshshshshshshshshshshshshshshshshshshshshs
shshshshshshshshshshshshshshshshshshshshshshs

Collom Nies has gone too far.

He fired his assistant for forging documents and misleading the Assembly. He's distanced himself from campaign contributors who face jail time for fraud, collusion, and insider trading. He's been present and accounted for at more elections than any conspirator ever. It makes you wonder why Collom Nies decided to work for the Assembly in the first place. He just doesn't get it.

Mae B. Noyes... she gets it. Mae B. Noyes is so forgery friendly, after a month on the job no one was certain if official documents existed anywhere anymore. Mae B. Noyes only associates with those who think talking out of both sides of your mouth doesn't involve enough sides. Mae B. Noyes thinks the only kind of trading is insider trading. Mae B. Noyes has missed so many elections, no one's even sure there is such a person.

Uncertain of who to vote for? Don't be. Vote Noyes.

Paid for by the Jack Paste-Ruby Group.

shshshshshshshshshshshshshshshshshshshshshs
shshshshshshshshshshshshshshshshshshshshshshs
shshshshshshshshshshshshshshshshshshshshshshs

Ladies and gentlemen, we're learning more and more about the Conspiratocracy from Charlotte Le Tannes. You've given us some idea how the candidates in this shadow assembly run campaigns, how does it operate?

LE TANNES: Needless to say, there are no formal buildings or offices, no hallowed documents or paraphernalia. Everything is secret and must remain secret. As soon as something, anything is revealed about the Conspiratocracy, that policy or procedure is no longer salient, no longer followed. It's rumored that when the Assembly meets, they do so in disguises, or they send doubles, dupes, sometimes random people off the street who immediately make claims of confusion, ignorance, and frustration; no one believes them because everyone at an Assembly gathering acts this way. The Conspiratocracy's meetings are *supposedly* never held in the same place twice and the locations are never revealed. It was once believed that their elections were held on April 1. This may've happened at some point, but it's entirely too obvious a choice. Another belief is that the Conspiratocracy meets on the blue moon. Being a variable day, this may be true, but is still unlikely. No matter when they come together, though, nothing important has ever happened at an Assembly meeting. Nothing.

Smoky back rooms and golf courses, then?

LE TANNES: Let me say this—as soon as you think you've pinned down the Conspiratocracy, it becomes something else.

The Conspiratocracy sounds like The Organization.

LE TANNES: I must disagree with you categorically. The Organization is open, completely open. We know where the headquarters is, we can go in and see what they're doing whenever we want, we just can't comprehend it yet. The Conspiratocracy is therefore the opposite of The Organization.

I see. But the Conspiratocracy sounds so labyrinthine, no one could ever possibly understand it.

LE TANNES: True, but remember that we're working with incomplete knowledge. Also, the Conspiratocracy doesn't have to be difficult, it just has to seem difficult. As long as a misleading, hopelessly elaborate narrative can be attached to or help cover up a process, a person, an action, then it's deemed significant. The operative word being misleading.

Thank you, Ms. Le Tannes, but we must send our listening

audience to the Hyperborean where... where... Oh my God! It's full of stars!

Your eyes are pulled toward it, though what *it* is, you're not sure. Everything else tries to take precedence, wants to take precedence, but never really does. For thousands of years we've worked to draw our attention away using myths and legends, figures that rarely resemble what they're supposed to be, the biggest cover up in history with red herrings and obfuscations galore, the kind of mystery where the answer's staring you right in the face, but somehow only the detective, the right set of eyes, is able to see it. How long can you look? What do you tell yourself you're looking at? When will the usual familiar comfortable bastions take hold, diverting you away? The stars, planets, satellites, comets, asteroids, all paste jewelry scattered across the surface, across the surface of what? Even the moon, that tyrant of poetry, the true god of the seas, big and pompous, now crowned by a module, a human descending, though like the constellations he barely looks like what he's supposed to be, robotically intoning, "That's one small step for man, one giant leap for mankind," yes, even the moon endeavors, in vain, to blot out this vast nothing...

"Cut!" sez the director, turning to a subordinate, quipping, "He finally got the line right." The crew fills the vacancy of space, at first, you imagine, walking in that slow motion, weightless style associated with low gravity, until the scene reverts to normal speed, the technicians killing lights, moving cables, inspecting set pieces, helping Neil out of the suit and back to his trailer, a flurry of activity almost impossible to follow, concluding with a mass exeunt, as if it were choreographed, leaving the sound stage under-populated: a middle-aged man, a teenager, and you, Wall.

"Thank you for joining me today, Junior Attendant," sez the middle aged man.

"Thank you for inviting me, Mr. General Counsel, sir," sez the teenager who, on closer inspection, is a younger Agent Asbestos; the middle aged man is his father.

"Do you know what you've just seen, Junior Attendant?"

"Is the sequel to... *2001* being filmed already, sir?"

"Are you being a smart ass, Junior Attendant?"

"I learned from... the best, sir." General Counsel Asbestos smiles and puts an arm around his son. The room, you notice, really does appear to be the surface of the moon right up to the point where the cameras are arranged.

"I invited you here today, Junior Attendant, because it's time you know... it's time you were a man."

"A man?"

"That's right, son. That's right. The time for childish games is over. Childhood is sweet lies and candy, but now the meat has been served."

"The meat?"

"It's rare and bloody. You know what you just saw? You just saw the moon landing, Junior Attendant," sez General Counsel Asbestos, moving away from his son, sitting in a chair marked STANLEY KUBRICK.

"Oh, a simulation?" sez Junior Attendant Asbestos.

"A simulation? Kind of," he sez, looking around, mumbling, "Models never are..."

"I heard Mr. Kubrick say Mr. Armstrong had gotten... his line wrong."

"He did, maybe a thousand times. He kept saying, 'That's one small step for a man, one giant leap for mankind."

"Uh..."

"What's the problem?"

"His version sounds... correct, sir."

"It sounds correct, huh? But here's the thing–it's wrong."

"Why? The one he said... it doesn't... make sense."

"His orders weren't to make sense," sez the General Counsel, glowering up at his son, then storming over to the Lunar Module. "His orders were no A."

"But *man* and *mankind* mean..."

"I can't wait for this..."

283

"…they mean the same thing!"

The General Counsel ascends the module's ladder.

"You know what, Junior Attendant, you're right. But man and mankind sound different, don't they? And I don't just mean phonetically."

"Well, yes, sir."

"Man sounds like it could be one group. Mankind is all of humanity everywhere."

"I don't think I… understand, sir," sez the Junior Attendant, standing at the bottom of the module's ladder, looking up at his father.

"I think you do, but you don't want to admit it."

The young Asbestos building his courage:

"Mr. Armstrong… Mr. Armstrong is… addressing one smaller group first and… then all of…"

"We're not going to the moon, Junior Attendant."

"We've… we've already… been there, haven't we, sir?"

The General Counsel nods.

"And… we weren't first?"

"Like the '45 Senators, second place. And it wasn't pretty. We were forced to make a pact with the worst kind of people. But there was no choice. This," sez the General Counsel, gesturing around the set, "is part of that pact. And it almost didn't happen…"

On a monitor nearby, Wall, you see a younger Owen G. Asbestos tracking what appears to be a walking silhouette.

"A rogue agent threatened to expose everything…"

The young Owen closes in on the silhouette.

"Though some said he was a spook—a ghost, not a spy. Someone invented to scare us, to make us think we couldn't win. Maybe the Soviets, trying to get a leg up."

The young Owen fires. There is the sound of a person falling to the ground.

"I even began to believe it myself. I spent so much time looking for him. But, in the end, what I found, what I delivered was real enough."

And yet, on the screen it's like the dailies for a movie, the director not quite sure which angle to use, which part of the alley, which lighting angles, though the shadowy figure crumples to the ground at the end of each.

"Now, we can move forward. And this..."

"This simulation will..."

"It's not a simulation, Junior Attendant."

"...placate..."

"For now."

"What would... happen if...?"

"World War Two. The real one this time. The war to end all wars. And right now, they might be the favorites," sez the General Counsel, descending the ladder, halting on the final step. His son, shaking, eyes reddening, looks to the side.

"B-b-b-but I thought you s-s-s-said..."

"Starting to stutter again. That pause I taught you is working..."

"*But*... I thought you... said... honesty is the..."

"When I said that, Junior Attendant, I was lying."

A long pause, the young Asbestos barely keeping himself from collapse, a battle is being fought on his face by voluntary and involuntary muscle groups.

"Why have you... told me... all this? Keeping this... secret, I'll be an... outcast. Cut off from... everyone I know. My entire world... turned inward. Everything a secret. Wha-wha-why?!"

"Because you're my son. Because there's no other choice. Because it's time to cut into the meat you've been served, Junior Attendant. And anyway, it may seem tough now, but later you'll think it was one small step for a man," sez the General Counsel, loping off the bottom rung of the ladder, "but one giant leap for mankind. Or, at least, it better be."

Junior Attendant C. Irving Asbestos, head down, looks as if he will crumple... but he does not crumple, he composes himself, seems to age a decade in seconds, a confident, adult professional, an agent. He straightens up, raises his head, nods, and walks off the sound stage with General Counsel Owen G. Asbestos, two Atlases bearing the heft of the world without even a twinge, letting on that they could carry others. While the door hangs open, inching to its original position, you feel weightless and alone there on the moon, Wall, floating away from all you've ever known. The stars having been switched off, there's only the light from the lunar surface, reflected from some unseen sun, glowing because it can't not glow, until you hear the latch click and all is dark…

Patient residents of Radioland, Edward R. Murrow has, once again, broken off from the narration. He appears to be going through some mental turmoil, though our own Madame Khryptymnyzhy is unable to connect with him right now, meaning we're not sure what the problem is. Currently, he stands in front of the one-way mirror and stares through, occasionally looking over his shoulder out the window. Meanwhile, Magam, behind the counter, appears to be sitting in a dugout waiting to return to the mound. It's apparent that he's more than just the pitcher in this ballgame. He's the manager, the umpire, the fans ordering peanuts and hot dogs and beers, the vendors selling the concessions, the true believer, the heckler, the indifferent boyfriend or girlfriend who got dragged along, the official scorekeeper, the legions of unofficial scorekeepers, the organist, the singer of the national anthem, the radio announcers, ladies and gentlemen, he's the entire baseball experience.

While our narrator stands entranced, gazing at the Hyperborean, and with no way to look into his mind, we turn now to investigative reporter Eve Z'droppe, who has acquired a private tape containing Murrow's thoughts on *Vayss Uf Makink You Tock*, which appears to be the manuscript, that is, appears to be the very root of his problem. And so, take it away, whether you want to or not, Ed Murrow…

"When I was first assigned to Senator Maris' project, I assumed it'd be like the other manuscripts I'd narrated. As I read through it, as I became more acquainted with it, honestly, I thought I was being put on. I thought it was a joke. And the joke wasn't funny. Even before I met Maris, I tried to

slough the script off on someone else, figuring that's when I'd learn it wasn't real. April Fools! Happy Birthday! Or whatever. I mean, CNS had never asked me to do anything like this before. I didn't know anyone who'd narrated anything like this before. Sure, maybe some other narrating company would take the contract, but not CNS. Only, they did take it. And they assigned it to me. Now, I've never rewritten a complete work. I've helped clients out with organization, structure, coherence, but I've never rewritten a complete work. Ways of Making You Talk *(I know, I know, I'm supposed to say it with that stupid accent… no one can make me, I just won't speak that way), it needed a complete rewrite. Maris wouldn't hear it, though. All of the impossibility, all of the insanity, all of the chaos, he wanted it in. And then… Well, then I had the freedom to do whatever I wanted. The client couldn't complain. Not only that, but I started to believe I was the only one who could present this material in such a way that… Listen: I know this sounds strange, not something I would normally say or even think, but I got the idea that this manuscript, this project was like a virus that attacked reality. And I had to do something to defend reality. That's what I've been doing my entire life as a narrator. Holding the real together. This time, though, well, each time I tried to change something in the manuscript, each time I tried to delete something that was implausible and replace it with something plausible… at least sort of plausible… the implausibilities would multiply. I now actually think my version is worse than Maris' was. But that's not all. As I continue on with the manuscript, the world around me seems less and less real. Here, conspiracy theories explain better than history books. I don't even feel like myself anymore. I feel like I'm watching the person who used to be me. From where? I don't know. Maris gave me the name* Edward R. Murrow, *even though that's not actually my name. The bastion of truth and I'm called what he was called. What an irony! Or maybe not. Could it be that Murrow took chaos and shaped it into order? Could it be that I've done the same, meaning we both worked in fiction, the type of fiction the entire world is based on, the type that's constantly being generated whether we realize it or not? Saying that doesn't make me feel better. Saying that feels wrong. It makes me think I've profaned the name of Truth. It makes me think I've tarnished the name of Edward R. Murrow…"*

That is the end of the report. Listeners, our narrator, Ed Murrow, continues to stare through the one-way, so we turn our attention to the mysterious condition Wallace Heath Orcuson currently suffers from, Agathopathy, thanks to *Youdunnit*. Recently, we spoke with folklorist and ethnographer Dasof Yore and our own Dr. DeMent about this psychosis:

YORE: Agathopathy originated in England during the interregnum between world wars. A culture-bound syndrome, it's often compared to Wendigo Psychosis–a condition specific to the Algonquian peoples of North America, wherein the afflicted begins to believe that the mythical Wendigo (rather like werewolves who feed solely on humans) are not fictional monsters, but real. And not only are they real, thinks the sufferer, but I am becoming one of them. As the psychosis progresses, the afflicted develops an insatiable desire for flesh and blood.

Dr. DeMent, can you tell us a bit more about culture-bound syndromes?

DEMENT: To be classified as a culture-bound syndrome, a condition must meet the following criteria: 1) it must be categorized as a disease in the culture, 2) it must have widespread familiarity in the culture, 3) there must be a complete lack of familiarity of the disease in other cultures, 4) there must be no demonstrable biochemical or tissue abnormalities.

YORE: Now, these syndromes are always connected to some problem facing the culture itself. The Algonquian peoples, for instance, live in remote parts of North America, and therefore often worry about starvation. For the English between the wars, it was the decline of the empire. Agathopathy, writ large, can then be seen as the delusion that the empire is dying *because I killed it.* Of course, that bit doesn't come out all at once. Instead, the afflicted feels guilty, but isn't sure why. And, indeed, characters in murder mysteries often feel and act guilty for unknown reasons, even before anyone's been killed. But as the sufferer's paranoia grows, he gets closer and closer to the revelation: *I killed the empire.* With this monstrous guilt on his conscience, the afflicted comes to believe he must cover up what he's done, and he does so by murdering anyone he thinks might have knowledge of his crime. Contrarily, while working to get off scot-free, the killer hopes for the arrival of the detective because once the detective has solved the case, order will be restored, and we will learn that whereas various subjects have been murdered, the empire is alive and well.

What about after the empire actually did die and the Golden Age of Detective Fiction was replaced by hard-boiled and noir fiction? For some reason, this condition remains, even though the original reasons for it are gone. Now, whatever the reasons were for our narrator's lapse, they must've been taken care of, since it looks like he's ready to get back to work. And so, ladies and gentlemen, we return the airwaves to Edward R. Murrow out there in the Pilgrim & Pagan. Ed...

Everyone reconvenes in the dining room where, it turns out, excessive apologies extended, there was no gun shot, just a highly pressurized cork that'd been popped by a cook. After the long hiatus, however, the dinner's ruined, no one really caring since most weren't in the mood for eating in the first place, least of all the detectives, who have completed their replica of the murder room, a stunning simulacrum that looks in all ways like a museum representation of the original. What is this, a game? Yes, to them it *is* a game and they're only picking up pieces of simulated evidence to convince those who're lower in life, it is a game because they've already solved the case, it is a game, sure, right, and for these flatfeet the game is afoot...

The Predicta sez: *Although it appeared that the ASA would protect us from the real Second World War, there was one man who scared everyone and no one even knew if he actually existed: Renato Fregoli.*

The dinner having been killed, the guests try to find something else to divert them, wandering out of the room, somehow ending up back in the library, where you see that "Senator" Maris' corpse is gone, having been replaced by Mr. E.'s kin: a chalk fairy.

Major Freytag and the Oberschütze butler are very pleased.

The detectives, when they finally notice, are not.

Somewhere a radio sez:

EUCHRE: …and that's it. The score remains 8-0…

shshshshshshshshshshshshshshshshshshshshs
shshshshshshshshshshshshshshshshshshshshshs
shshshshshshshshshshshshshshshshshshshshshs

Tu: A final thought for this inning: think about what it takes to make that decision, that decision to become a Knucklehead. They're frequently the least athletic looking players on the team, often the oldest. Every other kind of pitcher knows just about everything about their pitch; good knuckleball pitchers just don't. Hoyt Wilhelm himself felt he had no control over which way the ball broke; he couldn't so much as predict which way it would break after he released it. And because the pitch isn't trusted entirely, Knuckleheads are often traded, bouncing from team to team, which adds to their alienation. Not to mention there's a general prejudice against deception of any sort in sports (see the anger leveled against "floppers" in basketball and soccer, against signal stealers in football). But most of all, think of this—hitching your star to the knuckleball means accepting the unknown. The unknown, a terrifying notion…

shshshshshshshshshshshshshshshshshshshshs
shshshshshshshshshshshshshshshshshshshshshs
shshshshshshshshshshshshshshshshshshshshshs

Ms. Le Tannes, there's one question…

shshshshshshshshshshshshshshshshshshshshs
shshshshshshshshshshshshshshshshshshshshshs
shshshshshshshshshshshshshshshshshshshshshs

During this election season, you will face a dizzying number of candidates…

shshshshshshshshshshshshshshshshshshshshsh
shshshshshshshshshshshshshshshshshshshshshsh
shshshshshshshshshshshshshshshshshshshshshsh

...Ms. Le Tannes, there's one question I'm sure all of us have been wondering about: why does the Conspiratocracy exist? What purpose does it serve?

shshshshshshshshshshshshshshshshshshshshsh
shshshshshshshshshshshshshshshshshshshshsh
shshshshshshshshshshshshshshshshshshshshsh

...you will see a constant barrage of ads...

shshshshshshshshshshshshshshshshshshshshsh
shshshshshshshshshshshshshshshshshshshshsh
shshshshshshshshshshshshshshshshshshshshsh

I can't imagine that anyone approaches government this way. Conspiracy theories are for fringe crazies, not the mainstream.

LE TANNES: And yet, how many times have you been watching some sporting event, football, basketball, hockey, and heard someone say this: "It was fixed!" How many times have you heard that?

shshshshshshshshshshshshshshshshshshshshsh
shshshshshshshshshshshshshshshshshshshshsh
shshshshshshshshshshshshshshshshshshshshsh

...you will have to wade through the issues...

shshshshshshshshshshshshshshshshshshshshsh
shshshshshshshshshshshshshshshshshshshshsh
shshshshshshshshshshshshshshshshshshshshsh

LE TANNES: It is part of our DNA to distrust any system at all, no matter what. Earlier, I called the Conspiratocracy a shadow government, but that isn't entirely accurate. Actually, the Conspiratocracy is more like a shadow world. Governments, corporations, secret societies, religions…

Yes, yes, yes, there are conspiracy theories about all of them, but you're avoiding my question. Why does the Conspiratocracy *exist*? What is its *purpose*?

LE TANNES: Isn't it obvious?

shshshshshshshshshshshshshshshshshshshshs
shshshshshshshshshshshshshshshshshshshshs
shshshshshshshshshshshshshshshshshshshshs

…you will have to choose what is most important to you as a voter…

shshshshshshshshshshshshshshshshshshshshs
shshshshshshshshshshshshshshshshshshshshs
shshshshshshshshshshshshshshshshshshshshs

LE TANNES: Sure, if you've never seen your enemy's face, that can be terrifying. He might be anywhere, he might be anyone, he could be your next-door neighbor or sister-in-law or the cashier at the grocery store! But if you've never seen your enemy's face, and your enemy runs a vast cabal… Let me ask you, how do you know I'm Charlotte Le Tannes?

shshshshshshshshshshshshshshshshshshshshs
shshshshshshshshshshshshshshshshshshshshs
shshshshshshshshshshshshshshshshshshshshs

…and you will have to decide who you trust…

shshshshshshshshshshshshshshshshshshshs
shshshshshshshshshshshshshshshshshshshs
shshshshshshshshshshshshshshshshshshs

Please, Ms. Le Tannes, we've met many times.

LE TANNES: True, but have you ever run a background check on me? Have you ever had a detective look into my past? Have you ever even checked my ID? My name's Char Le Tannes, doesn't that name sound a little suspicious?

I know lots of people with strange names.

shshshshshshshshshshshshshshshshshshshs
shshshshshshshshshshshshshshshshshshshs
shshshshshshshshshshshshshshshshshs

...but luckily for you, I am here to tell you who you can trust. Me. You can trust me...

shshshshshshshshshshshshshshshshshshshs
shshshshshshshshshshshshshshshshshshshs
shshshshshshshshshshshshshshshshshshs

LE TANNES: Security. That's the Conspiratocracy's purpose. Security.

That makes no sense at all. The Conspiratocracy undermines security. It makes us question whether we understand anything at all about, well, any system or organization that happens to be in place.

shshshshshshshshshshshshshshshshshshshs
shshshshshshshshshshshshshshshshshshshs
shshshshshshshshshshshshshshshshshshs

...in the months ahead, you will often think that every candidate's lying, that every ad is making the truth more difficult to find. And you will wonder who you can turn to. But then you will remember. You can turn to me. You... can turn... to me.

shshshshshshshshshshshshshshshshshshshshshs
shshshshshshshshshshshshshshshshshshshshshs
shshshshshshshshshshshshshshshshshshshshshs

LE TANNES: You're wrong. If we didn't have the Conspiratocracy, we would have no order. With the Conspiratocracy, well, we have the security inherent in our systems, the security that those systems generally do what we expect them to do, and then the security that comes from knowing there are vast secret organizations (meaning these cabals are *organized*, not chaotic) that bolster the systems we know. These conspiracies may not do what we want them to do, but we believe someday we'll take them down. And we will... though they'll immediately be replaced by others. Order will reign supreme thanks to the Conspiratocracy, and no matter what anyone says, they're all complicit in electing this order. Because if we didn't have the Conspiratocracy, below our systems would be the swirling void, and anytime our systems didn't work, it wouldn't be on account of another order threatening the one we know, it would be on account of chaos threatening the one we know.

Ms. Le Tannes, I refuse to believe... What you're saying is...

LE TANNES: Mr. Station Manager, think about it. Can you really trust me? Whose pocket am I in? Whose interests do I represent? I've already told you my name isn't my name. Who am I really? Tell yourself a story. An acceptable story. An organized story. It's the answer, the answer you've been looking for. Now believe it, truly believe it. And when you do, fear not, *order* will be restored...

shshshshshshshshshshshshshshshshshshshshshs

294

shshshshshshshshshshshshshshshshshshshshshs
shshshshshshshshshshshshshshshshshshshshshs

The one you can turn to. The one you can count on. The one you can trust. Me.

My name is Owen G. Asbestos, and I disavow this message.

shshshshshshshshshshshshshshshshshshshshshs
shshshshshshshshshshshshshshshshshshshshshs
shshshshshshshshshshshshshshshshshshshshshs

Um… and… and now this:

§

MR. E.: Me? When I first appeared, I was barely myself. Not even an outline for what I would later become, which is an outline. Mr. E.? I wouldn't call myself that, though that is what I am… now. I could not tell you what I was then. All I remember are vague shapes. It's as if my head is empty; that's true, but misleading. *I* am empty. Emptiness. Not erased, an eraser. Later, I was like a model, only the opposite. Models draw attention, demand attention. They are there to be there. Not me. *My* presence expressed absence. In looking at me, you were invited to not see me, to think beyond me, though I was prominently placed. Before there had been something, too much something, entirely too much. Or, maybe not enough. Never enough. Insert more something here. To taste. Think about it, think about it, but not too long. It isn't anything; it's not quite the opposite. Whatever that would be. Let us call on the ones who know. No one knows. Let us call on the ones who do not know. *They* will hear our plea. Oh great uninitiated, obscure from this world as much of the light as you are able, so we can gape, gobsmacked, at the mystery of it all and become like you once again. In the name of whomever… A ritual. I was the avatar. The expurgated version. Something went missing when I arrived and would remain missing. I could never quite put my finger on what. I was like a detective, but the opposite. The more places I went, the more clues vanished. In the beginning there was ignorance. In the end, more of the same. Much more. I wasn't long for this life. The adepts were learning which made them inadept. I became a self-parody, a laughing stock. I was cast away. Written off. Taken out. I was dead. Murdered. The only thing left to do was no longer done. The case went unsolved. The investigators baffled. The more they learned, the less there seemed to be. A world, a universe had to be created to fill in the blanks. A legend. After that, we never saw him again, but there were stories… Oh, there *were* stories… And then, some blanks are easier to fill than others. When you want something done right… Some blanks you have to fill in yourself.

§

Dedicated listeners of Radioland, it appears absolutely anyone could have Agathopathy at this point…

STARCH: That'd be a twist *Youdunnit* hasn't tried yet. So far in the show's history, there's always been one clear culprit. For this episode, I assumed it was Wall. But maybe the entire cast has conspired to commit a murder, or maybe each and every person has killed someone, or…

WRYLY: Mmmm-well, sir, if this shall we say *entertainment* is to follow the rules laid down by S.S. Van Dine, there can be only one culprit, though any number of murders and suspects.

STARCH: Rules, Wryly? Do we appear to be following any so-called rules here?

WRYLY: Touché, sir.

Ladies and gentlemen, could this be true? That everyone is in on the conspiracy, or that everyone has committed a murder? We've only seen one body so far. Are others hidden behind the scenes? Has anyone actually been killed at all?

WRYLY: Mmmm-well, sir, according to the august Mr. Van Dine,

"There simply must be a corpse in a detective novel, and the deader the corpse, the better."

More rules... But what about the fact that some of our characters look different? To this point, we figured it was because they were being played by actors. Could it be that what we saw before was the performance? Could it be that what we're seeing now is the reality that performance was based on? Will any of our questions be...

Ladies and gentlemen, breaking news: I have been informed this very moment, quite aptly I might add, that our ambiguity expert, Polly Semmy, is alive! Or may be alive. Granted, the message came through the usual, well, no, there's nothing usual about anything Ms. Semmy does, so– the usual unusual channels, meaning we are not sure if it's legitimate or not. This report, however, is an upgrade from earlier when we were almost certain... yes, almost certain she was dead. As soon as we have some sort of verification... if such a thing is possible... we'll let you know, good people of Radioland. Until then, we return you to the simulcast of *Vayss Uf Makink You Tock/Youdunnit*, where it seems unlikely that clarity will be forthcoming. Ed Murrow, godspeed...

Flittering, flittering.

The first impression is of disintegration, though I don't have to tell ya, buddy, that word normally implies a quicker process. A gradual disintegration, a moderate disintegration, a moseying disintegration, a fixing-to disintegrate disintegration, disintegration in super slow motion, none of these works. Maybe it's more like this: if reality were thinking about falling all to pieces in some dimension beyond the one we see, only it hadn't entirely made up its mind, if reality came to the conclusion that it'd had a good run, but really, come on, enough's enough, if reality looked in the mirror and, in the cold light of an insomniac dawn, wondered what it would be like to just no longer be... but if, also, reality wasn't completely committed yet, wasn't foolhardy, wasn't willing to take the leap, and therefore decided to run some simulations, well *that* might begin to describe this ballroom filled with butterflies and dancers, the butterflies fluttering, the

297

dancers spinning, Hermes Pan and Busby Berkeley around here somewhere, that constant twirling of the revelers and pulsing of the wings creating dots of nothingness, vertiginous, will that piece of the cosmos be gone forever? Will others follow? Reality still unsure.

The Predicta sez: *After the fake World War Two, there was a surge of patriotism in the United States and the Soviet Union. The puzzle for the leaders of both nations, then, was how to dispel that unifying sense of allegiance.*

Meanwhile, way up there on those catwalks, in their own realm, full of despair, the detectives, believing no murder has been committed, have organized their own simulacrum of a crime scene, scattered clues to create a puzzle, positioned the body to point the police in the wrong direction, assigned roles (the shifty suspects, the inconsolable family members and friends, the apathetic acquaintances, the irate vengeance seekers, the baffled neighbors, the secret love interests, the stoic servants, the long-lost cousins/ siblings/children), prepared alibis and false alibis, planted red herrings, engendered the idea that the murder itself (which, again, doesn't appear to've taken place) is impossible and therefore can never ever be explained, well, unless we locate, yes, you know… and thus for their quietus the detectives have, in their infinite wisdom, so justice may be served, hired the only sleuths capable of cracking this case–namely, themselves. Who could argue with them? There will be no charge. It's a point of honor. This mystery *must* be solved.

The Predicta sez: *The answer for the United States was the horribly ambiguous, 'Making the world safe for democracy.' So we got the Korean War and the Vietnam War, conflicts that undermined the clear narrative we saw in the fake World War Two.*

This mystery of why there is no mystery? Well, no, that's not the one they're interested in. Instead, the detectives are running with the idea that a job worth doing is worth doing in a simulation first, an elaborate reenactment, the sleuths obviously no longer interested in the chaos below, in its lack of respect for the rules of decorum, in the country house's tripled population, in the fact that the lone dead body either wasn't quite so dead as previously believed, or in the fact that it's been moved, they've sealed themselves in glass, they've blocked out all the noise, mostly sounds like a band playing innocuous ballroom dance music because there is a band playing innocuous ballroom dance music, but there are other frequencies coming in too, quieter, more subliminal...

The Hazy-Hazy
You do something or other first,
Then you try a reroute,
You do an indescribable thing
Annnd you fill yourself with doubt.
You do the Hazy-Hazy
And you run yourself aground.
That's what it's all about (or so I'm told!).

Do the Hazy-Haaaaaaazy,
Do the Hazy-Haaaaaaazy,
Do the Hazy-Haaaaaaazy,
Yeah!
That's what it's all about (I guess!).

Sure, a dance craze that's sweeping, well not this nation exactly, maybe some other nation or even some other globe. Who knows? But that's not the sole transmission being fired out by KZZZ ("The only station you turn to unconsciously"), there's also, why not?, a ballgame:

EUCHRE: *The score's still 8-0, the Senators in the lead here in the sixth, and neither team has recorded a hit. What do you have for us this inning, Count?*

TU: *Well, George, "There are two theories on catching the knuckleball... unfortunately neither of the theories works." That's what the great hitting coach and former Major League catcher Charley Lau had to say, and this inning I'll be talking about the plight of the butterfly ball catcher...*

Can't imagine a soul out there's listening (though tomorrow, strangely, everyone will know the box score up and down), so many people cuttin' a rug, all of the world's Persians must be in tatters, folks in the textile industry excited on a level indescribable, unquantifiable, really only one way to express their joy, sure, and now they're jumping up, time to slice the carpets underfoot wherever they may be, I mean *everyone who is anyone* must be shaking what they got on that dance floor… so, yeah, come on! Is your last name actually Flower, Wall? You've been demoted. And the smart money, pal, well it can't augur how much more time you have, but if asked it wouldn't say, "Your *days* are numbered," nah, it'd probably go with hours, if not minutes.

WRYLY: Mmmm-yes, that may be.

What may be, Wryly?

WRYLY: Well, sir, there is a *fine* tradition of killing off minor servants to bolster the body count in mysteries. One would assume, reading such novels, that that was a servant's purpose–to be murdered and therefore decrease the surplus population, while simultaneously increasing the suspense. Wanted: Aspiring corpses. No experience necessary. Salary and benefits competitive, moot. Inquire at the Hyperborean, is how the advertisement would run, I believe, sir.

Oof! Uh, excuse me. Bound to happen, the ballroom being as packed as it is, and what with everyone whirling around, only a matter of time before someone smashed into you, Wall, turns out to be, is that? Yep, Ima Fregoli, who seems to think you were just trying to join her anyway, so she grabs your hand and your hip and…

The Predicta sez: *The answer for the Soviet Union was to become one of the most oppressive regimes in history. Hungary in 1956, Czechoslovakia in 1968, East Berlin and East Germany, the gulags, the millions of deaths due to population transfers. Anyone who thought the Allies had fought the good fight, anyone who thought that communism was a viable alternative to democracy…*

"My father…" sez Ima, and, well, it's like this: you're dancing with Ms. Fregoli, Wall (she's leading, you're hanging on for dear life), yeah, right there in the ballroom, but you can also see Ima talking to… is that Greta? In a husk of an old theatre, both of them sitting on the edge of the stage, you in the back row. "Well, the problem with most fathers is that they're there. In the flesh. Unmistakable. With all of their flaws and inconsistencies and prejudices. My father was never around and we loved him for it. Me and Iam. If he'd been around, he might've beaten us, or molested us, or hounded us, or manipulated us, or even actively ignored us. But with him gone, we could have any father we wanted, free of constant corporeal disappointment. So the one we ended up with, he couldn't be topped. Absolutely dependable. The man forgot birthdays, baseball games, recitals, spelling bees, rituals, traditions, and performances of all kinds; we knew, when we looked into the crowd to see who hadn't made it out, we could count on our dad to never be there. Really, the fact that he was so reliable, it made you feel like he was there with you, hand on your shoulder, even when he wasn't there... which was perfect because he was never there. Since he was such an excellent father, we were passionately devoted to him in a way that would've been unacceptable if we'd actually seen him on a daily basis, or really at all. Thank goodness, we always said, that he had the foresight to remain away. A prime example of his superior parenting skills. Now, you might say that the father we created was the same as our real father, though I don't think that adequately sums it up. I believe the reason our actual father and our invented father are completely the same is because it would be impossible to think of any progenitor greater than the one we had."

"What if your real dad had shown up?" sez Greta.

"We probably would've killed the bastard," sez Ima.

The Predicta sez: *The two sides even played off of each other. The United States attempted its own version of Stalin's Purges with McCarthy's Red Scare. It even had an acronym that'd make the Russians proud: HUAC. The Soviet Union matched America's nonsensical wars with Afghanistan.*

...and the theatre's gone, your orbit righted, Wall, as you spin and spin, maybe a bit of a wobble, could be why everyone around you appears, well, menacing, even the new arrivals look to be carrying, uh, okay, right, maybe a gun show booked this room and that's why there are so many revolvers, a cookware convention could explain the knives, a plumber's conference the wrenches and lead pipes, spelunkers the ropes, but the candlesticks, the candlesticks, the candlesticks, anything but candlesticks, what could possibly explain *those things*...

EPIFANIK: It appears Wall's got keirophobia along with Agathopathy now.

Ladies and gentlemen, joining us is our own station literary critic, Anne T. Epifanik. Dr. Epifanik, Das of Yore informed us that Agathopathy is a culture-bound psychosis connected to the decline of the British Empire...

EPIFANIK: And to the Golden Age of Detective Fiction, which is also long gone.

If both of the causes are gone, how can anyone, or, in this case, how can perhaps *everyone* have Agathopathy?

EPIFANIK: First, even though the Golden Age of Detective Fiction is over, our culture industry continues to pump out works that resemble it. Think of all of the Sherlock Holmes-inspired TV shows and movies, all of the Agatha Christie adaptations, and so on and so forth. The English Country House Murder Mystery is so common, people from all over the world are versed in it. And whereas the hard-boiled style, noir, was and is popular in its own right, it never achieved the same success as Golden Age works.

But what about the connection to the Empire?

PESTEL: That's completely gone, but then it's unnecessary.

In the studio with us now is Mortimer Pestel, our pharmacological expert. Why is it unnecessary?

PESTEL: Because Agathopathy is no longer a culture-bound psychosis; it's a bonafide psychological disorder brought on by an overdose of Narratol. The new Agathopathy has nothing to do with the Empire. Instead, it's the outcome of an addiction (an actual, chemical addiction) to hyperbolic, melodramatic narratives. Narratol, to be sure, increases levels of dopamine, serotonin, and norepinephrine. The norepinephrine raises the anxiety (necessary for any good narrative), while the dopamine (which plays a role in reward-motivated behavior) and serotonin (which regulates mood) increase the enjoyment of that narrative. MDMA (which goes by the street names ecstasy and Molly) affects these same neurotransmitters. Over time, anxiety levels continue to increase, as does the need for more superlative plot arcs, which ultimately leads to Agathopathy.

EPIFANIK: Consequently, a person with Agathopathy both acts like a character in a murder mystery, but also like a reader of murder mysteries. And if there aren't any murders being committed, and likely there aren't, then the sufferer knows how to deal with *that* situation…

Thank you, Dr. Epifanik and Mr. Pestel for that elucidating explanation. I am afraid, however, we're still having difficulty ascertaining just what is going on at the Hyperborean, so we've brought in pop culture guru William Bored. Bill, thank you for stopping by.

BORED: Hey, yeah, my pleasure.

Bill, although we've learned a great deal about Agathopathy, we still don't know very much about the show *Youdunnit*. Could you tell us a little more?

BORED: I can do that for ya. *Youdunnit*, when the producers got it up and running, dead in its tracks. Wasn't going anywhere. Now, 's got a cult following. Just… like… that. But how did it catch on? Whatta we got, bunch a third rate actors playing like this is some murder mystery so an actual killer full of Narratol can remember his crime? Someone describes that show to you, ya figure, rightly so, they're talking about a pilot never even got aired. Poor fool who pitched it, probably used his head to open the door when they threw him out. Big ol' picture of him posted in the guard shack: DO NOT ADMIT. Now, you expect me to believe 's been on for how long? Midway through the first season, that's when it all started, though. The theories. Ain't no way a show this lousy, and it takes dedication to be this bad, ain't no way… meaning *something else* had to be going on, something heinous, something sinister. How else could this show get on the TV and stay there? That's what the cult asks itself… and then it answers: *Youdunnit* actually kills people, no one's been on it more than once, the producers get the murderers to whack rivals, it's a front for who knows how many secret organizations, just watching increases the chances you'll get a delusional misidentification syndrome, subliminal messages in each episode make people more violent (specially toward English folks), gonna turn the whole nation, the whole wide world into a pack a ravening ghouls...

Bill, obviously none of these things are true.

BORED: 's what the producers of *Youdunnit* thought, too. Obvious. Problem was, only reason anyone watched this train-wreck, yep, that second script. One the audience wrote. One the audience added to during each episode. So whattaya do? Can't nuke the hands that shove cheese curls in your face. So the *Youdunnit* producers, oh they may suck at television, but they got this one right—they quickly denied everything. Was the way they said it, though, that kept the fire burning. Brighter than before even. Now, the cult revealed the producers were aliens, demons, angels from God who were testing us. Show itself was a red herring that covered up the nefarious plots and schemes the producers were running behind the scenes. Another part of the cult, they thought all of this fervor, it'd been planned, secret agents dropping stories, starting groups that'd binge watch and interpret everything that happened, but more importantly everything that didn't happen, creating mass delusions. Greatest marketing campaign of all time...

But it sounds like none of that's true either.

BORED: 's not. People who watch, most of 'em anyway, now, they ain't idiots. Don't even believe the supposed killer *is* a killer. Show's fiction. And everything about it's fiction too. Producers probably aren't even actual producers. Episodes themselves are almost beside the point. 's what you see on account of that second script... Somehow, *Youdunnit*, with all its layers a chicanery, flimflam, gammon, and outright bamboozlement, it seems real. Like some other kind a real. Not like a story you get caught up in. Not like a documentary or one a them feature pieces on the TV news. 's like because it's so completely false... it's absolutely true.

Of no help whatsoever, ladies and gentlemen, our former pop culture guru, William Bored. Good luck with your future endeavors, Bill. Now, it's back to the Hyperborean...

304

"When it comes to the conspiracy, Renato was a purist," sez Ima, and, sure, bilocation again, the theatre and the ballroom at the same time, though that doesn't keep the TV screens away.

The Predicta sez: *What we have to remember, though, is that all of these moves were predicted by the Lunarian Manuscript. Except for one: the Cuban Missile Crisis.*

...there's been a bit of a scene and cast shift, Ima and Kuzma right in front of you in your last row seat now, Wall, so it's the best in the house except, like teenagers at a movie, these two, making out and talking the whole time:

"Or so we thought. Having never met him. And his purism was his downfall. He'd watched as a grand conspiracy was hatched, an honest to goodness conspiracy, the very stuff of fiction unfolding before his eyes–only it was real! Repenting his earlier association with the Axis, Renato had a mission from God: to reveal the fact that the Nazis had colonized Antarctica and the moon and that the American-Soviet Alliance had covered it all up. With his deity-issued walking orders, Renato made speeches, recruited members, founded an organization, held meetings, formed strategies. He was monomaniacal. I think. This might all be conjecture. I wasn't present for a second of it. But there was a problem. Over time, people would leave. Drift off. People with fervor, fire, people who by all appearances were True Believers. Renato could never figure out why. He died ignorant and alone. Perhaps. I may be wrong. I'm not even sure I could be used as a tertiary source for this story. Later, me and Iam, we figured it out. Those who believe in conspiracy theories, they don't expect to be proven right. Ever. They believe so they can smugly proclaim the truth to the vast array of idiots who'll consistently ignore or deride them. Renato, on the other hand, appeared to be just the kind of charismatic mountebank who would lead a cult, but he was selling the truth. When his followers learned that, well, only a fool would expect them to stay. And Renato always expected them to stay. Or maybe not. I dunno. It's kind of like I'm talking about a person I've never met here. Someone I made up or someone someone else made up. But telling it, I can't help but think about my dad. It almost seems like he's here with me now, even though I couldn't pick him out of a lineup. It makes me feel safe, like I'm back at home."

TU: *"You don't catch the knuckleball, you defend against it," is what Joe Torre said, and that may be true. The 1945 Washington Senators, who had four pitchers who specialized in the butterfly ball, also combined for 40 passed balls, more than double any other team. All of the records for most passed balls in a game or inning are owned by catchers unlucky enough to be selected for dry spitter service. Men like Geno Petralli, Gus Triandos, and Ryan Lavarnway each have four. Jason Varitek holds the postseason record with three.*

A combination of things knock you out of that bilocation you've been experiencing, Wall: 1) the baseball game—for some reason it gets your attention, like a slight hiss of static that's always there underneath the music, a slight hiss you just forget about from time to time, and 2) Ima Fregoli, who obviously thinks dancing is a competitive sport and that competition takes place not between couples, but between partners (yeah, guess who's in the lead, pal), and well she's just dipped you, meaning as you snap back to the ballroom you're listening to Euchre and Tu call the game and you're gazing up at that orderly world the detectives have made in the rafters, everything organized, even the chaos the murder represents ain't as chaotic as all that...

The Predicta sez: *The Cuban Missile Crisis is the only significant deviation from the Lunarian Manuscript in the world's history. And it was brought about by one man: Renato Fregoli.*

Frustrated listeners of Radioland, certainly I don't need to tell you that, yes, once again, Edward R. Murrow has broken off from his narration of *Vayss Uf Makink You Tock,* now pacing back and forth between the one-way mirror and the Pilgrim & Pagan windows. And, at this time, neither Madame Khryptymnyzhy nor Eve Z'droppe have anything for us. So we turn to our own CNS insider, the undercover Heidi Larynx. Remember, ladies and gentlemen, Larynx is disguised in every way, nom de guerre, voice modulation, and the like...

Larynx: I'm going to tell you what I think about when I think about Murrow. The inside scoop is that when he first started at CNS, he was considered talented, very talented, but then all the new narrators were talented. And the group Murrow came in with, it was a big cohort. He was expected to be good, but who really knows if someone is going to be great someday? So imagine this group, imagine them all sitting at a conference table, an office like any other office, smoking cigarettes, drinking coffee and water, going through their voice exercises, waiting for the orientation to start. This group, or so I heard, they became tight. They thought the way most young people think; they were going to change the world; they were going to change CNS. During that Age of Heroes, the one who kept coming out on top was your man, Ed Murrow. There was even word around the office that Central Ops preferred him. He was their golden boy. Imagine Murrow moving to the front of that conference table, the office getting bigger. And for a while, he did a stellar job of keeping everyone together. But soon there was dissent. Why did Murrow get all the best assignments? He was good, sure, but he wasn't actually any better than most of the rest. The reason he was so well respected, then, was because Central Ops kept grooving fastballs for him. Murrow tried to keep things from breaking up, but that task would've required a god, and he was only a hero. First, there were the ones who just decided that narrating wasn't for them. They left for other jobs, or stayed on at CNS, but not as narrators. See the office expand now, growing bigger and bigger. Then there were the ones who were sick of Murrow, sick of CNS giving him whatever he wanted, so they went to rivals. There was also tragedy (narrators dying) and comedy (narrators falling in love, getting married, vanishing into domestic bliss). Now imagine that conference room, that conference table. The room vast, bigger than any other office (except one) in the entire building, and the table had more and more ghosts sitting at it, until the only living, breathing human left was Murrow. No one talked to him anymore. There was a rumor he'd gained access to Central Ops, something no narrator had ever done. There was a rumor he wrote his own voice work, something forbidden to

307

narrators. You could tell he'd been affected by the loss of his compatriots, but in a heroic way. Their sacrifice had built him up. Bolstered him. That's what we thought, anyhow. No one actually knew. So when he was charged with "Senator" Maris' *Vayss Uf Makink You Tock*, there was no one for him to go to. Maybe, maybe if he'd been given that project back when he was one of the gang, or when he was a junior narrator, his pals could've taken him down to the bar, a superior grandparent-like figure could've listened to his story, dispensing worthless, though soothing advice. That didn't happen. He wasn't the golden boy anymore. He was the Chosen One. And foax in the office weren't going to help the Chosen One out. Never even crossed their minds. They said it was a test. They said Central Ops thought Murrow was too proud, that he believed he was greater than the Central Operations Office itself, that he needed taken down a peg. The rest of us, we couldn't agree more. Jealousy. Spite. The usual. And now think of the man you call Edward R. Murrow looking at Maris' manuscript as it lay in front of him in that great big office at that great big conference table, sitting, even the ghosts gone now, sitting all by himself. Alone. And that's what I see, no matter where he is, no matter what he's doing. I see Murrow abandoned in a cavernous office, abandoned by his compatriots, abandoned by his god (Central Ops), abandoned by all of us, forced to contemplate this manuscript, this absurdity. There's no way we can imagine him as being happy.

Thank you, Heidi Larynx. We would love to discuss this more, but we have a breaking news bulletin: our ambiguity expert, Polly Semmy, is alive! Through the usual labyrinthine channels (usual only because we've never received information from her the same way twice), we've gotten word that Ms. Semmy emerged, a little worse for wear, having gone through the ringer, looking more dead than the opposite, but still–alive. Patient listeners of Radioland, we will bring you more when we have more. For now, we return to the Hyperborean, thanks to Ed Murrow. Take it away, Ed...

"I said we both loved our father, me and Iam, and that's true," sez Ima to, well, who exactly is uncertain, as she sits behind a screen backstage *and* dances with, you guessed it, buddy, can't stare up at the detectives' paradise forever... "But we are very different people. Iam seeks to expose the conspiracy; I seek to conceal it," and it sure looks like Ms. Fregoli's talking to a little speaker? "Right there, you'd assume that Iam followed in Renato's footsteps, while I stabbed the old man in the back. To my brother's credit, he works tirelessly to disclose the Nazi plan, making sure to implicate the United States and the former Soviet Union in the process. Moreover, Iam runs a newsletter called *Nouveau Brisant* that reaches proselytes everywhere, continues operating our father's organization, and even (this is a bit different than Renato's way) coerces people into joining his side. And whenever you ask Iam *what* he's doing, he'll say, without pause, 'I'm working to reveal the truth.' Sounds like Iam is Renato 2.0, right? But you see, Iam wants to expose the conspiracy because he doesn't believe in it at all." Yes, there's the little sign that sez Mr. Speaker. "Now, why would a person work indefatigably to divulge something that isn't true, that he *knows* isn't true? I can think of a few reasons. First, he wants to experience what it's like to lead a cult. My brother isn't above the baser impulses in life anymore than the rest of us. Second, a point Iam and I agree on completely, no one actually believes what everyone knows. If Iam exposes the conspiracy, then everyone will know about it and no one will believe in it. How can this be done? By concealing it in plain sight, using the Alternate History Channel, for instance..."

The Predicta sez: *Renato Fregoli, or so the story goes, had stolen the Soviet Union's copy of the Lunarian Manuscript and had amassed enough evidence to expose the ASA's ongoing conspiracy. Or, anyway, someone who was going by Renato Fregoli or who was being called Renato Fregoli had endangered the plot...*

"...In this way the conspiracy will be revealed and concealed simultaneously. Revealed because it will be out in the world. Concealed because everyone will know about it, everyone will accept it, so no one will believe in it. We saw this with the Kennedy assassination—the evidence was apparent, so it was immediately questionable. Nothing is more suspicious than clarity. But what's the point? Iam wants to expose this conspiracy, so we can move on to some other conspiracy, and then to some other, until we finally get to the truth, a truth he couldn't possibly comprehend, or so his thinking goes. And finally, the last reason Iam fights to expose this plot is because it brings him closer to his father. After all, when working with the resistance, Iam is most aware of Renato's absence, which brings them closer together. How can that be? Because, for us, absence is the only presence our father ever had. So Iam can't help but think Renato is there, watching over him, proud that his son followed in *his* footsteps, the world will be a better place because he created the resistance, yes, Iam imagines his father thinking all of these things, and it warms his heart to be gifted with such parental love that is right there, right here, so close by, just out of sight, always *just barely* out of sight, but there all the same, Renato bursting with pride, Renato a godlike figure looking on, giving his blessing, as Iam continues on his quest to completely destroy everything the old man ever worked for…"

Inquisitive listeners of Radioland, we have the first complete transmission from Polly Semmy since we announced she'd died. We only know the report is from her because we had to cobble it together from various snippets delivered to us by such a bizarre cast of characters, honestly, the message couldn't be from anyone else. And so, take it away, Ms. Semmy…

SEMMY: The Hyperborean building you are focusing on, in Area 51, is not the only one. Kapustin Yar in Russia; a section of the Gobi Desert called Dunhaung, Jiuquan, Gansu; Porton Down in the United Kingdom; the Kalahari Plaas in South Africa; Pine Gap in Australia; Wheeler Island in the Bay of Bengal off the coast of India. There are others. But the first one was constructed on Wainiwidiwiki Island. All of them are owned and operated by A. Parachroni, Inc. All of them are connected. All of them are built on deposits of Explodium. The simulations being run inside normally vary, but now they have all begun to overlap. *That* is why your Hyperborean seems overcrowded. The vast array is now driving to its climax.

That is the end of the report. But ladies and gentlemen, what could it possibly mean?

TU: …catchers, for years, have been complaining that all of those passed balls aren't their fault. And they might have a point. Here's why: the fastest possible voluntary reaction time for a human is around 150 milliseconds, and in that span a knuckleball can change course so much you couldn't possibly catch it…

"You know my brother seeks to expose the conspiracy because he doesn't believe in it," sez Ima, though you can only tell by the sound of her voice, so dark in here you're not even sure this scene's set in the theatre anymore, and the bilocation doesn't help seeing as how you jump between the ballroom's lighting and the blackness of what smells and feels like a basement, "and if you think I'm the opposite, you're right. However, normally it's assumed that since my father abandoned me, I'm out for vengeance. What better way to get revenge than by undermining your dad's life's work?"

The Predicta sez: *Terrified that Renato Fregoli would expose the conspiracy, the ASA was forced to create a narrative that would make all others seem insignificant. They chose the threat of a global nuclear conflict.*

"First, let me say it's my belief that a good parent should do whatever they can to better their children. My father's entire life was a masterful performance enacted to teach me how to expose the conspiracy. Proof–by never being there, I wasn't sentimentally influenced by Renato then and I'm not nostalgic for him now. Since he was distant, I was able to critique his actions, I was able to learn from him, instead of being hypnotized by him. Consequently, I came to understand an extremely important lesson: nobody trusts you when you tell them things in easily understandable language. People like to interpret, they want to interpret. So, when my father stepped forward and told the truth, that there were Nazis on the moon and the Americans and Soviets helped cover up this startling fact, his audience assumed he was a mountebank, just the kind of person they wanted to follow. When they learned he wasn't a mountebank, they left. Now I step forward. I know the conspiracy is true. I also know it doesn't seem like it's true. How can I convince anyone that something this difficult exists? Ah-ha! By discouraging them from believing in it. The more scorn they hear, the more misdirection they're fed, the more they know. But it's not enough to say, 'There aren't any Nazis on the moon.' I have therefore constructed a vast and truly difficult to manage meta-conspiracy that works tirelessly to cover up what I, the meta-conspiracy's head, want to reveal. It's not easy. But I think of everything Renato taught me, and through various channels my meta-conspiracy releases this idea: 'There couldn't be Nazis on the moon because there never were any Nazis. They were invented by authors and filmmakers, by con men who want us to think such villains could actually exist,' a statement so obviously untrue it'll take ages to understand how anyone could believe it. Holocaust deniers are merely racist. Nazi deniers? What colossal and omnipotent organization could've pulled that scam off? And, if I'm successful, it'll end, finally, with our audience recognizing both that there was a National Socialist Party and there still is, just not in Germany anymore, but underneath Antarctica and on the moon. Only reason most people don't know is because of the coverup, the coverup that was designed to reveal the entire conspiracy. I know my father's constant, ghostly disapproval is his way of showing how proud he is of me," sez Ima, and there, right at the end, lighting a cigarette, is that? Sure, it's Agent Asbestos, or someone who looks a lot like him, you think, anyway, since you're quickly pulled back to the ballroom, Ms. Fregoli seemingly headed to the lady's, the band having stopped, though the various KZZZ transmissions continue on:

TU: *Now, it's true, pitchers who decide to hitch their stars to the knuckler have accepted a certain amount of chaos. They realized they couldn't overpower their opponents like fastball pitchers, they couldn't outwit their opponents like control pitchers, and so they resorted to something called a junk pitch. But what about the knuckleball catcher? What unlucky stars align, what hex is cast that dooms a catcher to the butterfly ball? Because, normally, knuckleball pitchers have a specific field general assigned to them. Ray Katt for Hoyt Wilhelm, Doug Mirabelli for Tim Wakefield, Andy Allanson for Tom Candiotti, Josh Thole for R.A. Dickey. These men are damned because when the butterfly ball is really working, it just might be impossible to catch. But then maybe it's not so bad. As Bob Uecker (who caught Phil Niekro) said, "I always thought the knuckleball was the easiest pitch to catch. Wait'll it stops rolling, then go to the backstop and pick it up."*

As you drift to your usual corner, Wall, the crowded ballroom and the butterflies convince you that maybe it's time to get some hallway air, though your destination ain't easy to reach, what with all the TV screens:

The Predicta sez: *After the Cuban Missile Crisis, Renato Fregoli disappeared. If he ever existed in the first place. The earthbound superpowers, they dismissed his followers as fringe crazies. Paranoia, though, slowly but surely, became the most prevalent political stance in the world. And right at its peak, A. Parachroni filed a red herring prospectus...*

...then the band starts back up, and whereas before at different times you could hear the baseball game though it technically never got any louder, you just focused on it more for reasons beyond your understanding, well now it's "The Hazy-Hazy" that's caught your attention:

> You do something or other first,
> Then you try a reroute,
> You do an indescribable thing
> Annnd you fill yourself with doubt.

Finally, Wall, you make it to the hallway, the door slamming behind you, slamming louder than you think possible, as if that bang wasn't one door, but every conceivable door, one of those cartoon tricks, so you slide your hands across the surface, trying to get an idea of what it's made of...

> You do the Hazy-Hazy
> And you run yourself aground.
> That's what it's all about (sure, let's go with that!).

…until you hear a click and instinctively look down.

Ima Fregoli lies bleeding on the ground.

Mr. E. points his gun at you, Wall. And, sure, he doesn't have a face, but the smugness, oh the smugness. If he weren't an outline, you'd wonder how someone could so thoroughly and vigorously pat themselves on the back. You look to the detectives above, but they've lost interest in the lower world. They are in hot pursuit of their simulated murderer. And do ya find yourself, buddy, wishing you were up there? Would you be happier even if you were gonna be the corpse? As the life drained out of you, you'd know, you'd know that in the future, oh you wouldn't get to hear it, but in the future there'd be a perfect explanation, a summation of exactly what happened, and as you died you could take comfort in that. But you don't live up there, pal. Sorry about your luck.

Do the Hazy-Haaaaaaazy,
Do the Hazy-Haaaaaaazy,
Do the Hazy-Haaaaaaazy…

"With Senator Maris missing in action, it'll be easy to convince them he did it. And really, whoever you are, who's going to miss you? They probably won't even notice you're gone."

Yeah!

That's what it's all about (or something along those lines!).

And now this…

§

Euchre: Whereas things continue to go well for one Arthur W. Magam, fanning ten batters including another this inning, the same can't be said for Wallace Heath Orcuson. Old Wall's got himself in quite a jam.

Tu: He certainly does, George. Thus far, he's managed to out-snark his opponent, but that doesn't work as well when your opponent pulls a gun on you…

"Arty… Arty, for a while now I've had this fear. This fear that we were sinking into a pit of unreality. The world's story was… is unraveling. At work, as a narrator, I saw myself as an agent of order. I was helping put everything back together again. Ha! More like Humpty Dumpty. But recently, I thought if we're descending into unreality, then there must've been a time when everything was absolutely real. And there was. The Second World War. I realized everything that happened in WW2 was not only crystal clear in my memory, but it all made sense. It made sense in a way nothing else ever has. I suppose that's the danger in reaching the height of… actuality, of… authenticity…"

Euchre: Steee-rike three! Magam sends down a second, while Mr. E., for now, seems content to watch Wall squirm.

Tu: I have to disagree with you there, George. As we've seen throughout, Wall never quite does what you'd expect, or want. So he's mostly a block that a chalk outline's pointing a gun at.

Euchre: Yes, Wall's happy not rising above his name…

"…you can only go down from there. The luster from World War Two, though, that kept me going. I thought, 'We were there once…' I brought this sensibility to every project. You know what they called World War One? The Great War. Wrong. It seems like something from the Theatre of the Absurd. Trenches. Barbed wire. Gas. Worthless 'tanks.' Battling for days to move ahead a dozen or so feet. Advancing in a gentlemanly fashion toward the machine guns. Ask anyone why *The Great War* happened and they get that same look undergrads have after reading *Waiting for Godot*. Senseless. Meaningless. Formless. *Un*real… Anyhow, away from the job, with friends, acquaintances, passersby, I talked about the Second World War all the time. I played it off like I was a WW2 buff so I didn't scare anyone. 'I know, I know, I always talk about this. You'll have to excuse me...' But what I was doing, I was injecting reality into their lives, into our lives. I was reminding them, subtly, what the world *should* be like. Sure, sounds high and mighty, but I don't care—I was juxtaposing this fiction, this *fiction* that surrounds us every second of the day with the genuine article, with, and I'm not afraid to say the word, Truth..."

EUCHRE: *A routine fly to right field for out number three. Stretch time, Senators fans...*

"...only one problem. I wasn't alive for World War Two. I didn't witness a single second of it..."

TU: *...and that's what I want to talk about, our 7th Inning entertainment: "Take Me Out to the Ballgame." George, you'll be happy to hear it meets the first criterion of anthemhood: we don't sing the entire song. What we sing is the chorus, just the chorus, which is repeated twice in the original. The verses are about a girl who's so baseball mad that when her beau asks if she'd like to go to the theatre, she says, "No, / I'll tell you what you can do," and then she goes into the part we know from the Stretch...*

EUCHRE: *...Foax, while the Count goes on and on, I feel like I should tell you even the people in the Hyperborean are stretching, buying beers, hot dogs, peanuts, pretzels from vendors who are walking around, calling their wares...*

TU: *...and even though the song was written in 1908, it wasn't played at a Major League game until 1934... Now, being such an important song, the National Endowment for the Arts and the Recording Industry Association of America included it in their 365 top "Songs of the Century" with this entry: "Take Me Out to the Ballgame" by Billy Murray and the Haydn Quartet. Interesting, because even though Billy Murray and the Haydn Quartet recorded a version of the song, Billy Murray neither sang the tune, nor was he the author of it. The song was actually written by two men who had nothing to do with the Haydn Quartet or with Billy Murray...*

"...the most important, the most *real* time in all of history, and I'd missed it. I wasn't even born. Do you realize what that meant? Do you? Instead of spreading reality every time I talked about World War Two, I was spreading something else... a type of fiction..."

EUCHRE: Now they're singing "Take Me Out to the Ballgame."
Everyone is. Even Mr. E. Well, right, Wall hasn't joined in, but he is mobile.
And for him, that's something. Foax, he's walking toward the one-way mirror...

TU: The two men who actually wrote "Take Me Out to the Ballgame"
were Jack Norworth and Albert von Tilzer, both singers and songwriters back in
Vaudeville and on Broadway. Norworth said he was inspired by a sign he read
in a subway car: BASEBALL TODAY–POLO GROUNDS...

EUCHRE: ...Wall's looking around. He reminds me of a baserunner
thinking of stealing home. As if he expects, any second, for a hidden pitcher to
try a pickoff play...

TU: You'd assume the two men who wrote the most iconic baseball
song ever were fans. But as it turns out, von Tilzer wouldn't see his first game
until twenty years after he wrote the song and Norworth wouldn't see his until
thirty-two years after he helped capture the essence of our national pastime, a
pastime the two men had little experience with...

"Arty, when I first read *Vayss Uf Makink You Tock*, I thought it
was a joke. Then, I saw it as a challenge. When it proved to be harder to
deal with than I'd assumed, I began to believe it was a virus, a virus that
threatened to tear reality apart. Now, I see it as an opportunity. In this
world, I may be... no... In this world, I am an unwitting agent of chaos,
aiding in the constant expansion of mendacity. In there... well, sure, it's
pandemonium now, but I can be, I will be what I've always wanted to be,
always tried to be, while I await the coming of Truth, while I await what
was denied me in *this* life, while I await World War Two. Reality will be my
future, Arty, *my* future, not my nation's mythic past..."

EUCHRE: He's reached the mirror, foax, Wall's reached the mirror
and no one seems to care. They just keep singing. Wallace Heath Orcuson, now
searching for maybe one of those wrenches from earlier to throw through the
glass...

"...So, if you'll step out of the way, Arty."

"Son... Son, I'm sending you in there. And I know we're not
supposed to talk about what's going on. It's bad luck, they say. But think

317

about all the times that superstition hasn't worked. I'd be willing to bet every busted, uh, *you know what*... I bet they all followed the unwritten rules and it didn't matter a lick! Maybe some skipper should buck the tradition and talk about it every single inning. I'm afraid I'm not that man. I can't do it. Maybe it'd be better for you if I did. I'm sorry. But remember this, son–I'm proud to've managed a team with you on it, no matter if the tradition leads where it usually does, no matter what happens in these last two innings. I'm proud of you, son. Proud."

"Thanks, Arty. That means... Well, I have no idea what it means..."

"Now take this for good luck."

"Fine, Arty..."

EUCHRE: ...the mirror spins! It spins like a revolving door! Orcuson was searching, I figure for something to smash the glass with, when he tripped and fell back into the one-way. And now, with a last look at the Hyperborean, he starts to push his way through. Foax, he's stopped halfway... There appears to be someone else in the revolving door with him. They look at each other, nod, and continue on until the door stops revolving. Baseball fans, today has been a doozy! Even the 7th Inning Stretch was something!

"Hey, can I get some coffee?"

"Oh, sorry, Ed..."

"The name's not Ed. It's Wall."

"Like, yeah, man. I knew your like name wasn't Edward R. Murrow, right, man? It's like I told you. He's, you know?, dead... Oh, shit, man. Sorry, I'll get you a new cup. Fuck, we got like a broken cup on the floor and all this, you know?, paper everywhere. Maybe if I like say, 'We need a butler,' again into the uh Mr. Microphone one will, you know, appear, right? Maybe a sassy butler..."

"A sassy butler? Whatever, uh, can I call you dude, dude? Thanks. Huh. What's this coffee cup say on it?"

The Pessimist's Credo

As you stumble on through Life, Sucker,
Regardless of your Goal,
You'll hope to get the Donut,
But you'll wind up with the Hole.

§

Who narrates for the narrator? WHO?! Just who…

"With 'Senator' Maris missing in action, it'll be easy to convince them he did it. And really, whoever you are, who's going to miss you? They probably won't even notice you're gone," sez Mr. E. Maybe his head is full of dust, though, because he's hardly finished his speech when you're on him, uh, Guy? Let's go with Guy for now, sure your name'll pop back into the collective unconscious sooner or later, though by the looks of things there's little differentiation between you and the chalk fairy, grappling for the gun, crashing to the ground, until a shot fires…

Ladies and gentlemen… confused listeners in Radioland… we are trying to keep things together here at the station, but we are having… we are having… We've completely lost contact with the Pilgrim & Pagan and we're having trouble keeping any semblance of order. Davenport Starch, can you shed some light on this matter?

STARCH: *Youdunnit* is normally predictable. It focuses on a murderer, he or she "kills" again, and then we get the big reveal. Like watching that lousy old Bloopers and Practical Jokes show, only much more serious. When this episode started, I assumed everything was normal.

Are you saying…?

STARCH: I'm saying at this stage absolutely anything can happen…

WRYLY: Mmmm-yes, and cliffhangers are a common murder mystery trope. Right now, we're not sure *who* was hit by the bullet that was fired, if anyone. Granted, it seems obvious, since a lead slug could hardly cause a chalk outline much damage. When it comes to, oh, what was the title again?

319

Vayss Uf Makink You Tock, Wryly.

WRYLY: Mmmm-yes, when it comes to this particular radio drama, we couldn't be asked to predict the outcome. Either Mr. E. or… the other one… whatever his name is now might have been shot. If it was the other one, then this sequence may be his flashback before dying, a scene that will tell us a little more about him, while also telling us something else about the mystery at hand…

Again, listeners, as soon as we take care of these technical difficulties… for now we bring to you this uninterrupted portion of *Vayss Uf Makink You Tock*…

"I'm Renato Fregoli," sez a voice, but even though you can see someone stand up, he or she's too far away to be seen.

A radio somewhere sez:

Tu: *Batters make the knuckleball sound like it involves mystical powers. "Hitting that thing is like trying to catch a butterfly with tweezers." That was Tim McCarver's take. Willie Stargell described it like this: "A butterfly with hiccups." So what's it really like facing a dry spitter? And why do so many people claim the ball darts in dramatic fashion, like UFOs, even though we've already proven a blunt object can't move like that? This inning we'll talk about how hitters view the…*

The static is back, Guy. Or so you think until you open your eyes and find yourself lying on the beach, now staring at the ocean. Do you assume it's one of the ones on earth? And if so, why? Provide sources to strengthen your answer. Extra credit: the sun glittering on the waves–which star is that?

The Predicta sez: *On July 21, 2011, the space shuttle Atlantis landed bringing an end to the Space Transportation System.*

"They say everything happens for a reason," sez some guy, about average height and weight, wearing a loose-fitting white suit with no tie and a bag over his head, standing on the beach assumedly looking at you. His eyeholes are pointed in your direction, but he's just far enough away you can't tell. "I dunno. I'm not so sure about that. I mean who are They?

These They-people we hear about. Where do *They* live? *How* do They live? What are their plans? Why… why should we trust *Them*?" His voice sounds… distorted? As if it were many slightly different voices all speaking in unison. Imperfectly in unison. "As for this reason that makes everything happen, what is it? Is it singular? Has it always been the same? Who keeps the reason? Where is it kept? How was the reason decided on? Was there a committee? A subcommittee? A cabal? One jerk-off by himself? And why… is it hidden?" Something seems off here. There's the ocean, the beach, the birds, but it feels more like a movie set than a real place. "So maybe then *nothing* happens for a reason. Say it with me now," (is he talking to you, or to the extra voices, the ones that haven't been joining in so far, wherever they may be located in time and space?) "Nothing happens for a reason. That's the stuff. Sucks the skepticism right out of you, doesn't it? Everything happens for a reason, that makes us think of the religious, the spiritual, the mystical, the overtly political. Trusted members of the community who again and again prove completely untrustworthy. Nothing happens for a reason doesn't carry so much baggage. Only then we ask, 'What reason? Is there more than one? Are they always changing? And how do we know when it's happening? Can we tell? Is nothing happening all the time? Has it ever happened? Will it ever happen? Who decides? Who's… who's in charge here?'"

The man on the shore turns around (guess he wasn't facing you after all, Guy), removes the bag from his head revealing a face obscured by glasses with thick plastic frames, an obviously fake nose, and an obviously fake mustache; he walks towards you, and maybe he's a conjuror too because he suddenly has a cane. When you reach for his hand he extends a card that sez How Do You Do? on it.

"Where are my manners? My name is… well, I figure I need no introduction. And yet we always introduce those who need no introduction. It's one of the most common ways to lead in. 'A man who needs no introduction' is always followed by a name. No one ever just wanders off the stage after that line. Imagine if they did and the poor bastard who walked out was no one special to the audience. A real nobody. Meaning he could be anybody. If only someone would introduce him to us. If only someone would tell us his name… My name? It means 'born again' and 'everybody.' Everybody born again! I guess I could be here to save your soul. You have taken the wayward path and the Lord has sent me to… No. That doesn't sound like me. At least, I don't think it does. But then what do I sound like?" he sez, his voice echoing. "My voice never sounds like my voice. Not to me," and the echoing stops. "I've heard people say it means I'm a different person all the time. I dunno. I always feel the same. At least, I think I do… The best explanation I've heard is that I'm whoever I need to be in any situation. Isn't that fantastic? Only, whose needs am I fulfilling? Mine? Yours? Someone else's? And who decides who I'm going to be? It's all moot, though. I didn't name myself. Would be easier if I did, but I didn't. I was named long before I did anything at all. So, really, how much meaning could any name have? Completely meaningless. Except… they do have meaning. Truly, they do. There are books and books devoted to the subject. No matter what you go by, you can look it up. You'll learn everything you need to know."

"I'm Renato Fregoli!" sez someone else back in the arena. Wait a minute. They can't *both* be Renato Fregoli.

He walks past you, Guy, and, turning and following, for the first time you see where you are. But what makes you think if you grabbed one of the palm fronds, it wouldn't be a leaf in your hand, it'd be plastic? Why is it so easy to imagine this sand being trucked in? The huts made of fiberglass? The birds animatronic? You're getting cynical, Guy. Cynical.

"When I first landed on Wainiwidiwiki, the natives told me a story about the founding of their island. It wasn't unlike my own arrival. A man came ashore and said, 'Wainiwidiwiki.' The islanders informed him that was the name of their home. Undaunted by this unexpected response, he then said, 'You don't know what you have here. Look at the potential.' Immediately plans were enacted as if they'd existed from the beginning of time, everyone chipped in, everything leveled, new structures built, exotic plants planted, animals imported and let loose in the jungle, costumes distributed to the local populace, truckloads of sand lined the beach. Before Wainiwidiwiki was just another tropical island. Wasted potential. Now, Wainiwidiwiki had been transformed, using all of its potential, into what it could be, which was a tropical island. After they completed their work, they gave it a name: 'Wainiwidiwiki,' they said. What better words could be spoken?"

"I'm Renato Fregoli!" Maybe it's a reunion. Naw. A convention. Everyone dresses up as their favorite version of Renato Fregoli.

At the edge of the jungle you see what you were being led to, Guy: a coat tree holding a gray raglan and a gray fedora. Is it out of respect that you keep your distance? Or is there some kind of force field at work here? Whatever the reason, you stay back while your host puts on the coat and hat, places his glasses/nose/mustache costume on the coat tree (immediately unrecognizable), removes a pair of mirrored shades from his pocket, slides them on, and turns around.

"You'll have to excuse me—what with all the wardrobe changes. It's really quite a bother. But these disguises are important. At least, they are to the islanders. I'm ambivalent. Only, when I don't wear the costumes, the islanders get nervous. Extremely nervous. And I don't like that. Them getting nervous means me getting nervous, we're all nervous, it's a nightmare. They say, 'Sir, you are being hunted. Everywhere there are assassins and abductors. You must remain inconspicuous so no one will know it's you.' And so I put on these disguises and my friends calm down. Completely understandable. They want me to be safe. Wearing this stuff, who would know it's me? But then, I'm the only one who dresses like this. The only one on the whole island. I'm the most conspicuous inconspicuous person around. Nobody has any idea what I look like; everybody knows me when they see me."

"I'm Renato Fregoli!" Wait a minute. Are you thinking what I'm thinking? That these people look sort of, yeah, familiar?

Into the jungle you go, Guy, your host leading the way, and as soon as you enter you hear the sounds you'd expect to hear in a jungle:

screeching monkeys, singing birds, growling cats, hissing snakes, and a cacophony of clicking, clacking, whirring, grinding insects. You never see any of these critters. You only hear them. Up ahead is a clearing already (the island is quite tiny, after all), and as soon as you're out of the canopy, the only sound's the distant whoosh of the ocean which you can't see because of the wall of huts.

"You should know, the story I told you, the one about the founding of Wainiwidiwiki, I don't think it's true. It's more like a myth. Not an original one either. Appropriated. Synthesized. Remixed. The islanders now aren't descendants of the people from then. They're descendants of other people. People from somewhere else. For a long time the only inhabitants were birds. Well, they weren't really inhabitants. They just stopped here along their migratory routes to take a shit. All of Wainiwidiwiki was a crapper for our feathered friends. And then the natives came. At first, they didn't know what they had except for a lot of shit. Years and years and years of shit. You might think, 'That's awful. Why would anyone stay?' Probably the first people weren't so sure either. 'What are we doing here in this shit?' But for some reason, they didn't leave. No, I'm sorry. Not 'for some reason,' we know better," your host sez, leading you inside one of the huts. The interior's gray cinderblock walls and cement floors. You follow him up black, metallic mesh stairs. "Later, we'd find out why. Over time, all that shit had become phosphate rock. The entire island was the richest phosphate mine in the world. Fertilizer for all. 'What a lot of shit!' the islanders shouted joyously, realizing why they'd stayed. And so the natives dug it all out of the ground, selling it all over the world. The salesmen, when talking about this fine product from the Wainiwidiwiki Phosphate Corporation, would say, 'This is the good shit.' They were right. The fertilizer sold well. The island prospered. Everyone was rich."

"I'm Renato Fregoli!" They're not sort of familiar, they're absolutely familiar. You know every one of them, Guy. They've been here from the beginning. But how could they all be Renato Fregoli? Or why are they saying they're Renato Fregoli?

A radio somewhere sez:

Tu: Both hitting and catching in baseball are based on where we expect the ball to go. With the knuckler, we don't know where it's going to go, so we have no way of anticipating its flight path. That doesn't mean it follows an impossible trajectory, however. It just means we don't know where the ball will end up or how it will get there. So, perception makes us think the ball is doing things it isn't in part because we're trying to predict something that's unpredictable...

At the top of the staircase is a door that sez: Topside. There's also a table holding a set of buck teeth, large plastic ears, a fake beard (black hair), a wig (long, curly, blonde hair), an eye-patch, a Hawaiian shirt, a pair of green clam-diggers, and a pair of Chuck Taylor sneakers. Once your host has swapped out his disguises, he grabs the knob and pauses before throwing the door open.

The Predicta sez: *After the Cold War, the United States and the Russian Federation became allies of a sort for all to see. Secrecy was no longer necessary.*

"It turns out, there's a problem with strip-mining every last inch of your homeland, especially when it's so small..." From the roof of the building (the "hut" just being a clever façade), sure, there's the ocean, Guy, but below you is a dark and apparently bottomless chasm, making you wonder what, exactly, is stopping you from falling into its depths. "'We're shit out of luck,' the islanders said. It was a dark time on Wainiwidiwiki. The people wondered what it all meant. They had no answers. Luckily, I came along. When Explodium was found, the natives said, 'It's the new shit!'"

You hadn't noticed it before, but there's a clear plastic panel with a clear plastic button on it suspended in the air right at the edge of the roof. On closer examination, the entire contraption is held up by a clear plastic conduit. When your host presses the button, you hear an electro-mechanical sound and you see an illuminated arrow pointing down on the button. Soon an elevator arrives, there's a ding, the door opens, the two of you get on, the door closes, and the descent begins.

"You know, people sometimes say I don't exist, and they say it as if it were a bad thing. Existence, let me tell you, is the greatest handicap. Everyone alive is disabled. Think of all the rules you have to follow. Think of all the boredom you have to endure. Think of all the physical and mental problems you have to deal with. I don't have to put up with any of that. Since I'm not alive and never was, there's so much more I can do. Anything really. And, take a guess, who's had the greatest influence on humankind–those who exist, those who have existed, or those who never were at all? People, living people, look to us, the nonexistent, for guidance, for examples, they talk to us when they're lonely, they hope for us when they're lost, they mimic us when they feel their selves are not enough... We, the nonexistent, are constantly with you. We always have been. I daresay, we always will be. Our presence is so palpable, it's like we're actually there. And maybe we are. Not born, but called into being. Not alive, but living. Not a physical attribute of your world, but absolutely essential. You couldn't go on without us. If we decided to leave, you'd be gone before we were. But then, don't I seem to be here? You've been listening to me yammer on for how long?"

"I'm Renato Fregoli!" There's Greta, Asbestos, Bezopasnosky, Arty, Ima, Freytag, and Schmetterling. Heck, even Maris came back from the dead to be Renato Fregoli.

The descent finally ends, and the doors open revealing the bottom of the bottomless pit. Or so you figure, Guy. Here you can see that the island is held up by a plexus of metal cables so convoluted it's difficult to understand how anyone human built it. Certainly a race of gigantic titanium spiders spun this support web, saving Wainiwidiwiki from its watery grave. But then, did they also construct the... uh... contraption there? Best possible description for whatever it is you're looking at, pal. Mammoth isn't the word for this machine. Naw. Rhizomatic. Like pachysandra or kudzu. As if someone had dropped a couple of engines off down here and didn't bother to come back for around a millennium or so. Meanwhile, this thing was spreading, expanding, and from the looks of things updating itself. In certain sections there are enormous wheels, gears, belts, a steampunk conventioneer's wet dream. In others, there are walls of blinking, pulsing, tracing lights, everything touch-screen, probably friendly computer voices to help you troubleshoot that which needs troubleshooting. Tell us, though, are you thinking every square inch of this what-have-you should be stamped GNDN? Goes Nowhere, Does Nothing? Yeah ...

Your host leads you through this labyrinthine museum dedicated to the history and, sure, why not?, future of mechanical and electrical technology, and maybe it'd seem odd that your host, the chatterbox, has finally shut up, except the racket made by your environs is downright stentorian. Tell us, do you think you can see the sound waves, Guy? If you reached out, probably you could touch them. One question, though: how come you couldn't hear this up on the surface? The blare from down here would reach the moon if it weren't for the vacuum of space.

In the center of it all... center? Well, right, every point's the center of this machine, but colloquially speaking, in the center of it all is a skyscraper... though with no sky to scrape... never mind, in the center of it all is a tall building that bears the name A. PARACHRONI, INC. At about one hundred yards from the corporate office, your host stops at an engine and throws a switch. The noise is gone. Not lessened. And not just locally. It's completely gone. Silence. Except for the blood pulsing in your head; except for the ringing in your ears.

"I really hate that racket. It's completely unnecessary. Or, I wish it weren't so necessary. As you can see, the works is naturally silent. But the problem when we first started up—no one thought the works was achieving anything because it was so quiet. Indolent. Stagnant. Worthless. So then we experimented with broadcasting various levels of noise, and we learned the louder it was down here, the more people thought we were doing. Diligent. Industrious. Worthwhile. Generating all that tumult, though, takes a lot of energy, so the works is actually accomplishing the least when the foax upstairs think it's getting the most done. Come on..."

"I'm Renato Fregoli!" Will this go on forever? Is everyone who ever existed Renato Fregoli?

Your host bids you follow him as he keeps approaching the A. Parachroni building. Now that it's quiet, Guy, you feel like one of the islanders yourself. The silence makes you think that if you went wandering off in the wrong direction, you'd run into the rear screen this maze's being projected on.

"This, this is my masterpiece. A. Parachroni, Inc. Where did I get the idea? When I was a teenager, I went to art school. Like all art school students, I had to copy works by the masters. I chose Vermeer. I liked that Dalí had called him the only authentic painter of phantoms. Actually, I'd seen Dalí first and then Vermeer and not knowing the chronology, I thought Vermeer had been influenced by the Spanish surrealist. To this day when I see the Dutchman's work, I still think that it's barely withholding dreamlike horrors, a realism constructed desperately to block out unconscious urges. Anyway, I always got in trouble because I never copied exactly what I saw. I would slip in things from ancient times or from our own time or from no time at all. My teacher told me I wasn't following the assignment, but those insertions were all that saved me from complete boredom. Later, we found out the Vermeer I was copying wasn't a Vermeer anyway, it was a forgery by Han van Meegeren. Just like me, he never copied what he saw. He included that which couldn't possibly have been there. I was forging a forger. And to me, no matter what Dalí said, van Meegeren is the only authentic painter of phantoms because he is so inauthentic. Everything in a Vermeer belongs there. Everything in a Dalí belongs there. But in a van Meegeren, hiding, in a world created *by* someone else, in a world created *for* someone else, there's something that doesn't belong. A phantom. It unsettles you. It unnerves you. Though you likely don't know why. You start demanding explanations but there are none. The world you thought was so solid begins to sublimate. You grab hold of the vapor and believe you're the savior of humankind for doing so, when really all you have is a lot of hot air you think holds the universe together. Painting wasn't my calling, though. And, for the most part, that story came from one of the ID placards in one of our early art museums. It does get the point across. Even if none of it happened that way… Excuse me, I have one more disguise change…"

"That last guy who stood up, he's Renato Fregoli!"

Of all the possible turncoats, traitors, Benedict Arnolds, you are disappointed to find, at this moment of maximum humiliation, of maximum anxiety, of maximum despondency, where there's no escape, where you're enfeebled, unable to satisfy the crowd, unable to satisfy the… the…, where only now you realize you've been sucked in, suckered into a situation that's far worse than you imagined, at this climactic moment you are grieved to learn that the accuser points at you. Standing all by yourself. Thinking the spotlight would never shine in your direction. Comfortable in your true uniform. After a lifetime of devotion to the Real, in this blazing glare of scrutiny, you feel engorged with deceit. You are Renato Fregoli, and anything you say can and will be used against you because no matter the words, no matter how you craft your statement, you will only speak in lies.

Your host is stripping out of his costume, though you can't see a new one for him to put on. So is he just going to be naked? Hiding in plain sight as it were?

"Actually, everyone standing up is Renato Fregoli. Notice how I'm still sitting down," sez the accuser.

A shadow of himself now, an outline even, an outline!, and you're grappling with him, buddy, grappling with an outline, grappling desperately, Guy! Guy! he has a gun! he has a gun, Guy! and there's a shot!

A radio somewhere sez:

TU: *Another reason the knuckleball plays tricks on our eyes is because batters aren't used to seeing the movement of the stitches. This anomaly, that a batter can actually see the stitches of the ball as it approaches the plate, creates an optical illusion which makes the player think the ball is doing things it actually isn't. According to physicist Robert Adair, once you are able to figure out where the ball is going, a human can't react quickly enough to hit it. "A knuckleball can change so close to the batter that he cannot physiologically adjust, so in some sense it's impossible to make contact…" Except by luck.*

Keeping your eyes closed won't make the world go away, Guy. Nor will it cure gunshot wounds. That's right, take a look around. Sure, you're still alive. But that galoot underneath you wasn't as lucky. Yes, an actual human male. Well, a former human male. Who is he? Wouldn't want to ruin the surprise. Though luckily the detectives are so enamored with their model, they didn't see any of it. Feel like drawing a chalk outline around him? Kidding. Couple looks over each shoulder, no one around, and, right, just slide this handy couch overtop of the body and what could go wrong? Though how's come you're taking that gun with you, pal?

The Predicta sez: *Since outer space had lost its lustre and politics had become a way for corporations, the true ruling bodies, to make more and more money, it appeared that the American-Soviet Alliance had been successful. The Real World War Two would never happen. But one man would change all of that: Renato Fregoli.*

And now this:

§

A radio somewhere sez:

EUCHRE: *This is it, Senator fans. The ninth inning, 8-0, Arty Magam is three outs away from a perfect game.*

…but where that radio could be is anybody's guess since all you can see is darkness, darkness, and, just for you, kid, a little more darkness (don't say we never did anything for ya, huh?), until a spotlight from way off in the distance ignites, illuminating some guy in, yeah, sure, in the traditional uniform of a detective:

"In the insurance business, honesty is the worst policy. In life too. The whole world's based on the idea that everyone's lying all the time. Lies make up the backbone of society. The Truth… what's that? There's no future in it. Worse yet, if no one ever lied, I'd be out of a job. And if I never lied, I'd be dead. So honesty really is the worst policy. No one knows that better

330

than Greta Zelle. But she's more dedicated to this proverb than other foax are. She took a job at the Alternate History Channel because the only story that's forbidden there is the truth. Anyone surprised that Ms. Zelle worked her way up through the ranks quickly? It was like she was allergic to reality. Then she became friends with two secret agents. And what's a spy's job? Deception. But the big prize was 'Senator' Kipper Maris. Ms. Zelle didn't believe he was a senator, and he isn't... wasn't. She didn't know what he did. He told her something new every time. All the jobs sounded plausible because they were all implausible. She didn't know where he came from, since he seemed to be from everywhere, though he always said he was from nowhere. Ms. Zelle went to great lengths to make sure that her husband remained an absolute mystery. When they got married, she refused to look at the license because she didn't want to know his real name. Now, there was one thing, just one thing Ms. Zelle asked of the Senator who wasn't a senator: please, always tell lies. He promised he would. As it turns out, he was lying. Soon after, Maris brought Ms. Zelle a manuscript for her TV station. She loved it. It needed some cleaning up, but she put it into production on the double. Then one day she learned from Agents Asbestos and Bezopasnosky that the manuscript, it wasn't a lie. It was reality. And with Greta, as it goes with the rest of the world, honesty is the worst policy. In league with Asbestos and Bezopasnosky then, Ms. Zelle framed some loser who called himself Wallace Heath Orcuson (an opportunity for even more deceit) and killed her husband. She killed him because he violated their vows. She killed him because he didn't lie. She killed him because he told the truth."

There's a pause.

And then a volley of gunshots.

The detective slumps to the ground as the lights come up revealing the Hyperborean apartment, or at least a studio set that resembles the Hyperborean apartment. This "familiar, but not quite right" feeling pervades, seeing as how the couches arranged in their V shape hold up the asses of the actors playing Greta Zelle, Agent Bezopasnosky, Agent Asbestos,

Ima Fregoli, and you, buddy; since you don't exactly recognize yourself, the fact that everyone else seems to've been replaced by an impostor, well, you don't have a lot of room to talk, pal. As for "Senator" Maris and Mr. E., both of them are on the ground, one lying not quite lovingly in the other, since he's dead. Above, the detectives on their catwalks have built a spiral staircase that plunges precipitously to your level. And instead of a one-way mirror behind the Predicta, there's what sounds like a live studio audience, though now you get why performers don't interact with the crowd very much. The lights are so bright, who could possibly see out there?

The Predicta sez: *The Moon Nazi Conspiracy could not be hidden forever.*

Yes, everything's in place, and no matter that it's a studio, you can't help but think this is your apartment. I mean, it feels like home.

"Where are we?" sez you.

"Welcome, everyone, to America's favorite game show of detection—*Super Sleuth!* Featuring our house firing squad, Captain Richard Deadeye and the Crackshots, a host of detectives, and me, the voice from above, I'm Oberschütze Lorenz Schmetterling. Now, here's your host, always the biggest schmarty at the party, Major Gustav Freytag!"

Freytag runs onto the set, somehow pulling off both the stiff-legged Nazi and the nonchalant game show host, reaches the V, turns with military precision at the vertex, just as a gigantic banner unfurls behind him, it's that pyramid the Gestapo wear on their arms, and I guess this is the show's theme song:

Freytag, Freytag über alles
Freytag, Freytag over a-all
Above every other form
When for rising then for falling
Action we'll demand the norm.
From the Ground Sit-uuu-ation to the Vee-e-e-hi-cle
From the point of the Climax to the calm after the storm.
Freytag, Freytag over a-all
Above every other form.

Frey-tag... Frey-tag... o-verrr a-all
A-bove eve-ry oth-er form.

Davenport Starch, would you like to explain what's going on?

STARCH: No thanks.

Mr. Starch...

STARCH: Fine. Fine! Now we have *Vayss Uf Makink You Tock,
Youdunnit,* and some show I've never even heard of called *Super Sleuth!*
mixed together in one big stew. I can't imagine that we'll be able to tell the
actual people from the actors. Though I suppose this confusion might be
what *Youdunnit* is using to further confound the real murderer. Now that
I think about it, this might be the best episode of *Youdunnit* ever. Or the
worst...

"Willkommen, velcome Damen und Herren to ze Programm zat
asks ze Fragen. Qvestions. Unt expects Antworten. Answers. Or you get
shot!" Uproarious laughter from the crowd. Guess they really respond to the
dark stuff, huh? "Remember! You must provide ze correct murderer, victim,
unt reason for ze Verbrechen. Crime. To avoid being riddled with Kugeln!
Bullets!"

WRYLY: Mmmm-if I may, sir.

Go ahead, Wryly.

WRYLY: It appears that *Super Sleuth!* is to *Youdunnit* what the
summation gathering is to a normal mystery. Here, we have the possible
murderers gathered together in one space, all of whom are prepared to hear
the detective weave a narrative that will conclude with the revelation of the
guilty party...

Yes, Wryly, but with the added gameshow atmosphere and the
potential for detectives who give the wrong solution to be shot.

WRYLY: Mmmm-yes. Certainly there's no accounting for taste...

"Now, Detectiff Zwei! Die Bühne. Ze stage. Ist yours..."

The Predicta sez: *After the conspiracy was revealed, the Moon Nazis
destroyed every satellite they themselves did not control.*

333

Major Freytag cedes the stage to the second detective, who descends the spiral staircase, and...

"From the beginning, this case has seemed to me... overly elaborate. Murder, unfortunately, is commonplace. And if we found, dear friends, a dead body underneath a couch in the city it would be alarming, indeed, but we would likely be able to begin assembling the clues soon after, the solution would almost immediately follow that. Here we have a completely different problem. Or, I should say, series of problems. Why build this country house in the middle of the desert? Why bring together this mélange of assorted characters? Why pile the stories atop each other so high even in a helicopter we couldn't see above them? An expert killer keeps things simple, and yet simplicity is completely lacking in our case. Hence, I am led to ask myself–which of our possible suspects yearns for complexity? Let us hold off on answering that question for a moment and instead look at the facts. The victim was called 'Senator' Maris, though the title and the surname did not belong to him. Why 'Senator' when he was not, nor was he ever a congressman? Why Maris at all? So I looked into this moniker and learned that it means 'old man of the sea.' The old man of the sea is a mythological character with a varied background, but we need focus on only two of his powers: 1) he could change his shape to look like anything or anyone at all, and 2) if he could trick you into allowing him onto your shoulders, he would ride you like a horse until you died. 'Senator' Maris used these abilities on so many people, but for the sake of brevity we will focus on two; the first will be Greta Zelle. Oh, when they met, he was everything she ever wanted. Little did she suspect that his demeanor, his personality were calculated. He knew beforehand that Ms. Zelle loved obfuscators. Did she ever have trouble seeing through them? No. In fact, it's the easiest thing in the world for Ms. Zelle to spot a liar. Being so beautiful, so alluring, people (especially men) are forever trying to win her with fantastic tales, and yet her desire for fiction is bottomless. While they are lying, Ms. Zelle wants to see them lie and she wants them to lie well. Each attempt at deception is a private, one-person performance put on for her and her alone. With 'Senator' Maris, she thought she had found her master thespian. In a way, she had. From the very beginning, 'Senator' Maris played his part, and on this one occasion Ms. Zelle *couldn't* see all the way through it. Climbing onto her shoulders, Maris rode her right to ICU where he essentially left her for dead, having delivered into their hands, my God! she would never live it down, the truth! Or so she was told. Traitor! Scoundrel! Opportunist! Yes, to Ms. Zelle he was all of these things. But did she kill our victim? Or did she have him killed? No."

The Predicta sez: *Hoping to placate the Moon Nazis, the earthling forces continued to cover up the existence of our Lunar nemeses…*

"Now, before we can proceed to the second person 'Senator' Maris abused, let us think about this fact—people who can dramatically alter their appearance and do so convincingly are often characters in paranoid fiction. Paranoids revel in complexity. And in this case, paranoia abounds. But one particular conspiracy theory is at the crux: the Nazi invasion of earth from the moon. It sounds preposterous, even idiotic, I am well aware. Worry not, dear friends—'Senator' Maris didn't believe in it either. *He* believed in something far more sinister; he believed that the Moon Nazi Conspiracy is actually covering up another conspiracy so secret, no one even knows what it entails. What he needed to do, then, was expose the ersatz Lunar Socialist Party plot as a hoax to get closer to his Grail. There was a problem, however. Two members of 'Senator' Maris' family *do* believe in this outrageous scheme: his father and his sister, also known as Renato Fregoli and Ima Fregoli. For, you see, 'Senator' Maris is actually Iam Fregoli. It was easy enough for Iam to collect all of the information about the Moon Nazis because the book his father (along with others) compiled was willed to him and his sister. Iam stole his sister's portion and later vanished, though much as he rode Ms. Zelle's shoulders, he rode Ima's shoulders too by constantly exposing her schemes that were intended to keep the conspiracy secret, her schemes that took complexity to the nth degree and beyond, though again and again her own brother deconstructed them and laid them bare. Finally, through her contact, Agent Bezopasnosky, Ima was able to confront the heretofore 'Senator,' who was by this time crazed, a drunken fanatic who threatened to shoot Ima if she tried to stop him. She drew first. And so, I submit to you that Ima Fregoli killed her brother Iam Fregoli (the erstwhile 'Senator' Maris) in self-defense over the Moon Nazi Conspiracy."

There is a pause.

"No, no, I am sorry, Detectiff Zwei, that ist not correct, but ve haff some wonderbare leaden partink gifts for you."

Detective Number Two crumples to the ground.

The audience bursts into uproarious laughter.

A radio somewhere sez:

EUCHRE: *A towering fly ball, deep to right, this one might be… caught! Caught at the warning track! A few more inches and it woulda been outta here…*

"Hello… to you. I hope you don't mind if I smoke this cigah," sez Detective Number Three, absentmindedly scratching his head with the butt of the stogie. "I may be an old man, but I think it takes someone old to figure this case out. Those of you who can, I want you to think back to before… before the Wall came down. For the youngins, that's the Berlin Wall. The Cold War, seems like a fever dream now. Vietnam, the trouble in Cuba, the Iron Curtain, McCarthyism, never mind, never mind. We hid under our desks in case the Russkies launched nukes at us. Ha! You laugh, I see you laugh, yeah, I see you, but we did it. Both sides, we were positive the other side was up to something. It was a war of spies and secret maneuvers. To all you good people out there, I say, we, in different ways, sure, but we wanted, we never thought it'd be over, but we wanted it to end. And then it did. 1989. Problem came up afterwards, though. The U.S. of A., it was used to defining itself against an enemy. Didn't really have one anymore. Not a real one. You thought people were paranoid when the Soviet Union was around, never mind. That was nothin'. And Russia, what?, what happened to Russia? It became a void. Land a gangsters. Got to being that some folks, they thought the old days weren't so bad after all. Some folks like Agents Asbestos and Bezopasnosky."

336

The Predicta sez: *The earthbound forces refused to warn their constituencies. They claimed there were merely technical difficulties.*

"But how... how do you bring back the Cold War? It ain't like puttin' together a softball game, I can tell you. And this question stuck with Agent Asbestos, until one day the answer fell right in his lap. You see, Ms. Greta Zelle, she works for the Alternate History Channel. Ms. Zelle told Asbestos and Bezopasnosky about an upcoming show. Lightning struck! Asbestos knew what to do immediately. This story, Nazis on the moon and whatnot, it ain't new. Kinda old, actually. Like me. Only Asbestos, with Kuzma's help, was gonna make it young again. Fountain a youth!"

The Predicta sez: *And even when it became apparent that the Nazis were real, the earthbound refused to believe it, not because they were in denial, but because they didn't think such an enemy was possible anymore. It was too good to be true.*

"Here's how: first, they inform Ms. Zelle that her program, it ain't fictional. 's real. They know what this'll do to her. She's, what?, she's a bit dramatic. Likes everyone to be playacting all the time. But they're not sure if they can trust her, so they start right in with a plan to get someone to kill Maris. They even set some schlemiel up to take the fall. Good people, it doesn't stop there. Next, the two agents get in touch with the narrator of a radio play called *Vayss Uf Makink You Tock*. It's being broadcast along with the Alternate History Channel show. They tell him they've solved his problem. He needed some Gestapo agents, and Asbestos and Bezopasnosky, they said, 'Oh, we've *got* Gestapo agents. How many ya need?' The narrator's relieved; the agents hire a couple actors to play the SS. Now here's where it gets really screwy. After the Cold War, Kuzma, he met a woman who called herself Ima Fregoli, who said her father was Renato Fregoli. Our former KGB agent, he decides to keep her close because... because there never was a Renato Fregoli. He was a spook. He was made up. In fact, Bezopasnosky was the one who invented him. Meanwhile, Ima Fregoli, she has this cockamamie story about... about what? About Nazis on the moon! About a brother who's trying to wreck everything their father worked for... I told you it

337

was screwy, but once you get rid of the impossible, well, if you're left with buhlonie, you make buhlonie sachwiches… And so Agent Bezopasnosky convinced her that 'Senator' Maris was her brother Iam Fregoli. With the Alternate History show, the radio program, and this attempt at a cover up, good people, our former KGB agent, our current CIA agent thought they could bring back the glory days–the Cold War. Only this time, it'd be the earth versus the moon. And so I submit to you that… that Agents C. Irving Asbestos and Kuzma Grigorovich Bezopasnosky contracted the murder of 'Senator' Kipper Maris to bring about a new Cold War. Good people, I thank you."

There is a pause.

"You, Detectiff Drei, vill be leavink here today in a new Auto!"

Detective Number Three is cut down by a hail of gunfire.

"Unfortunately for you, ja, it ist a Hearse."

The audience bursts into uproarious laughter.

A radio somewhere sez:

EUCHRE: *An uncommon number of foul balls for this batter…*

"Perhaps, Damen und Herren, Detectiff Vier vill fare better…"

"Riiiiight. Darlings, I have a very different story to telllll," sez Detective Number Four. "But don't worry, even though I'm a *genius*, I'll talk *slowly*, so I don't confuse any of the cavemen and cavewomen at home. The man I wanta call your attention to today… man? I guess we can call him that… this *man's* been living a double life. Which is two more lives than any of my exes lived. Dolls, in one of them he's Wallace Heath Orcuson. Who?! I *know*. I've heard drunken pickup lines that were more convincing. In the other, well, who cares? The troglodytes are getting restless. So, baby, lay it on us already. What's your *real* name?"

The Predicta sez: *The conspiracy holders believed this would pass, believed they could appease the Nazis by saying no one would believe a show on ICU…*

"*What* is your actual name, honey?"

"Egbert," Egbert sez. And that's you, buddy.

"Egbert *Schtein*?!" sez Major Freytag.

"No. Egbert Murrow. I was named for Edward R. Murrow."

"Your parents *gave* you a different last name?"

"No. Edward R. Murrow's birth name was Egbert. He changed it later. My father told me I'd be even closer to the Truth than his hero."

"You see, ve knew your Name vasn't Vallace Heat Orcuson."

"Bra-vo, Major Freytag... Now, babies, let momma learn you good. Eggie here, he's a C-N-S narrator–that's Columbia Narratorial Services for the Cro-Magnons at home. A real Crusader this one, he's more devoted to his job than I am to gin. Now that, darlings, is *devotion*. And he *thought* he was making a difference. But then one fine day he was assigned to 'Senator' Kipper Maris. Horrorshow. Nightmare. Oh child, don't worry, it was all just a bad dream. Ha! You should *be* so lucky. But it wasn't Eggie's fault. We should have pity on him. He was *spoiled* by fate. Before, he *always* got what he wanted. Just. Like. Me. And if he didn't, Eggie-baby could make 'em think what he wanted is what they wanted too. Not so with Maris. With the Senator, the Senator *could* be called an 'it's my way or the highway' kinda guy. Cept the highway is named for him, and so are most of the other roads. Meanwhile, back at the ranch, that's CNS headquarters, darlings, Eggie had no one to go to. Aww, all by himself. The poor thing. So, he got it in his head that Maris was to blame. Maris corrupted Central Ops. Maris defiled CNS. And if Eggie wasn't careful, babies, Maris would tarnish our knight in shining armor too: Sir Eggie. Darlings, that couldn't happen. And so, Eggie, that's Egbert Murrow, killed 'Senator' Kipper Maris to protect himself and to bring new life to the place he was devoted to."

There is a pause.

"Damen und Herren, I would like to introduce to you der Gewinner. Ze vinner. Uf *Super Sleuth!*"

A hail of bullets cuts Detective Number Four down.

The Predicta sez: *The flying saucers, the Flugkreisels are on their way.*

"...vhen later ve haff found vun..."

The audience bursts into uproarious laughter.

"Zough, Damen und Herren, der Gewinner. Ze vinner. Might already be on die stage. You zee, zis episode uf *Super Sleuth!* is different, for zis time ze Gestapo are playink too!" Major Freytag sez, now brandishing a manila envelope. "Richard Deadeye, voult you please do ze honors?"

The Predicta sez: *The Nazis have superior technology, superior weaponry.*

The captain of the firing squad accepts the envelope with a smile, tears it open, blows inside, removes a piece of paper, hams it up to the audience that laughs on cue.

"Do I have to speak in your accent while I deliver the accusation?" The audience laughs again.

"I haff ein Akzent, Herr Deadeye?" Major Freytag, hamming it up himself. The audience approves the only way it knows how.

The Predicta sez: *We have lost the Space Race to an opponent many of us didn't even know we had.*

"Never mind, Major. Here we go. One-two-three-four. Fraulein Zelle, being an attractive woman and an important figure at ICU, had access to many circles. People may have found ICU ridiculous, but based on its ratings, they found it to be ridiculous in a very entertaining way. Not to mention because of her can-do attitude, they liked to have her around. Of the people she met, there were two in particular who were interested in her, two members of the intelligence community: Agent Asbestos of the CIA and Agent Bezopasnosky, formerly of the KGB. Asbestos and Bezopasnosky were interested in her because they suspected her husband, 'Senator' Kipper Maris, of being Iam Fregoli. Iam Fregoli, much as his father before him, was working to expose the Moon Nazi Conspiracy. If he was successful, then World War Two would've begun—the real World War Two. And then one day, it happened—Fraulein Zelle brought to the agents her series on the Moon Nazis. Agents Asbestos and Bezopasnosky let her know that unlike the rest of her shows, this one was the truth. Enraged, she entered into a pact with the two agents—they would have Iam Fregoli (aka 'Senator' Kipper Maris) murdered. In the meantime, ICU picked up the Moon Nazi series, filmed it, and began airing it. Contrary to what Agents Asbestos and Bezopasnosky believed, the Moon Nazis did take this broadcast seriously, meaning, for the Third Reich, the time for World War Two had come. The invasion, ladies and gentlemen, has already begun..."

The Predicta sez: *The ships are entering our atmosphere.*

"...We are everywhere..."

The Predicta sez: *They are pouring out of Antarctica.*

"...There is nothing you can do to stop us..."

The Predicta sez: *They are already here! They are already here!*

"...We may have been dupes in the trial run, but this time you are weak. Join us or be conquered!"

The crowd has finally found a new way to respond, as you can hear them rise up and begin to shout, "Heil, Freytag! Heil, Freytag! Heil, Freytag!" and the pyramid banner, which was already enormous, is now the very definition of enormity, and the major appears to be just as big.

"As for your Iam Fregoli, we had him killed because... he knew too much. And if we toyed with an innocent man, you can hardly blame us. That is what we do."

The "Heil, Freytag!" shouts resume and you feel like you're at one of those rallies from *Triumph of the Will.* This conclusion would be downright sickening if it weren't for the fact that you wanted it all along, Eggie. The Nazis may be the villains, but the villains have to take power in order to make the good guys look all the better. Consequently, you can't help but revel in the rise of Freytag, who now stands atop an impossibly tall platform, his shadow deeper, stronger, more stylized than any in *Dr. Caligari,* for the only way his being brought low makes any impact whatsoever is if he stands on high at some point. With him up there, with the obvious early victories by the Nazis elsewhere, the future is bright, finally becoming what you always wished it would be:

World War Two.

The *Real* World War Two.

"Now, retriefe Schmetterlink for me so he can bask in die

Herrlichkeit. Ze glory."

Ladies and gentlemen, patient listeners of Radioland, we have heard a good deal about Agathopathy today, but we have yet to learn how to treat it.

DeMent: First, if untreated, the afflicted will, in all likelihood, become a murderer. Luckily, it does take some time for the condition to advance to that stage. Early on, you might pick up minor symptoms, but these can easily be treated by weening the addict off Narratol. In the later stages, however, a specialized therapist is needed who can evaluate the narrative playing in the sufferer's mind and emulate a detective solving the case. After the story is brought to its conclusion by the psychologist, the patient is sent to a rehabilitation center where they are taught, once again, to live life without a major, melodramatic narrative.

Thank you, Dr. DeMent.

DeMent: There is one danger, however. If the therapist does a poor job of playing the detective, if he gives an unsatisfying summation, the afflicted *could*, he won't necessarily, but he *could* fly into a murderous rage committing acts worse than he would've committed otherwise...

"Now, retriefe Schmetterlink for me so he can bask in die Herrlichkeit. Ze glory."

A stagehand is dispatched to the booth, he throws open the door, only to find no one there. In the Oberschütze's place is a small envelope with the word Confidential on it, which the stagehand immediately opens.

"Brink Schmetterlink out," sez Major Freytag.

"I'm afraid he's gone, sir," sez the stagehand, looking up at the major on his gigantic platform. "And according to the confidential file, the accusation Mr. Deadeye read is incorrect."

The chants for Freytag stop abruptly, as Richard Deadeye slowly backs away.

"It wasn't my accusation. I was just reading it for the Major," he sez, as his firing squad gets into place.

"But vhere... vhere coult Schmetterlink haff gone?" The audience laughs uproariously.

"Come on, guys. Freytag's the one you want, not me." The audience laughs again.

"Schmetterlink! Schmetterlink! Vhere are you?" shouts Freytag, as he's brought back to ground level.

"I'm your captain! I command you to stand down!"

There is a pause. Did 'Senator' Maris' corpse move, or are you seeing things, Eggie?

"Richard Deadeye," sez Major Freytag, suddenly refocused, "ve are goink to send you to Paradies…"

The former captain is cut down by a hail of bullets. Maybe you are seeing things because you could've sworn…

"…or to Hölle. Hell. Vhichever." The audience howls with laughter. "Schmetterlink…"

"MURROW! Look! Look what you've done!" Who is that? Well, yeah, sure, it's your old pal "Senator" Kipper Maris, looking a little stiff, but then wouldn't we all be a little stiff coming back from the dead? He grabs the back of your neck, Eggie, like you're a dog who took a shit on the floor and now the Senator's gonna rub your nose in it. "You had a simple fucking job! A *simple* fucking job! And now look what you've done!"

"What I've done? What I have done? You wanted me to narrate a program about some worthless slacker who was being harassed by the Gestapo in the twenty-first century! You might not've noticed, but the Gestapo went defunct in 19-fucking-45! You know, when World War Two ended?!"

"Was this your first job? Your first day? Do we need to show you where the goddamned water cooler is? Run through the orientation tells you about your insurance and all that shit? You're a narrator! You, and tell me if I'm going too fast for you here, you narrate! Whatever's set in front of you, you *narrate*!"

"Look, I don't know who you bribed, who you slept with, who you have dirt on, but CNS never gave me a project like this until you came around! How did you do it?"

"I have a message for a Major Gustav Freytag," sez a Western Union representative.

"Schmetterlink. Vhere ist Schmetterlink?" sez Freytag.

"Like I'm going to explain myself to the help," sez Maris. "At least this trainwreck is just about over. You… you've fucked everything…"

"Over? How could it be over? We don't even know who the dead man is yet," sez Murrow.

"Dead guy? There *is* no dead guy. Didn't you see me stand up? There's a chalk outline, but that's it."

"Should I just read this telegram?" sez the Western Union representative.

"There *is* a dead man! He's under the couch," sez Murrow.

The couch is moved aside and underneath there is, indeed, a dead body. Everyone, even Major Freytag, stands silently staring at it, until the Western Union representative decides it's now or never.

"Okay, I'm just going to read this telegram. It sez it's from someone named Schmetterling. Here we go: The dead man is Edward R Murrow [STOP] The butler did it [STOP] That is all [STOP]."

Immediately there's a frantic search performed on the body. In one pocket's a set of press credentials that identify the man as Edward R. Murrow; in a small fob pocket sewn into the inside of his jacket is a tiny little scroll that bears these words: Tamam Shud.

"That's all" is repeated various times in wonder.

A radio somewhere sez:

EUCHRE: *One out in the top of the ninth. This is the twenty-sixth batter faced by Arty Magam. But even though the knuckleballer has an 0-2 count, the number of foul balls is just phenomenal…*

"Alright. Seize that man," sez Maris, as the firing squad swoops in and handcuffs you to a conveniently placed post, just as all of the original players enter. The real Greta, Asbestos, Bezopasnosky, Ima Fregoli, but then there's also the guy who called in sick who was supposed to be the butler, and he looks like a faux-Schmetterling.

EUCHRE: *...and here's the pitch...*

Ladies and gentlemen, to better understand our erstwhile narrator and the company he, perhaps, no longer works for, we are joined once again by Heidi Larynx.

LARYNX: Let me start by saying a little bit about a narrator's environment, something we rarely think about. Narrators inhabit a mysterious realm, standing somewhere between the author and the audience. No matter what type of narration they're using, narrators are part of the world being created, while also being part of the so-called "real" world, which is to say they're actually a part of neither. This is obvious for third person narrators, but less so for first. And yet who are they talking to, writing to, or, as the case may be, thinking to? First person narrators seem to know that someone is out there, yet in the world of the work, that should be considered insanity. So, Columbia Narratorial Services is private because it houses these people we'd rather not know about. We treat them like characters (merely like characters, I should say), or like the projector at a movie theatre, instead of truly separate entities off in some other space. The secrecy surrounding CNS, then, is not the same type used by, say, the freemasons. Instead, it's an unconscious collusion between those on the inside and those on the outside. Well, until now, I suppose...

What about the narrators themselves?

LARYNX: We can think of narrators like secular prophets. A narrator has been in contact with and now serves as an intermediary for an author, who is like a god in this analogy. That isn't to say authors are omnipotent themselves, far from it. But in the worlds they create, they are all-powerful (or as close as it gets) and their narrators speak for them. Because the two work in close proximity, people confuse authors and narrators all the time. If a narrator is foul-mouthed, then it's assumed the author is, when actually it might be the case that neither the author nor the narrator regularly deal in expletives. Instead, it is the merger between the writer and the speaker that creates the narrator, and that merger is accomplished through the manuscript.

It sounds like a mutual partnership, and yet we've seen problems. "Senator" Maris and Egbert Murrow for instance...

LARYNX: Gods and prophets don't always agree either. In order to be a good narrator or prophet, you have to be completely open. The best, then, have no personality of their own. Authors make narrators say things they wouldn't ever say, do things they wouldn't ever do. No matter how bizarre a program may be, the one person you can always trust is the narrator. Granted, there is the "unreliable narrator" technique, but to be honest unreliable narrators are often even more reliable than the disembodied voice narrator. The disembodied voice is convinced it knows all, but that is impossible. An unreliable narrator, on the other hand, is pretty obviously unreliable from the beginning. Reliably unreliable. It is rare when a truly unreliable narrator is created because then we'd have no idea what's going on at all.

You said that the best narrators have no personality of their own. What about those who do have personalities?

LARYNX: It's rare for any human being to have no personality. But as long as a narrator checks his or hers at the door, then everything will be fine. The trouble comes in when a narrator gets so frustrated with a particular script that he or she rewrites it. Now, narrators can offer criticism to authors, and oftentimes they do. A rogue narrator, however, creates chaos. How? When the narrator reads the new manuscript, Pandora's Box is opened–the original comes out, the narrator's version comes out, and every potential version too. I'm sorry to say it, but your Egbert Murrow appears to have done this.

Does the analogy hold? What if a prophet was unhappy with the message his or her god handed down?

LARYNX: Then that person was a false prophet. And the punishment was death...

"All I wanted was something... real," sez you, Eggie. "A coherent narrative. Something... the way *life* is actually *lived*. Something connected to the Truth. What you gave me was madness. I didn't think it could get any worse. So I tried to make your story make sense. I tried to make it reasonable..."

"I warned you about reasonable explanations, Murrow. But I'll give you what you want. Exposition: Egbert Murrow was a namby pamby narrator who was so goddamned lucky, he got to work on the same kinds of projects again and again. The Turn: And then one day Murrow got assigned to 'Senator' Kipper Maris. At random. Because that's the fucking way assignments have always been given at CNS. The Rising Action: Instead of doing his goddamned job, Murrow violated every rule in the CNS handbook and tried to rewrite Maris' project. But that wasn't enough for this poor excuse for a narrator. So he fucked Maris' wife too..."

EUCHRE: *It's a slow roller to the first base side that'll stay fair! Magam will have to cover first!*

"Climax: Having ruined everything, Narrator Numbnuts even accidentally killed some poor bastard. The sentence for being a false narrator is death. There. Realistic enough for you? Your panties unknotted themselves okay? Do you have any goddamned last words?"

"At least it makes sense. I didn't get World War Two, but at least, in the end, it all makes sense."

EUCHRE: *The first baseman barehands the ball, spins, and throws!*

"Proceed, gentlemen," sez Maris.

"Ready, aim..."

EUCHRE: *It's gonna be a bang-bang play!*

"...FIRE!" The guns roar, and certainly this must be a delusion, but you think you hear someone shout:

"But it wasn't him! The butler did it!"

You slump forward, wondering how it will feel, wondering what the last moment will be like, will you be conscious of it? And you look into the audience, trying to see someone, anyone, who might make your last moments on earth..., but no, because of the lights you still can't see them, you can however hear them, you can hear them howling in anguish like

347

you, as your life force slips... No. They are not howling in anguish.

Euchre: Heeeeee's out! Two down! What a play, foax!

They're laughing.

Uproariously.

Like they have every single time.

"Now, I've ruined your story too," sez Maris, undoing your handcuffs, Eggie, but what's that look in your eye?

DEMENT: I don't think Murrow likes this solution...

Eggie, you, uh, realize there's a gun in your hand? And that it's, right, pointed at the Senator?

"Woh. Woh, chief. Come on. You can't deny you broke every rule in the book. Aww, who you kiddin', you ain't gonna shoot..."

The Predicta sez: *There are those who might say none of this has happened yet. But it will. This is the history of the future.* And then it dies. Elvised.

"You're right, you're right. Just, don't kill me and I'll tell you everything. Lay it all out for you..."

"I don't want to hear anything else out of you," sez Egbert Murrow, and he fires, spinning Maris around, the Senator falling perfectly into the chalk outline he was lying in earlier, only this time he's dead. What... what have you done, Eggie? Everyone looking at you, wondering where you got that...

"This is America. Everybody has guns."

Hey, what're you doing now? No, no, no, maybe they'll go easy on you. That Maris was pretty awful, Eggie, put the, put the gun down, Eggie. Put it...

A shot rings out.

But you're still standing.

More uproarious laughter. Only this time, the crowd's joined by all the detectives who were shot earlier, even Richard Deadeye. The Predicta's fine too, though I guess ICU is signing off because they're playing the national anthem for some alternate America. Finally, Maris stands up. He holds a remote, hits a button, the lights dim, and you can see the "audience." Mannequins. Another button they laugh. Uproariously. Another they chant for Freytag. Another blames the butler. Another you can see the moon in its various phases.

The only body still on the ground is that of Edward R. Murrow.

"How'd he die?" you say, Eggie.

"I don't remember exactly, but I think it was lung cancer," sez Maris.

"Lung can... lung cancer?"

"Now, there's only one button on this here remote I haven't pushed yet..."

"Lung cancer? He was murdered! Who did it?"

"Didn't you hear? The butler did it," sez the Senator pushing the last button on the remote.

Ladies and gentlemen, brave listeners in Radioland, what could this possibly mean? Wryly, Wryly, we've just learned that... I can't believe I'm about to say this... we've just learned that *the butler did it.*

WRYLY: Mmmm-yes, we have, haven't we?

At least, at least give us some context. What was happening in *The Door* when Mary Roberts Rinehart had a character utter that line for the first time?

WRYLY: You mean, *the butler did it,* sir?

Yes, Wryly. What are we talking about?! Yes.

WRYLY: Well, sir, Mrs. Rinehart never had a character speak that line.

But you told us... Wryly! You told us... ladies and gentlemen, I apologize. You told us, Wryly, that she did.

WRYLY: Mmmm-no, I said no such thing, sir. I *said* that Mrs. Rinehart was *credited* with inventing the line because a butler commits the murder in *The Door.* In fact, according to the august S.S. Van Dine's "Twenty Rules for Writing a Detective Story," it was considered bad form to have any servant commit the murder or murders.

349

But it's a cliché! Wryly, it's a cliché. For something to become a *cliché*, it has to've been overused beforehand.

WRYLY: Mmmm-indeed, sir. It's such a cliché that everyone always suspects the butler. However, it was not a staple before *The Door*, and it was only the norm in parodic works after *The Door*–Damon Runyon's short story, "What, No Butler?" (1933), for instance, and later Wodehouse's *The Butler Did It* (1957). *The butler did it*, as a cliché, then, has always been an alternate history, one that described some other world...

Chalk dust and sand float in the air. It's almost beautiful. The Hyperborean is outlined on the desert ground where you and Kip sit joined by a... servant? valet? former stagehand? We'll go with former stagehand. He's opened a briefcase that contains paraphernalia from a bar. He's making drinks.

"I guess that last button detonated the Explodium," sez Eggie.

"Explodium? Hell you talkin' about? Sounds like a made up element," sez Maris.

"Fiction..."

"That's right, Murrow. And I knew you'd bring it off. The right way. I just knew it. Wasn't possible without you."

The former stagehand finishes making the drinks, pours them into two stainless steel cups.

"Singapore Sling?" sez Maris.

"'s what I'm always drinking, Kip," sez Eggie.

Both take long pulls from their cocktails.

"Tastes... well... you think it tastes anything like the original, Murrow?"

"I doubt it..." Maris looking at you, Eggie, almost a little nervous. "But, close enough, Kip. Close enough."

A radio somewhere sez:

EUCHRE: ...strike three! Magam has done it! Magam has done it! The first knuckleball pitcher in history to throw a perfect game. But that last pitch, that wasn't a knuckler.

TU: *No, it wasn't, George. It was an Eephus pitch.*

EUCHRE: *Eephus! An Eephus pitch! You've had so much to say about the butterfly ball today, what do you have to say about the Eephus pitch?*

TU: *There's only one thing to say about the Eephus pitch, George.*

EUCHRE: *What's that?*

TU: *Nothing.*

And now this…

Double Zero

The Case for the Flying Saucers

"Arty! Arty! Arty! Arty!" says… says the thousands of fans rushing onto the field? Reporters hoping for the first interview, pushing their way to the mound where teammates have mobbed the victorious knuckleballer? Foax at home already imagining themselves at the game, ready to tell future generations they were *there* when…? No. "Arty! Arty! Arty! Arty!" says none other than Arty Magam, his own cheering section.

The game being over, someone changes the station on the Predicta. The Predicta? Well, not exactly. It's not a Philco. It's a plasma update made by Telstar called the Corona. The flicker of the screen, along with the abundant neon flashes brilliantly against the darkness outside the Pilgrim & Pagan. And darkness is the topic of discussion on this here channel, whatever it is, showing a news program apparently, what with the scrolling ticker at the bottom of the screen, the shifting captions beneath the impeccably maintained talking heads, the logo, the overuse of unnecessary technology that makes the entire enterprise appear to take place on some starship even more futuristic and far-flung than the *Enterprise*. But all goes still in this antiseptic atmosphere when a rumpled, sweaty, befuddled spokesperson addresses the topic of this persistent darkness, informing all of the members of the press and the viewers at home that what's going on isn't just nighttime, no no no, this is *permanent*. The sun is gone. Silence. And then an uproar, questions shouted over questions, misheard answers transcribed imperfectly, phone calls that couldn't possibly result in actual communication by either party interrupted anyhow (and instantaneously retried), lamentations at the lack of information, the lack of cell service, the lack of sunlight for Chrissakes, where are we? It's like a tomb in here! In short order, the spokesperson's ushered away, the reporters flood out, the story is disseminated (though the various versions are disparate, the gist is the same), a panic spreads. At first, the people want to blame the government, but find it hard to believe their elected officials could be this powerful. Are you kidding me? Destroying an entire star? Not a chance. The people then turn to the obvious source: the shadow government. Much as in the past, however, the shadow government is impossible to find either because its leaders are good at hiding, or because it saw this coming and enacted various baroque contingency plans, or because it doesn't exist, in fact never existed. So the people turn to religion, incorrectly citing ancient, apocryphal, prophetic texts that, if interpreted in just such a way (the right way), reference this very situation. In no time, with sects all over the world, a sun cult emerges, attracts followers, anoints priests, forms colossal prayer circles that grow more massive by the minute. The clerics, in their prismatic vestments, in their polychromatic headdresses, entreat their god to rise up, to shine the light of truth upon this world of lies; the terrified proselytes zealously assent, repeating in sometimes bold, sometimes quavering voices what was said before, while questioning in their hearts when this horror will finally cease.

And then, as it appears to every morning, the sun crests the horizon.

The ecclesiasts in their absurd getups shout prayers of thanksgiving, but no one's having any of that.

The ancient, apocryphal, prophetic texts are mocked, ignored, fall once more into obscurity.

The shadow government rests comfortably in its underground bunkers, orbiting space stations, nonexistence.

The actual government issues apologies, retractions, makes claims of ignorance, bad information, good intentions, you know, doing what they always do, proving they're back in... power? or what have you, their words falling on deaf ears anyhow.

As the sun rises, though, something's different. It seems bigger, brighter, its rays *not* providing the light of truth, heh heh heh, naw, *this* is a bedazzling luminescence that... blinds? No, but a disabling glare now surrounds everything and everyone making them seem somehow more real than they ever seemed before. A mirage. A trick. Yet very few acknowledge what's happened. They accept this new real as *reality*...

Wait a minute. What station is this? Oh, sure, it's the Alternate History Channel. Went back to its old name, though must be hard times because after this is a glut of reality TV shows about... who cares? Not Wallace Heath Orcuson, since he's switched the Predicta off.

"Arty, that was a hell of a thing," he says shaking Magam's hand as the sun rises in the sky higher, ever higher, firing its light down on the Pilgrim & Pagan, cauterizing the world. "The first perfect game by a knuckleball pitcher! I mean, kind of embarrassing, but, uh, would you mind, um, can I get your autograph?"

"Like, you know, anything for, right, a *fan*, buddy," Arty says, grabbing the manuscript and signing it. "Yes, and yes. Anything, anything, like, for a fan, you know? And you, you should, right?, hold onto that. It might be, I dunno, it might be like worth something someday."

"Thanks, Arty. You don't know what this means," says Wall, clapping the donut clerk on the shoulder, nodding gravely, taking the battered manuscript. Then, without looking back, he leaves, stopping only to put on a pair of sunglasses.

"Foax, President Gerald Ford once said, 'I watch a lot of baseball on the radio.' So thanks for watching this season, everyone. We hope to see you again next year when perhaps we'll finally make it to that promised land, that afterlife, the post-season. Until then, this has been George Euchre for KZZZ, home of your Washington Senators. We now return you to your irregularly scheduled programs." Though, just for a moment, on the Corona, at least according to our resident clairvoyant, Arty Magam sees himself being carried off the field by his team...

The 1942 Chrysler De Soto sits in the parking lot, the sun reflecting off its surface, but the shades protect our man from the glare. Wall, in the driver seat (at last), tosses the manuscript to the passenger side, airs out the car, inserts the key into the ignition, the engine coming to life just as a hand appears next to the pull chain of the PLOT NOW sign. Soon it'll glow no more. Wall swings the car away from the donut shop and onto the road, a long, straight strip of asphalt that extends to the horizon, perhaps beyond. He pauses. A drag racer waiting for the lights to... And there he goes! Wind floods the car and papers begin to blow around until they're finally sucked out into the desert. Wall doesn't appear to care. Behind him pages from the mangled manuscript fill the two lanes, and who knows but maybe they've found their way to you? Organized. Reorganized. Disorganized. From our view on the road, the car roars at blinding speed, seems to soar off, maybe heading... does it pull up into the sky? Almost impossible to tell. Just so blurry. *So* blurry. And tomorrow, according to our prophetic correspondent, an even blurrier picture of this blurry event will be used, once again, to argue that extraterrestrials exist, are among us, will be used, once again, to argue, that people are foolish, gullible, but who knows how many hands are controlling these marionette factions, who knows what narratives back these two (or however many) camps, who knows but that both sides, all the sides, every possible side, seen–unseen–unseeable, might be watching you now, waiting for your response, poised to take the necessary action. Against that day, ladies and gentlemen, we all prepare. Until then...

For Madame Khryptymnyzhy, William Bored, Dr. A.O.K. DeMent, Sirius Simoleons, Blaise Algonquin, Munn E. Pitts, Theo Reticle,

Dusty Buchs, Water Wordsworth, Eve Z'droppe, Gorgias Georg Sofiztri, Anne T. Epifanik, Baron Monopoly, A. Phil LeBustre, I.M. de Mann, Heidi Larynx, Aiya Noh, George Euchre, Count O.N. Tu, Otto Graff, C.U. Tomorrow, Colon Bownde, Ben Blotto, Mortimer Pestel, Kelvin Klone, Brahma Gupta, Davenport Starch, Loman Drab, Charlotte "Char" Le Tannes, Norton Thales, Uwen Farr Oarbytt, Paisen DesGuise, Pierce Wryly, Marmaduke Ekudamram, Citronella Fogge, Chic Manley, Dasof Yore, and for the elusive Polly Semmy wherever she may be, this is Egbert Murrow saying:

"This is Edward R. Murrow saying:

"'Goodnight, and good luck.'"

Acknowledgements

I would like to thank James Tadd Adcox, Paul Albano, August Evans, Carl Peterson, and Brooke Wonders for reading and commenting on this book as it was coming together. I would like to thank David Welch, who listened to me talk endlessly at the Black Rock about working on this novel. I would like to thank Scott Schulman for designing such awesome covers. I greatly appreciate the blurbs from two writers I admire to the moon and back: Laird Hunt and Michael Martone. To Jesi Buell and everyone at KERNPUNKT, I thank you so much for bringing *The Big Red Herring* to life and for being so amazing to work with.

And I am deeply indebted to Lewis Moyse, who read and provided feedback on every single draft, no matter how rough. This book wouldn't have been possible without you.

Finally, for John Schloman, who I know one day will grow up to be… Abraham Lincoln.

Andrew Farkas is the author of a novel, *The Big Red Herring* (KERN-PUNKT Press), and two short fiction collections: *Sunsphere* (BlazeVOX Books) and *Self-Titled Debut* (Subito Press). His work has appeared in *The Iowa Review, North American Review, The Cincinnati Review, The Florida Review, Western Humanities Review, Denver Quarterly*, and elsewhere. He has been thrice nominated for a Pushcart Prize, including one Special Mention in *Pushcart Prize XXXV* and one Notable Essay in *Best American Essays 2013*. He holds a Ph.D. from the University of Illinois at Chicago, an M.F.A. from the University of Alabama, an M.A. from the University of Tennessee, and a B.A. from Kent State University. He is a fiction editor for *The Collagist* and an Assistant Professor of English at Washburn University. He lives in Lawrence, Kansas.